a site visit

A novel by C.S. Beck

ISBN -13: 978-1479399116

Cover shot & design by C. S. Beck

Dedicated to Deidre, Mark, Alexa and Luke – with much love!
In memory of William, Grace and with special appreciation, Uncle
Jack

"Hurry to build your home, for there is so little time to perfect this creation of heart and soul before the fragile light of life may be extinguished"

Contents

Grace & William

Chapter 1 - Site Selection

A solitary woman stood in front of a rusted steel break wall, which held back the seaweed layered sand and lapping water, looking out across the dark lake to a distant shore lined with trees. The thick foliage of ancient willow and oak trees concealed the slate roofs of historic mansions, their locations only revealed by slashes of gray in the felt green palette. These elaborately carved and gilded buildings had once been prestigious sentinels along the shore during the golden age of the city and their manicured lawns still unrolled themselves past neglected gardens and gazebos out toward the water's edge. In front of the stately houses the choppy steel blue waves beat a steady pounding rhythm against the rocky coastline as the wind, blowing in from the southwest, whistled a tune through the willows draped along the water's edge. The wave action had eroded away beach along the coast and as a result the lake bottomed out quickly to the channel where freighters cruised year round. These waters also hid many secrets in their murky depths; old trucks with their cargos of boot leg liquor, railroad cars, model T's, lumber on sunken steam ships along with the bones of their passengers. It also hid an invisible line that separated two countries. The woman on the shore could not see this crucial demarcation, the border, despite the hours of gazing, but she felt its presence in her breast and her conscious intellect. She had been banished from that distant shore and those she loved deeply were on the other side.

From above, the woman appeared to be quite ordinary, her hair the color of aged wood, light brown with the faint hints of silver. Her skin, Anglo Saxon pale was folded with soft lines at her eyes and sprinkled with freckles across her nose that were now beginning to blend together. She had a narrow face, clear grey eyes and a generous mouth with a thin upper lip. Her teeth, when exposed in one of her broad warm smiles, were straight and white. Her hands, with their long fingers, bore the calluses of using hammers and tools but the nails were squared off to better press a computer keyboard. She did not wear a wedding ring but the faint impression left by one from years ago was a reminder. She was a good height, not domineering yet not diminutive at five foot eight and her body was quite toned and slim from both exercise and physical labor. She wore a pair of dark jeans; a white tee shirt and a black crop jacket which made her look younger than her thirty nine years. Her arms were crossed to protect herself, hold herself together, but it appeared to be only a reaction to the wind and chill in the air.

The woman, Lee Harding, was actually born on the Canadian side of the demarcation, the land on which she stood. Her family history was one of skipping across this border like a step dance over a jagged crack in a concrete floor. One side of her gene pool was supposed to have come from a band of fleeing British Loyalists, escaping the very shores that she watched, their true histories forgotten, the passage of time eroding the nature of these ancestors. Their hopes, ambitions and accomplishments lost beyond documentation of births and deaths on court records. How they truly existed was only a vague notion, whispers in conversations grasped by a curious young mind. The matriarch, the remaining puzzle piece at over ninety, had lost the thread of memory. The names of even the children she bore were questionable day by day let alone the past characters of her lineage. She spent the remainder of her existence in a corner of Alabama, tenderly cared for by her only daughter, both now widowed, in the very country that her forbearers fled. The idea of putting her into a "home" being passed about quietly over the phone lines between siblings, soon to gain head way like water approaching the falls.

Lee's mother was descended from a family of working class people from the small town of Braintree in Essex County of England. It was originally a hamlet that grew at the intersection of two Roman roads nestled into the patchwork of fields along a river. Braintree, known also as Brachetreu in the Domesday Book of 1085, meant "town by the river" and it was where pilgrims stopped over on their journeys. A marketplace had developed and the area grew when Flemish merchants set up a wool trade in the 17th century. Once that industry died out then silk manufacturing was introduced and the village survived on agriculture and textiles into the twentieth century benefitting from a rail line to London. But jobs were scarce as the textile industry slowed and work, when found, was hard. It was in this humble backdrop that the Steward family had been settled for generations working their way up from serfs to builders to carpenters and craftsmen.

Lee's great grandparents Lucy and Archibald Steward had

married young and started their large family immediately. A child was born every year or two until they had eight and they took in Lucy's sister as well when her parents died. They all shared a cramped leaky four room row house flat on Coggeshall Road near the town center. It is either an amusing irony or an intentional pilgrimage that these immigrants wound up in Essex County of Ontario, Canada. Nine children and their mother, the youngest one only five years old and Lee's grandfather just seven, made the crossing by ship in 1913, first landing in Montreal then traveling by train to the English speaking Windsor. This was as far south as can be achieved without actually leaving the colony. The city is geographically south of Detroit, on a tilted peninsula of land encased by a chain of waterways feeding the Great Lakes. Archibald, head of the clan, had been a sash fitter for Crittall in Braintree but he had left two years earlier for Canada, leaving his vast family in order to make preparations for a better future for them.

Archibald first tried to find employment in Toronto and then he moved to Windsor to work with his brother, who had immigrated years earlier and eventually become President of Truscon Steel. He spent his time earning money for the family's passage and building a small house for all of them on Windermere Avenue. The dwelling was a narrow dark red brick structure, within walking distance of the small downtown, tucked tightly between the identical neighboring houses. These buildings all had concrete stoops with wrought iron railings, lined up in a row, from which to conduct daily business. Upon arrival, the formidable Lucy immediately sent the oldest children to work while the younger ones were put into local schools. Through sheer determination, this woman did not lose a single child, in times when infant mortality was still quite high, and each of her children would live on into their eighties until they disappeared like fall leaves, quietly and peacefully, except Reggie the oldest boy, who died as a pilot of a bomber in WWII.

The children thrived in their new country, each heading in their own direction but still connected to the modest hub on Windermere. They had inherited an inner strength, learned to survive the harshness of the streets in the poor tenement district of their first home and strived to always prosper. Their main example was Lucy who eventually managed to purchase the store she so often patronized, having so many mouths to feed. She set some of the children to help in the store on a regular basis and she expected them to work hard. The younger ones were pushed to attend school and taught that education was equal to any business fortune but both were important. Lucy encouraged them in their own business enterprises as well which sometimes led to unexpected surprises, like the real estate mogul scheme. Several of the children had decided to pool their meager earnings from peddling telephone books or mowing lawns to purchase land, the least expensive real estate investment. The problem with this idea became quite obvious when the tax bill arrived and the raw land offered no income for payment. Lee's grandfather laughed as he recounted this childhood story but the family took this experience with its inherent lesson and moved on to other more memorable successes.

Throughout all of these ventures, the family worked as a unit, unusual in their companionship and co-operation, successful primarily due to their optimistic good natures, work ethic and inherent honesty. They were basically kind, and down to earth individuals with some exhibiting Lucy's determination and stubbornness. They had good humor and played pranks on each other, though harmless ones. The children all married eventually and several had large families of their own. Through their children, they passed on many of the Steward physical features and character traits, including a long face culminating in a recessed chin which tended toward jowls as the owner grew older and a thin nose with narrow set intelligent dark eyes on either side. The faces were open and guileless with warmth and compassion. William, who possessed these typical features as well as an extra dose of his mother's determination, was one of the first to take advantage of the bounties of the United States just across the river.

William attended University of Detroit on a co-op system that allowed him to go to school for two weeks then work in engineering, his field of study, for two weeks. He would walk the narrow streets from his home amongst the older brick structures, toward the docks to go to school each day. The main street of the city, Ouellette Avenue, offered a vista directly toward the skyline of classic stone high rise buildings of Detroit across the turbulent waters of the Detroit River buffeted between the steel and concrete encased shorelines. William would catch a ferry for a nickel to cross and then board a bus, included in this fare, to carry him the rest of the way to the university. William's job during the school work program was that of a rear chain man in a surveying company. He eventually became crew chief but his real enjoyment occurred during the winter months was when he was paid seventy five dollars to play basketball for the school. Though only five feet tall in high school, he grew enough through college to reach six foot and play for the college varsity basketball team.

It was during his second year at college that William met Grace Collins, the American whom he would eventually marry. Grace, a high school student living in Detroit, was visiting her cousin Helen who lived on the eastern side of Windsor, when they decided to go for a drive along the river. The two girls were riding in an open car with Helen's date Stan at the wheel when they passed William out walking along Riverside Drive. Stan pulled over when he recognized his friend and invited William to join them. He hopped into the back of the car next to Grace and was immediately smitten with the petite brunette visitor. During the ride the two chatted and laughed amicably and William slipped in a request for her phone number before they parted. He then called Grace the next day and after their first date, they began seeing each other on weekends and at games during basketball season.

Grace was a person with wonderful style, a regal bearing and proper attitude though she had experienced a very difficult childhood. Grace along with her mother Florence and grandmother had fled to Detroit from Cincinnati following a violent attack on them by her drunken grandfather. In the last scrimmage, Grace had just escaped with her life after she crawled out of a skylight of her grandparent's small top floor flat, where her mother and she were staying, after her grandfather had come after her with a shot gun. The women moved in with Grace's uncle in Detroit where her flamboyant mother got a job working the switchboard at the Book Cadillac Hotel. This suited Florence's personality very well, since she had a fascination with the various gangster types who prowled the hotel and she was popular with them as well.

Florence had a variety of suitors, husbands and other beaus throughout her life. Her family never really knew which ones she was actually married to except the first, Grace's father Stephan Collins, a banker, and the last, a one armed character who was a former bookie, Joe Hamel. Her first husband was a respectable man from a middle class family who had attained a position at the bank in Cincinnati where his father had labored all his life. Stephan was intelligent and worked hard but he didn't enjoy the career. He found it dull work and he longed for a more exciting life. While in his small office he would dream of making a change but he didn't dare consider acting on this desire, until the day Florence swept into the customer area of the big hall.

The woman appeared as a vision to him, so bold in her colorful dresses and stylish hats. She had a confidence in her stride, a wide smile and a lively personality which represented to him a breath of fresh air. He would watch for her each Friday when she came in to the bank to deposit her earnings from her job as a shop assistant. One day he gathered his courage to approach to her, introduce himself and ask her to join him for a coffee. Florence did not find the thin, prematurely balding man to her taste but she spotted an interesting opportunity and accepted. Despite her poor background and his parent's objections, Stephan pursued Florence like a thirsty man seeking water. He courted her with flowers, small gifts and carriage rides, which amused her but also made her, feel special. Finally he was able to convince her to marry him and after a couple years, the couple were blessed with a beautiful daughter they named Grace.

This new life was not for Florence though. She missed the rough and exciting areas of the city, the camaraderie of the pubs, her girlfriends from the seedier section where she grew up and she missed her mother. Her husband did not want her to go back to her former home and the couple had fierce arguments about it until Stephan finally put his foot down and forbade his wife to go. Florence, who wasn't fond of being confined or kept away from her family, listened to his ultimatum but considered him a fool. So once the baby was old enough, Florence would slip away with her during the day and stay in her old neighbourhood until just before Stephan got back from the bank.

Stephan found out about Florence's exploits from a neighbour one afternoon when he had come home early. He had then waited in their house for her to return, his rage building as the time drew out. When Florence finally entered the house with Grace in hand, her cheeks pink from adventure, he pounced with harsh words. In a moment of unchecked fury, he swung his hand to strike her across the face, back and forth. He was only trying to stop the belittling insults she was hurling at him, and ensure that she followed her husband's wishes before it went too far; but of course, he had gone too far. The very traits he had initially admired in her were the ones he now fought to contain.

Florence immediately packed her belongings and her daughter into a cab, and left for her parent's house. Stephan was crushed. Guilt, pain and loneliness assailed him during the weeks that Florence stayed away. He missed his wife and daughter and when his messages to her went unanswered, Stephan tried to see her in person but he was turned away by her brutal father. The man was a common laborer who drank too much and while he was usually disdainful of his daughter, he disliked this uppity son-in-law law even more. So he defended Florence's wishes not to see her husband. He had never liked Stephan, who thought he was too good for Florence's family. They knew that he had tried to keep Florence away from them too. As the weeks wore on, Stephan realized that his wife was not coming back and desolation set in. Finally, unable to function any more, he decided to take action. He bought a gun and ammunition in a small pawn shop near Florence's house and asked for direction on how to load it. The shop owner, a hunched skeletal old man with stringy hair and dirty fingernails eyed the neatly dressed man for a moment. Then with a shrug of his shoulders and cash in his hand, he showed the customer how to load his purchase.

After another week in a state of depression, Stephan brought the gun to the bank, concealed in his briefcase. Stephan worked methodically at his desk until the time approached when he used to watch for Florence's entrance. He scanned the hall as people strode past but knew she would never be coming into the bank again. Shame and remorse filled his mind and shattered his heart. He withdrew the gun from his briefcase and with tears spilling down his cheeks and a shaking hand; he aimed it into his mouth and fired. The bullet, which was a small caliber, did not end his life however. Instead it had taken an angle that had partially severed his spine and left his body paralyzed from the neck down. It was said that after this incident his sister took him away to Texas for care and Grace never saw her father again.

Florence's last husband, Joe, a dashing, handsome man whose original name was Horace Dinkle, had enlisted in the military at fifteen by lying about his age and presenting false paper. This allowed him to solve two problems at once; how he would support himself after escaping the servitude of life on a farm and how to get rid of an embarrassing name. His parents had died when he was just ten years old and he had then been taken in by an aunt and uncle. However, they only saw the boy as an extra set of work hands for the farm and ignored any of his other needs like affection or an education.

As soon as he was old enough, Joe had run away to enlist was eventually was deployed overseas to fight on the front in France in WWI. He had distinguishing himself in battle enough to have been decorated as a war hero but when he came back to New York at the end of the war, all he could do to made a living was become a tough, a bookie and overall shyster. He bragged that during this period he had become a partner with Jimmy Durante, the well-known comedian, in a comedy club that they had started. But when the next war broke out he enlisted again, perhaps to escape another sticky situation or maybe out of pure patriotism as he liked to tell. Due to his age he was put in non-combative jobs. He boasted that he was eventually assigned as a driver to Eisenhower, the Supreme Commander of the Allied Forces in Europe, and they had become friendly. He returned the States again but this time wound up in Detroit, the reason for which he never told anyone.

Stories were Joe's hobby and the family didn't know which ones were fiction and which were factual. When they challenged him about his connection to the General, he apparently made a phone call to the White House which was put through. He then proceeded to have a grand chat of old times with his former military boss, the recently elected Eisenhower, 34th President of the United States. Of course no one else was allowed to get on the phone to verify the call was really legitimate. One year Florence, Joe, Grace and William drove to New York for a vacation. While in the city, Joe insisted that they go see Jimmy's Durante's show since he was playing at a nearby club. Joe got the group seats up front, settled them in with drinks and then left for a few minutes. He returned just as the show started with a tuxedo clad announcer introducing the star. When Durante, a balding man with a large nose, lopsided smirk and heart of gold, walked out on the stage, he recognized Joe in the audience and called out.

"There is my old partner right in the front – that guy helped me get started. Let's have a round of applause for Joe"

It had astounded Grace and William who hadn't believed that particular tale of Joe's.

One story the family didn't question was how Joe had lost his arm. It was not during a heroic act of bravery but ironically it occurred when he was racing his convertible too close to the side of a stone bridge. He had tossed back a few too many drinks, and lost control of the car while hanging his left elbow over the side, a popular gesture at the time, where it was crushed as the car veered out of control. For the remainder of his life, he wore his well pressed suit jackets with the left arm sleeve neatly pinned up to his chest.

Joe outlived Florence by a few years and was well taken care of by his wife's family. Lee would go with her mother to visit him in the brownstone apartment they had arranged for him across from her Aunt Penelope's. He never went back to the United States or had contact with his own family and when he couldn't take care of himself any longer, Lee's family moved him into a nursing home. Even at the home, Joe had apparently never stopped his showmanship and unusual antics. This was made evident when shortly after his death, a young Philippine nurse in her twenties came to see Anne at their home to offer condolences and inform the family that she had been engaged to Joe. She explained that she had been the one to care for him over the last year and they had grown quite close. This news brought more amused surprise than consternation from Lee's mother, who did recognize the girl from the nursing home. Anne invited the slim figure into the front hall of their large house and explained.

"Joe, though an entertaining man, did not leave any estate if that was the purpose of your visit. You are however welcome to any personal effects of his that you would like"

The girl, who had appeared genuinely grieved over the loss of her companion, now seemed even further hurt by this assumption and declared in broken English.

"Joe say he not have anything to give but also say dead wife's family had been good to him. It is duty to honor his family in time of grief. May God bless you and your family"

Then she turned and left; her back straight and proud. Lee had witnessed all this from behind the railing of the stairs where her mother couldn't see her. She waited to see if her mother would mention the visit to her father later that night at dinner, and explain what she really thought of the woman. Anne did tell Joseph about the visit, suggesting that the girl may have been hoping for some financial support. They would never know if she had been telling the truth about the engagement. She ended the story by shaking her head and wryly saying that it could have been possible since you never knew what that man was going to do next.

The family's lack of exact knowledge about Joe and his history became apparent when at the funeral home after his death the undertaker had asked, "Where was he born?"

"We're not sure, wasn't it somewhere out west," replied Anne and her sister Mary together.

"Who are his next of kin?"

"We don't really know if there are any," was Mary's reply.

"How did his parents die?" was next question.

"We believe that his mother died when she fell down a manhole while walking home drunk from a bar," said Anne.

"And didn't his father die in a brawl at the foundry where he was working when a fellow thrust a steel pole right through him," piped in Mary.

Then the two women looked at each other and collapsed in fit of unsuppressed mirth at the sad absurdity of the situation. They didn't know if any of it was true, they only knew that Joe was quite a character and he would be missed.

Chapter 2 – Excavation & Forms

In 1931 Grace and William were married, then honeymooned in Montreal and began a long stable relationship which produced three children, all girls to the chagrin of their father who had been hoping for sons to play basketball. Their start in life together occurred towards the end of the depression and William took jobs in construction for a few years when he could find them. He had learned some carpentry from his father and gained more experience as an apprentice on the various building jobs. He followed the money around the province, in order to help put food on the table, while Grace stayed in Windsor working at a bank. Once their first child came into the world, a premature baby discovered to have Cerebral Palsy from lack of oxygen to the brain during her birth, they settled into a house on Turner Road.

This child, Penelope, was to be an American since Grace had been driven across to her homeland to have the child. The couple had believed that the hospitals in the States would be better for a premature or difficult birth and when the baby decided to come early, they headed across the border. It had been a hard labor even though the baby was small and she had suffered distress. The doctors had saved her life but she was damaged. These complications from the birth forced the couple to leave the child in the hospital for the initial months, during which time William drove Grace across to Detroit every day to give the baby breast milk. Grace would hold her sweet baby while she feed her and sadly ponder what sorrow and pain was in store for this child.

Once the baby was allowed to come home, William, who wasn't working, thought that he could care for the child while Grace went back to her position at the bank. Grace had been lucky to keep her job since it was still hard to find work. William had tried to find a job in construction again but no one was hiring. In a pragmatic gesture, he had offered to stay home with the baby while Grace went back to work, though it was very unusual for men to stay home with a child in this era. After one exasperating day as care giver for the handicapped child, William knew he couldn't continue. Once Grace was able to take a day off he went out to each of the prominent employers of the area, the big three automotive manufacturers, offering to do whatever they could find for him. He was finally offered a job. "Here I was an engineer and I was pushing heavy trolleys loaded with car parts across a thousand foot long warehouse and I was glad for the work." was William's description of his new job. It was excruciating work that left him in pain most nights and having to soak his feet upon coming home to reduce the swelling so he could get them back in his shoes for the next day. Eventually his intellectual assets were recognized and he was moved into various positions throughout the plant until he had the experience he needed to move on.

The baby was a very difficult burden on the young couple both financially and emotionally and she would continue to be for the remainder of their lives. Although Penelope was able to attend regular elementary schools and could walk fairly well for the first couple decades of her life, her progress did not continue. At some point she had become enamored with a young doctor, who promised her that she would be able to walk normally if she had a couple operations that he recommended. Her parents were against it but Penelope had reached her majority and she had decided to go ahead with the painful and brutal surgeries. This doctor had proposed breaking the bones in each leg and realigning them. It was supposed to be an innovative surgery procedure which the doctor assured the girl would be successful.

The operations did not work and Penelope wound up with her knees twisted and her legs at different lengths. She eventually had to use crutches and terrible envy of her sisters and bitterness for her handicap was all that remained of her nurtured beginning. It was especially tormenting to the couple when Grace was told that she shouldn't risk having any more children because of her heart condition. She had been an only child and extremely lonely growing up and since William had come from a large family, they had hopes of having many children. Instead they had two more healthy girls, both highly intelligent and gifted, before Grace succumbed to advice of medical science at the time and had her uterus removed.

Throughout all this turmoil in his life, William continued to play basketball and in 1935, he was appointed the Captain of the National Basketball team. He was the highest scoring player for Canada and expected to lead the team to the Olympics. He was however unable to go to Germany the next year for the Games since he had collapsed during practice just before the trip in extreme pain and had to be rushed to the hospital with a burst appendix. While recovering from the surgery, he developed nosocomial pneumonia and the infection decimated his body. This form of pneumonia, contracted in hospitals when the immune system is vulnerable, is also deadly. William was the most celebrated person in Windsor at the time and his physician, Dr. Ross, was very concerned that his patient might not pull through. His athletic training had helped him survive to this point but the infection was causing damage to his lungs and his health was deteriorating quickly. Fortunately, during the period of William's convalescence, Dr. Ross, was to attend a convention for physicians in Detroit. He was debating whether he should leave his patient to attend the event, when he realized that this offered an opportunity.

Upon arrival at the convention hall, Dr. Ross asked the speaker at the podium if he could address the other doctors in appeal for assistance in a high profile case across the border that might ruin his reputation if the patient got any worse, let alone died. His request was accepted, and at midnight, a group of six specialists from the States, all in tuxedos, voluntarily came across the border to attend the case at Hotel Dieu in Windsor. They each examined William, conferred between themselves then offered a prognosis and treatment. Dr. Ross followed the suggested procedure and William was soon responding well to the treatment. He recovered slowly over the next few weeks and was able to leave the hospital to return to his family. Meanwhile during his hospital stay, the Canadian basketball team, his own team, played with distinction in Germany and won the silver medal for Canada.

William retired from playing basketball after his recovery and went on to Coach Men's basketball while still working for one of the big three car companies. After a couple years as coach, his team won the Ontario Championship then went on to become the Canadian National Champions. He had the golden touch and it was time to use this talent in his working life. His brother Len, a former basketball player as well, had begun dabbling in various entrepreneurial ventures, which reminded William of their childhood land speculation since he was not having much success. This was evident in a warehouse space Len had leased which was filled with unsold boxes of aspirins in one corner and diapers in another from a couple of failed business start-ups. William was intrigued though and felt that he could figure out the puzzle to a new and successful business idea. So he threw his lot in with Len, expanded the lease of that same section of warehouse and started a new company in 1941, Steward Packaging, in order to package engine parts for the war effort. These parts were to be wrapped in waterproof paper then dipped in wax to be floated onto some foreign shore. William's experience at the car companies had come in handy and the available inexpensive female labor force helped launch the company. The Second World War was on in Europe and jeep parts were in high demand.

It was a time of shortages which ingrained in many, including Grace, a lifelong habit of frugality and conservation of materials, something lacking in following generations. As Grace interacted later in life with her grandchildren, she would especially scorn the use of paper towels, the failure to finish all food on a plate and the purchase of any luxury items. She also developed a deep religious commitment to the Anglican Church and the bible. She frowned on any poor manners, negative attitude or spoiled behavior and as a result, her daughters Anne and Mary tended to shield her from their children's bad antics when possible. The grandchildren were taught to avoid discussing unpleasant topics with their grandparents and the girls tried to perpetuate an aura of contentment at all times. Grace's perspective may have been the result of her upbringing in a volatile and unsettled situation or just the challenges of raising three unique girls. Anne did recall however, that in her childhood that her mother had chased her around the dining room table with a broom for misbehaving. It later came out that Grace abhorred conflict and only did the disciplining at her husband's request. So all the mistakes of her grandchildren and bad judgment of these teenagers were concealed and when Grace accidentally overheard disciplinary measures, arguments or intercepted a letter from a grandchild discussing sex, she would pray even harder that day.

When the war ended and the work in packaging was slow, William and Len bought the Windsor Arena, a former twenty year losing venture, and turned it into a highly profitable business. They sponsored events such as concerts for various stars branching out from Detroit including Sammy Davis Junior and Lena Horn, Bingo tournaments and they founded the semi-pro Spitfires Hockey team. The arena was revived and became a focal point of entertainment for the city but the work load was too much. During this period of entrepreneurial management, William had three massive coronary attacks and was told by his doctor at age forty five, to either quit the hard life of smoking, drinking and working so much or he would die.

William chose to live longer by quitting smoking, limiting his drinking, eating low fat foods and when he was in a meeting that got difficult or stressful, he would get up and leave. Since he had already secured his first million before he was forty, he began to give out his salary as bonuses to the other relatives and staff. He also bought a small condominium in Pompano Beach Florida, across the street from the ocean, and began a semi-retirement pilgrimage south for six months every year as a retreat from stress. He was probably one of the first true snow birds and he lived to the ripe old age of eighty six with only a minor stroke in his mid-sixties from which he recovery completely and continued to play golf three times a week for the next twenty years.

Chapter 3 - The Footings

Lee's first remembered experience occurred when she was four with a black foul smelling mask being lowered over her mouth and nose, producing a silent terror, as she was prepared in the hospital for the removal of her tonsils. This was a standard procedure done on many children at the time and Lee's mother never questioned the need for the operation. Lee recalled being given ice cream while convalescing in a bare shiny yellow hospital room laid out on a hard narrow bed with white curtains to separate her from a half dozen other little girls. Her early memories also include fleeting images of her great grandmother Florence propped in a bed with her white hair framed against the dark wood headboard and her fascinating paper-like skin on her smiling face and folded hands. The elderly woman was living in Lee's grandparent's house because she was dying of cancer. Florence had beaten, or held at bay at least, cancer thirty years earlier becoming one of the first recipients of a colostomy bag as her permanent token of the encounter. She and Joe had lived quietly in Windsor for years after the procedure, taking car rides across the providence with their Cocker Spaniel named Penny for entertainment. Unfortunately the cancer eventually came back and took her after all in 1962 leaving Joe to live on his own.

The back of Lee's grandparent's house had a great expanse of well tended lawn, sloping gently down to the Detroit River culminating in the low steel break wall which enclosed a boat well and empty lift. The house, a one storey ranch with a red brick base and almond siding, was built for Grace by William, his gift of love to her. The yard facing the river, the front of the house as people on the river called it, had a view across to lush Belle Isle, home of several yacht clubs, and the side yard was adjacent to Mackenzie Park, a popular lover's lane. A high rock garden at least a hundred feet long, braced the hillside against the park fence and was a source of great adventure to the small grandchildren left to entertain themselves. Narrow pebble paths wove between small colorful heathers, delicate lily-of-the-valley and bright marigolds. Rock walls bordered the edges that dropped off more severely to the next level of path below. Grace made sure that the children were warned of water rats and snakes near the break wall, just to prevent any overly curious youngster from straying too far from the adults or too close to the river's edge. The children who visited included Lee's sister Cathleen, younger by eighteen months, with silver white ringlets and an instantly charming smile; the dark skinned round faced cousin Barry, with his concealed hurt, and his wiry energy charged sister Jessica, youngest by two years but always in the thick of things. Lee was the leader though, by age and disposition. She would charge off, unhampered by the constricting fancy dresses they had to wear and lead a foray into the gardens. The children would imagine adventures with pirates, hidden treasures and tight escapes. Inevitably, Cathleen would get insulted, head off and pout while Barry would wind up fighting with his feisty sister and the day would end in relief for everyone when they bade goodbye.

At this point William, who had lost most of his hair except for some fringe along the sides exposing his imperfectly shaped skull, appeared to be a contented man. His long agile fingers, once used to encircle a basketball, were now covered with finger puppets or paper pieces when he did the classic "Dickie Bird" skit for his grandchildren. His neck hung with jowls of extra skin connecting his chin to breastbone and his face held deep lines with highly polished tanned surfaces between. He often sat with this glasses intentionally perched upside down on his nose while he watched the television until a grandchild would point out his mistake and insist that he put them on correctly. It was another game and everyone would chuckle as the child would climb up on William's lap, take the glasses from his face and try to "fix" them for grandpa. They all loved their grandfather who was an honest and kind man. They knew that people always spoke well of him and when the children would ask for stories, William's dark eyes would twinkle with delight and he would entertain them as they wished. Only rarely did these eyes turn away to transmit his displeasure at someone's mistake or bad judgment.

Grace was small in stature, strong limbed but bird-like in movement with a well proportioned face and a halo of silver hair as she aged. She was never happy about being just shy of five foot, especially with a tall husband, and constantly commented to anyone over five foot five that they were "So blessed". She had wonderful compassion, humor and took the brunt of criticism or difficulties, physical or emotional, quite stoically. She eventually had many physical ailments including an unknown disease that eventually left her blind in one eye, even after various operations. This eye wound up becoming milky in color, instead of the original clear blue, and the lid sagged especially when she was tired. Grace's grandchildren were always told that her eye damage was a result of bacteria from touching a wild bird. This scared the children away from picking up feathers off the ground. Despite the loss of depth perception in her fifties, Grace continued to do fine embroidery, travel abroad, study art history and the scriptures. Arthritis eventually limited each of these hobbies but she would replace it with another that she could handle without complaint. She also suffered a broken arm that would never mend properly from a car accident. The driver, an elderly friend was fiddling with the radio and went through a red light and was struck in the side by an oncoming car. Her arm was finally secured in place with metal plates through surgery, the bones being too fragile to mend and it had to be carried in a bent position for the remainder of her life.

The home in which Lee was raised, was a large waterfront brick and wood siding salt box with multiple dormers, an attached garage and small concrete stoop at the front door with planters on each side. In the back yard there was twenty feet between the steel break walls restraining Lake St. Claire from the closest part of the house, the sun room. The home was originally built by a Chinese couple on the lake near the mouth of the Detroit River but Lee's paternal grandfather had attained the property through his investments and allowed his younger son and wife to live in it without rent. The street leading to it, wound along the river, past cottages, the water treatment plant and multi-storey red brick industrial buildings with high stockpiles of stone and sand left by the great freighters. The small worn out cottages were grouped together on wide beaches between the stately homes for year round residents. This pattern of modest and massive structures continued along the waterfront to the edge of the city limits and eventually tapered to rows of similar uninspiring average dwellings as the road extended into adjacent communities. Lee's house was at Stop 26, the last stop for the bus line for eastern Windsor.

Across Riverside Drive, the two lane road in front of Lee's house was a collection of humble worker homes owned primarily by French immigrants called "The Village". Here the names Labute, Souilleur and Pillette were predominant. The inhabitants, having intermarried, were a close knit and gregarious group. The older generation, some who did not speak English, usually received a basic public school education before quitting to farm while the younger generation tended to complete high school and sometimes go on to community college for trades. Their families still primarily lived off the land through farming to put food on the table and hunting to supplement it. They also worked at the car manufacturing plants, including the more dangerous stamping plant nicknamed the "Finger Factory" for all those who lost digits there. This plant paid well so the villagers were enticed to risk their hands to pick up the generous pay check. Their houses were one or two storey boxes with siding of white or various pastel colors on neatly kept small lots usually separated with chain link fences, quite in contrast to the grand lake homes with their large expanses of lawn in front and wide side yards between neighbours.

The center piece of the Village was the convenience store, a landmark which stood on the axis to the gravel entry road. The partially stone clad structure, with its broken concrete steps leading to the angled glass entry door, had a wood plank lined interior, dark warm surfaces well lit from the large plate glass storefront windows. Here the proprietors displayed fresh garden items such as shiny red peppers, bunches of deep purple grapes and large smooth leafed lettuce in wooden crates. There was a small butcher shop in the back which sold thick cuts of red meat, farm raised chicken while the rest of the shelves were canned staples.

On the front counter were old fashioned glasses jars of candy, row upon row, filled with rainbows of brightly colored sweetness. These were what Lee longed for when she got to visit the store. Her mother would take them when she had to pick up an item and she didn't want to drive to the grocery store. The children would press their faces up against the glass counter while standing on tip toes to see the jars above and hope that their mother would be generous that afternoon. One day when she was about nine years old, Lee went into her mother's purse, took a ten dollar bill then crossed the busy road by herself to buy some of the wonderful candy she had not been able to taste yet. Unfortunately, the shop keeper immediately called her mother to question whether the girl had permission to spend such a large sum and Lee was hauled home and punished.

The main sources of entertainment during Lee's childhood was the lake behind the house and the new black and white television which held Lee's attention with "I Love Lucy", "Leave it to Beaver" and "The Twilight Zone". The Twilight Zone and later, Star Trek were her favorites. She could still recall the episode of Twilight Zone where a couple of astronauts newly landed on a planet were working through debris to get to a higher point to assess their situation. Suddenly a huge creature started attacking them, swooping from above and the astronauts began to defend themselves. Just as the viewer was inwardly cheering for the pair, the camera zoomed out to reveal that the hillside the men were climbing was actually furniture in an attic and the creature was an old woman with a broom swatting at what she thinks are pesky insects. It was a lesson in perception and Lee learned that one should see the overall picture before establishing an opinion.

Lee also loved Star Trek because she believed everyone could be equal in that future world. Intelligence and honor were important and greed could be substantially eliminated if only everyone had a replicator, which could produce any physical object including food. Then all the material items that humans longed for could be produced at will and we would learn to value love and friendship more. Lee also hoped that eventually humans could telepathically transport themselves anywhere they wanted to go just like the show, since she dreamed of traveling far and wide in this world. She wanted to get away from her small confining life.

Despite her time in front of the television, Lee was a physically active child. She was in the water constantly whether skiing, swimming, fishing or just sitting on Turtle Rock, a large flat perch a few dozen yards out from shore that could hold four children at a time. Turtle Rock was named by the eccentric artist who lived in a low caramel colored brick bungalow with large windows facing the rock. Mr. Barwell was just three doors down from Lee's house and he liked to get the lake children to study the washed up tree roots or clouds in a contest to see who could find the most images. The children would point at a formation call out the word "elephant", "horse" or "old man". He encouraged them to stretch their imaginations, while he was throwing back a number of gin and tonics.

Mr. Barwell was also responsible for Lee's first job, designing logos for pleasure boats which would be parked on massive trailers in his driveway while he worked on them. Mr. Barwell would tell her what name and image the owner wanted and she would do a watercolor painting of the design so he could get approval. Then he would paint the image and letters onto the sleek polished wood hull of the boat with elaborate brushstrokes by hand. Any stripes along the water line would have tape set on each side so the lines would be straight and crisp then it was removed when the paint dried. When he finished one of Lee's first designs, Mr. Barwell invited her over to see the final results. As she walked around the large sailboat with the beautifully curved hull, and saw her design on the sides and across the stern, she felt a great sense of pride. This was Mr. Cecil's boat, a wealthy family friend, and he was so pleased with the final work that he hired Lee to do her first commissioned painting for him. Once she completed the painting Mr. Cecil thanked her and handed over a new one hundred dollar bill, the first one Lee had ever seen. Lee felt a thrill as she held the crisp elegant bill until it was snatched from her hand by her father and tucked it into his pocket.

"This will contribute toward your room and board," he stated.

On Turtle Rock, Lee, her sister and the other neighbour children would imagine that we were in a great sailing ship being pounded by the massive ocean waves when in actuality, the small lake rollers were just trying to toss their scrawny bodies off the submerged granite. One time as a great storm was rolling across from Gross Point on the Michigan coast to the north, the sky became incredibly deep green with black edges where lightning was crackling along the distant shoreline. The children, who were never supposed to be in the water when they saw lighting, were galvanized by the sudden change to the elements. The water seemed to immediately become warmer than the air and it glowed in a bright green illumination against the black clouds on the horizon. They became absorbed in the challenge of staying on their little perch throughout the onslaught of violent waves until a parent spotted them and waded out to help them back to shore to accept deserved punishment. Shortly after this, Turtle Rock was removed by dynamite because of its potential danger to boats and the children lost a beloved playground.

In the winter Lee would sit in her house in a room facing the lake and watch the ice boats, skaters, hockey players glide by and even an old Volkswagen drove past one winter on the smooth ice, to her surprise. She would see all of this from the sunroom which had views on three sides and projected closest to the water's edge. It was a former screened porch that her parent's had glassed in and it was Lee's favorite room.

Eventually, the US government sent cutters through the main channel of the lake right in front of the house to keep it open all year for the freighters and the ice was never as strong again. They still skated but the ice was more unpredictable and the children often lost boots, skates and legs down the shockingly cold dark holes that suddenly formed as the ice collapsed beneath them. Dangerous packs of ice crumbled and shifted along the edge of the free flowing water of the river passage. The children were never allowed to venture that far out though they would always see the line of continuous moving ice piles and wished that they could go climb on them.

Chapter 4 - Weeping Tiles

Lee achieved her basic education in a small four classroom brick school with single glazed windows set in peeling iron frames surrounded by orchards about a mile up the road toward the city. Coleburne Elementary had a total enrollment of about sixty students from various sections of the county but few from the Village since they attended the catholic school. Most teachers taught two grades per classroom since there were not enough students of one particular level to fill a room. In kindergarten, Lee had to lay on a towel on the floor of the gym that doubled as a classroom for a nap. In Grades One and Two, she suffered under the tutelage of a thin and homely spinster who thought that correct spelling would solve all future problems in life. Rows of words were formed with meticulous care on a long roll of paper hung on the pine supply cabinet to be copied with mindless obedience. Each week the teacher introduced several new words and went over their meaning multiple times, teaching to the lowest level in the class and leaving Lee's attention far behind.

Lee did not excel in this atmosphere which only added to the nightmare of Grade Three and Mrs. Willard. This woman stood about five foot tall and about five foot around with a cleavage that had to have measured a foot long, at least the part that was exposed above the rim of her scoop neckline dresses. Her grey steel wire hair was styled short and wavy and never shifted even when her jowls were in rapid movement. Mrs. Willard always perched her cats eye glasses at the end of her short nose, braced her body with thick banded arms, hands placed on each side of the first desk, as she leaned forward and scowled contemptuously at the class. Her incredible mass and the intensity of her beady eyes set in layers of wrinkled mottled skin alone usually quelled even the most obnoxious student, but this was not enough for her. Her raw anger was often appeased only by the sight of a child crying after being taken to the office and hit with the thick leather belt that she had hidden in a drawer.

Lee was the recipient of that belt. The first time was a surprise since Lee had never imagined that she would actually be punished this way. Mrs. Willard yelled at her regularly claiming that she was disrupting the class even though she rarely spoke. Lee accepted the harsh words with a lowered head since she feared the teacher but part of her knew this behavior was wrong. She knew that she wasn't as useless as this teacher made her feel so she would peer up through her bangs to glare at Mrs. Wilson with defiance. Mrs. Willard read this on the girl's face as plainly as if she had written it in large letters on the chalkboard. She was not getting the respect that she felt deserved from this child so she decided to tame her belligerent spirit.

Her chance came one day when Lee had accidentally dropped her lunch box while retrieving it from the top shelf of the coat rack and it hit her best friend as it fell. She had apologized and claimed that it was an accident but Mrs. Willard decided that she had done it on purpose. So Lee was hauled to the principal's office where she watched with trepidation while the big woman opened the top desk drawer and pulled out a thick brown leather belt. Mrs. Willard then demanded that Lee was to lay her small hand upon the desk palm up. She then swung back her massive arm and lashed the leather strap downward with a crack. Lee was shocked by the pain as well as the helplessness and unfairness of the entire situation but she was determined not to show it. She had never been hit that she could recall and couldn't believe that this woman had the right to do this to her. She braced herself and while the smack of each following blow was painful, she did not cry out. Mrs. Willard tried again, her face getting a deeper red with the effort until she was panting and had no more energy to lift the strap. Since Lee failed to cry upon this punishment of the belt, Mrs. Willard was unsatisfied.

"Next time you will cry," she stated with her narrow eyes promising this threat and Lee didn't doubt it.

The second time Lee was given the strap it was in punishment for the audacity of reading ahead in her reader when she had finished all her assigned homework before the other children. Mrs. Willard couldn't bear that this girl would work ahead of her curriculum so she had put elastic bands around Lee's text books. This was supposed to prevent her from working ahead of the class but Lee would slip the elastics off and read the text books held in her lap hidden from view below the desk top. Mrs. Willard of course noticed this and would haul Lee off to the principal's office where she would lay on the belt again. Lee knew that she risked being punished when she had opened the book but she loved reading and was bored when she finished her work early. Mrs. Willard had directed Lee to always sit in the classroom with her hands folded on her desk until everyone else caught up. In the big picture, they would never really catch up and Lee was punished until she was finally broken and shed the tears that Mrs. Willard wanted. Her saving grace being that Mrs. Willard retired the next year.

"That is an excellent picture - you are truly talented," reverberated in Lee's ears in Grade Four.

A miracle had happened; good teachers started being sent to Coleburne Elementary School. That year, besides getting a young enthusiastic teacher who enjoyed children, Lee was tested for being gifted. She hadn't answered all the questions on this IQ test in the time allotted, but she must have scored well since she was selected to attend classes for gifted children. Every Friday, Lee was the only one from her small school to be transported by bus to a large city school where a group of a half dozen children were given special lessons and allowed to create projects in their own areas of interest. This new group of bright children, along with the educational freedom was a bit unnerving at first to Lee. The other children were all from the same school so they knew each other, leaving her an outsider. The teacher, a serious thin balding man had given them the assignment to pick a topic of interest and create a project to best demonstrate the characteristics of this subject.

Lee watched as the other children quickly immerse themselves in their projects, and eventually she selected a topic. She had decided to do one on various species of Lepidoptera since she could represent the topic best graphically in pastel drawings and photo collage. Soon the other children noticed her art work and came over to watch her in action. They were impressed and began to think that she might not be such a loser after all. One girl invited Lee to sit with them at lunch so she wasn't as lonely in the classroom any more. The year was a turning point and Lee blossomed with the knowledge that she was special – she had intellectual and artistic talent. She was not just the girl who feared what was under the bed, or the one who forgot to bring her lunch sometimes or the one cornered by the frightening six foot tall special education student who tried to kiss her.

Lee could not recall the reaction of her parents to any of her accomplishments. Her mother Anne was often busy though she did drive the girls to activities including their ballet classes, Pioneer Girls and speed swimming practices. Lee was not very graceful and couldn't remember the French terms for the steps so she failed her ballet tests. In Pioneer Girls, a type of Girl Guides, she got the most badges in the city every year and won a free week at camp but she turned the trip down preferring to stay on her own lake all summer. The committee had to find a bracelet or necklace to give her instead. In contrast, competitive swimming which she started when she was six years old was where Lee found a good fit. She did well due to her natural athletic ability, long limbs and strength. Backstroke was her favorite and she was soon the fastest in the city in her age group and eventually one of the best in the province.

Her hair became bleached blond with white ends where it broke off, while her shoulders widened and her hips narrowed. The swim work outs were at six am in the morning to start then twice a day when she reached high school. She was strong and sinewy but still shy, so she kept her head dropped, hunched between her wide shoulders. She wore baggy boy's shirts to hide her blossoming figure and kept her face free of makeup. She just wanted to be invisible except when she was with other swimmers. The swimmers were a close group and they had many good times traveling together by bus to swim meets across the province. Lee would win blue and red ribbons as well as tall trophies to bring home and stack in her closet. She was sometimes invited to go with a very talented family of swimmers, the Ramsey's, over the border to practice with the Detroit swim team in their older gloomy Olympic size pool which was a privilege.

Despite the outdated facility, the US swimmers were faster and had more serious training so it was a great advantage to swim with them and experience their work out. When Lee went to swim practice with the Ramsey's on Saturday mornings she was invited to go to their house early for breakfast. She enjoyed camaraderie of these tall lanky outgoing people at the table. They teased each other, laughed and discussed in detail the work outs, times and swim techniques for the upcoming practice. Lee envied the attention and interest that these children got from their parents as they sat around the big round table in the modest kitchen.

When Lee went home her sister would be hiding in her room, her father golfing and her mother would be busy working on some project. No one would ask her about swim practice. This cross country training ended when the Ramsey's were pulled over at the border for a random check one time when Lee was not with them and a joint was found in the back of the van. The family tried to explain that other kids sometimes got into the van at the high school and used it without permission. But the family was banned from the USA until further investigation and the van could never return across the border. The a site visit

Ramsey's were eventually cleared of drug charges and they were free to cross again, though not in that van, but by then Lee had quit competitive swimming.

Chapter 5 – Foundation Walls

Lee's father Joseph was a reticent man. He was tall, thin and blond, with a serious look to his narrow face, which would break into a wide grin when he was making a sarcastic remark revealing small even teeth. Lee loved and respected her father so she hungered for any sign of attention from him, but it was not easily forthcoming. He was an accountant and his nature was well suited to this career since he was both meticulous and cautious. He had gone to University of Toronto to study for a degree but he had gotten sidetracked by fraternity parties until he had failed out in his sophomore year. Upon returning to Windsor he was able to get a job at a local accounting firm through family connections. He was to apprentice for five years before writing the exams to become a CPA. After qualifying as an accountant he was then encouraged by his father to help run a business he had invested in years earlier. It was the Capital Night Club and Joseph agreed to work as a manager for a while to please his father.

It was during this period that he met his future bride Anne Steward when she was the maid of honor in his best friend's wedding. He had been the best man and when the male attendants were asked to dance with the bridesmaids, he was paired with the lively and popular young woman with the dark pixie hair cut he had noticed earlier. Once they were dancing Joseph had been intrigued by the girl. She seemed intelligent, easy to talk to and she enjoyed boating and golfing which were two of his favorite activities. He had not dated many girls, they were all too frivolous and uninteresting to him, but this one seemed different. So he decided that he should take advantage of this opportunity and asked her out on a date. It was a logical step in his mind.

Anne had been impressed with the thin, attractive but serious older blond man who invited her out on his boat. None of the boys she knew owned a boat, they just borrowed their parents. She was less impressed however when he arrived on her door step a few days later in loud plaid shorts which exposed skinny white legs that looked like they had never seen the sun. She had to hold back from bursting out in laughter at the sight of him that morning since she had always dated muscular tanned athletes. But it was a nice day and she had agreed to this date, so they left for the marina in his sports car. Once they were out on the lake though, Anne grew to admire this man who seemed so confident and in control at the wheel and the couple began courting with approval from each of their parents.

After they were married, the newlyweds settled into the salt box house on the lake that Joseph's father owned. Anne had quit college after just one year at University of Detroit to marry Joseph but she would go to the Club to help out as hostess once in a while. When the couple had children, the girls were sometimes brought to the Club when their mother worked, where they played on stage behind the thick curtain.

The children would peek between the drapes to watch their parents as they seated diners, checked liquor supplies and restricted the prostitutes to the regulars only. William was not pleased with this lifestyle for his daughter and his grandchildren so when the Club was closed during a labor union dispute, he offered Joseph a job as the accountant for the family business. Joseph did not want to disappoint his father but he knew that this was a better opportunity for his family. It was a position that Joseph would value and hold for the next forty years. His conservative and wise decisions guided the business through calm waters as well as rough storms. His role was as important as the rudder of a ship seeking a safe harbor and the business steadily grew and prospered. He eventually took over as President of Steward Packaging upon William's death and stayed in that position for the rest of his working days.

Shortly after Joseph had joined the Steward family business and the girls went off to school, Anne had gone back to university. She had been nineteen when she had quit school to marry, so she was determined to complete her degree in Interior Design. The girls knew that if their mother wasn't home when they got off the bus after school, they were to go to the milk chute to get the key to let themselves in the house and occupy themselves until their mother returned. Lee used this free time to search her parent's room, as though trying to unravel a mystery. She would go through their drawers, especially her father's top bureau drawer which held the small valuable items such as watches and cuff links as well as curiosities like small black and white photos, coins, metal objects and old keys. Every time she opened the drawer there emerged a strong musty cedar odor blended with her father's Old Spice. She would breathe in deeply as she ran her finger over the items in the drawer and wonder where they had come from. She imagined the keys opening secretive vaults or doors to ancient places. She imagined previous generations of her family touching the same items.

Lee also hunted through the night stand and under the bed where she would find her father's stash of Playboys and read them to glean knowledge of sex and intimacy so forbidden except in these pages. She read about fore play and erections. She studied these women fondling their own breasts, spreading their legs and touching their moist places while slyly glancing over their shoulder with bold eyes. They were so brazen, at ease in their nudity and sensuality that it was riveting to Lee. She read the articles to understand more about the human body, a subject never discussed in her house. She found out about penises, scrotums, clitorises and parts that she had never imagined existed. The crude aggressive writing described the Playboy way of life which was lustful and seemed decadent and selfish to Lee but the message was that this is what men wanted. It was a world so far from her limited experience that she couldn't really understand it. She tried to relate this information to those she knew in her life, her father's friends, her male teachers, the man at the store but all she could come up for a match was the neighbor and his strippers.

Next door to Lee's house was a rental property that had tenants living on each level of the house, including a man on the upper floor who had opened the first strip club in Windsor, according to the conversations that Lee had overheard. She knew the French family below with the father who rarely wore a shirt and habitually styled his hair by pulling the long pieces on the side of his head over the front of his balding pate then securing them into a ponytail. There was also his loud cheerleader daughter and a red headed freckle faced son who wouldn't talk but tortured small animals with his pocket knife. Lee had seen the boy do these things when he thought no one was watching. He de-scaled fish then threw them back in the water or caught birds and pulled their feathers out then dropped them in the water. So she thought that he was cruel and avoided the boy.

The boy would die young though, the year that Lee had left for college. He had chosen to walk across a traffic bridge in a snow storm that winter instead of using the adjacent pedestrian bridge. Apparently, a car lost control on the ice and slammed into the boy pinning him against the rails. He was killed instantly. This was tragic but it did make Lee wondered about karma and whether the world was spared a worse fate had he lived. The boy and his family had spent a lot of their time in the yard since the father was home all day living off welfare or "poggey" as her father had called it. At some point though, they stopped going outside as much, perhaps the man got a job finally. Instead every once in a while, a bevy of beautiful young women could be seen sunbathing on the neighbour's lawn, walking on the dock or splashing each other in the lake. Most of them had long blond hair, curvy figures and tiny thong bikinis. They were visiting at the invitation of the man upstairs.

When these girls first started coming over, Lee would find her father in the breakfast room with binoculars trained on the figures in the adjacent yard. When her mother entered the room, all Anne did was frown, said "Joseph" in a disapproving tone, and walk out. Lee felt embarrassed that her father was obviously leering at these girls and she thought that her mother should have said more but she feared her father too much to comment herself. She also couldn't imagine the neighbour from upstairs with all these girls to himself. Did he date any of them or maybe all of them at once like the magazines had said she wondered; though that didn't seem right. Then one day while Lee was outside working on her bike in the driveway, she heard a soft voice speaking to her from overhead. As Lee craned her neck to look up, she met the gaze of one of the most beautiful women she had ever seen in her life. The woman had bright blue eyes, set in an oval face of pale smooth skin with waves of chestnut colored hair falling around her shoulders. She was in a simple blue oxford shirt open only slightly at the neck, but on her it had the most flattering shape.

"I am Julia, your new neighbour from upstairs"

Lee's mouth dropped open as she tried to figure out who this stunning woman was and why she had approached her. Julia went on to explain that she was engaged to Randy, the man who lived upstairs and they would be married soon. She asked Lee about her school, how old she was and what she liked to do. She had a gentle nature, kind smile and soon they were laughing and enjoying each other's company. Lee found out that she worked as a legal assistant in a law office where she had met Randy. He had so many legal issues with his new business that he had to go to the law office regularly to resolve them and eventually, just to see her. They never discussed Randy's business but Lee was glad that Julia wasn't a part of it. Maybe she was wrong about all the girls who came over, maybe they were only visiting to enjoy the lake. Soon Lee was so anxious to see Julia that she would go outside and linger in the driveway just in hope that she might come downstairs.

Julia made her feel special because she paid attention to her and seemed truly interested in her. She also felt pretty because Julia complimented Lee, something that her parents rarely did. She told her how certain colors would bring out her beautiful eyes and how her hair was such a lovely thickness and how she was so clever to be able to repair her own bike. Just being around Julia was a gift. Their special friendship continued for many months and Lee hoped the couple wouldn't move once they were married. Then for a week she didn't see Julia and wondered if she had gone on a trip before her wedding. She asked the downstairs neighbour if he had seen Julia recently. He told her in his wheezing accented voice, that earlier in the week Julia had suffered a brain aneurism. It was a condition that she may have had since childhood and they would never know what had triggered the bursting of the blood vessels in her brain at this time. She had died the next day. Lee was shocked and so disappointed that she turned and ran for the tree house to hide for a while. She would miss Julia fiercely and regularly think of the kind words that the woman had spoken to a shy insecure young girl.

Chapter 6 – Utilities & Systems

Lee would always be grateful to her parents for the one incredible gift that helped to mold her adolescence, a motor speed boat. It was twelve feet of curved aluminum with a nine horse motor to power it over the ricocheting waves in the river and the turbulence of the shallow lake. While it was not a thing of beauty, she tried to make it a symbol of personal expression by painting it with fanciful waves along the sides starting in a deep Prussian blue layered up to a frothy white - it represented her freedom. The little boat wasn't very deep and Lee had to be careful not to get swamped by the wake of the the massive lake freighters that sweep past in the river. She also had to be cautious when she maneuvered the boat for docking. The level of the lakes had dropped and the dock was now at least four feet above the water surface.

Lee always felt a little anxious when she approached, at full speed of course, and then had to throttle down to a stop right next to a great steel leg that stretched to the dark underside of the massive metal and wood structure above. She would grab onto the slimy seaweed covered leg post, step onto one of the benches crossing the boat and then hoist herself up over the edge in order to tie the ropes to the cleats above. It was also difficult if she had to take the motor off the boat since she did not get any help from anyone lifting the awkward monster onto a lower step in the well while the waves rocked the boat, then hoisting it from there to the top. She was always worried about dropping it in the water but she was quite strong and that never happened.

Her boat gave her access to a slightly bigger piece of the world including shoreline of Detroit and the deserted Peche Island, or as everyone called it, Peach Island. It was here that she first began her search for archeological evidence of buildings and their foundations. She was told that there had been an estate on the island once and stories circulated about the owner of a famous liquor company who had tried to develop the island for his summer retreat. While circumnavigating this island, Lee had stumbled upon a series of canals, originally built before the turn of the century but now blocked by fallen trees. She found that her shallow boat could make it past these obstructions if she rowed strongly toward the canal, quickly stowed the oars and then ducked into the hull. She could then use the tree to pull herself through the low gap in the foliage. Once inside the island it was extremely quiet except for the croaking of frogs or small fish jumping, their splashes breaking the mirrored surfaces. Meanwhile just a few hundred yards away, Canadians and Americans alike had their boats pulled up on the beaches of the island to have picnics and drink tremendous quantities of alcohol before heading back to their prospective marinas to continue the drinking while docked.

The discovery of the ruins of a building at the entrance to a ten foot wide canal was very exciting and magical to Lee. She had been towing her boat under a fallen tree when she had noticed nearby a section without any tree coverage. So she pulled her boat over into an indentation on the bank and disembarked. The area was carpeted in vines with slightly geometric shapes protruding under the patterns of filtered sunlight. She used a stick to pull the vines away and uncovered stone forms which must have been foundation walls. A little more effort uncovered some much narrower rows of stone just over an arm's length apart. She spent some time mulling over these pieces until she realized that they must have been part of a stable.

Lee had read historic accounts of life during the later part of the nineteenth century and remembered that horses were the common form of transportation before Henry Ford's model T. They were also used for recreation by the wealthy even after the car became popular. She imagined that the section where her boat was on the bank might have been a dock and these were the stables to get your horse to ride to the main building. She began to research books and articles about the island at the public library. She found that the island was first inhabited around 1780 by a French Canadian family named Leforet. This family was from Gross Point, the American side, but they had settled under a land grant from Louis XV and built barns, houses and cultivated about twenty five acres. They shared the island with the local natives and tried to barter livestock with them to secure ownership of the island but in 1857 it was transferred to the Crown by the Chippewa Indians.

A couple decades later the island was purchased by the liquor baron who built a fifty four room summer home, pump house, stables, ice house and a carriage house on the land. He also cleared canals to bring in supplies and ensure the flow of fresh water. Private yachts were used to bring guests from the distillery offices on the Windsor shore to the island. When he died the Detroit Windsor Ferry Company then bought the island with the intention of developing it as an amusement park. The president of the company was using the mansion as his residence when he died on the island and it passed ownership again. The mansion was then burned to the ground by vandals and the island remained deserted until 1962 when another private developer envisioned a grand resort on the island and built docks, harbor buildings and brought power, water and telephone to the island. When he wound up in debt, the government of Canada bought it from him and attempted to turn it into a public park with various concession stands and ranger offices but that too failed and the modern wood structures and docks were left to rot and eventually be reclaimed by nature.

Lee was determined to find the rest of the buildings that had been listed in the documents that she had read, so she started mapping the structures on a crude site plan. She also asked some local people for information. She had a friend in the village, Karen, whose house she used to visit to play and once in a while stay over for dinner. During one evening meal, her friend's Uncle Joe started telling stories of the grand building on the island that had burned down. All that remained was the stone foundation which you could find if you hunted in the middle of the island. He also said that the rich man who built the mansion had forcibly taken the island from the French Canadian family who had lived on it for a century and they had cursed him which must have been the reason for the island's misfortune. Just as he had the group leaning forward at the table in anticipation of his next story, he did his trick of wiggling his ears and popping out his fake teeth, which sent the family into bemused laughter. Lee enjoyed going to this girl's house - it was so warm, loving and crazy. The small house was always filled with relatives, friends stopping in, people hugging and laughing, while her house was large and quiet with people who rarely touched each other and stayed in separate rooms.

Karen's family kept rabbits in a hutch in the back yard, which the girls had to chase when they got out. They spent hours feeding and playing with the large brown rabbits, though they both realized that these soft sweet creatures were meant for the dinner table. The girls also ran through the rear neighbours high corn fields, between rows of grape vines heavy with small purple and green fruit trained on posts. If the farmer saw them in his fields, he threatened them with a shot gun and French curses. They also unwillingly assisted another neighbor, a woman who yelled at them in her foreign tongue and gestured with her heavy arms for them to help pluck chickens. She had beheaded several and had them soaking in a pot to loosen the feathers. Lee had never been exposed to anything like this but she was fascinated rather than disgusted. The woman then reached in the pot, grabbed a headless bird and thrust towards Karen who immediately began pulling feathers off. Then she pushed one towards Lee indicating that she should do the same. Lee held it tentatively at first, the cold rubbery neck in her fist, while she followed Karen's movements to remove the pin-like wet feathers. While she worked, she watched the woman kill another bird which ran off without its head until it collapsed ten feet away from the block. This caused her to burst out laughing because she hadn't known that they actually did keep running after losing their heads. Then Karen glanced at her, looked at the scowling woman with her hands on her hips and joined in the laughter until their sides hurt. Lee was so fond of these experiences but somehow she knew her family would have disapproved so she never talked about them with her parents or her sister and they never asked.

After finding no more evidence of structures along the canals, Lee decided to explore the west beach for the mythic pump house. She had driven her boat past this beach many times but never noticed a structure so she picked a midpoint and landed her little boat on the empty narrow rocky beach. The beach on this end was unprotected from the wind and large waves so boaters rarely stopped here. It did however have the most panoramic view of the open lake, the lighthouse and the facing country's shorelines. After securing the boat lines to a large tree, she started hiking along the beach edge lined with thick undergrowth and elegantly sloping trees creating archways. When she didn't see anything along the beach she strode further inland and tried to cut her way through some of the foliage. Eventually she did find a section of vines that were higher than the rest. She walked around the form, poked it with a branch and removed as many vines as she could. Underneath was the remainder of the stone walls of a small structure.

The building was square in footprint and the walls were almost intact except for some crumbling stone on the water side, the roof having collapsed long ago. Inside the square space was a series of disintegrating pipes with one stretching out of the wall and extending into the woods, soon lost under the forest floor. This she knew would have lead to the main house and that meant that she had found the pump house and she had a direction for the main ruins. She carefully mapped out the location of the pump house on her drawing, then packed up and went home for dinner.

A few days later, feeling like a true explorer, Lee decided to go into the heart of the jungle to find evidence of the main house. She packed some food supplies, a jacket, her map and pencils into a backpack, loaded it onto the boat and set off straight toward the island. Lee was a sight - a determined young girl, fiercely clutching the handle of the motor, face set forward with the wind flattening sun bleached hair, racing across the calm early morning water. The whine of the motor could be heard all across the lake. She decided to dock the boat in the interior rather than the exposed beach, and set out with her compass, in the direction she believed would intersect the pipe.

As she moved into the foliage it immediately got darker and she was engulfed. The smells of the damp earth became stronger and the calling of the birds intensified while the lap of the waves disappeared. It became difficult to part the branches and weeds since there was no path so she held her backpack in front to protect her face. Her legs were constantly getting caught in the undergrowth as vines tripped her and slowed her progress. Her spirit was sinking in the struggle. She needed a machete, like she had seen in the movies that would slice through these vines. Finally, after hours of effort and the day coming to a close, she couldn't go any further and retreated in defeat back down the tiny path that she had cut.

She was back a few days later, heading in the same direction on her new path but making better distance as she wheedled a sickle in front of her. She had found it at a garage sale down the street and used all the coins she had saved to buy it. Then she hid it in the garage behind other tools so her parents won't find it. Lee was sure that she was headed the right way, though she spent more time looking around her for clues than she had the last time. She especially listened to the birds, as they acknowledged her intrusion and called their warnings ahead. While paying attention to these calls, she noticed the most unusual sound in the background. It was a low tone, a deep throbbing vibration. She made a slight turn toward the direction of the sound and cautiously waded through more underbrush until the noise grew in scale. It was frogs, so many that their croaks had blended to a single chorus from farther away. She found herself on the edge of a huge vivid green space, the size of a soccer field, without any trees. As she bent down to examine the forest floor, she noticed that the green was a kind of small leafed water plant that totally covered what seemed to be a pond underneath. She was amazed by the density of the plants since they looked more like a carpet. She had never seen anything like it before.

Lee decided to circumnavigate the pond since she couldn't understand why there would be such a land locked body of water in the middle of the small island. It was hard to move around the pond because the forest wall pressed close to it and kept forcing her every step almost into the water. She tried to use her sickle to measure the depth of the pond at the edge to see if she could wade through it and was surprised to find that she couldn't touch the bottom. Then she dropped her hand to feel along the sides and realized they were made of stone, man-made stone. She had found the foundation of the main building of the estate. When the building burned down, all that was left were these foundation walls deep enough to have been below the frost level. This excavation had eventually filled with water and created the pond. The pond attracted the frogs and grew over with thick water plants, hiding the surface beneath. Lee had uncovered its mystery, and while it wasn't what she expected, it was an amazing sight and she was very pleased with herself.

For all her time on the island, Lee was lucky to never have been discovered in such a secluded spot by one of the drunken brutes who frequented the island, until she was thirteen. One afternoon during a visit to the island, a man surprised her on the path near a popular beach, tackled her to the ground from behind and held her down with his weight. Lee had screamed and fought, which only brought laughter from nearby boaters thinking that the noises were part of a wild party. She continued to fight but grew frustrated with the knowledge that she was so helpless under the strength of a two hundred forty pound adult male. She then changed her tactics and threatened him with charges of jail time since she was underage but he continued to hold her by the wrists over her head while he groped her body.

Lee moaned the word "No" when she felt him fumble to pull down her shorts. She could smell the liquor on his stale breath as he panted into her face and she began to yell even louder and twist to get away. At one point she saw another man emerge on the path so she called out for help but he just looked directly at her, then turned chuckling and walked away. The man on top of her told her to shut up, forced his forearm across her neck and began to press down. Lee felt her esophagus compress painfully and soon she could not take in any more air. Her eyes opened in alarm as her muscles clenched in desperation to get oxygen. Wheezy sounds came from her throat as small amounts of air made it down the passage but her lungs could not fill fast enough. Just as suddenly as he had blocked her throat, the huge man removed his arm so he could get back to opening his zipper. Lee gasped as the air filled her starved lungs.

She didn't scream any more after that and the sweat soaked man on top of her got even more excited by her unspoken admission of helplessness. He felt powerful as he held the girl down and began to pry her legs apart with his knee. He then began to pump his member into the tight space at the top of her thighs searching for the cleft opening but after a few minutes he spilled prematurely before penetrating the girl. He grunted in satisfaction, then collapsed and rolled slightly to the side of Lee but still pinning her, exhausted by his efforts.

As he shifted his weight, Lee grasped the opportunity to pull her hands free of his loosened grip and squeeze out from under him. He didn't resist; he had what he had wanted. She then kicked as hard as she could into his body and quickly jumped up to race away. She headed straight for her boat without looking back, though she heard his amused laughter follow her as she ran. She vaulted into the boat and yanked on the pull cord of the starter. The engine kicked to life and she muttered a quick prayer then steered the boat out of the harbor to head home.

Her body shook with fear as she rode, bouncing over the waves while she lifted her fingers to touch her bruised throat. Tears streamed down her face the whole way but she didn't notice them. She was lucky to have escaped with her virginity intact, let alone her life, but the humiliation, helplessness and the degradation of the experience would haunt her for many years. She believed it was her fault for going on that path and for not fighting harder, so she never told anyone about it and the island lost its magic for her forever.

Chapter 7 - Waterproofing

During this period in the late sixties and early seventies, Lee's parents were caught up with the styles and trends for families of this era. Her father wore wide flowery ties with wide lapel suits and her mother wore short A-line dresses and a bouffant hairstyle. Joseph came home at night to sit in front of the television with a martini as the undisputed lord of the house. Her mother would be busy in the kitchen preparing dinner that he would expect served at six o'clock precisely each night. Lee would set the table in the sun room and often sat to eat her whole plate piled with food before her father even moved to the table. Lee's mother rarely joined them since she tended to eat while she cooked and was often dieting. Lee would then have to stay seated and watch her father finish his meal, slowly methodically moving the fork from the plate to his mouth until he was finally done before she was allowed to leave the table.

In order to fight her impatience and boredom, Lee would try and find amusement in her father's actions, such as the way he ate corn on the cob. He was just like a typewriter, moving the cob back and forth, creating precisely four straight sides. They often sat in silence except for her sister's complaints about why she had to eat something she thought was unpleasant. This was the moment when Lee decided that she did not want this life for herself. She could see that her father wielded power and her mother yielded to him; but that didn't seem right since her mother was as smart as he was and worked pretty hard. Lee just knew that she didn't want to be like her mother; less respected and someone who was always serving others who do not appreciate the effort.

Her parents had a good social life at the country club and gave lots of parties with heavy drinking, party games and food that Lee's mother had made weeks in advance, kept in the freezer then thawed just for these events. Their guests were often curlers, or golfers, professionals and doctors who couldn't drink when they were on call. The other guests when drinking liberally would sometimes get a bit carried away. Some became overly affectionate with each other causing minor scandals and indignant spouses while others merely entertained. One very serious surgeon, when able to drink, would quote poetry, line after line of Emerson, Whitman and Frost that he had memorized as a youth while living in a tough area of downtown Toronto. He also told of his success as the horseshoe tossing champ of the city at age twelve.

Another friend of the family, a teacher whom Lee had been encouraged to call Uncle Randy, though he was not related, had tried to assault Lee at one of her parent's parties. She had been in the sunroom away from the other guests when he found her, grabbed her arms, forced his mouth on hers and stuck his tongue between her teeth. Lee was so shocked at first that she couldn't react. She had grown up knowing this man all of her life. His grip on her was strong, bolstered by the alcohol, but she had a flashback of her fear that last day on the the island and recovered her senses enough to push hard against him to break his hold and run out of the room. She ducked into the bathroom upstairs and locked the door, the sounds of the party still breaking through the safety of the room.

She was ashamed and repulsed, trying to assess what had just happened. As she sat with her head in her hands, she didn't see that she had any choice since she again couldn't tell her parents. She was too embarrassed and thought that they wouldn't believe her. So she stopped joining the parties and avoided being around this man again. The episode also changed her view of these "Uncles". She started really seeing, for the first time, their flirting with waitresses and secretaries and she wondered about the lunches at the "strip clubs". She now heard in their teasing of each other, hints of something even more secret that may have happened during their golf trips. Some of these Uncles would never again be as funny as they had once been to her before.

One of Lee's favorite people at these parties was Aunt Rachel, a wonderful boisterous character with a raspy voice, who would recite Irish drinking limericks when in her cups. She could rattle off one complicated lyrical ditty then immediately swing in to another tongue twister while tilting her head back and drawing the listeners in. Sometimes her limericks were rather naughty and she winked as she told those tales. The whole crowd listening would laugh and cheer her on. She loved the attention and Lee admired her optimism since she suffered from so many health problems all of her life which would have defeated a weaker person. She had bad knees, painful swollen feet and shoulder problems, each requiring multiple operations every few years. These constant setbacks, to her consternation, would interfere with her one true hobby, the beloved game of golf. Aunt Rachel got pure enjoyment out of facing a long manicured fairway and belting that little white ball as far and straight as she could. She loved the challenge of finessing the ball over gapping sand traps and onto undulating greens. She watched every major golf tournament to see how the pros did it and then she would try these techniques herself, to limited success, but it didn't deter her. She wanted to be out on the course as many days as possible and this was easily accomplished since she was a popular golf partner. Through the pain, she would smile and tell a series of self-deprecating jokes worthy of a professional stand-up comedian during the round, reducing the other members of her foursome into stitches from laughter. She would often declare, her chin up and voice strong.

"God did not give you this body to lay a nicely preserved specimen in the ground to rot when life was over. You were supposed to wear it out before you go and I plan to follow these instructions"

Aunt Rachel was also Lee's grandfathers' niece and her family had a reputation as big partiers. Her three sons were considered quite wild and they spent a lot of time in the northern Muskoka Lake Region at their cottage where they would throw drunken bashes and when sober, put on ski shows. It was said that the boys could each dive off a lifeguard tower while clutching a ski rope as the boat took off and emerge to the surface, in a position on their elbows and knees, spray blasting against their faces, to ski across the entire lake. The crowd of vacationers who craned their necks to watch would be enthralled. The boys would next jump off the edge of the lower dock with feet extended forward and holding the rope, as the boat took off at high speed. They would hit the water with their bare feet planted as substitutes for skis, and circle the lake in that position. Water would shoot out the sides of each foot like a rooster tail and their arm muscles would bulge with the strain. Eventually they would hook the ski handle into the elbow of one arm and use their free arm to wave as they passed the cheering audience on the shore. "True showmen in that family," Lee thought!

Aunt Rachel's gregarious husband Frank was the manager for Steward Packaging's Brampton plant. He was a hardworking and valuable employee for over forty years. Many other businesses tried to lure him away but he was loyal to the family. The business thrived under his direction but he also played hard and eventually became a full blown alcoholic. At the age of sixty, he was told that his liver was so stressed, that one more drink would kill him. He decided to voluntarily go into rehab where he eventually emerged sober, quiet, and thinner.

The greatest change was that he didn't have his standard bulbous red nose. His appearance was so altered that when he bumped into William at a Christmas event, the older man didn't recognize his long term employee and tried to introduce himself.

Frank attempted to live within his new sobriety but unfortunately, he could not resist temptation and began drinking again which caused his early death. He was missed terribly by Aunt Rachel who remained single, living in a senior's apartment complex in Naples, Florida the rest of her life. She had been born American and hadn't given up her citizenship all the years she had lived in Canada with her husband so she could become a resident now instead of a snow bird. She didn't have to return to Canada every six months like her friends. So she continued to play golf in the Florida sunshine between operations until her own demise at the age of seventy six, well worn out by then.

Meanwhile, in the States, the Vietnam War was in the headlines of the newspapers constantly and on all the televisions stations that the residents of Windsor picked up from Detroit. For the first time, the war was brought into the public's living rooms. Canada however was a cocoon of safety while it viewed the anguish and struggle of their neighboring country torn apart. They saw the riots in Detroit, the soaring increase in violent crime, women's rights protests, the black power marches and the gang wars but all these injustices and prejudices seemed to bypass the Canadians. Windsor still maintained a low level of crime with very few violent incidents, even though it was only one tunnel ride away from the murder capital of the United States. The influx of immigrants from former British Colonies like Pakistan, Jamaica and Hong Kong brought diversity to Canada. Increased numbers of mixed marriages then helped with ethnic tolerance, something that did not exist in most of the States.

The laws preventing hand guns may have also helped prevent crime in Canada but there were also seemed to be fewer desperate people and no real urban blight or slums. This socialistic country paid high welfare distributions to those who were unemployed, had laws in place about equality of pay between the sexes and strong employment protection as well national health care; but someone had to pay for all of this. These benefits came at a high economic price and taxes could soar to over fifty percent for individuals in the upper income sectors. Also, all Canadians and visitors would eventually pay the infamous GST tax on goods and services of seven percent on top of the already high provincial sales taxes. The health care system sometimes floundered under lack of funding forcing the closure of some hospitals, limiting new equipment and delaying treatment. Even so, crossing that border was still a huge attraction for those who wanted to avoid service in the Vietnam War. The draft dodgers spilled into the border cities of Canada and the population of Windsor grew steadily, flush with newly arrived Americans as well as immigrants. The city flourished and thrived across the narrow stretch of water, as though the war, poverty and conflict were a disease and they were immune.

Chapter 8 – Sill Plate

At fourteen, Lee entered Riverview High School imbued with feelings of curiosity, trepidation and naivety. She decided to keep her head down to avoid attention, especially during hazing week for freshmen and this way she was able to avoid being forced to climb the flag pole or sit in a garbage can each day. One of the sophomore girls recognized Lee from the bus route and took Lee under her protection which initially boosted the girl's confidence as well. Susan was a tall dark haired outspoken girl with a streak of head strong ferocity. She took Lee places that she would have never ventured with her timid nature. Susan's house was only a block from the school so Lee began "hanging out" there and avoided going home until late each day. Susan drank heavily and smoked pot in her basement while her elderly parents were upstairs, and Lee had to rescue her many times in her drunken adventures out on weekends. Lee stayed a sober companion and watch dog most of the time. Unfortunately, Susan also had a mischievous streak that played itself out on all around her and their friendship went off course many times. She loved to play pranks including sinking fellow basketball player's shoes in the toilet while they were in the shower or telling Lee a certain guy was interested in her when he wasn't or breaking into the visiting basketball team bus and starting it up. What she would have done with the bus Lee never knew because the ensuing chase by the police had them climbing chain link fences and running through neighbours yards to avoid capture. Lee had never been so scared of getting in trouble in her life.

Through Susan's influence, Lee grew more daring at school and she joined some of the sports teams including track and field, swimming and volleyball where she became captain of the team. The girls also both played tennis and basketball with the senior boys after school most every day. They were "tom boys", if that meant that each of these girls loved physical activities, were bold in action and could play any sport that the boys could and often better. They believed that they could do anything with their lives and they didn't accept the previous generation's restrictions and limited expectations of girls. They had been given freedom of action, thought and consequences, which boys had always taken for granted, and it changed them. It was a new generation of baby boomer women emerging to challenge the status quo by getting greater education, joining the work force, choosing to marry or not and when or if to have children. Most colleges were becoming co-ed and jobs that had previously banned women, such as construction, military and aerospace opened their doors inch by inch. Opportunities were becoming available to women that had not been available in the past.

The Suffragettes of the nineteenth century had finally gotten the vote for women in 1917 in Canada and 1920 in The United States and Lee could only wonder why it took so long. Only in this generation were women allowed to fully explore their natural gifts of intelligence, artistic talent or athletic ability openly. It was the time of Gloria Steinham and the Women's Liberation Movement, who rallied to ensure that women's rights, including equal pay and equal representation, were put into law and ratified. Lee would later learn that these rights were fragile, when Iran, a fairly modern society under the Shah was taken back into the dark ages by radical Islamic fundamentalism lead by the Ayatollah Khomeini.

Women who had been professors, doctors and professionals were restricted from teaching, practicing or even getting an education. Even more basic rights such as choosing their clothing, driving a car, wearing makeup or traveling unescorted were limited as well. It became apparent that countries with more equality between sexes were actually the more prosperous nations. They had taken advantage of all of their human resources instead of expending such energy and efforts to restrict half of their population so the other half could be masterful. When women became lawyers, they also became law makers and politicians so they could protect their rights and influence the future. As Lee traveled more in her life, she began to understand that women's rights require constant vigilance and should never be taken for granted.

Lee and Susan did not consider themselves "Women Libbers", slang for the Women's Liberation Movement, but they also didn't fully understand the history of the fight for rights that their sex had only recently inherited. Lee knew that her father ridiculed and reviled the Women Libbers, so she avoided ever using that terminology or associating with the group since she loved her father and wanted his approval. She didn't understand that her father's remarks probably came from his upbringing as well as possibly the fear of change. Susan had a brother and Lee had a male cousin but they had never considered these boys better or more entitled than themselves. They looked at other kids by their personal traits and talents. They knew that Mark Conner was an amazing athlete in basketball and track, but so was Julie

Smith in volleyball and tennis. It was a naive view to assume that a person could achieve whatever they were willing to work hard enough for in this world despite sex or race or religion, but that is how these two thought at this time in their lives. Their misconception would later cause them each frustration, anger and pain but they would better understand the value of the gift of equality. The challenges in life would approach each of them, as though they were a ball in a pinball game that is buffeted from all sides and at other times lulled and enchanted by deceiving calm and easy advancement.

The girl's friendship however took a final twist toward ending when Susan expected Lee to lie for her to the volleyball coach about missing a practice. They had gone to the curling rink instead of volleyball practice since their coach was going to be out of town even though before leaving she had instructed all players to attend the practice on their own. Lee and Susan decided to use the time for another practice instead. They were both Skips on curling teams, which is the team captain of a four person team, and they had their first tournament of the season the following weekend. They needed to practice.

So Lee went out on the ice to practicing her throws while Susan joined her to call the throws. Curling is a truly popular Canadian sport, where each member of the team takes a turn swinging the "rock", a polished granite stone with a handle on top, then releasing it to slide towards the bull's eye at the end of a sheet of ice the length of a hockey rink. This technique is done from a swatting position, with the thrower pushing off a stationary block with one foot then sliding on their extended foot, in a Teflon-coated shoe. During this push the curler gently releases the rock with a twist to glide down the ice. The intention of the throw is often to knock out the other team's rock or land in the bull's eye like shuffle board. The points are made by counting the closest rocks to the bull's eye. Sweepers with brooms are stationed on each side of the rock as it glides down the ice, to vigorously sweep in front of it and cause a slight melting of the ice that speeds or turns the rock. The Skip at the end calls this action and leads the team to victory or defeat. While Lee defended Susan's choice to practice curling, she would not lie about where they had been. Susan then would not forgive Lee for getting her kicked off the volleyball team and they stopped calling each other.

This incident did end the female friendship but it also started Lee looking to her male basketball buddies with new interest. She started to see these boys as more than just fellow athletes and began flirtatious teasing with a tall shy volleyball player named Alan who reciprocated her interest. This interest in each other eventually led to a first kiss. Alan had begun to ride his bike with Lee home after they played basketball or his volleyball team had practice. They would pause at the separation point, talking under a street light, drawing out their time together. Finally, one evening he leaned forward and his lips met hers in a sweet kiss. Lee was so excited afterwards that she rode the long dark route home without worrying about the bugs flying at her face, which was set with a broad smile. She couldn't wait to see him again and wondered whether they would kiss again. Her excitement was short lived though when the next day she watched Alan collapse on the volleyball court during a game as the ligaments in his knee tore and he couldn't stand again. It was like seeing an antelope after being shot, confused as to why its body wouldn't allow it to rise. There were no more bike rides or basketball games after school and Alan spent most of his time after his operation in therapy or catching up on studying so he could graduate in the time.

After this awakening to boys, Lee began dating with mixed results. One date involved a cocky good looking fellow who asked that her mother drive them to a movie theater downtown where he rather aggressively tried to grope Lee in the dark. She pushed his hands away and they had a silent embarrassing return home in an over lit city bus. Flirting, crushes, insecurities, fear. A first regular boyfriend the summer before sophomore year, a secretive street wise fellow who would get Lee to do some furtive necking on the dock, in his car or in the basement of his house, while his family were upstairs. He disappeared when school started and Lee never saw him again.

After this, Lee dated a British boy with long blonde hair whose brother was in her electricity class. She had wound up in electricity due to a mistake. She had signed up for architectural drafting, for first semester of her freshman year, in the tech wing, a dark oily smelling section of the high school. She had been encouraged to take drafting by her explorations of mapping the island and watching her mother build models for interior design classes. Lee loved the drafting class and she knew right then, that she wanted to be an architect. The selection for second semester tech classes was based on a lottery and you could not take the same class twice. The person with the highest marks from the first semester had first choice and Lee, whose grades were the best, had chosen auto mechanics. When the class lists were posted though, she was not in auto mechanics, as per her request, but electricity which was her third choice. When she confronted the Dean of Technology about this mistake, a portly man with dyed black hair, he told her that no girl could be in auto mechanics.

"A girl in that class would be a hazard to herself and her fellow students," the Dean exclaimed.

Lee then pointed out that there actually was a girl on the class list, Kathy Black, a rather stout androgynous looking girl. The Dean's patronizing smile drooped a little. He sputtered then defiantly stated "That seems to be a mistake" which Lee recognized as a lie. Then he told her to just take the course she was put into - electricity.

So Lee joined the electricity class which actually gave her a new skill set. She spent the semester getting hands-on wiring training under a severe German teacher who was determined to protect her from her fellow students by throwing his collection of keys, probably weighing in at fifteen pounds of metal, at anyone who looked at her. This meant her boyfriend's brother came within an inch of having his head cracked open many times. This teacher had also intentionally paired her up with the most harmless student in the class as a wiring partner, Johnny Wells. Johnny was a very sweet fellow but a bit out of place in this tough environment with his lanky swaying build, crisp ironed shirts and wide naive smile. As partners, they had assignments which included the wiring of an open wood frame room that had a working electrical panel in it.

Lee and Jonny's room was on the mezzanine, away from the rest which suited Lee since she wanted to figure out how to run the wire on her own. One thing she did learn right away was that Johnny wasn't very coordinated or talented in electrical installation. He couldn't figure out how to run the wiring, especially three way switches but he wouldn't allow Lee to take a lead role. During one project, Johnny refused to check whether he had shut off the power before the teacher came to inspect the work even though Lee had warned him about this. He resented what he saw as her superior attitude, so he ignored her suggestion. Lee just decided to back away when the teacher came to inspect their work. As the teacher was sticking his fingers deep into the multi-colored wiring of the panel to check the connections, he suddenly was thrown back, wide eyed in surprise. As he recognized the culprit, with extraordinary control, neck bulging with veins, face red in fury he quietly told Johnny to turn the power off next time and retreated to his office to gather himself. Johnny later went on to become a general contractor with lots of opportunity for repeat performances.

In sophomore year Lee settled down emotionally when she started a long term relationship with Rene Lebuff, a tall handsome dark haired fellow from the village. Rene had worked up the courage to skate over to her one evening when he had spotted her in her back yard while he was playing hockey on the lake. She had been barbequing steak for the family's dinner, a chore her father had her do all year round, when she saw the well built boy approach skating smoothly with the hockey stick casually in one hand. This boy was one of the best looking but extremely shy fellows in the school. He had never been seen with any girlfriend so Lee was intrigued. They chatted for a while, both shyly studying the other before Lee was called to bring in the steaks. She apologized that she had to leave but he asked if he could call her and she agreed, secretly excited.

Although she knew that he might not go far in his education, Lee could tell that he was a good person and she soon looked forward to his phone calls and visits. Lee's grandparents also enjoyed seeing Rene because he reminded them of Joe Namath, the famous quarterback for the New York Jets, thus they nicknamed him Joe. To entertain her grandparents, Rene would twirl a basketball on his index finger then pass it back and forth between fingers and then across hands, to William's delight. Rene was from a small house in the back of the village and his kindly mother, always neatly dressed with her dark hair curled, was very good to Lee every time she visited. Rene's sister was always home as well since she was sick and couldn't go outdoors without losing her breath. She had been born with a hole in her heart and was not expected to live long. She was a frail, toothpick thin, pale girl, with blue veined skin and red rimmed eyes but she loved Elvis and got excited every time his songs were playing on the radio. She was both her mother's joy, in that they were very close, and her extreme sorrow, in the knowledge that one day she would have to bury this lovely girl.

It was in the spring of Lee's junior year that Mrs. Lebuff had a horrible accident. She had been cooking for the family when a grease fire started in the pan and as she tried to grab the handle to move the pan to the sink, it spilled and the burning grease went onto her hands and down her leg. The problem with hot grease is that it keeps burning deeper into the layers of the skin and the pain is continuous, the doctor explained to Rene and Lee at the hospital. Mrs. Lebuff had suffered severe second and third degree burns but she was getting daily baths and skin grafts so that she would be able to go home in a few weeks. Her arms and legs were covered in gauze when Rene and Lee went to visit and they had to wear gowns and masks to lessen the risk of infection to her exposed flesh. While in the hospital, Lee was amazed by the number of children in the burn unit. They were playing in the halls, pushing toy trucks or bouncing balls. One little boy riding a tricycle, who couldn't have been older than four or five, stopped Lee to ask if she wanted to see his "owee". She agreed and he immediately lifted the back of his pajama shirt to expose a mass of red welts, blisters and scaring while watching her reaction with wide blue eyes. She held her composure; even though she suddenly felt sick to her stomach, and remarked that it looked like it was getting all better and he should be able to go home soon. This pleased the boy and he peddled off to his room while Lee went into the nearest washroom to sob.

Lee also spent a lot of time with Rene at the Sportsman Club across the street, watching him practice archery for hunting or just hanging out with his friends. It was an older low roofed concrete block building with a big bar in one end and an open meeting room in the other. One night when they were at the Club, a few camouflage clad men came in to announce that they had just got back from moose hunting and they had their prizes outside in the trucks. Everyone poured out to examine the carcasses of two moose, one young one in the flat bed of a pickup and the other, head only mounted on top of a U-Haul since the body was inside. Lee watched the excited men move closer to touch the poor animal's face below the open glassy eyes and pull out the tongue. The men continued to congratulate each other about the kill and discussed the distribution of the thick steaks that would soon be prepared and she realized that even though she felt incredible remorse for this animal, she was not the person to judge these men. Lee did not agree with hunting as a sport but she was also not a vegetarian.

Chapter 9 – Floor Joists

The first pull towards the arts that Lee felt was when she saw the charcoal sketches that her mother brought back from her figure drawing classes at Wayne State in Detroit. Anne would encourage the girls to use her supplies and sketch pads to draw alongside her as she worked on her projects. She then enrolled Lee in painting and drawing classes at the coach house on the grounds of the stately old stone mansion called Wilmsted in the heart of Old Walkerville. There Lee worked on easels in an elegant Tudor styled stable with clerestory windows that had been turned into a studio. The students sketched in charcoal and ink on reams of large vanilla colored paper and eventually graduated to oil painting on stretched canvas. Painting was a rewarding hobby but Lee could sense that there was something else she could do with that artistic ability. It was when she took her first architectural drafting class in high school that she found an outlet to combine the flair and creativity of art with a practical application. She saw designing as challenging intellectual puzzles and she admired the new modern white houses that she saw in magazines. These concepts were like a breath of fresh air.

Lee didn't know it at the time but this aesthetic was a result of the modern movement in architecture. In America, the architect Frank Lloyd Wright had introduced long low roofs stretching across continuous lines of windows and concrete walls. Mies Van De Rohe and Philip Johnson had taken this concept even further with houses entirely of sheet glass walls between thin steel columns supporting a flat roof that appeared to be floating. The Glass House designed in 1949 by Johnson became an icon of this era. Still the most popular housing style for the average consumer was a bastardized version of historic Georgian, Victorian or Queen Anne styles with pitched roofs, dormers, shutters and casement windows. These were built throughout the sprawling new suburbs in North America as the middle class became more mobile and left the urban cores. Lee was enraptured with the modern look though, and for her class project she designed and drafted a long sleek white house stretching across a river with large sections of glass under flat cantilevered roof panels. It was her drafting experience in this class that helped with her first job at Richard Architects for the summer. Her Uncle Jack arranged this opportunity for her since George Richards, the principal architect, was his good friend.

Uncle Jack was an unusual looking fellow, though very admirable in his character, and Lee adored him. He had been born with Osteogenesis Imperfecta, known as brittle bone disease. As a result, he had been bed ridden until the age of twenty when he was told that he could finally stand and potentially walk with newly developed steel leg braces. He had to choose between spending the rest of his life in bed or walking with the braces and crutches which invariably lead to accidents, falls and pain. When he chose to learn to walk, he knew it would cost him in broken bones and he would eventually have fifty four fractures in his lifetime. He had to always be careful since if he even tensed his muscles too tight, it could cause a fracture. Jack was very intelligent and he had been home schooled by a kindly aunt who had once been a teacher.

He eventually completed his high school certification through correspondence but he missed the excitement of a regular school education. He was a highly social individual and enjoyed the company of any visitors who came to see him, entertaining them with humor so they would stay longer. The rest of the time it was a lonely existence. His brother was busy with his friends and his parents felt guilt wrap itself around them any time they sat too long in the quiet room with their aging son. Jack's view into the world was from his window and through it he would hear the children coming home from school, their laughter seeping through the cracks in the frame, and he would envy them their strong working legs.

Jack Sherman stood about four foot six inches when he was upright, with a broad chest and muscular arms. These arms had developed even more as he relied on them to walk with his new crutches since his legs couldn't hold his weight very long. He would place the crutches on either side of his weak thin braced legs, allowing them to steady his body before swinging the sticks ahead with rhythmic precision to create a smooth forward action. It took courage to leave the cocoon of his room and emerge in a harsh world where every step he took was painful and risky. He trained himself to ignore the rubbing metal chaffing his skin, the bruised tissue and strained muscles - he was determined to walk. Despite everything, he was optimist by nature and he had decided to make the most of this short life despite the cards handed to him. His good spirits, laughter and sharp mind drew people to him and his social circle expanded. He was also a dignified man with thick dark hair that thinned and went grey as he aged, but it was always neatly combed above his tortoise shell glasses which framed bright blue eyes and a constant smile.

Once he was mobile, Jack decided to get his insurance license and started his own insurance company. It wasn't a large practice but it did provide him with a modest income. Shortly after this he met Lee's Aunt Penelope at a social gathering. They courted for a year then Jack asked Penelope to marry him. The couple was thrilled to have found each other, especially with their understanding of each other's infirmaries and challenges. As the years wore on though, Uncle Jack began to travel frequently for his various boards and committees while his wife preferred to remain home and withdrawn from company. His friends were intellectual people - doctors, lawyers and architects and he was a prominent figure in the community. He became the driving force behind the formation of the Windsor Accessibility Advisory Committee which worked to create building codes for a barrier free environment for the handicapped. Eventually these codes, that promoted accessibility for the handicapped, would spread worldwide.

Uncle Jack took his concern about improving opportunities for the handicapped even further when he campaigned to get a new community development built for disabled people in different stages and abilities so they could live together and support each other. This was an architectural project that his friends helped him design and his niece was fascinated to hear about as it was built. He was a great story teller with his teasing manner, and Lee enjoyed visiting her uncle in the single storey house he had built specially designed to support he and his wife. In this house there were no stairs, the counters were all lower and there was a space under the sink for a wheel chair to roll in so Penelope could reach the water when she had to abandon her crutches. The bathroom was larger than usual to allow for the turning radius of a wheelchair and grab bars were mounted on the walls at the toilet and shower. This sanctuary, with its dark comfortable den, was where Lee would find herself listening to Uncle Jack's deep sonorous voice with his heartfelt laugh. She would watch his hands, the nails irregular and yellowed by his disease, with familiarity and love.

Lee's last visit with Uncle Jack, in a hotel in downtown Toronto, after he had just found out about the cancer that had invaded his crippled body, was very profound. She was struggling with some decisions at the time and Uncle Jack told her that life was far too short to not get all she could out of it. He implied that it was all right if she had to leave an unhealthy situation like a marriage or a job, in order to be happy. He also talked of people supporting each other, helping one another, and how important this concept was to humanity. He encouraged her to go out and provide service for other people; this was the way to find peace and happiness. Jack followed this by a story about a colleague, a woman who had become a quadriplegic due to a car accident. Though she was trapped in a metal chair, using her mouth to guide it, she still traveled and worked on boards to improve the plight of other handicapped people. She had determination and will power to overcome incredible obstacles especially after such a change in circumstances.

"I have not known anything different," Jack said as he leaned in toward Lee to explain "But she had her life destroyed"

He further said that he liked to tease the woman when they went out for dinner after a committee meeting, that if she fell out of her chair then they would both be in trouble since he couldn't get her back into it. Falling is one of the great fears of the handicapped and assistance without pity was important to Uncle Jack. This story led to his last words of wisdom to his niece.

"I have felt my whole life that I was waiting for something to happen, anticipating better times or circumstances, but I realize now that the current moment is all there is - there is nothing else to wait for"

Uncle Jack passed away on Sept. 22, 1983 after a long battle with cancer that eventually spread throughout his frail body. He was 55 years old. Lee was unable to attend the funeral but she was in the hall when the community honored Jack by showing a short documentary film that had been shot of his life a few years earlier. The film opened with a camera view of Jack from behind as he swung his crutches along a broken concrete sidewalk to maneuver himself toward his small downtown office. The film had his voice as narrator talking about how people would stare at him when he was in public but he knew that they didn't mean to be cruel, they just didn't understand and may not have encountered someone who looked like him before. It was at this point that Lee burst out sobbing, for her uncle, his kindness, and for the difficulties he must have faced that she didn't know about. She could not be consoled and soon people around her were backing away and asking who she was.

"This is Jack's niece who has been away," a deep voice explained to the crowd.

Lee tried to wipe away the tears, gain control of her grief and peer up at the person who must have known her. It was George Richardson. He said hello, offered his condolences then proceeded to try and talk her into opening a branch office for his architectural firm in Toronto. Lee was appalled at the poor timing for this offer but held her outward composure for Uncle Jack's sake and said that she would think about it - but she would never work for the Richards again.

She was sixteen when she started at Richard Architects part time after attending summer school classes in the morning for extra credit. She drove to their stylish offices in downtown Windsor for her first real paying job and she was nervous to be in such a quiet formal office with so many older men. At the beginning of her employment, she was sent down into the damp ammonia filled basement to clean out old drawings and run blueprints. In the dank room, the old mold covered block walls were plastered with every Playboy centerfold since the magazine's inception. She tried to avoid staring at the naked bodies all around her as she ran the blue print machine, ammonia seeping out of the paper like a mist as it emerged from the roller.

Lee had thought that she was entering a distinguished profession and instead she saw disillusioned stooped men bent over drafting boards pumping out drawings in an assembly line fashion. To top it off, they were all supervised through an opening into the drafting room by a sleazy fellow with oily hair and a barking voice, probably the one who posted the centerfolds. He had positioned Lee in the desk closest to him so he could stare at her backside or peer down her blouse when she wasn't running prints. She rarely saw Uncle Jack's friend, George Richardson, since he didn't venture up to the second floor drafting area until one day in August. The whole team was surprised when the tall stooped figure in a grey suit ascended the stairs. He went straight to the senior draftsman and handed him a small magazine photo of a modern wood siding house with clerestory windows and overlapping shed roofs. All the other draftsmen were pretending to draw furiously but they each were listening and watching the interchange. George spoke with a nonchalant authority to the senior draftsman.

"This is what I want my house to look like – draw it up"

It was plagiarism Lee realized - how could an architect not want to design his own house she thought. She watched incredulous as the partner scribbled a basic room layout on velum then left the drafting floor. He would then come up every few days to scan the progress and change a few details. It should have discouraged Lee from ever entering the profession but she maintain a belief that this was not the standard architecture firm and she could find one that suited her, never thinking that she might have to form her own practice to do this.

Lee was just starting to get a sense of her foundation, her moral compass. She knew that the things she was being exposed to at Richards were not right but she had no confidence to speak out about it. One day though as she was with the family at her grandparent's house, she blurted out that she had "swiped" some drawings from the office. This was not really true, the drawings were being sent to the garbage but it sounded more exciting to word it that way. She noticed her grandfather turn away from her and immediately her mother was off the couch and pulling her out of the room. She hissed "You are lucky that your grandfather didn't smack you for such a remark!" This shocked and embarrassed Lee who couldn't image her gentle grandfather hitting anyone. But the lesson was learned and it imparted in her a desire to never disappoint her grandfather. She swore that she would never steal and always be honest in future. She kept this oath, to the best of her ability, for the rest of her life.

Eventually at Richards she was able to work on the drafting board and prove her skills. She knew the art of carefully twisting the lead pencil tips across velum or Mylar to get crisp clear lines. Some draftsmen, including Lee at times, actually used an adjustable triangle set against the parallel bar of their drafting table to ensure that all letters of the text were slanted at the same angle. Velum originally used for working drawings, was an ancient type of paper historically made from calf skins and used by the monks to write biblical texts. Lines made on it were hard to remove, often causing holes in the sheet especially if the draftsman used the new electric eraser. Lee loved the luminous quality of the translucent new plastic film called Mylar. It was a recent invention that was more forgiving for mistakes and easier to erase than the lighter fragile velum, though she couldn't wear nail polish or she would risk spreading lines of color across the spotless clean sheets.

These drawings were works of art created as a guide for the contractor to piece together a building and all its systems. The sets started with cover sheets loaded with information on the building's site, dimensions, codes, general notes then moved to floor plans, reflected ceiling plans showing the lighting and ceilings types. Next there were elevations of all sides of the building, wall sections sliced through each different wall construction type, plan details such as window sections, built-in desks or furniture and finally the interior material schedules. They were road maps to be followed precisely or the contractor would be lost and Lee was learning how to assemble the routes.

The following summer, Lee worked at a marine construction company owned by a stout, good natured Italian man named Bruno. Again Lee was one of the few females at the firm but here she was fully accepted by the crew, the rough necked construction workers, the white collar salesmen and accountants. They encouraged her as she produced drawings of bridges, docks and crawled over the heavy machinery to design the remote control housing for a dredging crane. She did ink sketches of the tug boats and barges for the company marketing brochure which they requested she design as well. Since there weren't many pictures of their finished projects, Lee arranged for a photographer and small airplane to fly over the lake and shoot the various marinas and bridges they had built on Lake St. Claire for the brochure.

Lee had never seen any of these projects in person so she studied the map of the lake and asked a lot of questions until she thought she knew where to direct the plane. After the door of the plane was removed to facilitate the camera action, Lee, supported only by a seat belt, would lean out to direct the pilot to the narrow end of the lake with the grand marina, or over a river with a rotating bridge or past a shoreline with an extended steel dock bisecting it so the photographer could get a good shot. Afterwards she went over each picture with the photographer to pick out the best. When she had assembled all the graphics, writings, renderings and photos into a final proof, she sent it out for printing. Boxes of the finished copies, bundled with their bright red covers, were sent to the firm and once opened for inspection, everyone who saw them congratulated Lee for doing a fine job. She was glad that the brochure had been a success but she was more grateful for the camaraderie of the people at the company and their faith in her abilities.

Chapter 10 - Anchor Bolts

During the winter of 1975 Lee approached her parents with a request. She had found a city wide organized high school trip to Europe and she wanted to go but it was a thousand dollars for the airfare, hotel and food. She enthusiastically showed her mother the information, who then suggested that if Lee contributed half the expenses from her summer earnings, perhaps they would pay for the rest. Anne then approached her husband with the idea and planted the seeds of acceptance. Her husband did not make decisions quickly and when forced to it, he needed a lot of documentation and information to analyze before his commitment. So when Lee approached her father, she made sure that she was prepared. To her surprise, he was receptive to the idea, perhaps even thinking it was his own idea by then, and she was allowed to go. When the time approached, Lee took the train to Toronto where her Aunt Mary picked her up at the station and took her to their modest red brick suburban house to stay overnight before leaving for the airport.

Mary, her mother's oldest sister, the middle child, had grown up in Windsor as a popular, good hearted girl, nicknamed Sweet M, who attracted boys like bees to a succulent flower. She was eventually persuaded by one tall handsome boy named Daniel, to go steady in her sophomore year of high school and this arrangement lasted through her years in college as well. Daniel was flamboyant, daring and loved to dance which Mary enjoyed as well. She had dreamed of being a competitive skater as a young girl, enjoying the flowing, graceful movements gliding over the ice, and she had hoped to compete in provincial then national events. After years of training and hard work, she realized that she didn't have the drive and competitive nature to win and eventually settling on being a judge while others competed. She volunteered in that capacity as long as she lived in Ontario and volunteered for many other kind hearted endeavors her entire life.

The young couple spent evenings in a flurry of activity, social engagements and innocent fun. After several years, Mary was still not sure about marrying Daniel even though he brought it up on a regular basis. There was no passion in the relationship though they were so compatible. It was not talked about in those days but the relationship seemed far too platonic compared to her girlfriend's lustful dates. Then one day, while acting as maid of honor for her sister Anne she met her future brother-in-law's best man, James Miller, and Daniel's proposals were pushed aside. James, an engineer by trade, was average height and weight, a good looking man with dark hair, a small nose and round cheeks, but his main attraction was that he was the life of the party and that was where Mary wanted to be. She and James were married after a short but intense courtship and the couple settled into a small house near the river where they were blessed with two children, a boy followed by a girl. James had been invited to join the family business, where he would work the rest of his career, and when the work spread to Brampton, subdivision outside of Toronto, to paint parts for one of the big three auto manufacturer's, Aunt Mary and Uncle James volunteered to relocate.

At the airport, Aunt Mary steered Lee toward a large group of young people and started chatting with some of them until she pulled Lee toward two girls who looked like they would welcome a third. Aunt Mary's uncanny social skills were successful once more and the three girls roomed together in Paris, Amsterdam and Brussels. The trip was so very exciting for Lee since she had rarely left Windsor on her own. Adult supervision was almost non-existent so after touring the Louvre, Eiffel Tower, Champes-Elysees in Paris, various museums, grand squares of Brugge and the quaint windmills and canals of the Netherlands, Lee and her roommates spent most of their nights at discos and bars. Here they could drink even though they were underage back home, dance, meet all kinds of cute boys and stay out beyond curfew.

One night, as Lee went up to the dance floor with a dark attractive fellow, she looked back at their table to see a couple boys still seated in the booth with an undeniable look of mischief on their faces and body language of collusion. The next morning she discovered that her American Express checks had been stolen from her purse. The money that had been tucked inside of the checks was still there, so once she replaced the checks she didn't really have a loss but it taught her a lesson. She felt foolish that she had been so flattered to have all the boys at their table last night, while some were really there to deceive her. So she stopped carrying a purse and instead switched to a man's wallet and she used her pockets to stuff lipstick and coins from then on.

At another dance spot, an older man grabbed Lee and spun her out on the floor in a tight clutch, his one arm encircling her and the other on her hip guiding her. He pulled her even tighter until his hips were grinding into hers to the beat of the music and his hand moved down to grab her buttocks. He then put his lips next to her ear and asked "Do you love the love?" in an accented English. Shocked at the suggestion, she tried to pull away but he held her tight. He tried to kiss her but she turned her head and just waited until the song ended to get away from this scoundrel and back to her table. But she never forgot that assertive titillating question. When she finally she broke down and conspiratorially told her friends what the man had said, they didn't let her forget it for the rest of the trip either.

In Amsterdam, the girls visited the edge of the famous red light district with the scantily clad prostitutes in welcoming poses displayed in the picture windows of row houses. The women looked bored and even the low tinted lighting couldn't conceal their hard looks. The girls also went into bars that had back rooms with the drug of your choice available but they were content just to drink without being carded. In one dark stone walled bar, Lee was approached by a very handsome boy with limited English but a great laugh and wonderful light brown curls. He was a Swedish engineering student on a tour with his class, thirteen in all. Lee and her roommates couldn't believe their good fortune and spent the evening together with the boys though they retreated on their own later after rejecting the boy's entreaties to come to their rooms. The girls were all virgins or claimed to be in order to comply with cultural expectations, and mention of a liaison so bold was surprising to them. This was their first independent exploration of the world and they were experimenting with tasting, smelling, touching and slowly stretching away from the protective grip of their parents.

The girls later found out that European men chased American women due to the widespread belief that these women were all sexual liberated since the development of the pill. The good girls in their countries would not be frolicking under the sheets, especially the Catholic ones who were viewed as the most pure. They would never be allowed to use birth control by their religion. The pill enabled freedom in one sense, changing a whole generation of women, heralding in the free love sixties and promoting equality in the work place when women could chose when they got pregnant. This also created unreasonable expectations, moral dilemmas and wider spread of STD's.

Lee never doubted that she would use birth control when the time came, but she had not clearly formulated her thoughts related to which birth control device. There was the pill but she had also heard about the diaphragm and IUD. She had a vague idea how these worked but she did not feel comfortable asking her family doctor more about them. She had also not considered what she would do if she did decide to become sexually active and risk an "accident", that unexpected spark of new life; would she consider abortion, adoption or keep a baby. These questions were land mines to be avoided unless foolish decisions and fate steered you straight toward them.

Summer jobs and European travel were great experiences but they were also good for the college applications Lee had to start filling out in her senior year. Architecture was a tough major to get accepted into since the number of applicants was high and the acceptance rate was sometimes only ten percent. Lee sent out applications to the three colleges in Ontario which had schools of architecture and she applied to one university in the United States within driving distance that she had found in a book in the guidance councilor's office. She organized portfolios, wrote paragraphs and attended interviews but she was rejected from each school she applied to in Canada.

One of Lee's problems lay in the fact that Windsor's teachers had gone on strike three of her four years of high school and she was missing critical aspects of the English requirements for college. Lee knew she had been accepted to University of Waterloo's architect school, her first choice, because a fellow she knew from school was on the admissions committee and he had looked it up. He didn't attend her interview, claiming a conflict, but he told her that the committee had been very impressed with her. They liked her artistic skill, admirable grades, her poise in the interview and especially her letter of recommendation from a Mr. Jack Longman. It had described every accomplishment she had ever achieved, even ones she had forgotten. He had also praised her character as honest, hard- working and creative. The committee had mentioned the letter during her interview and she sent a silent prayer of thanks to Uncle Jack for his support.

Unfortunately Uncle Jack's letter was not enough, she had failed the English entrance exam at Waterloo and upon learning that her applications to the Canadian colleges were turned down, Lee was devastated. She felt that she would never become the architect that she aspired to be and she had no backup plan. A despondency set in until a couple days later, while slouching in her chair in English class, Lee glanced up to see her mother, smartly dressed, waving at her though the narrow sidelight window adjacent to the classroom door. Anne beckoned her out to the hall where she explained that she had contacted Miami University, the school whose earlier acceptance into architecture Lee had ignored, and they would still entertain the possibility of her enrollment if they got her acceptance that day. The two women jumped in the car and headed south across the border. It was a five hour drive through dismal industrial towns; each one more soot-covered than the last until leaving Toledo. Then fields of lush waving green corn stalks or golden yellow wheat began to stretch across the view over the hood of the paneled station wagon. As the hours passed, the relief at leaving the hideous urban sprawl was replaced with the fear of being dumped in a totally isolated insignificant school began to permeate Lee's thoughts. After all, she had never really heard of this school in Oxford, Ohio before.

Lee was taking her turn driving through the undulating corn fields when they unexpectedly emerged over the crest of a hill and were confronted with the most extraordinary collection of buildings that she had ever seen. They were neatly organized matching two storey red brick Georgian style structures with gleaming white rows of Doric columns, like soldiers, in front of stone steps guarding massive wood doors all organized around the large lawn of a central park. This distinguished campus was what she had pictured a school like Harvard would be visually. She was enthralled, even more when she saw handsome preppie boys crossing the street in front of the car. She immediately turned to her mother and announced.

"This is the college for me!" she said with a large smile on her face.

They continued driving through the campus until they found the building where they had an appointment with the international student councilor. He was a distinguished gentleman with neatly combed white hair and dark rimmed glasses, who welcomed them and explained that Miami was founded with a land grant made for it by Congress and signed by George Washington in 1809. Besides being one of the top public universities, and the 10th oldest, it was nicknamed the Yale of the West. Lee was impressed and anxious to ensure her ratification as an accepted student. The councilor went over the school's expectations, class information and housing with Lee then stood up and extended a hand to shake - she was admitted to Miami School of Architecture.

When they returned across the border, Anne suggested that Lee sit down with her father and discuss with him the tuition costs since Miami's out of state fees would be a lot more than the Canadian colleges. Lee prepared the material and caught up with her father the next night after dinner at the table where she spread out the information the councilor had given her. Lee was very excited and after making her presentation with high enthusiasm, Joseph asked her what the tuition cost. She told him twelve thousand US dollars, not including room and board which was another four thousand. He then looked up, stared straight into her eyes and declared.

"It was only sixteen hundred when I went to college so I guess you aren't going to Miami"

Lee blinked, looked at him one more time to determine if he was serious. His mouth did not turn up in a smile, in fact it was pursed in a frown which sent a shock through Lee, that maybe he really wasn't going to help her go to college. This was yet another hurdle to overcome in the emotional roller coaster. She wasn't eligible for scholarships as a foreign student and she might not be able to get a student loan due to her parent's income so she burst into tears and ran from the room. Lee stayed in her room that night too upset to talk to anyone until her mother, who had witnessed the exchange, came in her room to tell her that she had talked to Joseph and they would certainly be paying her university costs so she could go to architecture school.

Chapter 11 - Wall Framing

Lee entered the School of Architecture at Miami in the fall of 1976 under the status of an international student. She assumed that this was the main reason as to why she was able to get into this school without writing the SAT and after the acceptance deadline. Lee had attended an orientation weekend in the summer where she stayed over in a typical dormitory while touring the sprawling, well groomed campus. She saw Alumni Hall; the historic dome topped architectural building situated in the center of the green where she would have most of her classes. She was led to the new stadium, the quaint downtown and the fraternity houses, brick Georgian or wood Victorian styled. These were a huge tradition since many fraternities were founded at Miami including her father's Phi Delta Theta.

During this orientation Lee had roomed in one of the three storey red brick girls dormitories in the freshman quad. She had been amused to watch the other girls, many blonde and tanned, parade in curlers and skimpy pajamas up and down the hall seeking out friends from cheerleading or drill team camp. Lee didn't even know what a drill team was so she definitely felt like a fish out of water. No one wanted to be a cheerleader at Riverview High and the few spectators at the high school football games were often carrying flasks and got drunk during the game since the legal age in Ontario was eighteen. The apathetic attitude of the average Canadian extended from politics, religion, through most sports except for hockey, so Lee was quite surprised to hear the enthusiasm applied to these US college events and teams.

Her first football game was an awakening to American patriotism and pride. Miami was in the Mid - American Conference and was known as the "Cradle of Coaches", as Lee had learned during orientation. There was a buzz before the game, rallies to boost school spirit, signs everywhere, group's organizing for pre-game events, rushes to get tickets and tailgating before the game. The bleachers of the stadium were packed solid with students and alumni while the cheerleaders, both male and female, were doing their stunts on the steps to the seating. A diminutive girl in a red and white uniform was tossed in the air from an upper level, tumbled into a somersault and landed in the arms of broad shouldered male cheerleader down the aisle. The crowd was excited and celebrating even before the play but respectful during the national anthem, most with their hands over their hearts. Lee didn't know what to do during this pause so she eventually put her hand over the left side of her chest, tilted her head toward the flag like the people around her, and concentrated on trying to understanding the words in the song by the deep voiced singer at the microphone. The air was crisp with fall colors, smells and vibrant sounds and the day couldn't have been more perfect. The marching band decked out in bright red uniforms and white boots, kicked up their knees as they swiveled into various positions before leaving the field from the end zone as the players raced in. Their names were announced individually and each one was followed by great roars from the crowd. The Americans were doing this with full exuberance.

That first year also introduced Lee to other rituals and pranks such as the panty raid. During evenings of the first couple weekends, after fortification with illegal stashes of alcohol, the boys would congregate at the base of the girl's dorm singing songs and calling out for panties. Then some brave soul's would try to scale the brick structure in order to retrieve a pair of panties, often with a phone number written on them, from the hands of a smiling bright faced freshman leaning out an upper storey window.

Later in the semester, during a floor meeting for the girls in the resident assistance's room, Lee heard her phone ring in her room so she raced back to answer it. The strange male voice on the other end told her to check outside because there was a gift for the girls in the courtyard. Lee told the rest of the girls at the meeting and a few of them joined her to go see what was going on while the rest leaned out their windows to watch. There on the snow lined sidewalk, was a shopping cart with a naked boy in it. The girls were angry at first so they gave the cart a push until it careened down the icy sidewalk and eventually tipped over. The boys watching from their building across the courtyard howled with laughter so that made Lee think that the joke might be on the boy in the cart and not them. She approached the shopping cart and saw the boy had a gag in his mouth which she removed. He explained that his girlfriend was about to call him and the guys had tied him up and put him out here to prevent him from taking the call. The girls removed the binding ropes and the poor boy sprinted back to the dorm, his bare back side disappearing in the dark, to take his call.

Lee had a room that was part of a suite so she and her three roommates had their own kitchenette and washroom, which was a luxury. Her bunk mate, Pat, was a sweet natured country girl with bobbed blond hair who had brought her horse to Oxford and was mucking stalls to pay for its board.

Unfortunately when Pat returned from the barns, she stored her boots in the closet next to Lee's bed and the smell of manure would drift into the lower bunk bed and hover there so that when Lee's parents visited, they were so offended that they could not stay in the room to visit. Lee didn't spend much time in the room though. Her studies in the architecture building were so intense that most students built themselves make-shift beds under their desks so they didn't have to leave the building. The architecture students took classes in art history, science, calculus, materials & methods, design theory, architecture history, structures and landscape design but the main class was design studio. This six credit hour course was the focus of the architecture program for each semester. It was here that the students were given assignments meant to open their minds and challenge their creativity. At project deadlines, the students would hang their boards, set their models and present their work in a Charette to the other students and professors. Often the student was lacking sleep due to working through the night but still wired and nervous enough to be cognizant while explaining his or her ideas in public. One student bragged that he hadn't slept for three days with the help of stimulants, but he still did not finish his project in time.

Soon Lee was familiar with basics of architectural theory and terminology including "Post modernism" and "Neo classical". She was drawn into the history of architecture studying the famous sites including the first man-made arch discovered in Mycenae, the Greek acropolis in Athens, the Roman coliseum and the impressive domed Hagia Sophia and Blue Mosque in Istanbul, Turkey. Following this was study of the medieval castles for the crusades in Cyprus, the squat crude Romanesque cathedrals built in the dark ages which lead to the soaring light filled pointed arched Renaissance cathedrals such as Chartes and Notre Dame in France. In Italy, Palladio had done designs based on Greek and Roman styles that used symmetry, porticos and stepped windows that eventually influenced styles in England and North America. The students were also told about another Italian, Brunelleschi and his design for the Domo in Florence.

The Domo was a church that had been completed in the early 1400's except for the dome which no one could figure out how to build. It was to be larger than any other dome ever built, including the Pantheon in Rome. The problem was that buttresses, which normally supported domes at that time, were not allowed in Florence. The city then announced a competition to find a solution and Brunelleschi, who had been a gold smith then builder, won this competition with an ingenious design. The men competing for this design were first asked to find a way to make an egg stand on end without emptying the contents. Brunelleschi announced that he had the solution. The fellow competitors had wrestled unsuccessfully with ideas and when they asked him what his solution was, Brunelleschi then demonstrated by crushing the bottom of the egg on the table so it stood up. The other designers then exclaimed that they could have done that, but Brunelleschi pointed out that it was the idea that was unique. This was the same way he approached the Domo. He had discovered that by wrapping a large chain around the base of the dome it would hold the structure in compression and support the double layered brick dome above. This was pure genius; simple in its concept but with sound structural principals and the impressive dome still stands today.

Lee was inspired by these famous architects and their prominent buildings. She learned about Mies van Der Rohe, who helped start the Bauhaus school of modern design in Germany, LeCorbusier, the French architect who designed bold forms in white concrete, Arthur Erickson the Canadian with eastern influences in his design, and Sullivan, mentor to Frank Lloyd Wright. Wright had designed the first cantilevered concrete structure in 1935 for a house perched over a stream called Falling Water in Pennsylvania. Lee's class made a pilgrimage to visit the historic house which appeared lower and darker inside than Lee had imaged it but the exterior was breathtaking. It also had surprising unique elements like a live tree growing through the hall, natural rock left in place and a stair through glass panels in the living room that dropped to a platform hovering just over the water.

It was said that the contractor had added extra steel reinforcing against Wright's wishes and even so, the workers had refused to remove the supporting concrete forms so Wright had to knock them out himself. He was also known an eccentric who had affairs with some of his client's wives and actually ran off with one to Europe leaving his wife and six children behind. This affair nearly destroyed his ability to practice in the US but after a short time in Italy, he returned and built a house for himself in Spring Green, Wisconsin next to his mother's property and he named it Taliesin. There his mistress and her two children were killed when a deranged manservant set the house on fire and used an axe to kill seven people. Rumors around the architecture school described the servant as swinging the axe to cut off the head of the mistress as she ducked under a Dutch door to escape the fire.

In this intense atmosphere, Lee began to experiment working hard to create outstanding presentations and designs. She bought colored boards and used ink, watercolor and collage to develop a unique look for her work. One day in the middle of her freshman year, she had just hung her boards for a presentation of a tree house design when the school's most revered professor, Kevin Malloy, a compact, bespectacled man who usually sported a wickedly boyish grin under his mop of dark hair, emerged through a doorway adjacent to her project. He glanced over the walls, as he had for years, taking in the batch of new student work. A board on his right, Lee's presentation, immediately caught his eye. He paused briefly to study it. Then he turned toward the entourage of adoring students following him, pointed a thumb back at the project over his shoulder and declared.

"This is good," before he sauntered off.

To Lee, it was a turning point. She had never imagined that her work could stand out so clearly, though she had secretly hoped. This recognition put her among the top designers in the school, a position she would work very hard to maintain throughout the rest of her years at Miami.

As Lee threw herself into her design work she noticed that her social life was fading away. She had started college attending freshman events with her room mates and neighbours but they all began to branch off into their areas of study or into sororities. Lee had been asked to join a sorority but she saw them as mostly helpmates, party coordinators and free cleaning staff for the fraternities. So she decided to start going to the gym to play squash and attend the hockey games since they reminded her of high school.

She began to become familiar with the members of the hockey team and while she was in the Cincinnati airport on her way back home for spring break, she spotted one of the players sitting on a window sill in the light filled walkway between terminals. She had recognized the reddish curls of the strong, good looking fellow as he intently studied the book in his hands. He looked quick, intelligent and totally unaware of his appeal. She walked towards him and asked him for the time, lingering long enough to casually inquire if he was on the Miami hockey team. He was surprised she knew this, and then he felt flattered, and she was able to draw him into conversation. They talked for the hour while they waited for their planes then exchanged phone numbers and promised to touch base when they returned to school.

Mike did call her and they started dating which continued through the next two years. Soon, they were spending all their time outside of school or hockey together. Mike was a serious student and a member of the honor society so he didn't go to bars which suited Lee. Instead he practiced hockey to work up to first string on the team and Lee loved going to the games as the girlfriend of a player. It made her swell with pride when Mike smiled at her in the middle of a game or waved to get her attention. She had also taken a photography class and would shoot the players for class assignments. When they saw her at the glass, they would take off their helmets in the middle of play and deliberately pose for her.

Lee spent a lot of her time the next year at the apartment that Mike shared with the other players. They teased her that she was a fifth roommate. In return she would cook for them and help clean up the place in payment for the food she ate and the room she shared with Mike. She was so grateful to feel like a part of such a close, popular group, so different than the intense self-absorbed architecture students. She also had a dorm room across the campus that she rarely visited except when her parents came to the college on parent's weekend. They would admiringly notice how tidy her area was, comment on the drawings and projects on her desk and then frown as they saw the mess on the other side of the room where her art major roommate would have dumped her clothes and paint supplies. Lee kept up this charade since she didn't think that they would approve of her current lifestyle.

That next semester Lee took an airbrush class and was immediately engrossed in this new technique using frisket to cut shapes and then layering color over the page with a spray of paint from a pen attached to a compressor. It produced a fine gradated finish with a professional look to a rendering or machine drawing. Towards the end of the semester, a local firm came to visit the class looking for inexpensive talent to work at air brush assignments on a contract basis. The teacher introduced Lee, his star pupil, and showed the two men samples of her work. They immediately offered her a job working whatever hours that she could spare. She could do some of the work at the school but the rest would have to be in Hamilton, twenty miles outside of Oxford. Sometimes she would borrow Mike's car to drive to the office and other times she would get a ride on the back of a heavy BMW motorcycle owned by a fellow employee who lived nearby. He was a local man with long stringy hair, a beard and a gimp leg and Lee was always a little uncomfortable around him but the job helped pay her expenses and she got to use the huge graphic camera to photograph her projects for her portfolio.

Lee had to admit that the motorcycle also made her nervous since she knew so many people who had died on them. Craig Harrison, the son of a family friend and a boy she had known all her life, was knocked off his bike by a car when he had missed a stop sign crossing an intersection on a country road. His friends, who were following in a car, had jumped out to help him and block traffic. Craig was sitting up and called to his buddies that he was fine but probably needed an ambulance just when a drunk driver veered around the blockade of friends and mowed Craig down where he sat on the road. The driver had then raced away and when one of the witnesses chased him down in his car, he had switched places with his wife. Craig's family did not survive the grief very well. Craig's mother became an alcoholic, as a way of escaping the pain, and his father retired early from his medical practice.

Then there was Jim Sanders, the son of a minister, who was riding a rented motorcycle out in California with his new bride on the back when a car, whose driver didn't see the two on the bike, pulled out in front of them. The impact threw Jim into a post which broke his neck. His wife survived her launch off the bike but was seriously injured. Lee only had one scare on the big BMW bike, and that was when a car in front stopped too fast while they were on a two lane highway. When the driver jammed the brakes on the big bike grinding it to a skidding stop, the back of the bike lifted into the air, like a bucking bull trying to toss Lee off its back. But she managed to hang onto the seat handles for her life, which she used so she didn't have to put her arms around the driver, and it had saved her from becoming a projectile.

On Christmas break that year since it was getting more expensive to get home especially with the Canadian dollar dropping compared to the US dollar, her parents decided that she should take the bus back to Detroit where they would pick her up. The bus ride itself was uneventful but as Lee was waiting for her father to arrive at the bus station in downtown Detroit in the vestibule between the double doors. A couple policemen circling past her on their route asked her to step inside the building.

"I am in the building" she told them, confused by their request, but they only looked at her hard.

"You will get hurt out here" one of them said to her.

She suddenly felt very vulnerable and exposed in the yellow tile interior and immediately turned to go farther inside but as she pivoted, her eyes picked up a movement across the street and she recognized her father's car as it pulled into a parking lot. So she ran past the policemen and crossed the street to meet her father. As she approached the car, the parking attendant, a thin wiry black man had come to her father's window and asked for eighty five cents for time in the lot. Her father dismissingly told the man that he was just turning the car around. The attendant got even more insistent and started raising his voice asking again for the eighty five cents. Lee's father obviously thought this didn't make logical sense and became even more stubborn, keeping his eyes straight ahead and ignoring the man screaming in his window. Lee had just pulled open the passenger car door when the attendant turned away and strode back to his booth. As she leaned to get into the car she saw the man returning with a gun in his hand and a woman hanging onto his arm crying "Don't do it!!" The man then took the gun and smashed it against the car mirror and the side of the new Lincoln repeatedly while threatening her father with screams.

"I am going to hurt your sorry white ass if you don't give me my eighty five cents honky"!!

"Hey, don't do that," her father responded from the leather clad interior.

The situation was at an impasse, and Lee realized pride would topple both these men so she leaned into the car and yelled at her father to pay the man. This seemed to jolt her father to action and he retrieved his wallet from his back pocket and slowly found a dollar bill and cracked the window to pass the dollar out. Incredulously, he waited for change with a shaking open palm while Lee, tense with prayer that they would get out alive, watched the movements of the attendant. All of this was in slow motion, taking hours, days, and years in Lee's mind. It was only when the car was moving that she felt the overwhelming relief from a close call as they rode in silence back across the border to safety. She did not take the bus again and her father never acknowledged the event ever took place.

Chapter 12 Insulation

School began again in the fall and Lee decided to try to finish her degree in Environmental Design in three years instead of the standard four since she almost had enough credits to graduate early. She had always taken summer classes as well as worked. She didn't know what she would do once she got out but she was tired of Ohio. During one visit home to Windsor, Anne's cousin Peg was visiting from Detroit and she suggested that Lee try an Ivy League college for graduate school.

"With your talent honey, you could have your pick of schools," Peg gushed.

Lee certainly had never thought that she was good enough for a prestigious Ivy League university for grad school but if Peg believed she could do it then why not apply. She had checked with the Dean of the Architecture Department but he said that the school would not allow her out early unless she got into one of the best graduate schools. So she filled out the forms for Harvard and Yale along with creating customized portfolios for each school. Her mother even helped by sewing ultra-suede covers for the portfolios so they would stand out both visually and tactically. Then she checked with her father to confirm if her parents would help her financially should she get into grad school. They agreed this time without resistance then she waited.

She had found an apartment that year in the upstairs of a small white clapboard house near campus and her roommate for the year was Sandy, another architecture student who was also a member of a sorority. Sandy was an attractive tall and willowy girl with a sweet nature and Lee was fascinated by her stories of working as a construction administrator on a project job site during the summer. Lee couldn't quite picture her friend in a hard hat having to deal with the contractor and workers daily but Sandy said that it had gone well and she enjoyed the work. Sandy was dating a handsome well built, arrogant fellow and Lee was still seeing Mike, though with less enthusiasm. The relationship was becoming more one sided as he made hints about a future together, invited himself over to eat at her place often, began to depend on her attention more than ever. With her focus on future goals, Lee was not thinking much about her relationship with Mike. They had been dating for almost two years and they had a routine of seeing each other between studying, projects and hockey which had worked out well for these two driven people but Lee hadn't really contemplated what would happen to them when she graduated. He was handsome, intelligent and hardworking but there was something in her feelings for him that was slipping away. She had never been in love with him but now he was getting so serious and they never did anything spontaneous or fun anymore.

Mike didn't come from a well off family so he was careful with money, which Lee admired, but when he began bragging about being cheap and adding derogatory remarks about Jewish people, this started to bother her. Lee had never understood prejudice so she had been surprised. She was exposed to more of this same kind of talk when she had visited his home in Cleveland Heights and met his attractive but domineering mother. Shortly after their introduction, Mike's mother had grilled Lee on her religion. Once she established that the girl wasn't Jewish, she went on to make snide remarks about her Jewish neighbors and their penny pinching habits, while imitating the exact same traits.

Then Lee found out that Mike's mother lived on the first two floors of the house while his father, older than his mother by almost twenty years, lived in the attic space and only came down for dinner. The pair had separated years ago but couldn't afford to divorce so they continued to split the house and his retirement money. Mike's mother also made constant negative remarks about his father, subtlety poisoning the boy against him and obviously just waiting for the poor man to die.

Lee eventually met Mike's father when he came down for dinner that night and upon seeing the bent backed grey haired man, she felt only pity for him. His wife and son ignored their elderly dinner guest and spoke only to each other and Lee. But Lee couldn't join in since she was so overwhelmed by the awkward situation. She dropped her head while glancing furtively at Mike's father slowly ate his meal. Once finished, the gentleman stood up, thanked his wife, nodded to his son and Lee before retreating in a shuffle back upstairs. The tension in the room eased and everyone relaxed except Lee who remained thoughtful while the other two chatted. Even when they returned to school, the visit remained with Lee and she could not forget the pettiness and intolerance that had permeated Mike's house. It had made her very uncomfortable. So when she started seeing similar behavioral patterns emerging in Mike, she could not continue the relationship.

When Lee told Mike of her decision to break up he did not take it well. Apparently he had assumed that they would finish school and get married. He kept calling her and started showing up at the architecture school, waiting for her in one of the recess of the atrium late at night, which startled her. He pursued her girlfriend Marty to ask what had happened and how could he get Lee back. Marty could not help him since she didn't know what had triggered the break up. He followed her parent's car when they came to visit in the spring and stopped them on the highway on the way out of town. He asked them what he could do to win Lee back and they certainly didn't know what to tell him.

Meanwhile, Lee was busy with her design work and focused on the future. She hadn't been to any parties or met other boys except architecture students for so long that she didn't know what to do to kick start her social life. Her roommate was still dating the same boy and they actually did seem to be headed for marriage. Her sorority sisters had a goal of getting their M.R.S. degree, in other words marriage, while they were in college and admired Sandy for snagging her catch so early. When these girls had a meeting in their apartment, Lee was usually absent but Sandy invited her to stay one time. The sorority girls all came clamoring in, well groomed and giggling. They said a polite hello to Lee, sat themselves down on the couch then enthusiastically began discussing the color of pompoms for a float, streamers for a fraternity party and dresses for a ball. Lee could barely keep her eyes open during the meeting and it confirmed her decision that a sorority was not for her.

In March of 1979, Lee received her letter of decision from Yale University. She had been nervous opening up the thin off white colored envelop with the gold embossed shield in the upper left corner with the words "Lux et Veretas" embedded in it. She hadn't really decided what she would do if she didn't get into Yale. She had always wanted to do a semester abroad or she could take the flying lessons like Mike had, but these were just fall backs if she was stuck at Miami another year. She finally sliced open the envelope with her fingernail and screamed with joy once as she read the introductory paragraph welcoming her to join the Yale Graduate School of Architecture! Lee immediately launched herself out of the apartment, with the letter clutched in her outstretched hand and ran directly to the architecture building. Once in the rotunda, she threw her head back and began turning circles calling out.

"You have to let me out now. I got into Yale"

The Dean and his secretary came out of the office to see what the commotion was about, and with a warm smile and a hand shake, the Dean congratulated Lee.

"This has never been done before at this school, graduating a year early. You have achieved something remarkable"

He then told her that she just needed to complete one more design studio in the summer but she would miss the formal graduation ceremony unless she came back. Lee told him that she didn't mind missing it and thanked him for all his help. She then quickly organized extending her lease with her agreeable landlord and found a new summer roommate, a quiet spoken attractive English major. Lee also began to answer all the correspondence from her new school, research her courses and prepared to move to New Haven, Connecticut.

This last summer in Oxford turned out to be relaxing yet exciting for Lee since she wasn't worried about grades anymore and she had a new focus, a destination whose time was approaching rapidly. She was extremely pleased with the path of her life and it showed in her face as she walked to her first summer class, basking in the rays of sunlight on the familiar route. On her return to the house, after class, she spotted a small playful black & white dog on the lawn of the corner house across from hers. As she walked past she paused and bent over to pet the pup. Its owner on the other end of the leash leaned down and introduced himself. James was a well groomed, handsome young man with a long square jaw and wide smile. He was wearing an oxford cloth shirt and well pressed khaki pants, the uniform of a frat boy. When he spoke it was with a heavy nasal drawl, a mid-western accent. He was from Chicago, a political science major and after some chatting, he asked her to diner.

Lee laughed then said "Using the dog for a pickup was very clever," and she accepted.

James was a gentleman; attentive, kind and very good to her. Their relationship developed over the summer with outings for picnics, concerts and trips in his car to Cincinnati. He had never known anyone like her and it fascinated him. He was used to sorority girls who traveled in packs and talked about fashion and parties. They were tanned, dressed in short skirts and tight tops. Lee was pale from so much time in the design studio, she dressed in sloppy painter pants and she didn't care about going to parties. He also knew that he was not her top priority. She was enjoying his company but he sensed that he played only a minor and probably temporary role in her life. This was again unusual compared to the girls he had dated previously and intrigued him even more. He was impressed that she was headed to an Ivey League school, a fact that he dropped in conversation with this mother to give a favorable impression of this new girlfriend. His mother was a strong, independent woman and she didn't think anyone was good enough for her son. James's father had died in a car accident when he was twelve and she had never remarried. Instead, she had opened her own high end fashion store in a wealthy Chicago suburb and she had done very well with it.

When summer school was over and the students went home, James invited Lee to come visit him in Chicago. Anne approved the idea and suggested that Lee take the train since it was least expensive. Lee agreed since her only experience with trains was the modern system between Windsor and Toronto. The morning of her departure, Anne drove Lee into the seedy section of downtown Detroit near Tiger Stadium to the Michigan Central Station. Lee stared wide eyed at the elegantly proportioned Beaux Arts style building, with its massive Corinthian columns, ornate carved pediments and large arched windows framing the entrance.

It was built in 1913 and designed by the same architects, Reed & Stern, who had done Grand Central Station in New York. The opulent large vaulted spaces inside were meant to resemble a roman bath, all lined with marble. When Lee entered the building, despite her awe at its design, she felt that something was wrong. It had an empty feeling to it even before Lee noticed the shops were closed and boarded up, the central areas were void of people, the walls were coated with black grit and skylight broken. She hesitated, asking her mother if she really thought that this was a good idea. Anne continued walking briskly to the gate for the train to Chicago, pointed her daughter to the waiting train and waved goodbye.

Lee entered the train at the front compartment with trepidation and noticed that each bench of seating was occupied with at least one passenger, who would slide even closer to the aisle as she passed, to prevent her from seating next to them. She crossed to the next car and the same thing happened. She was the only white face on the train and many of the other passengers made it clear that she was not welcome in their seating area. When she had passed through the entire train, she stopped at the last section of seating, turned to the woman in the last row, and begged "Do you mind if I sit next to you". The woman glanced up with a guarded look and invited Lee to sit with a gesture of her hand and a shrug. Lee was very nervous now and grateful to the woman for sharing her seat. She thanked her, lowered herself onto the end of the vinyl seat and tried to stay as small as possible.

Her seat mate, a broad hipped woman with a tight cap of dark curls, dressed in a worn but clean skirt and blouse, had been watching her, noticing her discomfort and correctly interpreting it as nervousness rather than racism. She felt a pang of pity for the young white girl alone on this train, so she kindly asked Lee where she was from and why she was traveling. Soon the two were chatting amicably, exchanging stories about family, siblings and work. Lee relaxed and enjoyed the conversation with the woman who was obviously very intelligent but living a life very different from Lee's sheltered existence. This woman had not completed high school, gotten pregnant early, worked a variety of jobs and even though she was only in her mid-thirties, her three children were already out on their own and one was expecting a baby.

Lee had been so engrossed in the conversation that she hadn't noticed the nasty remarks being hurtled towards them from the furthest seats of the car until her seat mate jumped up suddenly, twisted to point a threatening finger toward the back and angrily shouted.

"I'm going to whip your ass if ya don't shut yur trap?"

She then calmly turned around and sat back down leaned toward Lee to continue their discussion as though nothing had happened. Lee was shocked by the explosive transformation in this seemingly soft spoken woman. Her language had morphed from grammatically correct to Urdu slang cursing and her body language had converted from intimate to aggressively hostile instantly. Lee realized that she must have been the reason for derogatory remarks due to her race and the fact that her seat mate was talking to her. Either way she was extremely grateful for this show of protection but also regretting that she may have caused this woman some difficulty.

"We are now going through South Chicago" her seat mate explained. "Those high rise buildings are housing projects and if you ever entered one of those buildings, it would be an act of suicide"

Then the woman demonstrated to Lee how to hold her bag, clutched tight to her side with one arm over it, so that it was harder for anyone to steal it from her.

"She is helping a suburban hick heading to the big city," Lee thought, but she was again touched by this act of kindness. Upon arrival into Chicago, her seat mate jumped down onto the platform and after a quick grin and wave goodbye, she disappeared in to the crowd. Lee's eyes followed the woman's receding figure as long as she could then the thought occurred to her that she had not even gotten the woman's name. She would however, never forget her.

When James spotted her on the platform, his face lit up and he rushed over to give her an encompassing hug. As usual he was smartly dressed and Lee felt a bit inadequate in her brown tee shirt and jeans but he didn't seem to care. He told her that she looked beautiful as he escorted her to the car. He continued to beam his affection at her as they speed along the highway in a new black Cadillac convertible but he allowed some creases of concern to cross his brow when she relayed the story of her unusual journey on the train. An hour later they pulled up the driveway of an attractive sprawling modern brick house with extensive gardens spilling across the edges of the property and hugging the corners of the building. They got out of the car and James walked her through the house to the pool in the back yard, where they approached a stylish woman laying in a lounge chair reading a magazine. James introduced Lee to his mother and the woman rose from her seat, turning to them while peering over her large black framed sunglass. She was elegant in her movements, thin and darkly tanned with sun bleached blond hair. She looked hard into Lee's face then moved her eyes up and down Lee's frame.

"Why she's quite sweet" she said to her son.

This scrutiny caused Lee to blush deeply and though she resented that the woman was talking about her as though she were a child, she controlled the flash of irritation and smiled in response.

James was a gallant host. He took Lee to the city center to see the Sears Tower which was the tallest building in the world, the plush department stores like Lord and Taylor and I Magnum that Lee had never heard of. They also strolled along the waterfront, visited various museums and the Hard Rock Café. Lee enjoyed it all but she was especially thrilled when James mother offered that she could go to her designer boutique and pick out any outfit she would like. The next day James drove Lee through the tree lined streets to a quaint boutique, unlocked the door and ushered Lee inside. She was awed by the long rows of beautiful clothing, flashing colors in rich silks, flowing taffeta and fine wools with the tags of the great designers Valentino, Gucci and Halston.

Lee was a kid in a candy store and she wanted to try them all on, just this once. She poured over every rack, pulling out the unique and beautifully tailored garments that she would never be able to afford. The suits and long dresses were thousands of dollars each when Lee opted to look at a price tag. She toyed with the idea of requesting one of these expensive couture outfits but subdued that greedy thought. James was wonderfully patient, helping find outfits that he wanted to see her try on and complimenting enthusiastically over the ones she wore when she emerged from the dressing room. Finally she chose a modestly priced ivory short sleeve top in raw silk by Harvey Bernard. When they got back to the house, Lee presented her selection to James's mother and thanked her profusely. James mother replied that she owned that same top as well and it was a good selection.

Later in the evening, the two dressed up to join his mother for dinner at their country club, a stately sprawling Greek revival styled compound around a manicured golf course and putting green. They ate succulent oysters, thick red steaks and luscious deserts of chocolate and fresh fruit. Afterwards, they sat outside under the ivy covered colonnade, with a warm summer breeze ruffling their hair while they listened to strains of music from a dance floor. It was a day of quality and high end living that Lee was not used to and she felt a stirring of unease and insecurity below her calm facade. She did not feel that she deserved this setting or was worthy of it.

Everyone she had been introduced to was most gracious to her but she felt out of place around the highly sophisticated close knit crowd. She began to wonder if she would find it the same at Yale - what if all the other students were so brilliant, rich and well-connected that she would be an outsider. James reassured her that she had done very well that evening, as he tried getting her to agree to let him sneak into her room later. She told him no, in respect to his mother down the hall, and she departed the next day, giving a long kiss to James at the station. She boarded the nearly empty train for an uneventful returned to Detroit where her mother picked her up at the dilapidated station. After passing through the tunnel, clearing customs and immigration, she was once more back in Canada.

Chapter 13- Subfloor

A few weeks later Lee's parents drove their overloaded station wagon once more across the border for the eleven hour drive to New Haven, Connecticut on their first visit to one of the most prestigious universities in the world. The first impression of the city with its dark, grimy streets, brutal concrete high rises lining part of the central Green was not favorable and Lee got nervous. Tough characters sauntered along the streets harassing Lee with explicit comments as she and her parents walked past them from their hotel to the campus. Once within the Yale campus though, the group was overwhelmed by the beauty of the stately buildings. Each block formed a quad, with grey stone Gothic or red Federal style brick buildings wrapping their protective arms around green inner sanctums.

The university had been established in 1701 and was one of the oldest universities in the United States with a rich history of Presidents, inventors and scholars who had attended the institution. Stone and brick structures with elaborate carvings, ivy filled moats and dormers protruding out of slate roofs faced each street. These blocks of dorm rooms turned inward, away from the city and had lockable gateways to enter. The library was set majestically, at the end of a larger center green space and it was explained during a tour of the college, that the tower was supposed to be higher than its eight stories but the architect or structural engineer had forgotten to allow for the weight of the books and the tower size had to be cut back.

The gym was a massive grey carved stone structural sprawling several blocks and housing various pools, rowing wells, gyms, lockers and squash courts. A short walk from the gym was the Law School and across from it was The Hall of Graduate Studies or HGS for short, where Lee would live. HGS was an imposing gothic styled stone clad building with a high tower and two courtyards surrounded by pointed arched windows and separated by an entrance colonnade. Lee was overwhelmed but hoped one day that this place would feel like home.

As her parents pulled away, without a backwards glance, from her new place of residence for the next three years Lee immediately felt deserted. Once she began to attend classes and got used to the campus she started to feel more comfortable. She learned to be cautious about where she walked and she avoided the section of Chapel Street where the prostitutes lined the corners. Some of these prostitutes were actually transvestites but Lee didn't know this until friends from NYC pointed it out to her. These sections of New Haven were eventually cleaned up and the town was transformed but it was different while Lee was there. The architecture building where she spent most of her time, designed by Paul Rudolf, was a harsh vertical shaft of concrete and due to its low lighting and lack of street level retail, it was the area of highest number of muggings in New Haven. Lee didn't mind the hard edged building and enjoyed her classes with the high profile architects from around the world who came to the school to teach and mentor. Her first year studio was with Charles Moore, the famous Californian architect who designed Sea Ranch and launched the quote "Less is more". Sea Ranch was a collection of wood structures with sloped roofs sited to blend with their windswept cliff environment. It was a new concept for housing and it inspired the next generation of designers.

Charlie, as he liked to be called, started the studio with a tour of New England. The class all loaded up in their cars and drove along the coast through New London, Boston, Providence and Newport Rhode Island. They were shown the heavy Romanesque designs of a library by HH Richardson, and the Tennis Hall of Fame, a stick style clap board structure with colonnades wrapping in a half circle around the grass courts in the center. They toured the great mansions in Newport on the jagged cliff frontage including the Breakers, a massive twenty thousand square foot colossus and Marble House which, like its name suggested, was covered entirely in marble at a cost of eleven million back in 1904. These were built during a period of extravagances by industrial barons like Vanderbilt, Rockefeller and Whitney before the great market crash. The Newport Historic Society now owned the buildings with their extensive landscaped grounds and they were open for tours by the public at a cost that assisted with their expensive upkeep.

Charlie also walked the class through the modest Newport downtown district where small brightly painted clapboard homes and offices stepped down the sloping streets toward the harbour. He pointed out their plaques marking them on the Historic National Register and explained that when they were renovated it had to be with matching materials and period consistent techniques making it an extremely expensive undertaking. He showed them the custom forged nails with their flat angled heads, which had been hammered out on an anvil, and the circular or star shaped cast iron plates on the walls that capped long metal bars running through the houses to hold them together during earthquakes.

They ate at local seafood restaurants, small well-worn places with lots of character and fresh catches. When Lee was at his table one lunch he ordered a type of mussels called steamers, which had a penis like shape and required the diner to pull off the foreskin before consuming the meat. Charlie then asked if the group wanted the watery remains once the mussels were gone. When they shook their heads, he grabbed the bowl, tilted it back at his mouth and swallowed the rest of the gritty liquid. He was a gourmet, well-traveled guide and also a kind and compassionate designer. There were rumors that he was gay but these were ignored and he was enveloped with incredible loyalty and admiration by the students. Former students lined up to work for him in satellite offices around the country so they could be associates. He emphasized putting a collaborative team effort into design work and he was never judgmental, as many other professors were. Lee was fortunate to have him as her first studio professor.

Although Lee spent her class time in the studio, she had vowed to enjoy herself more, not limit herself to architects as friends and to especially not do any more all-nighters. The easiest way to achieve this was to work on her projects in her dorm room. This way she would be more efficient and have more time to socialize with other grad students. Besides, she loved her room with its dark wood trim, antique gothic windows and stone fireplace overlooking the small courtyard filled with ivy. Finding friends in this dorm became a challenge since on her first day in the lunch room, a massive thirty foot high space with stone floors and stained glass, she wound up at a table of linguists whose conversation was limited to semantics.

While she as interested in this, it just didn't hold her attention for an hour and she fought to suppress a yawn. Her dorm neighbors were always busy as well, though one British girl did invite Lee over when an especially good band was playing at the Toad, a night club next door whose music spilled into her room. Lee rarely took her up on this offer except when Stevie Ray Vaughan was playing.

Eventually, she gravitated to a table of students, who she noticed laughed and joked with each other a lot. They saw her hovering and invited her to join them. Soon she was one of the gang, bantering and teasing them as much as they teased her. The members of this group were Charles, from a wealthy NYC family with wicked sense of humor, Will, a tall lean coffee colored boy from Brazil, Tim, an English major from Ireland who fancied himself a "ladies man", and Mike, a gregarious botanist from Louisiana. A handful of other people joined them at times but these were the core of the group.

Lee also became involved in the HGS Social Club through Mike and Will and she was paid a small stipend to help organize parties for the graduate students. She eventually became co-chairman with Mike, who initiated the ideas for events while she did ink sketches for the advertising posters and drove the car to get the kegs of beer. They enlisted their friends who were music majors to give recitals and organized parties with other professional schools like the Law or Medical schools. In order to get those parties off to a big start, the three social committee members, Mike, Will and Lee would go to the middle of the room with drinks in one hand, passing a joint with the other while dancing to the rhythms of loud reggae music to entice others to join them. Their parties were huge successes and soon the dorm inhabitants were looking forward to the next event posted. They decided to branch out and try a party with the undergraduates. It would need a big draw so they used some of their earnings from the other parties to hire a band.

Mike researched the bands on campus then had Lee join him to visit the dank basement rehearsal rooms in various quads to audition the undergrad bands before they selected a popular one. On the night of the party, Lee helped the group set up in the HGS cafeteria and was amazed when their amplifiers were finally in place and blasted out the music. The atmosphere for the party was electric and a huge number of undergrads came to the event. Will manned the bar and got so sloshed sampling his wares that he forgot to close the tap of the keg. The entire floor was soon covered in an inch of beer and the keg emptied. When the undergrads heard that the alcohol was gone they started protesting and Lee was forced to drive to the nearest store and buy cases of beer in order to keep the party going.

At one point during the party, a student from the Art History class that Lee taught approached her to chat. Lee was a teaching assistant for the well-known historian Vincent Scully whose flamboyant, sexually charged lectures drew over three hundred students every semester. The graduate student TA's were in charge of the individual class room teaching, giving out assignments and grading papers. This student, who she knew was from California, had brought along a friend. She was a short plump girl in an unshapely outfit with light brown hair cut to shoulder length. The boy was a good looking surfer type, with longer hair, an earring and a cool way of dressing so the girl didn't look like his type. Then Lee remembered who she was - Jodie Foster, the movie actress. The school had been in a buzz ever since John Hinckley had attempted to assassinate President Ronald Regan in March 1981, in order to impress this girl. Jodie had been in movies and advertising since she was a baby but it was the movie Taxi, in which she played a street smart child prostitute which had apparently resonated with Hinckley.

After Hinkley was arrested and mentioned Jodie as his motive, the journalists descended on Yale desperate to get an interview or photo of this small girl who was world news. What they didn't report, which the head TA told all the rest of them, was that she was a brilliant student and straight A grades for her major in French. She eventually had to take a year off school to avoid the publicity but came back to graduate Magna Cum Laude.

During the first few months of grad school Lee had clung to James, through phone calls for support and encouragement. He called often at first but he had moved out to Oregon to become an assistant to a senator, so he was not free to visit. Slowly their communications broke down and calls became fewer and farther apart until they just stopped. Lee had also started keeping company with another architecture student, a tall thin boy from NYC. They had been part of a group of architecture students who shared design studio together, but slowly the group began pairing off into couples and by the end of the fall semester, Lee and the tall boy were on their own.

Lee called this fraternizing "incest", since the architectural students all worked, ate and spent most nights together in the studio for three years. Some of the couples were also highly unlikely pairings, such as Lee's friend Shelly, the stylish but wild red haired girl from California, who was going out with Bruce, the egocentric preppy clad Princeton graduate. Lee had met Shelly the first day when they were in line together to register for classes. The two girls felt an instant bond as they chatted with each other. Both were unique personalities, independent, highly talented and both attractive and good humored. They were also outsiders, from far off places compared to the other New Englanders and NYC dwellers.

Shelly was an only child, who had been given incredible freedom as a teen. She owned a convertible sports car, which she had been given on her sixteenth birthday, wore expensive designer clothing and had never had a curfew. Shelly said that her parents were too busy with their own lives, sailing and working together in their insurance company to pay much attention to restraining her and as a result, she didn't get into trouble. She had turned out highly responsible and never had the drunken escapades of a typical teen.

At the end of first year, the architecture school held a competition for the students to design a public building and Lee's class was assignment the international conference center for the Boy Scouts of America. The winning design would be built by the first year as part of their two week construction project participation required for every student. Lee's friend Shelly and her Princeton beau were part of the team whose design was selected and the class packed up and headed to Winsted Connecticut once the term ended.

Lee and a couple guys were the first to arrive on site, settle into the small cabins in the woods and start the digging of foundation holes for the concrete caissons. Each of the holes for the posts had to be four feet deep to below the frost level, by thirty inches wide. They were being dug by hand since heavy equipment could not get into this location without taking down too many trees. It was hard sweaty work, with only three of them digging along with Gus, the project manager, a tanned, thin white haired man, who had been hired by Yale to supervise the construction.

Once the holes were finished they were filled with concrete, the forms removed after curing then the beams for the suspended floor were set on top, spanning between the caisson footings. Lee, Gus and the other boys then wrestled the long 2"x12" floor joists onto joists hangers supported on the beams and the floor system was ready for the plywood subfloor. When all the other students arrived, the main wall framing was built on the ground and lifted into place. The roof trusses were then set on top of the walls and Lee, who didn't mind heights, volunteered to climb to the top of the trusses and straddle the top beams to drive the nails and spikes to secure the members.

Lee enjoyed the work and Gus who had taught her many tricks of the trade, noticed that she was quite adept with hammer, skill saw and nail gun. He complimented her on her skills, her work ethic and then he offered her a job to stay on as a carpenter after the school assignment was finished. She was not used to such praise and she gladly accepted the job. Her classmates had been staying during the weekdays in the cabins, taking turns cooking in the big commercial kitchen, then returning to New Haven or New York for the weekends.

They set up a communal keg of Guinness Crème Ale and each day after the work ended, they all hung out on the porch of the dining hall and drank together in great camaraderie. One of the students, Dave, was an excellent cook and made fragrant apple strudel with a light flaky crust for breakfast and deep dish lasagna and pies for dinner. When Lee was left at the camp for the weekends, she would head to the lake to swim and fish. It was supposed to be a stocked lake with good sized rainbow trout which she tried to catch with a worm or hot dog for bait, but she had little success. One day while she was fishing off the shore, a local fellow in a baseball cap and flannel shirt, beached his aluminum boat nearby and asked her how the fish were biting. She backed away slightly, ready to run, and told him that she wasn't catching much. He saw her hesitation, introduced himself as Eddie and kept his distant while explaining that these were farm raised fish who had been feed corn niblets.

"They jump at the toss of a line with a kernel of corn on the hook," he continued "You are welcome to use some of my bait"

Then he held out an open tin of nib let corn and motioned for her to help herself. She approached slowly, grabbed a nib let then stepped back. She looped the corn onto her hook so it wasn't visible, as Eddie had demonstrated, and cast her line into the dark water. Soon she was catching the sleek striped fish with most every cast and she grinned up at Eddie, who was fishing nearby, each time she did. It felt like cheating but it was a lot more fun than her previous attempts. She had reeled in several beautiful fresh trout to cook for dinner when she finally stopped. The best part was when Eddie explained that she only had to scrap off the scales, slice the fish down the middle and scrape out the guts to have them prepped for the grill. She followed his instruction and the rainbow trout were delicious when she cooked them up for dinner that night. After this Eddie became a regular fishing companion pulling up to the shore any time he saw her out there after work. She also went to play pool with him at the local pubs and met a cast of characters from the area which enriched her experience.

Once the other students left, Lee was the only one living in the Boy Scout camp full time. The main framing had been completed so a local carpenter and Lee worked on installing wall panels, plank flooring and other finishes for the kitchen and washrooms. She also began spending more of her free time with Gus and his girlfriend, Cherri who came up on some weekends. She was a beautiful fine boned woman with large green eyes and salt and pepper hair. She was living with Gus in a house that they renovated on the waterfront just outside of New Haven. They had been together for many years and Lee admired the calm respectful nature of their loving relationship. They did small things together that brought great joy, such as exploring a country store or watching the sun set. They playfully teased each other and often left each other presents in the form of wild flowers or a carved piece of wood. There was an earthy quality to their lifestyle and a freedom from materialism. They were the first people Lee met who grew their own garden vegetables without pesticides, refrained from chemicals in their home and had a vegetarian diet.

At the end of the project, the couple hosted a party for the class at their house on the bay. They first gave a tour of the well-built but modest wood structure, pointing out the handmade furniture by Gus and the embroidered pieces by Cherri. They served a wonderful salad from the garden and homemade pasta with a pesto sauce of fresh basil from the garden, Lee's first experience with his aromatic herb. The evening was filled with laughter and excellent food. Lee also learned about yoga and morning meditation for prayer and stress relief. She began to understand that her family and background had sheltered her from exposure to this unconventional and probably healthier lifestyle. There was so much to learn outside of Windsor she mused.

Lee finished up her next two years with a solid showing in her design work and passed all her classes, something that almost half the class did not achieve. Her last semester design studio was under visiting architect John Hejduk of the New York Five, a well-known group of NYC architects, and it was her most successful. They were given an assignment of designing a masque. The first masque was a literal one in which the students built elements that could be held on the face or head to tell stories about themselves. After this they were asked to describe a more elaborate history of themselves in a shoe box, similar to the art created by Joseph Cornell, the famous American sculptor. The students were to use "found objects" to express their inner most feelings and attachments with family or friends, all arranged in a very small space.

Next they had to design a masque as a building or structure to express something important to them. Lee decided to base her masque on a recording of classical guitar song that she had become enthralled with recently. She designed a pathway that started with a swirling pattern, reminiscent of the musical figure of a clef which begins a composition. Next the path crossed the symbol for infinity in stone, representing the unlimited sounds that are possible. This led to a structure that was a series of boxes within a box, each one indicating layers of music in the guitar piece. Hejduk was so impressed with the work that he clapped at the end of her presentation, looking from side to side to encourage the others to clap. The students slowly began to applaud. There were fewer clapping for her project than had clapped when Shelly presented her expandable and collapsible maze but Lee did not mind though, she knew that she had struck a home run.

Chapter 14- Studs

After graduation, which her parents attended, Lee packed up her worldly goods, said goodbye to her friends and went back to Windsor with her parents to prepare for the next phase of her life. She had been so driven with her ambition in school that she hadn't really thought beyond the goal of attaining a higher degree. Now she had to confront the practical notion of getting a full time job, but she knew that she could not live in Windsor again. She had already seen so much of what the world had to offer that she craved more. Her mother had made the sad statement "I always wanted to be an architect" at her graduation and she did not want to have regrets like that.

New experiences were essential to Lee and she would have to be in a larger city like Toronto to support herself. Her classmates had all scattered around the world but many had stayed in NYC trying to get positions with the most famous firms in the city. She had thought about doing the same thing, but her drive to be the best in the architecture field had burned out. Now when she thought about it, she really just hoped that one day she would have a good career, children and travel. She had always felt alone in the world and thought that children of her own would perhaps help fill that void. She didn't know if there was a soul mate out there for her and she didn't believe in a knight in shining armor, because she had known enough boys to understand that they were fallible creatures, but she hoped that she might find someone worthy, who would win her heart one day.

While she reviewed her next step, she was living in a farmhouse that her parents were using while they built a new house on the lake just outside of the city limits. The City of Windsor had expropriated her childhood home under Emanate Domain to turn it into a city park. They had slowly forced all the families along the waterfront to forfeit their property and then demolished each house as they acquired it, and planted grass. All that was left of the only home Lee had ever known was a gnarled willow tree gracefully draped over the steel break wall. She had used the hanging leaves of that tree to swing out over the water and drop into its murky depths. In future years, she always looked nostalgically for that tree every time she visited her parents.

While at the farm, Lee tried to get some advice from her father by asking his opinion on jobs or investing but he avoided her questions and would bury himself in the newspaper. Her mother was rarely home, busy supervising the construction, buying materials or golfing. Soon Lee was extremely bored so she decided to leave for her Aunt Mary's house and look for a job in the Toronto downtown area right away. She had originally approached her grandfather asking to get a job in the family business, but he had told her that if she was interested in the family business, she needed to go work for their competition first so she could understand their techniques and bring new information to the company. Lee didn't understand this since no one else in the family had been asked to do work elsewhere first. In fact, Grandpa had built this business to provide security for the family and everyone had been welcome to work there except for Lee apparently. Once she recovered from her disappointment, Lee decided that it may have been a good thing she got turned down, since this would force her to move out of Windsor and stay in architecture. So she typed up what she hoped was an impressive resume then set off to hand-deliver them to the most prestigious firms she could find in the yellow pages.

Wandering through the chic Yorktown and the intimidating high-rises of Young Street to drop off the summary of her achievements to date, she felt overwhelmed by complexity of the urban center. Toronto buzzed with vibrant energy from dense packed swarms of pedestrians to bright retail markets and storefronts overflowing with retail goods. Cars, taxis, buses congested the highways and their honking filled the narrow streets. The city was known to be clean, safe and culturally rich with theater, museums and music venues but her Aunt Mary's suburban house was twenty miles outside of the main city center. The house was a red brick split level ranch, lined up with identical copies marching down the newly developed street, most likely built by the Italian immigrants who were expert masons.

By the time Lee returned from downtown, there was a message from the firm of KOL and she was pleasantly surprised. They were one of the most prestigious firms in Toronto and their landmark projects included high rises such as the Colony Bank Plaza and the CAT Tower. She called them back immediately to set an appointment with the senior design partner for the next day. Lee had learned over her summer jobs, that as a female she had to work harder and perform better than her male counterpart, so for her interview, she reviewed her material, practiced her dialogue and planned her clothing to be conservative. As she strode out of the house the next day in her dark knee length suit, Aunt Mary waved from the small concrete porch and wished her luck.

Lee entered the contemporary, slick lobby of KOL, gave her name to the smartly dressed receptionist and took a seat on the authentic leather Bauhaus chair while the girl called the partner. A middle aged bearded man in a tweed jacket ushered her into a glass walled conference room. He was curious to meet the person described in the impressive resume since the firm had rarely had an Ivy League applicant before. Upon seeing how attractive Lee was in person, he relaxed and leaned forward while the girl described her previous work experience at construction companies and other architecture firms during summers. He noted that she was well spoken and professional, if a bit nervous, and for a quick moment, he fantasized about asking this young woman for a drink.

Refocusing his attention back to the interview, he decided to offer the girl the position right away and hope she could join them immediately. Lee accepted and she was secretly thrilled to have found a position so quickly. It was a long commute every day and it didn't seem to matter whether Lee took the VIA train, subway or drove her car to the tightly packed urban core of the city, it was always took an hour and a half each way. The firm was in Yorktown, a haven of historic buildings converted to offices and residential condominiums mixed with slick modern in fill projects. Lee loved the vibrant atmosphere, the cafes spilling out onto the sidewalks and the fast pace of this section of the city center. She was very excited and nervous to be working at one of the top firms in Canada with such amazing projects.

Her job turned out to be design assistant to the project manager of a 30 storey high rise to be built in Montreal. Her desk was located in the design department on a mezzanine overlooking the drafting floor below, both under a massive sloped glass ceiling. A dozen designers looked down over a hundred draftsmen and engineers who would take their ideas and make them hard line drawings that would allow the contractor to bring them to life. Lee was glad to find a couple other girls in the design department besides secretaries. She immediately gravitated to a pretty blond with wide set blue eyes and a sweet disposition. Tracy was a great help getting Lee familiar with office policies, break times, lunch spots and general gossip. She described the role of each partner, Martin the overweight diabetic who could have been a classical pianist, Hiram the stylish egocentric whose wife's connections brought in Jewish clientele and Ryan, the partner who had interviewed Lee, ran the day to day operations and was going through divorce.

Lee's project manager was a dark haired scruffy looking bohemian who Tracy said was not very friendly to anyone. She was glad to hear that it wasn't just her that he ignored. Still, he had to be one of the best designers to be in such a position at this office. The designers were the royalty of the firm and sat at drafting tables lined up in rows under the north facing sky lit roof so the soft indirect light poured over their boards. They used thin yellow onionskin or velum for sketching and then thick Mylar for final drawings. When designing these high-rises, Lee was instructed that the grid was critical and all elements had to fit exactly within the dimensional structural bays. The core of these buildings served as the spine and held the washrooms, plumbing, mechanical riser shafts and exit stairwells, like the blood vessels and organs of a body. The glazing on the exterior was a skin stretched across the skeleton of the steel beams and columns and the great HVAC air conditioning cooling towers were perched on the very top.

The high rise that Lee was working on actually had a gothic style to it which complemented the adjacent church. An agreement with the church on the sale of the land to the developer required a connection be built between the buildings, both above grade and below, so a cloister connected them above while an underground retail shopping center connected them below. The entire stone church was going to have to be held up on piers and shoring while a multi-storey retail mall was built beneath it. It would be an amazing engineering feat but it also seemed a bit sacrilegious to be praying over the bustle of commerce below, though the Canadians didn't seem to mind. At least the beautiful stone Catholic Church was not going to be torn down. Once Lee was at KOL for a couple months, Hiram, who had no real job function beyond socializing, started to get more aggressive about harassing the women.

One day Hiram came into the design area, leaned against the rail, arms crossed, looked beneath the desks and began to rate the women's legs. Drafting tables are set higher than normal desks and they have a step to set feet on which elevates the thighs, so he had a pretty good view under the women's skirts. He also began to tease the beautiful Tracy once he found out her name. He said that he knew her name had to be Tracey, Stacey or Bambi and what was she doing in an architect's job when she should be staying home and having babies. Tracy usually laughed off these remarks since she felt that she had no recourse beyond quitting, but they bothered her. Lee started wearing pants to avoid the comments but Traci liked wearing her skirts. She had a boyfriend who she would meet for lunch and she wanted to impress him so she continued to bear the brunt of Hiram's lustful rhetoric.

One evening after Lee jumped on the subway at Bloor to get home after work, she looked up to see a young man at the end of the compartment watching her. The fellow was in a light blue oxford cloth shirt that was slightly creased, with a tie hanging lose and the top buttons splayed open as though it could not contain his body. He was a tall well built man, more slight than she remembered but he was still an imposing figure and his smile broadened when he saw that she recognized him. Robbie had been one of her students in her History of Art class at Yale and they had seen each other on campus occasionally after the class ended. Being two of the Canadians at the school, they were always pleased to see each other and chat about what was going on back home. She had forgotten about him until this moment. The two each expressed surprise at bumping into each other then tried to catch up on their lives as the subway sped closer to their destinations. Just as the car slowed for his stop, Robbie suggested that she come to a big party for some athletic clubs the following weekend. She was intrigued and said that she would try to make it. He quickly gave her the location and time then he jumped off the train and waved to her as it headed to the next stop.

The party sounded like fun but she was too shy to go to an event like that by herself so she invited her girlfriend to come along. When the night approached, her friend Shannon drove over to Lee's apartment, which was in a twelve storey white concrete high rise in Brampton and near her Aunt's place. After reassessing their outfits and touching up makeup, they both drove together into the city. The party was in a large hall with a stage up front, banners were hanging from the ceiling, the lights were low and it was quite crowded by the time the girls arrived. Alcohol flowed freely and the buzz of various conversations grew. Lee had dressed carefully in her tightest jeans and a stylish flattering top, but she felt self conscious standing in the middle of the room with Shannon so she started to look around for Robbie. When she couldn't find him, she assessed the clusters of groups to see they could join one.

Lee spotted one fellow in the shadows of the dark room because his head was raised above all the shifting figures around him.

He was a commanding presence in the sea of people and this drew her curiosity. She gathered her courage and suggested to her friend that they edge over toward that animated group. They moved through the crowd until they were near the tall figure. Lee paused to pick up the thread of conversation and then the group widened to include her and Shannon. As the other boys continued to banter back and forth, Lee took the opportunity to look over the tall fellow with the deep laugh. He was not a handsome man, with his large head, marked skin, small squinting eyes and uneven teeth, but he stood with his shoulders thrown back, full of confidence and strength which were attractive to Lee.

Curtis Richards was a highly observant man and his tracking blue eyes followed the movement of the girl with the long dark hair edging towards his area. He had assessed her slim figure with the rounded shoulders, thick hair, narrow face with angular features and he was intrigued. He hadn't seen any other girl show any interest in him and it had been a long time since he had been laid. As the girls got closer and joined his band of friends, Curt, as he liked to be called, began to subtlety shift his position until he was next to Lee then he then leaned down and asked her if she wanted to dance. She nodded agreement and as they moved toward the gyrating bodies on the dance floor. He laughed and said that they had been on opposing sports teams in college. His team had actually won the National Championships against Robbie he bragged with a laugh.

The two continued with other small talk, comparing backgrounds, work, travel, and eventually, Curt asked Lee out to dinner. He never tended to date women for very long, and was perfectly contented with one night stands, so he didn't extend much thought to where this would go, beyond the potential of a good tumble, but Lee wasn't aware of this. She had already begun to contemplate the variety of possible scenarios where this introduction might lead. Curt and Lee had stayed close together, chatting when possible and dancing when the music was too loud, so it was a natural gesture at the end of the evening for Lee to pass her card to him after he asked if he could call her to confirm dinner.

Their first date occurred a few days later and Lee was excited about it. Curt pulled up to her apartment building in a low black Porsche and he was well dressed in an expensive jacket, white shirt and jeans when he came to the door. He brought her to a small elegant restaurant within a short walking distance where he had made reservations, and she was immediately impressed. They were lead to an intimate corner table and fell into easy conversation, leaning toward each other, laughing. The time slipped away and Lee was surprised to look up at some point later in the evening and find that they were the only customers left as the waiters impatiently circled trying to clean up. The couple left the restaurant holding hands and wandered along the quiet streets of the quaint downtown in the warm evening, content in each other's company.

They continued seeing each other, meeting to play tennis, go to movies, concerts and out for dinner. They were both athletic, active and found that they enjoyed each other's company. He was a strong personality who guided them in a direction that seemed to be in keeping with her own goals so she was pleased to continue with the relationship. Within a short time he was adding new experiences to her life including trips into the country to visit his parents and skiing. Lee hadn't skied much but Curt was a ski instructor for children with Down's syndrome and other handicaps so she went along to the mountains with him.

Curt had only gotten involved in this group in order to entice a girl to sleep with him Lee found out later, but after the girl had left the program and his attentions behind, Curt had stayed and brought in some of his high school friends as instructors as well. Lee was fascinated watching these children so excited to expand their abilities and joyful in the new experience of gliding down the mountain. One boy, who had no legs, used prosthesis metal legs with skis attached to weave down the slope in a very masterful style. Another heavy set Down syndrome boy labored to remain upright on his skis and had to have an adult hold him from behind the whole time down the bunny hill but he could not hold back the huge smile on his innocent face.

Curt Richards liked things that were new and shiny and he did not like Lee's old Thunderbird sitting in the driveway of his expensive townhouse. He decided to change that and eventually talked Lee into buying a new car from a friend of his who worked at a Volkswagen dealership. Lee's car did need an expensive brake job she found out after she had purchased it as well as various other repairs that kept coming up unexpectedly. It was however, fully paid off so she wasn't thrilled about going into debt to get a new car. But Curt was persistent and arranged everything before she could object. He also sold her old car to the mechanic who had given her a quote for the brake replacement. The deal didn't seem right and the amount that she got was so small and a bit suspicious but it was too late. Curtis claimed that amount was all she could hope to get in his opinion and since he had bragged that his father had owned a used car dealership, she believed him. So Curt helped arrange for her first car loan and Lee was the somewhat proud owner of a shiny new Jetta. The only problem with this new compact car was that it was manual and she didn't know how to drive a stick so Curt gave her a few lessons on his Porsche. It was a huge treat to slip behind the wheel of the sleek black machine with the scent of leather permeating the interior. She felt wonderful but also guilty when she stalled the car while trying to release the clutch at an intersection or when she heard the grinding of metal as she tried to shift into a higher gear without having the clutch fully engaged. As this happened, Curt would burst out screaming instructions but often he just cringed and ended the lesson.

The day she was supposed pick up her new car, Curt had gone out of town with his friends to go white water rafting and Lee was supposed to drive up on her own to join them. She was extremely insecure about having to do such a long drive north after just getting the car and with only a few manual driving practices but Curtis had insisted that it would not be a problem. After trading the cashier's check for the Volkswagen Golf's keys, she slid into the car and made a silent prayer that she remembered all she needed to get the car out of the driveway without humiliating herself. She let the car coast down the driveway, waved a goodbye and jerked the car down the road as she tried to shift. Once on the freeway, relief swept over her that she didn't have to shift for a while. She still had to find the exit, steer through winding two lane roads then on a gravel road into a remote campground.

Lee's new car was taking a beating but all she could do was concentrate on was trying to park without stalling or smashing into another car. After successfully maneuvering the car into a space, Lee exhaled a breath and tried to ease some of the tension of the last few hours. She then locked the car and set off toward the wooded area to find the group who were all gathered around a camp site busy regaling each other with the adventures of their first day of rafting. They were so caught up in their enthusiasm that Curt didn't pay much attention to Lee's arrival. She sat quietly on a log wondering why she had bothered coming. When the group decided to head to the main building for dinner Curt hung back talking with his close friend Ned, ignoring Lee, so she headed up the path by herself. As she was strolling between trees with her head down and eyes on the dirt trail, one of the rafting guides stepped up next to her and starting chatting. He was kindly and soon he had her smiling again. The path snaked next to the lake and Lee was growing more relaxed and pleased that she had made the drive after all. As they neared the dining hall, Curt suddenly appeared at Lee's side, grabbed her arm and led her away from the guide with a threateningly intense look. He bent over her, not quite out of hearing, and lashed out with comments about her embarrassing him and being inconsiderate.

"How could you talk to another guy in front of my friends," he yelled at her.

She was so surprised at his anger that she made no reply in her defense. She recognized the jealousy but couldn't understand the reason for it. Curt would not let up until she appeared more humble and apologetic, his control asserted once more, they proceeded to join the rest for dinner. Lee was once again quiet and Curt exuberant.

Lee did eventually forget about Curt's behavior, as he charmed her back into his control, and mastered driving her new car, out of sheer determination. Her job however left her less than satisfied. She had been getting frustrated with her position at KOL since the head designer had refused to share the design work, leaving her with only the less appealing parts. She was in charge of arranging the meetings with the elevator supplier, the window washing company and the fire alarm company, then adding their information to the drawings. This meant that she was only working on the maintenance and mechanical items of the double peaked high rise, a design she was not impressed with at all. She didn't understand how anyone could design a building that it looked like it had dog ears. The consultants started calling it "The Dog" and at those times she was glad that she was not listed as a contributing designer.

Despite being disappointed in the job Lee had not been looking around for another position when a small architectural firm approached her with an offer that she couldn't turn down. Her cousin had been golfing with a buddy if his, Kamal Khan, who was in partnership with a British architect by the name of Robert Adams. Kamal mentioned that they were looking for a good architect so Lee's cousin summarized her resume and potential availability. Kamal had then called Lee the next day to find out if she would be interested in a position as head designer and potential partner. When she said that she would be glad to meet with him to discuss the possibilities, they arranged an interview. On the day of the meeting, Lee took the subway up Young Street at lunch time to meet with the partners of Adams Architects in their small but tidy office near the 401 highway, with exhilaration in her step.

Kamal and Robert were in their late fifties but opposites in many ways. One was shorter and rounded with dark skin and black hair from Indian heritage, in a golf shirt and slacks and the other, a distinguished Brit sported white hair, wire rimmed glasses, an ascot and hounds tooth jacket. These affable men had met when they were both teaching drafting at the local community college and they complimented each other both in personality and responsibilities. Kam, who was not a registered architect, played golf with the clients and oversaw the drawing production, while Robert, the stamping architect, did presentations, design work and the office management. The company was located in a modest office unit and they had five staff members, all draftsmen they had trained at the school and one secretary. They were both kind hearted, good humored gentlemen and after the interview they offered her an enticing salary with a guarantee that once they retired in five years, she would be a partner in the firm, along with a second partner to be selected. It was a nice fit for all three of them and Lee accepted.

Once Lee had changed jobs the hardest part was not seeing Tracy as much. Lee had spent a lot of time at Tracy's house since moving to Toronto, but it was harder to get together when they worked in different parts of the city and lived even farther apart. Tracy was also getting quite serious with the fellow she had been dating for a couple years, Matthew, a handsome blond who had been her high school crush. The girls tried to arrange double dates but it soon it became apparent that Curt and Matthew did not seem to like each other's company. So Lee and Tracy would meet without them for lunch or dinner.

One day while they were at a café, Tracy told Lee that she was ready for Matthew to propose. She had waited long enough for this man she had always adored, and now she wanted a commitment. Tracy was a little afraid that Matthew might start looking around so she felt that marriage and children would seal the deal for her. She planned to surprise him with a hotel room for their dating anniversary and greet him sprawled on the couch of the sitting room in just a fur coat in order to entice him to propose. This sounded so bold to Lee, such a methodical sexual approach, and she wondered if it would really work.

She could understand Tracy's motivation, since she would also like a family, but not her method. Shortly after this however, Tracy was sporting a large solitaire diamond and a big grin.

It did not surprise Lee that Matthew did not get along with Curt since they were such different personalities. Matthew was a smooth talking, thin, naturally stylish man who looked good in anything while Curt was very confident but forceful, brutish, with a thick chest and waist on thin hips and legs. He had to select his clothing carefully to be flattering and he got his suits custom made for his build. He also liked to throw money around to impress and often stated that "Someone has to pay retail" a quote that carried heavy significance for future financial compatibility but was lost on Lee at the time. Matthew was frugal and careful in his selections. Curt also possessed a cynical sense of humor that confused people who didn't know him. They couldn't be sure if he was laughing at them or with them when he tilted back his head and unleashed a deep burst of laughter after making a blunt and often critical observation.

His group of friends shared a similar humor and regularly made unsavory remarks about various girls from Curt's history in front of Lee. There didn't seem to be any steady girlfriends in the past, just passing flings. Curt's sister, who was part of the group as well, told Lee that she was the first long term relationship for Curt. On hearing this Lee felt rather proud; as though she had broken a pattern and that she was special. This thought was shattered shortly afterwards by a girl in the group who called herself the Queen Bee. She was a rather overweight, plain, round faced woman with an unattractive bowl haircut and she bragged that she had been the first sexual experience, or "lay" as she termed it, for most of the guys in the group when they were just fourteen. Lee was floored when the girl made this proclamation in public but none of the boys denied it. The girl's chubby bespectacled boyfriend, who later became her husband, also didn't utter a word, he just smiled.

-100-

Chapter 15 - Top Plate

The design work that Lee produced at Adam's Architect had begun with small projects of industrial warehouses, office condos and retail stores but it slowly grew to larger developments. Industrial work had been their bread and butter before Lee arrived. The team had done all the drafting work by hand but they had just gotten a taste of the new computers coming into use when one of their employees, Maury, had asked to try to build one for the firm. This draftsman of Polish descent didn't have much understanding of hygiene, thus his desk was in a remote corner, but he seemed to think that he could set up a system very cheaply and maintain it himself. He started by inviting a software representative to the office to sample their AutoCAD drafting program.

After the salesman left, the grinning Maury indicated that he had secretly copied the program and they wouldn't have to pay the three thousand dollars the supplier was asking for it. This bothered Lee and she mentioned it to Kam but he ignored her copy right concerns. Meanwhile, the self appointed IT fledgling was constantly pulling the computer parts out of the metal case, examining them, reconnecting wiring and generally looking busy. He monopolized the machine and gave the impression of secret knowledge and skills. The rest of the employees had never touched a computer and were in awe of the complicated looking device with its tangle of exposed wires. They were however interested in learning to use it but they never voiced this around Maury. His smug satisfaction on hearing this would have been too much to bear, though he did guess it. The older draftsmen weren't convinced that the new fangled computer really would save any time over good old hand drawing so they were the most reluctant to embrace the technology change. Adaptation was harder with age but they would have no choice eventually.

Lee had a drafting table on the second floor of the office where she sketched and prepared designs for presentation to the clients. She didn't have to do the working drawings any more since there were young kids fresh from the college for that work. Instead she was able to be creative and solve problems all day. She met with the clients, determined their programs and laid out floor plans, elevations and perspective drawings in color and ink. Once the designs were approved she saw them to fruition by supervising the work of the draftsmen and going on site visits to watch the construction. The projects got bigger and more complex as well and the office had to hire more people. One day Robert came to her with a high profile resort project in Beaver Creek, Colorado. He said that he was working with a fellow who had inherited a prestigious residential practice from an architect who had died in a plane crash.

Christopher was not a registered architect, just a well trained and talented draftsman who had been second in command of the firm for many years until the accident. Business had now grown to the point that he had more work than he could handle. He also needed an architect since the projects had grown from custom homes to commercial projects for one of the wealthiest men in Canada and they had to be stamped by a registered architect. Robert could provide that architect's stamp and additional staff for Christopher so the collaboration was set up in the Adam's office.

However, the client for the Beaver Creek project had required that Christopher travel in his private plane to meetings and site visits to Colorado but Christopher had a horrible fear of flying, exacerbated by the accident. He often sent Robert in his place and sometimes at the very last minute. He would get to the airport and attempt to get on the plane but back out of the flight terrified. Eventually the client insisted on Christopher attending, so after extensive therapy sessions he tried again and eventually overcame his fear of flying to in fact become a frequent flyer.

While Lee's work was flourishing, so was her personal life with Curt. He grew tired of driving out to the suburbs to see her and suggested that she move in with him. She had never thought she would consider this but she was fond of the lively section of the city called the Beaches, and she was falling for Curt. She was pretty malleable at this point in her life, soft clay open to sculpting but still with an intrinsic backbone of work ethics and morals. She was slowly gaining direction and a sense of self, but she still felt a great desire to bond with another human. She wanted to have children to fill her life and give it purpose. Curt had absorbed her into his life with the blending of activities. They were compatible in their family backgrounds, ambitions and sports as well as sexually. He wanted her constantly and that gave her a heightened sense of her own sensuality. She felt more attractive when he touched her waist to let her know he was next to her or rubbed her thigh in the car.

Curt wasn't overly demonstrative with affection but they did hold hands sometimes when they were out together. The only problem was that he touched other women as well, always in a jesting manner though so she was not sure of his intent. It bothered her to see him ogling and commenting on another fellow's girlfriend with a large chest or a woman in a bikini on the beach. She would mention to him that she didn't like his lusting after other women so openly but he would laugh it off as her own insecurity.

Lee was definitely insecure, as were most people in some way, but Curt did make it worse on her with his behavior. She felt a slight fissure in her trust in him when this happened. Shouldn't she be with someone who made her feel secure, respected and good about their relationship instead of fearful? Then she would think about the parts of their relationship that worked well and her hopes would rise. Still, she began to contemplate Curt's past in a different light which raised the question as to whether he would be capable of staying true to one woman and respecting her.

When Lee moved in with Curt in the summer of 1986, the first items out of her car were a skill saw and tool box. Curt made the comment that not many guys can say that their girlfriend moved her tools in first. She didn't know if he was pleased with this or being sarcastic again. She was very proud of her ability to fix things and work with her hands. Her mother had built her own kitchen and bathroom cabinets. She had a new router and jig saw so Lee's phone calls to Anne often consisted of listening to facts about laminates, plywood and router bits.

Lee felt it was important to be self sufficient in this world and she was very independent, her nature right from birth according to her mother. She was also curious about centuries past when people had only their own skills to keep themselves and their families alive. So she read books on the founding of the west in the US, the awakening of Russia under Catherine the Great and of course, the British navy and their adventures to isolated areas of the world in the 19th century. Tall ships, their rigging, sails and structures had always fascinated her and the paintings she did were often of these statuesque emblems of ocean travel. She liked to read about the hardships that were overcome by tenacity and intellect. Curt did not read much so while he would watch TV, Lee would settle in on the couch with her paints or a book to keep him company, though she had little interest in the TV and its noise.

Their life together merged well at first. Curt was working at one of the large brokerage houses and he was in an elite group of twelve fellows who had been pulled together by their leader, a persuasive gregarious mountain of a man who also made big money and intended that all of his group do the same. Tom had started at the bottom of society, a tough impoverished childhood, and he had fought hard to get to what he perceived as the top. He enjoyed his success and flaunted it with custom tailored suits from the best designer shops, gold cuff links in French handmade shirts, fine dining at the most exclusive restaurants and expensive cars. He kept a picture of his wife on his desk, a high school sweetheart with blond hair and a sturdy six foot build, in a frame that had the words "My First Wife" written around the edges. He was known for satisfying his extracurricular sexual desires with secretaries, waitresses and any woman who caught his eye although he was at least relatively discreet.

The group adopted this attitude of indulgences and spending for sake of "image". Confidence permeated the air around them as they flashed large bills at hostesses to get prime tables or seats at sporting events. Lee and Curt would go out to events with this group where each couple would try to outdo the other with fancier clothes, more jewelry and better Rolex's. They talked about the huge houses they owned or wanted to own and the expensive furniture they bought. Lee found it extremely superficial but she was also caught up in the yearning and couldn't turn away from looking at the babbles. Most outings though, were just the boys at a bar after work and the only part of those evenings that Lee would hear about were the cigar smoking and hints of tall tales.

Lee liked Curt's duplex in the Beaches, although it never felt like her place since Curt had not allowed any of her possessions to occupy it except her clothes. He had suggested that she throw her furniture out instead of bringing it with her since the place was already fully furnished. She had been given a beautiful Chippendale dining room set from her grandparents to remember them by so she refused to throw anything out and instead stored it in the lowest level near the garage. The Beaches was a cluster of former cottages on the shoreline section east of the downtown. The streets were narrow, one way and followed the roll of the hills. Lee loved to walk the busy café filled sidewalks, buying groceries at the local health food store and wander the boardwalk along the water's edge. There were pathways through the park, basketball courts and hockey rinks used for lacrosse in the summer. This was a sort of hippie tinged place where people wore earth shoes, flowing skirts, love beads and shopped at stores smelling of incense. Many buildings had wild flower power paintings on the front and sides. It was a rough gem hidden in the massive grid of urbanity. The living spaces were tight and the population so dense that everything felt compressed. The buildings were constructed over underground rivers and they leaned near each other, sometimes touching. These tight living areas drove people out into the wide open spaces of the parks, neighborhood squares and shopping areas and so the streets were always teaming with people of all nationalities including many mixed ethnic couples and foreign nannies with strollers. Lee enjoyed the exotic and intimate feel of the area – it felt like home for now.

One advantage of living near the lake was that Curt could practice his wind surfing when the wind was in the right direction. He used a short board with a Mylar sail which had to be moving fast to carry his weight and it required a lot of strength and skill. In deep water the short board surfers did a water start which required floating next to the board with one foot in a strap on the top and one dragging for stability. Then they would crack the sail up so it would catch the wind and it would yank their body out of the water. Once up the rider would have to jam their second foot into the back strap and hook the harness belt onto the draped line on the boom attached to the pivotal mast. This required extra concentration to get the hook connection while racing downwind but the harness prevented the surfer from being thrown over from strong gusts or getting overtired arms so it was worthwhile.

Curt reveled in the macho nature of this sport. Few women used the short board due to the strength required but the ones who did were very good. However, Lee had read about a female architect who had died while windsurfing in Georgian Bay. She had been thrown from the board, hit her head on the mast and drown. Still Lee did not want to be left behind so she asked if she could try the sport. There was a lot of expensive specialized equipment involved, such as sails of different sizes for different wind conditions, custom boards, booms, skegs, clew, pullies, fins, harness and a collection of other lines and hardware. Lee could not afford any of this herself so she hoped to use Curt's equipment since he had duplicates of many pieces. This worked out at times when Curt would assemble a second board so Lee was able to learn to get up and sail out at exhilarating speeds. But more often Curt was busy with his own rig and left Lee watching rather than riding.

At one point Curt suggested that the boys were going to Hatteras North Carolina to windsurf and asked if Lee wanted to come along. It was one of the best spots in North America to wind surf and Lee was up for any adventure. They drove fourteen hours down through New York State, Pennsylvania, Virginia then past Kitty Hawk along the North Carolina coast to the Outer Banks of the barrier island. The road narrowed and wove between sand dunes and brown waving grasses. They passed tall grey weathered wood houses on stilts until they turned into a driveway of one of these vacation rentals.

Lee was the only girl in the group but that didn't bother her since she had always been the only girl in many situations. Curt rather enjoyed having his girlfriend on the trip especially since she was such low maintenance. His friends seemed to like her company as well so he relaxed and even felt a bit of pride. On the first morning of their trip, the guys all went to the Canadian Hole on the bay side of the barrier island that stretches the entire length of the North Carolina coast. This side had smooth protected, shallow water with a steady breeze that made it easy to sail directly west into the bay and then back to shore so it popular for windsurfers. The other side of the narrow spit of land was exposed to the harsh breaking waves of the Atlantic Ocean, dark and foreboding. This was the side that interested Lee and after she got bored watching the guys launch their boards and sail off, she wandered over to investigate.

After observing the crashing waves for a while, Lee decided that she could have some of her own fun here. So she went back to find Ned, a high school friend of Curt's who didn't wind surf, and suggested that that they grab their boogie boards and cross the dune. The water was chilly and the waves were enormous on this side so Lee entered the surf cautiously. Ned waited out into the surf but paused to see how she would do it since he was not a good swimmer. It was difficult for her to swim out past the breakers, diving under each crashing wave dragging the board behind on its tether.

Finally Lee was able to fight her way out to where the water was just gathering in a swell before it began rolling to escalating heights. Lee hadn't used a board like this much and as she paddled to catch an especially large wave, she realized that she wasn't sure where she should be positioned. The wave however picked her up and moved her to the top of the crest. As it rolled to the beach, she realized her mistake too late. She should have been riding the middle of the wave, closer to the water's surface and less exposed than at the top. It felt as though she was ten feet in the air as the wave finally ran out of power and flung itself onto the shallows of sand and rock in its shadow. She briefly glimpsed the shocked look on Ned's face as the wave drove her past him and she was tumbled head over heels and lost in the spray. She hit the bottom and was jarred by sand and rock still tumbling with the wave as it rushed to the top of the beach.

It felt like hours of constant movement until she finally stopped on her back in the foam even though it was only minutes. The wind was crushed out of her lungs and she had been paralyzed by the violence of the washing machine action. Finally she pushed herself up on her elbows and gulped a deep breath of air. Then she took inventory of her limbs and realized that she did not feel any unusual pain anywhere. There were no broken bones or lacerated skin. Some instinct had made her relax her body as the wave crashed at the end, and in the harsh reality of danger she became an un-resistant puppet, which is what saved her. She looked up to see Ned rushing toward her through the surf, a worried look on his face that changed to a grin as she gave a thumbs up sign. "That was a thrill" she called out, as she vowed to herself to never do that again.

As Ned and Lee returned to the bay side, the group was still out wind surfing and would continue for another hour then it would take them an additional hour to disassemble and pack the equipment. It was a labor intensive sport but the guys were still in their adrenaline rush when they got in off their boards and jocular as they packed up. Lee settled down gently on her towel, careful not to further hurt anything, with a book to recover and wait. She did not tell Curt of her boogey boarding incident on the return to the rental house since he would have teased her. But later that evening when the group was at a tavern having a few beers, Ned had enthusiastically painted a harrowing picture of an incredible wave ride. He made her sound more in control of the wild ride than she had felt at the time. The group then all gave her affectionate slaps on the back, toasted her bravado and allowed her to feel some of the camaraderie they were seeking in their testosterone filled adventures. Curt scrutinizer her during this exchange; watching the happiness of acceptance cross her face and the full uninhibited laughter spill out. He was not pleased that she was getting this attention. He had brought her along to watch him succeed, to see how good he was at this tough sport and for a good romp at night afterwards, not for this. So he interjected.

"Well, if she was able to handle a real board then she wouldn't be over there playing with the baby boards"

The group hooted with laughter at this and conversation moved back to recalling the days more memorable wind rides. Lee was hurt and looked at Curt quizzically but his attention was back with the boys even though he knew that she was watching him.

As the wind surfers geared up for the second day, Lee tentatively stretched her battered but thankfully unbroken limbs. She had also grabbed a harness and wet suit to take to the beach. The guys assembled their boards and sails on the sand then towed their full rigs out into the shallows. They slipped their feet in the stirrups, cracked sharply on the sail to snap it full with the wind, stepped easily on the top of their boards and raced away to join the other butterflies skimming across the light blue surface. Lee waited until they were gone then grabbed the pieces of equipment that Curt had left behind and used them to assembled a suitable board and sail.

Lee carried this makeshift rig to the shore edge for final adjustment and in the shallow water along the curved of the bay, she grabbed the boom, hooked her foot in and step onto the board to take off as she had seen the others do. It was a surprisingly presentable launch and soon she was flying, the board digging into the water threatening to fling her off its back. Curt had given her some pointers before and she had tried his board a few times from a water start but never doing everything herself - this was a challenge. She knew that balance wasn't a skill of hers so she just clung to the boom with all her strength, not attempting to hook in her harness, just thrilled to be sailing. Of course her arms were already getting torn from her shoulders and she knew they wouldn't last long without the harness so she slowly moved her waist so the hook latched onto the boom rope. It took several tries but she was finally hooked in and moving smoothly across the short chop of the bay. A huge smiled crossed her face and though she wasn't fond of all the work this sport entailed and how sore she would be the next day, she was proud to have succeeded. "This is not a baby board" she thought as she took off after the rest of the windsurfers.

Chapter 16 – Mechanical Systems

The young couple's relationship continued to develop at a steady pace and soon Lee noticed that she was spending all her free time with Curt and losing touch with her friends. Tracy still tried to get together but with the underlying tension between Curt and her fiancé, it was hard not to feel torn between loyalties. Lee enjoyed her friends but Curt made subtle detracting comments about them, criticisms of their behaviour or the way they dressed or spoke. It embarrassed Lee to hear him speak like this and made her feel uncomfortable. She tried to defend her friends but then Curt would get even more abusive and the day would be spoiled. Lee didn't enjoy conflict of any kind so she made the choice to not argue and of course, the seed of doubt about her friends was planted whether she wanted it there or not.

The toughest situation was when Lee was invited to be a bridesmaid for Tracy in her summer wedding at the prestigious Royal Canadian Yacht Club on the island in the Toronto habour. Matthew had pulled some strings and was able to book the popular spot a year in advance. The yacht club, a British sailing tradition, was founded in 1852 and had acted as an auxiliary base for the Royal Navy. The beautiful two storey white Victorian styled building built in 1919 would be a wonderful backdrop to their perfect wedding. Tracy was even sewing her own wedding gown, a strapless number with chiffon layers, floating crinoline hoops, thousands of seed pearls and a long satin train. Tracy sewed every pearl in place herself and even made a jacket to match. She also bought mauve silk fabric and dress patterns for the bridesmaids. Then she asked that each girl make their own dress or employ a seamstress to make it for them. Lee was constantly updated and shown the progress of the beautiful wedding dress by Tracy and she was excited for her friend.

Lee had cut the pattern for her bridesmaid dress but she had not started the sewing when Curt had proposed the trip to Hatteras. Unfortunately for Lee, he had called her late at night and said that the group was leaving on the night of Tracy's wedding so they could drive through the night and windsurf the next morning. He demanded an answer immediately and Lee was torn again. When Lee told Tracy of her decision to make the trip, her friend was very unhappy with her and asked Lee to relinquish her position as bridesmaid. Lee explained that she would still be able to attend most all of the wedding festivities before leaving but it was the act that Tracy saw as a betrayal in choosing the trip over her wedding that made her ask for the dress material back. Lee and Curt still attended the wedding, which was very traditional, long but perfectly planned. The bride was stunning and the groom extremely attractive in his tux. The bridesmaids dutifully stood by Tracy's side all day and Lee felt some relief that she didn't have to bake in the sun but she also felt regret and knew that the relationship was damaged. Their friendship cooled and was never as close again though they still visited each other. Lee had been forced into making a difficult choice and she was disappointed with herself so she did not blame Tracy for pulling away.

Once back in Toronto, Lee felt the loss of her close friend, but work was quite busy and it distracted her. She had also found a local athletic facility, the Lakeshore Club, where she could go play squash and swim. Curt would meet her at the club sometimes to work out as well. Once, after he had finished his gym work out early, he had sat behind the glass wall of the squash court and watched her practice. He had never played squash but thought it looked easy so he suggested that they play a game. Lee was excited about this and taught him the basics of the sport. He had played tennis so he had the bad habit of a big rangy swing instead of the tight wrist movement of squash. This was tricky for Lee since it meant that she could get hit by his racket which happened several times leaving her badly bruised.

They practiced mostly then played a few games until Curt realized that he couldn't beat her as handily as he had first assumed. Their games then tapered off until he would say that he was too busy to play anymore. It happened that way with other sports as well. They would decide to swim or play tennis together and after volleying the ball for a while, Curt would get competitive and suggest a game or want to race in the pool. Lee didn't really have any desire to beat anyone, but Curt was so insistent that she complied and tried her best. Once Lee drew on her natural athletic ability, her opponents would be challenged and often bested in agility or speed sports. This did not sit well with Curt to be beaten by his girlfriend and soon Lee was forced to find new partners for these sports at the club.

One of the new friends Lee had found was a woman who she had met at the firm. Laura was an interior designer originally from Quebec. She was eight months pregnant in a loose but stylish top when Lee first saw her. She was designing the interiors on one of their office projects when Richard had steered her over to meet Lee. Laura had a sophisticated beauty with her thin face of flawless skin and large dark intelligent eyes framed by layered highlighted hair. She also spoke with a heavy French accent but the two designers had immediately seen in the other, a kindred soul. Laura was a very athletic, talented professional and she lived in the Beaches area with her husband, who was tennis professional at a private club.

Once Laura had delivered her first child, a beautiful blond curly haired girl, she was eager to get back in shape and she took Lee golfing at her country club or they played tennis at Lakeshore. Laura was a fiercely independent business woman with her own commercial interior design firm so Lee really enjoyed their time together. Again, Lee tried to double date, but Curt did not fit in well and avoided the outings. He did not dare speak poorly of Laura though since he was actually intimidated by her, but he was also frustrated by the attention Lee gave to the woman. This soon led to some tension in their relationship but Lee wasn't worried, she just felt that it would get sorted out over time. She was very happy with her new friend and did not want to give up this one.

At the firm, Adam's was getting so much new work that they had to hire even more draftsmen and Lee's projects had moved into multi-storey residential condominiums, restaurants and even a seven storey medical office building. Lee designed them all and even when she had little experience in a certain building type, her logical understanding of function, spatial design sense and knowledge of building construction techniques helped her through. She was the merging of a practical technician and a conceptual designer/artist, though she didn't feel that she had mastered either. Architects who had both skills were rare though.

The firm finally outgrew its rental space and moved to a building on Sheppard Avenue which Kam and Robert purchased privately and leased back to the company. It had been a private house on an extremely busy street so the partners got it re-zoned to commercial and asked Lee to design a new facade and interior renovation so that it looked more like an architect's office. She was thrilled to take on the challenge in such a prominent location and she spent many hours designing and sketching until everyone was in agreement on the final product. Lee had used a layering of different height walls in the front to give the building more complexity and screening. Then she removed the existing low sloped roof, set floor joists for a second floor and added a high pitched roof with exposed bow trusses for the new upper studio space. She also cut in new windows and added skylights to get north light into the studio. Then the group decided together on a unique color scheme of grays and smoke blue to ensure the building stood out amongst the adjacent typical red brick homes. This was her new work place and she was proud of it.

Things were not as smooth on the home front for Lee though. Curt had decided that he was not happy with their relationship and one evening after work, he confronted Lee, told her the situation was not working for him and then asked that she move out. He said that some of her habits had started to bother him and they just didn't seem to fit as a couple any more. She asked him what he was referring to so she could understand. He told her that she was not as tidy as he would prefer, she didn't smile enough and she swore sometimes. Lee was shocked by this bizarre superficial list which was apparently the cause of the break-up of their nine month co-habitation. It was true that she had some of her painting materials in the guest room and it had a messy studio quality to it. But she was the one who kept the rest of the house clean and tidy.

When she had first moved into the townhouse there were year's worth of serious grime in the bathroom and kitchen which she had used Brillo pads to remove. As for the other two comments, she felt like a very happy person and smiled often though once in a while she did use the English term "bloody" in jest. But that wasn't much of a swear word. He had to have been making excuses for other more important issues, like loss of attraction perhaps. She tried again to ask if he would like to talk things over to try to work them out but he just shook his head and said no. This rejection hurt her badly but she hid it from him. She then took a breath to stay under control and focus while her mind digested all this surprising and disturbing information.

Lee was surprised at how the rug could be pulled out from under her in such a quick movement and she hadn't seen it coming. Then she realized that she had nowhere to go on such short notice so she humbly asked him for some time to find a place. He agreed to this with a sigh then turned and walked away from her. She couldn't believe how harsh and without warning or discussion this break up was, but she would not let him see how upset she was right then. She willed herself to proceed upstairs where she grabbed most of her things out of the master bedroom and hastily moved them into the guest room on the same floor. Once in the room, she shut the door and silently wept for her loss, foolishness and difficult predicament. She buried her head in a pillow to muffle any sounds while going over in her mind any signs that she may have missed of a serious problem between them. This self pity didn't last too long, and she got herself up and moving. She forced her body, through shear will power, to appear to function as usual. She went through the motions of making up the bed, of putting on a tee shirt for sleep, then going to the bathroom to brush her teeth. There was an awkward moment when Curt came to the door of the bathroom to use it as she was coming out. When he saw her, he had flinched and moved back as though afraid that he might touch her. Then she saw that he was wearing a t-shirt when he normally walked to the bathroom in boxers only. This wounded her again so she brushed her teeth quickly and hastened back to her new room. She was now determined to find a place quickly to end this uncomfortable situation, no matter what it cost, so she could begin to heal.

Through newspaper ads, Lee found a narrow two storey wood siding house a few streets over and up the hill. It was too big for her alone and the rent was a little steep, but she had decided to take in a roommate. Moving wasn't difficult, especially with Tracy and Matthew helping while they tried to hide how pleased they were about the break up. Once settled, she placed an advertisement in the local paper for someone to share a house in the Beaches. She had however, forgotten to specify which sex she wanted so after a couple days, the only call she had gotten was from a deep male voice with an Australian accent. She stumbled through several questions about his background before agreeing to his request to come see the house. She made sure that Tracy was at the house when the potential boarder came to visit.

At about eight o'clock on the appointed evening the door bell rang and Lee approached it alone while Tracy stood in the hall behind her watching. Tracy was prepared to start screaming or run for help out the back of the house if the guy turned out to be unbalanced or dangerous. As Lee opened the door, it revealed a very well built, handsome young man in a suede bomber jacket with short cropped dark hair and a huge smile of perfect white teeth. "Gooday, I'm Warren, the fellow who called about the rental". Lee was amazed, he was so good looking and likeable that she immediately invited him in. Then she turned to Tracy and saw that her friend's jaw was dropped open in surprise and her eyes were huge. The girl had imagined all kinds of scenarios for the evening but this was not one of them. Lee introduced the dumbfounded Tracy then she showed Warren through the house. When they went upstairs and Warren went into the common bathroom to check it out, Tracy grabbed Lee by the arm and pulled her aside to ask.

"How are you ever going to have a shower then walk back to your room in a towel with someone so great looking in the house?"

Lee just grinned and when Warren emerged, the deal was made.

Warren was the perfect roommate. He was considerate, kind hearted, tidy, upbeat and always invited Lee to join him after work when his office group went out for drinks. He worked at one of the world's largest advertising agencies which explained why he had been able to transfer for a year overseas to their Toronto office. His work group tended to be mostly women and while he enjoyed their playful company, he remained loyal to his girlfriend Shelley who was still in Sydney. In fact, he would often come home from a bar and pull out pieces of paper that women had shoved in his pockets with their phone numbers on them. He never seemed to call these women, he just laughed when he found the notes. He did comment that people in Toronto were not as attractive as Australians. The Aussies spent most of their free time outside playing sports so they were tanned and in great physical shape while the people in Toronto were pale and out of shape by comparison. Warren was a surfer and despite the scars from collisions with the board and coral, he had smooth bronzed skin, clear blue eyes set in an open well proportioned face with a strong jaw. He may not have understood why the girls were so persistent but Lee knew - he radiated a beautiful person inside and out.

Warren was also a popular fellow and over the months a steady stream of Australians traveling through Canada on their world wide treks, would stop in at the house to visit him and crash. Since Australia was so far from other continents, the young Aussies would set out during a break in college or right after graduating to travel across the globe for months at a time. They were a happy, affectionate, gregarious group who added an element of camaraderie and fun to the house. Lee enjoyed their company and welcomed their laid back good nature. In return, they included her in trips to Niagara Falls, karaoke clubs and outings to the lake but the reason also may have been that she was the only one with a car. Finally Shelly had called to announce that she was coming to visit and Warren was very excited. They had only started dating just before he left for this trip so the relationship was new. He described her as a tall thin and beautiful girl with long dark hair who had worked as a model and been hired as an extra in the Mad Max movie. When Lee looked suitably impressed and asked how she got the part, he explained that it was her similarity to an Auschwitz survivor that caught the eye of the casting director. Lee raised her eye brows in surprised, picturing a pale stick thin emancipated waif, but Warwick just kept singing her praises.

Shelly arrived one autumn day and while she was exceptionally thin, she also had a darker completion that gave her a healthy glow. She was attractive but not beautiful in Lee's opinion especially since she was awkward in her tall frame and she had an unfortunate over bite which dominated her small face. Once Lee had a chance to get to know her, she also found that Shelly was not the smartest or the most considerate person. Lee did not say anything to Warren especially since he had been so looking forward to her arrival but the girl was constantly irritating. Unlike the other Aussies, she didn't pick up after herself, cook or clean up to contribute to her share of housework.

Eventually Warren must have gotten tired of this as well and he announced that Shelly would be heading west to see Vancouver on her way back to Australia. After she left, Lee noticed that Warren seemed to seek out her company more. He asked if she would like to join him for breakfast and he would make her a steak since he was cooking his own anyway. Later he would ask if she would join him to watch a show on TV even though she rarely watched TV. She agreed since he must have been unhappy about the break up and he was always good company. Lee also noticed that he seemed to be sitting a little closer to her which made her very conscious of every movement of his body, especially when it touched hers. She shook this thought off since he had always been an affectionate, open natured person to all his female friends. Besides, he was younger than her, leaving Canada soon and in the looks department; he was certainly out of her league.

Meanwhile, Curt had started to stop in, with the excuse of dropping off the mail for her that hadn't been redirected. He had heard about the good looking guy living with her and he found that it actually made him jealous and interested in seeing her again. He was surprised that she hadn't just collapsed when he broke up with her and he grudgingly admired her fortitude, though he would never say it out loud. Instead he had shagged any girl he could find, including his boss's secretary though none of them lasted more than a night or two. After each encounter he would feel deflated and his mind would always return to Lee. She was much better company once the lights were turned back up since he could actually talk to her. The fact that her family had some money was also a big incentive to rekindle things. He finally decided that he had to come up with some way to ease back into that relationship again without appearing to be crawling back. The mail delivery was a good idea. So instead of throwing out the letters that came for her as he had been doing, he saved them up then waited until he knew she would be home by checking that her car was parked in front before knocking on the door.

At first he wanted to appear uninterested and just draw her into general conversation then leave quickly. Then he slowly brought up good memories of past trips and mentioned a few potential new ones to see if she expressed any interest. When it seemed that she might be receptive, he closed for the kill and used his formidable persuasive abilities to let her know that he might have made a mistake, he missed her and still cared for her. This hit its target because despite all the people staying at her house, Lee was lonely. She yearned for a deeper emotional bond to another human being. She wanted that connection and even just the small act of talking to someone about her day or planning trips to the grocery store seemed so attractive to her. Most of all she still wanted children. She had achieved so much in her professional career but it paled in comparison to the idea of starting a family. Children would be hers to love and enjoy. It was a natural next step, a primordial pull and she knew this was what she needed in her life.

While Lee understood that she hadn't had a deep connection with Curt, when he started coming to the house to drop off the mail, she imagined that things could be different. She thought that maybe he would change once they were more committed. He might become more dedicated, kind and concerned for her. So with this naive and optimistic thinking, she let him sweep her once more into his sphere. Before she knew it, she was back spending most of her time at the townhouse, cleaning it, cooking and trying to share the queen size bed with a two hundred and twenty pound man who didn't really know her or care to understand her.

Chapter 17 - Headers

Once they had gotten back together, Lee had refused to move back in with Curt and stated that she would only live together again if it was in a marriage. Curt pretended to ignore this and shortly after they reunited, he had suggested a wind surf vacation to the Dominican Republic with some of his friends. The group all flew down to the north side of the island to Playa Plata then caught a taxi to a remote surfer beach area and booked into a small beach front hotel overlooking a protected bay. Lee and Curt spent the next few days wind surfing off the beach, drinking frozen Pina Coladas at the grass thatched beach bar and riding a motorcycle along the surf. They got to know a local at the bar who invited them to a special meal at a private restaurant in the mountains and they agreed to go.

After the fellow had rounded up a dozen interested tourists, loaded them in a van and drove for a half hour up steep switch backs until they pulled next to a colorful wooden structure with a large open air dining patio, replete with a spectacular view across the mountains. The group was fed more drinks and a tasty meal of spicy marinated lamb, chicken and roasted potato while they watched the sun set over the lush green landscape. A lone guitar player soon joined them on the patio and some couples danced to the Latin beat. They returned in great spirits, safely deposited at the gate by the bartender, who probably got a cut of the profits. The guide waved to the security guard, who held an ancient shotgun across his arm while he paced in a circular pattern around the compound, then sped off to the next hotel to find his next patrons, or victims.

The next night, even though the guests were warned to be careful not to leave the hotel grounds at night, Curt announced that they were going into town for diner. Lee slithered into a tight red dress, which garnered many admirable glances and comments, and they set off in a taxi that Curt had found down the street. They arrived in the modest city at dusk and were dropped at a restaurant that the taxi driver recommended. After an uninspired meal in a loud room with strong lighting they set off to explore the small main street and the casino. Curt suggested to Lee that they return to the hotel and take a walk on the beach. Once on the soft sand beach and out of the glare of spot lights, he had taken her hand in both of his and proposed. She looked up at the large man expectantly watching her and said yes. Curt then pulled out a large diamond ring and slid it onto her finger. She looked down at the solitaire diamond sparkling in the reflection of the moon. The monumental moment was over with surprising quickness and it just didn't feel the way she thought that it would. Curt then grabbed her for a kiss before tugging her toward the water where he threw off his clothes and encouraged her to do the same. Lee was shy about skinny dipping but in this private area she complied and followed her future husband into the surf, full of the happiness for the moment but trepidation about being lured to do something she was not comfortable doing, perhaps in more than one way.

Once this decision was made, Curt moved with precision. He suggested that they start trying for a baby right away and begin looking for a new house. Unfortunately housing values were on the rise and it was a seller's market. Decent places in the Beaches were bought before they got on the MLS listing service. They would need a fare amount of cash for a deposit so Curt went to work on his parents to secure a loan of forty thousand dollars. Then when Lee had suggested they go to Windsor to tell her parents of their engagement, he saw the opportunity to solicit more deposit money. Curt and Lee drove from Toronto south on Highway 401 through the lush green pasture land and farming communities of southern Ontario with their modern well kept farm buildings. They didn't talk much on the route and soon pulled up to the imposing new house that Lee's parents had built on the water across from the country club on the outskirts of Windsor. The driveway stretched in warm red pavers to the concrete steps of a modern two storey brick and glass structure with balconies and a double storey glass entry.

When the front doors were opened, the view was through a cathedral ceiling living room with faceted windows overlooking the manicured lawn out to the lake. Lee's mother had helped design it with a builder then she organized its construction. Anne loved her new home and never tired of giving tours. She welcomed the young couple in then immediately began talking about the family business, her other children and various domestic subjects until Curt interrupted her to announce that Lee and he were engaged. She looked at him blankly since of course she already knew this. He went on to explain "My parents greeted us at the door with congratulations and flutes of champagne for a toast when we went to visit them after the announcement". Anne still didn't get his point but she offered to go get some champagne if Curt would prefer. He turned away, rolled his eyes and said "No thank you Anne". It was not an auspicious start but after Lee's father got home from golfing, Curt offered him a hand shake and suggested that they all sit in the living room. Lee and Curt sat on a sofa facing the lake while her parents sat together on the adjacent couch looking puzzled. Lee hadn't grouped her parents for a talk like this before and she had never asked them for anything beyond college. She knew that Curt was going to request money and she didn't want anything to do with it but she understood that Curt's parents were loaning them money for a deposit on a house so she wouldn't stop him from trying.

He started his sales pitch with a boisterous "How would you like to invest in a great property in Toronto for your daughter".

Lee cringed inside but kept an outward calm, waiting to see how her father would react to this. Curt continued to pitch the advantages of the investment until he finally paused and waited for Joseph to speak. Lee's father then looked up from under arched eyebrows and said that he was not interested in a house as an invest but that he was willing to loan the couple money for a down payment especially since Curt's parents had done the same. He then suggested an amount above what Mr. and Mrs. Richards had given them but he would require a promissory note signed by both of them.

The couple left Windsor with Curt feeling relieved and Lee anxious. Curt hadn't told Lee but he knew exactly which house he wanted to o purchase. It was a few doors down from the place Lee was renting and it was for sale by Owner but they were asking higher than market value so it hadn't sold. Curt was convinced that he could talk them down in price and took Lee over to see the place. Lee was disappointed because the house was already renovated but still looked extremely unattractive from the outside. She would not be able to use her skills to fix up the place to gain sweat equity and when she saw the wide open floor plan, she predicted that they would actually have to spend money to build rooms back and expand into the porch when they had children. It was on a postage stamp size lot only twenty five wide by one hundred feet long with an eight foot wide shared driveway between houses. The other side yard was only eighteen inches from neighbouring house except at the roof line where the two gutters actually touched. The structures leaned toward each other like tired boxers. The narrow house was eighteen hundred square feet on four floors so it was like an oversized elevator shaft with light from either a bay window on the front or skylights and tall windows facing the back yard. It also had a basement apartment that would help with the mortgage, Curt encouragingly explained to Lee so she would go along with his scheme.

Curt began negotiations with the owners but since he had not seen any other house that interested him and did not want to wait to see what came on the market, he lost his patience and wound up settled with them for the asking price. It was quite a bit higher than he had told Lee they would pay but she wanted to trust him since he was so sure of himself and convincing. She was rather nervous about having such a high mortgage especially since the rate was almost ten percent but Curt told her that they could refinance when the rates dropped which would happen soon he reassured her. So Lee went into the bank with Curt, filled out the information about her income and signed the mortgage papers. She could not believe how easy it seemed for such a large amount but they were now the proud owners of a house that the people in the neighbourhood called the Ponderosa.

The real Ponderosa was a cheap steak house that was recognizable due to its olive green wood siding on every one of its locations. The moldy green siding on this house was the reason for the nickname and that would be the first thing Lee decided to change once the closing went through. She then had to sublet her rental house since Warren had already been invited to move into a penthouse at Young and Bloor with the offspring of a wealthy industrialist. So Lee advertised in the local papers and was able to get a new couple to take over the rental in short notice.

It was soon after the house signing that Lee realized that she had missed her period. She immediately bought a pregnancy kit, urinated over the little piece of tape and was then both pleased and a little apprehensive about seeing the positive confirmation. This was it - now she was really committed. A couple weeks before the wedding, while Lee was still dazed by her pregnancy, Curt announced that he was headed up north with his buddies to wind surf for the weekend. Lee was surprised by this since there were so many things to be done with the house closing, both of them moving and the wedding approaching. Then she started to get suspicious when one of Curt's friends accidentally mentioned that the guys were probably going to a party with some girls. One last fling before the knot was tied. Curt had claimed that since she hadn't made any plans for them, he might as well accept his friend's invitation to windsurf. He then brushed it off when she asked for more information about their trip and wouldn't answer her questions. She didn't press the point but once Curt had left, Lee could not get the evasiveness out of her mind. Deceit was not a good way to start a marriage and Lee thought long and hard all that weekend. She thought about whether she really trusted him, if her feelings were deep enough to weather future problems and whether she thought he really did love her. Her instinct told her that she shouldn't trust him but she had already invested so much into this situation. Could she back out and consider being a single mother, taking a big financial loss by selling the house they had just bought and continue to look for a soul mate. Then she realized that Curt must not be the right partner if she could even consider this scenario. So with great resolve, she made her decision and accepted the potential fallout as she pulled the engagement ring off her finger.

On Sunday afternoon, she let herself into Curt's townhouse and left the ring in an envelope on the coffee table with a note explaining why she just couldn't go through with the marriage. Then she went to the club to do a light work out before just collapsing on the couch at home, torn between relief and worry before she closed her eyes overcome by exhaustion. She woke up later in the dark to the sound of her door bell ringing repeatedly. In a slightly groggy haze, she moved herself toward the door and when she swung it open, the frame was filled with the outline of Curt's body. She was startled and backed away in fright, but then he had thrust a letter towards her and said.

"You need to read this" Before he turned to leave.

She watched him walk down the sidewalk as she shut the door then went into the living room and sat down. Lee gingerly opened the envelope with dread overcoming her emotions, and read the letter that had been enclosed. It started with his hurt and disappointment at finding her note and the ring. Then the letter swung between protestations of love and accusations that she was inconsiderate, unreasonably suspicious and unfair. He said that his friend and he had only gone out to a bar and didn't talk to anyone else - what did she think he was doing? She began to feel guilty and question her assumptions. The note made her wonder if she had been wrong, which played heavily on her compassionate nature, pulling at her subconscious toward atonement. He was forceful in his writing and told her to think this over then call him so they could talk. He said that he would respect whatever decision she made.

She was humbled and embarrassed when Curt had knocked on

her door after she had called but she had opened the paneled door wider to admit him to the living room. He moved gingerly for such a large man to the patterned sofa and then waited until she sat as well, in a matching chair across from him before he asked her to explain why she had given the ring back. She fidgeted under his gaze then looked up into his face searching for the right words to try to express her thoughts.

"I am uncomfortable that you had not told me about trip ahead of time and your friends had implied that there were other reasons you were going. I don't want to live my life always wondering what is going on behind my back"

"I also don't want to compete with other girls for your attention, as I feel like I am doing now. When you make sexual comments about other girls and ogle them, it is not good for our relationship"

She further explained that things were moving too fast for her to understand and she just wasn't sure enough to commit to such a big step right now.

Then he started talking, telling her that she was mistaken, that he had no intention of deceiving her and he would never fool around on her. She wasn't sure she believed him but he was pulling her in. He chided her for foolishness, getting her to question her reasoning again, and then he talked that smooth reassuring salesman talk. That convincing voice, describing their future with their baby, their new house and their great new life together, He talked until he had her back on his side of the room in a powerful clasp and she let him put the ring back on her finger.

They were married on a beautifully restored paddle boat in the Toronto Habour on a clear warm evening in July of 1987. Curt had chosen the venue, the date, the minister and put down deposits for the boat and food. Lee had gone with him to tour the boat and help pick out the menu but Curt did most of the selecting, cost being of little concern to him. They had also agreed to hire a quartet to play during the cocktail period before the service and then a DJ for dancing afterwards while the boat cruised between the harbor islands in the evening. They had made up the guest list together but since the wedding was in Curt's home town, Lee agreed that he could have a larger number of invitations. This offended Lee's mother, who would have liked to have invited more of their friends and relatives, but Lee didn't know this until years later. The minister was a jovial, white haired

Scotsman who was retired from preaching but he did services once in a while. He had been recommended by Curt's family friends. He didn't have his own church so he had asked that the couple meet with him at his apartment at least once before the wedding.

Curt refused to attend premarital classes, which most ministers required, so this fellow was an easy selection. The couple went to the man's small apartment and sat perched on a velvet couch while the minister, in his leather lounge chair dressed in a black shirt with clerical collar, asked questions and offered some advice. Lee had been a bit nervous since she hadn't attended church for a while but once she realized that his questions weren't going to be religiously oriented, she relaxed. She also noticed that he seemed to have a reddened nose and a glass of scotch on the table near his seat, which seemed odd to her for a minister. However, he still seemed in control of his wits so she ignored this. As the minister probed their understanding of the vows and the seriousness of this commitment, she began to feel slightly reassured. She was sure that she would be a good wife and honor these vows; she just wasn't sure about Curt. But when she looked over at his confident posture and determined smiling face, she decided to finally put her trust in him. The last thing that the minister said just before they left, with one bushy white eyebrow raised and a piercing look directed at Lee was a warning.

"It takes two to marry but only one to end a marriage".

The bleeding started two days before the wedding. Lee had been in the kitchen preparing dinner when a sharp piercing cramp struck her lower abdomen. She felt immediate fear as she recognized the potential source and then the wet dripping down her leg. She really didn't have to look down to know that it would be blood. The pregnancy had been so easy, no sickness or nausea and she hadn't gotten bigger in the waist much at all for being almost three months along. Curt rushed her to the hospital but she thought that she had already lost the baby in the mess in the bathroom. An overwhelming sense of sadness came over her as she lay alone in the curtain enclosed examination room of the emergency area. She hardly registered the incredible pain of the probe with the speculum that an inept intern was trying to jam inside of her. It was something he had never done to a live patient before and he botched it each time until another doctor had to be called in to perform the simple procedure and check her for complications. She was then sent home with an appointment to see her doctor the next day and told to rest. But that was not possible with the house closing and the wedding so soon. Instead she busied herself in details, making phone calls, unpacking and she forgot the sensation of loss and failure until she had to face it when she changed the blood soaked pads.

It was a perfect warm evening with a clear sky when the wedding party boarded the festive green and white trimmed boat and greeted their guests. Everyone was elegantly dressed for the boat trip, in sparkling long dress, tuxes and dark suits. Lee had her hair done at the house by a hair dresser in the bathroom with her mother and friends hovering about happily chattering. Then she squeezed into the beautiful long gown with their help. They were all so supportive and loving that Lee had felt better about all her past concerns. She had then gathered up her veil and bouquet to ride with her mother in the white stretch limo that Curt had arranged to drive them to the harbor. Anne spent the entire limo ride complaining about her father's driving during their ride to Toronto but Lee tried to block out her voice so she could savor the moment and feel special on this day. Twenty minutes later, they had stopped on the wharf and Lee had emerged from the limo to an ovation from the guests peering down over the high railing of the boat. She smiled and blushed, since she had never been the center of such attention.

Lee was wearing a strapless sheath dress with a black sequined bodice and clinging long flowing white skirt. It was not a typical wedding dress but she hadn't wanted that anyway. She had hunted for a dress with her mother throughout Detroit and finally found this one in a quaint dress shop in the high end neighbourhood of Grosse Point. On the paddle boat, which gleamed with polished teak and shiny brass reflecting the twinkling lights, she felt elegant. Glistening cocktails were passed around by waiters in white jackets while sweet tones of violin music wafted between the voices of animated conversations. Lee found Warren, looking even more handsome in his suit, if that was possible, and gave him a big hug. Her sister Cathleen had brought a very proper gentleman as her date who exuded old money and looked down his nose at Lee. She was surprised at her sister's choice of escort but by the end of the evening her date was so drunk that he had even made a pass at Warren.

After many bottles of wine, the minister signaled to the wedding couple to take their position. Curt took his place next to the minister, while Lee went with her father to the back of the boat. The quartet had packed up their instruments, so as Lee moved through the crowd she realized that there would be no music for the bridal walk. She mentioned this to the best man who was helping move the already intoxicated guests to clear a path and he said that he would take care of it. So Lee put her chin up, felt butterflies leap in her stomach and got into position next to her father who looked very distinguished in his tux. She put her arm though his, kept her eyes straight ahead and proceeded down the makeshift aisle.

As they walked the length of the deck the crowd on each side began humming "Here comes the Bride". Lee smiled as she approached Curt, standing so straight next to the minister and smiling broadly at her. She was happy at that moment, basking in the glow of alcohol and warm wishes from so many friends and people who loved her. The minister then asked that everyone put their drinks down, "Not for reasons of religion, but because if I can't drink, then you can't either". This brought the expected laughter as he proceeded to read the service that the couple had selected. He asked them if they accept each other and after the typical "I do" then he pronounced them husband and wife. Curt then leaned Lee back in a dramatic prolonged kiss until she felt that she might fall onto the deck if he let go.

The crowd rushed forward to congratulate the couple, hugging and smiling and then soon the music from the DJ started up. Curt led Lee out onto the section of the deck that had been cleared for a dance floor. There he took her in his arms and kissed her again while he pulled her in a slow circling motion under the stars. Lee and Curt's parents came out onto the dance floor next and began to dance together which brought out some of the other guests. Once the music picked up tempo, all the young people crowded the floor and some of the older folks went back to their tables to watch and reminisce. Lee excused herself and headed off the floor toward the stairs.

As she was passing her mother and aunt, they grabbed her and rushed her toward the washroom. They explained that she had a large spot of blood on the back of her dress and they helped her wash it in the sink. She was vaguely aware of being grateful that the dress was washable and not silk, then concerned about the image of her dancing in front of all those people with this embarrassing mark of tragedy so obvious. Fortunately her mother said that it wasn't noticeable on the dark dance floor but that it was bad timing to have her period right now. Lee didn't correct her statement but instead helped squeeze out as much water as possible from her dress then dry it under the hand dryer before she headed back on deck where the evening breeze would finish the job.

At around midnight the boat docked and the party disbursed. Curt and Lee checked into the harbor front hotel next door for their first night as a married couple. Lee took a shower to clean herself up while drunken guests banged on their door and then left notes under it when they weren't invited in. The rest of the night was filled first with a clumsy consummation of the marriage then exhausted sleep. In the glare of morning, Lee got herself dressed to go to the doctor's appointment while Curt claimed that there was nothing he could do at her gynecologist's so he was headed back to the house. They hadn't booked a honeymoon trip, since they couldn't afford it, so they were going to just work on the new house.

However once Lee was at her doctor's, the woman suggested that she be admitted to the hospital next door immediately for a D&C. She was then escorted down the sidewalk, checked into the hospital and moved to a small room where the members of the operating team introduced themselves and asked her some questions. Afterwards she used the phone to call Curt to tell him that her doctor had recommended the D&C right away and she would have to stay overnight. Curt didn't seem to mind and said that he would pick her up in the morning. She was put under anesthesia and wheeled into the operating room where they scraped her uterus to remove any vestige of the birth that might cause infection. In the recovery room when she came out of the anesthesia into consciousness, she was in the middle of talking but she had no idea what she had been saying. She looked toward the nurses on each side and blushed at the thought of babbling to these strangers without any filter or awareness. Her awakening was as though someone had snapped their fingers and a hypnotic trance had ended.

She was dressed and ready waiting on the edge of the bed when Curt came into her room the next morning. She didn't like hospitals and couldn't wait to leave even if it meant being rolled down the hall in a wheelchair. Curt walked next to the wheelchair and made joking remarks to the nurse pushing it until they were through the sliding doors and into the waiting car. Lee was quiet on the drive back so Curt made up for it by telling stories about what his friends had done after the wedding. He explained that the group who left the note had actually booked a room in the hotel on the same floor and continued partying all night. They had hoped that Lee and Curt would have come down the hall to join them. A couple of these friends dropped by the house once Lee was back and settled on the couch. She had still not really recovered and none of these guys had been told about either the pregnancy or the miscarriage so they were animated and celebratory while Lee felt rather despondent. She only showed some interest when one fellow in particular, Rob a high school buddy, began teasing Curt about the bachelor party. There had apparently been a very well endowed stripper with red hair called Bush Fire who had danced around Curt, rubbed her breasts in his face until he tried to grab her. The guys laughed as they recalled Curt's fumbled attempts to get his hands on her. Then they recalled Mr. Richard's fascination with the girl since the white haired man had followed her around while she had danced.

"He was practically drooling in her wake"

"The old guy even tried to pay for her services afterward but the girl had refused"

The guys chuckled as they recalled how appropriate that stage name Bush Fire was for her and that Curt had exclaimed loudly in a drunken stupor how much he loved that kind of bush. Lee was disgusted. She had not known that any of this had occurred since she had lost the baby on that day and forgotten about the bachelor party. When Lee was quiet the guys assumed that she was tolerant of the banter and the stories got even worse while Curt just laughed and puffed up in pride at the attention. Lee felt sick and excused herself. How could she have married someone who would behave like this! She was so humiliated. Obviously her instincts had been right after all but she had let herself be convinced by Curt to ignore them.

However, the next day Lee felt a little better after a good sleep and decided that she had to make the best of this situation. She began to focus on the house and had selected a Cape Cod Gray solid stain to paint over the green siding and opaque white for the trim. Curt had decided to work on the yard so she was glad to be alone with her own project. She started on the long side of the three storey house and worked her way around each side. The ladder didn't always reach so she was fortunate that she could stand on sections of lower roof to reach more difficult peaks. Finally after a couple days, she stood in the front yard covered in paint to inspect her handiwork. It was perfect - just what she envisioned. She had painted the front door Chinese red to emphasis the point of entry and added shutters, white trim to the roof peak and brackets for the eaves.

Curt had decided to lay pavers for the driveway and he and his cousin packed the area with sand then set the beige and red pavers in a herringbone pattern. Next Lee and Curt worked together to build a small shed in the back. Lee showed him how to build the walls on the ground then lift them into place. Lee then calculated the pitch for the roof and laid out the frame for the rafters. She installed a small window and planter box for flowers in the side wall. They also built a six foot privacy fence and Lee pained it the Cape Cod Gray. The place had been transformed and would never be called the Ponderosa again.

Chapter 18 - Nails & Connectors

In the beginning of their marriage, Lee found that it was usually quite easy to keep Curt happy. He just needed good food, a clean house and night time attention several times a week in order for him to feel "like a man". After that Lee was relatively free to do what she wanted, or so she thought. She went to work, where she was head of design and still in line for partnership, she played squash at the club and saw her friends for lunch regularly. Her family visited once in a while and she went to see them fairly often. Then Curt started to show some jealousy. He told her that he didn't want her playing squash with guys any more, she should only have female squash opponents. His argument was that she wouldn't want him meeting with a girl to "supposedly" play squash once a week.

Lee had no idea where this suspicion had come from since she had never looked at other guys the way he implied, let alone contemplate anything more, but she agreed to this demand just to keep the peace. Then he slowly started needling her about playing squash with other partners at all. So she began to limit the number of games she played. Then he went after her family, subtlety disparaging them and ridiculing her visits, making sure that his disapproval was clear. She ignored it for a while but the seed of discontent was sown. She began to feel that she had to choose between her husband and her family. Then she found out that she was pregnant again and the issue was pushed aside.

This time she was sick, gloriously sick. The minute Lee woke up, she had to run to the kitchen to get some toast in her stomach or she would be nauseous for the rest of the morning. She began to feel bloated and tired but she was elated by the thought that she had a baby growing inside. She had gone to see her doctor who confirmed the pregnancy with a test and she had recommended prenatal vitamins to take each day. Then she had asked that Lee fill out a questionnaire about the miscarriage in order for doctors in research to learn more about the subject. At first Lee was hesitant because it brought back the bad memories but then Dr. Treland explained that the last pregnancy was not the development of a baby. It was a collection of cells that were not forming correctly so the body rejected them. In fact, fifty percent of all pregnancies ended in miscarriage she said, we just didn't realize it when a period was late. Lee felt relief fill her as the guilt she had held tight to her chest was lifted and cast away. She hadn't even been fully aware of how much she had blamed herself and now she knew deep inside that she was not responsible for the miscarriage. It was cathartic and healing. The questionnaire had pointed out to Lee that she had not been sick or gained weight the last time as in a normal pregnancy. It was just a collection of cells as her doctor had said, not a baby. So she grew more confident that this baby would make it to full term. Lee was feeling much better when she left Dr. Treland's office but she was still cautious about telling anyone until she got past the twelve week point when it was less likely for the pregnancy to end in another miscarriage.

There was one problem with the timing of this pregnancy, and that was a trip to Thailand. Curt had been trying to sell over a certain amount of Excuala mutual funds in order to win a free trip to Bangkok that the company was sponsoring for brokers. He had just passed the mark in time to qualify for the ten day tour leaving in October and announced to Lee that they would be going. Lee was very excited about the trip but she was going to be just over two months pregnant when they left so she wouldn't be able to drink alcohol, she would be nauseous and she would have to be very careful about health issues.

It was short notice as well for the required vaccinations but after some research, she was able to get all of the shots in time, she just couldn't take any malaria pills because of the baby. The nurse practitioner advised that she not go anywhere outside of the cities and use lots of bug repellant to ward off virulent mosquitoes. She took this advice to heart as she prepared for the trip. She also researched the historic sites that she wanted to see and a little about the culture. She loved travel to explore other cultures, architectural surprises and artistic wonders. Her soul yearned for new experiences where she was challenged by something beyond her cocoon-like background, whether it was religious or spiritual or socio-economic. There were other points of view and options to consider in this world.

The trip started with the twenty five qualifying couples being flown from Toronto to San Francisco for a couple days stop over before heading to Asia. After settling into the Hilton, the brokers, who were all men and one woman, were escorted to a conference room in the hotel to get a pep talk about the Excuala company and its funds. As they entered the room they were greeted by the San Francisco 49er's cheerleaders all decked out in their tight short skirts, bright white smiles and pom poms. The spouses were then taken into an auditorium where the celebrity host Robin Leech gave a talk and slide show along the lines of his popular TV show "Lives of the Rich and Famous". The couples all came together again for dinner at a posh restaurant with granite countertops, crystal chandeliers and an extensive wine cellar. They shared war stories of the day and the market. The men in Curt's group told of Mrs. Chow, whose stock picks were always the most accurate even compared to the daily recommended stocks by the firm's in-house analysts.

After Mrs. Chow called in to her broker, Ben, he would circulate her latest selections to the group and they would buy for their clients. Lee was uncomfortable with this information since it seemed unethical and it also pointed out that the brokers did not know what to pick themselves, something she hadn't realized. She had always assumed that stock brokers knew the market enough themselves to help clients. Of course, if that was the case then they would all be wealthy themselves instead of pushing stocks all day she finally reasoned. She also found out that since they worked on commission, the more they moved a client's stocks, the more money they made. So even though it might be in the client's best interest to leave a stock in place, the brokers would call a client and entice them with a new offering, expertly manipulating the uninformed by tapping into their greed, like an addict to a blood vessel.

After more wining and dining at top restaurants, the group was taken by limousines to the airport to catch their flight to Bangkok. Twenty two hours of travel later, they touched down in the early afternoon at Suvarnabhumi Airport, cleared customs and were whisked through the teaming streets of the city, with noisy three wheeled motorbikes, battered taxis and buses spouting diesel fumes, to the first class Riverfront Hotel, a white high rise hotel right on the river's edge. They were told that this was a central area and they could get to the River Market and temples easily by water taxi. Curt and Lee were given a penthouse suite which had a balcony overlooking both the beautiful turquoise pool and the adjacent dirty brown winding Chao Phraya River.

The group was then asked to freshen up and come down to the pool level for cocktails at six. Curt and Lee descended in the elevator and were surprised at the bottom when the doors opened to reveal a baby elephant in the lobby in front of them with its trunk raised, and its head and back covered in colorful silks and beads. A thin dark trainer stood next to it welding a stick and watching anxiously with a forced smile on his face. The open doors also brought the smells of sweet jasmine, frapagini flowers and dung to Lee's nose. After moving in closer to admire this marvelous beast and pet his trunk, they were directed to walk under waving palm fronds being held by beautiful young girls in silk sarongs on a path leading to the outdoor gardens.

Once through the palm arch, Lee shockingly noticed that they were passing a large tiger sprawled on the grass next to the sidewalk. Its tawny legs and large paws stretched on the ground but its head was raised and it's eyes shrewdly watching them. There was only a single chain around its neck leading to a spike in the ground. Lee did not trust this flimsy restraint, even though the animal was probably drugged as well, so she moved quickly past the cat and its handler. As they approached the pool, men wearing white turbans bearing large plates, bent to offer them colorful fruit drinks and succulent delicacies as they circled the area. Lee was amazed by the beautiful patterning of the slivers of fish, seafood marinated in lime juice and vegetables arranged by rainbow color on the plates. Around the pool there were also other animals such as tiny brown faced monkeys, multi colored parrots and even a camel. She had Curt take pictures of her with a huge yellow boa constrictor wrapped across her shoulders, then feeding the parrots and riding the camel around the pool. It was an exotic dream.

The following days were spent taking rides in the narrow long-tail boats through the busy canals. These boats were equipped with automobile engines mounted on the back with extremely long drive shafts for steering by the boatman. They motored past elaborate golden temples, floating markets and thatched huts on posts where lightly clad klong people washed clothing in the mud dark water. The people also swam or scooped water for cooking and drinking from the same filthy source.

One excursion brought them deep into the canal system to see a snake show. They had another couple along with them and the group all sat in the front row of the handmade theater seating at the edge of the show ring. The snake handler came out holding a snake by the head in each hand while the bodies wrapped around his outstretched arms. It was explained by the ring master that these were poisonous vipers commonly found throughout Thailand and their fangs had not been removed since they were milked for their poison to use in medicines. The next act he declared included one of the most poisonous snakes in the world, from which there was no antidote. He said that this snake would be amongst four snakes that the handler had to catch with just his hands, feet and mouth. The dark, scared handler came out for the second act with a simple cloth bag from which he tossed the angry snakes out onto the green carpet. At this Lee became acutely aware that there was no barrier between her and these snakes. She immediately climbed higher up the bleachers until she was at the top. The rest immediately followed her move. From her new perch Lee watched the man catch each snake until one was hanging from each of his hands with his fingers pinching the heads, one was curling from his mouth and the last was pinned by the toes of his left foot. Handlers must die regularly here especially since the nearest hospital was over an hour away by boat. Lee realized that this kind of show would never have been allowed in the States.

Life was cheap in this country and short unless one was very fortunate. Lee made sure to leave a large tip before they climbed into the boat for the ride back. On the way back she was struck again by the unbearable poverty in Thailand in stark contrast to the incredible luxury of their hotel. When they left the hotel for walks they were surrounded by masses of people who wandered the streets, some were looking for work, some begging and others laboring as street vendors, selling cheap tourist goods. Others sold dangerously ripe skewers of unidentifiable meat off of carts, often set up in front of elaborately ornate palaces or temples. All of this chaos and humanity was reflected in the sleek glass walls of high rise office buildings.

One evening the entire tour group was treated to an exquisite six course meal served to them at tables under the stars on a private estate where the owner collected historic buildings. He had various important temples, palaces and humble wood structures moved and rebuilt on a hundred acre property just outside of Bangkok, with winding rivers and a man-made lake in the center. They were told that the only other westerner to be invited to this estate previously was the Queen of England. At the end of the lovely evening, everyone was given a simple lotus shaped paper boat with flowers and a candle in it called a krathomg. Then they were asked to light the candles, make a wish and then send the boat off to the center of the lake as an offering to the Goddess of the Water and to ward off bad luck. Lee closed her eyes as she sent the boat out onto the lake and prayed for the baby.

The group also visited the landmarks of the city including the Grand Palace, with its magnificent throne room, shrines and audience chamber within in a walled royal residence, as well as the adjacent Wat

Pho compound which featured the giant gold plated Reclining Buddha. The architectural styles were so distinctly Thai with their high pitched gracefully arching rooftops covered in gold filigree and adjacent layered bulbous domes stretching to needle points high into the air. The styling was almost a melting pot of the Russian onion dome, the Chinese wood carved temples and the Japanese pagoda emerging as a unique fantastical form of architecture.

The next evening Curt encouraged Lee to go with him to Patpong Road, the famous entertainment district specializing in the sex trade. Lee was hesitant, she had an aversion to sleaze and human degradation, until he told her that it was featured in the musical Miss Saigon and then her curiosity was peaked so she agreed. When the cab dropped them off, they were immediately accosted by men describing outrageous sex acts and pushing brochures with extensive graphics at them in order to tempt the couple to go into the club they represented. Lee was overwhelmed by the flashing colored lights, the shouts of callers and the pushing of other foreigners. They first went into a dark bar that had naked girls wandering around taking drink orders or dancing unenthusiastically in cages to loud western rock music.

Curt sat on the edge of a booth with Lee on the inside. A server immediately approached and seemed to lean into Curt to fondle his upper leg while she told him how handsome he was. Lee drew the girl's attention, explained that she was his wife and gave her a drink order. The girl did not stop her advances but it was dark and Lee couldn't be sure what was going on under the table. Lee had been to strip joints in the States but this had none of that sexuality. It was flat, blunt and businesslike. The girls, who seemed so small and young, gave off feelings of tedium, never looking directly at the men while they moved their hips or balanced their trays, but perhaps it was the apathy of drug use.

Lee had read that these girls were often sold by their parents, out of desperation, into the sex trade which brought out compassion in her and a sense of shame. She put an extra tip on the table and asked Curt that they leave immediately then prodded him toward a cab. But he had been tempted by an advertisement for a live sex act so he pulled Lee through curtains of the next building into a dark room featuring a small stage with a poster bed in the center. Soon a young girl of small stature dressed in a silk wrap came out on the stage, circled the bed and then theatrically lowered herself onto it. She was followed by a thin young man in silk pajama bottoms with the protrusion of a huge erection. He slowly undressed the girl then himself. Then he slowly rubbed her between the legs with one hand as she laid spread before him, automatically fondling her small breasts with the other before he thrust his great length into her. He began to rock, his body changing positions every few minutes, hovering over her, then to the side but always with his eyes shut and his body gently slamming against the girl.

Lee was amazed that a man so slight could be endowed with such an organ. She felt sorry for the girl because it had to have been painful and tearing in the beginning. Women didn't always want it bigger. She looked over toward Curt and saw that he was mesmerized. Once climax, whether fake or real, was attained the program ended quickly and the couple left Patpong and headed to the famous Night Market. Here they wandered under the strings of party lights, between booths of gaudy colored silk scarves, teak carved souvenirs and imitation designer purses before they returned to the hotel. Once in their suite and in bed, Curt began rubbing Lee's back down to her buttocks to inspire her for love making. Lee then realized she was actually uncomfortable with the idea of mimicking the earlier act of the evening. She needed some time to remove the images from her mind, but Curt didn't care, he was driven by the memories and used her hard that evening.

On the third day, Lee started getting sick. The smell of the breakfast buffet, with a heavy fish spice on everything, made her even more nauseous than the pregnancy. After breakfast, on the bus ride to the airport to fly up to Chang Mai in northern Thailand, Lee was sure that she would not be able to hold down her food and grabbed a bag to use just in case. The flight was short but the landscape outside of their windows when they landed had transformed entirely. Chang Mai, the largest city in the northern area of Thailand, a trading link to the north and east, was nestled into a bowl surrounded by lush green mountains. It was a paradise of jungle and clear streams winding around thatch roofed buildings, white painted temples and jumbled but enticing shops. Villagers in brightly colored wrap skirts welcome the group with smiles, flute music and a shuffling dance expressed through elegant hand movements and Lee forgot about being nauseous.

Founded in 1296 as the capital for the Lanna kingdom, Chang Mai was originally enclosed by a large moat and wall to keep out Burmese. These precautions were unsuccessful so the city remained in turmoil and even abandoned for a period until King Taksin drove out the Burmese in 1774. Chang Mai then became part of Siam and began to flourish into a prosperous modern city with a population of over a million people. It had also retained its heritage and there were over 300 temples scattered throughout the city and hillsides. The majority of the people were Buddhist who cherished their temples and the humble teachings of the prophet Buddha. Their orange clad monks with shaved heads lined up and begged for food each morning. However, the Excuala group was here to sightsee and to ride elephants, not to worship.

The group boarded another bus and drove a half hour north of the city to the Elephant Nature Park which had about thirty rescued elephants in its care. Then they were lead through heavy jungle to a river where several elephants were bathing and spouting water while thin dark mahouts were standing by with sticks to direct the massive beasts. Lee and Curt were told to mount a set of stairs while a driver brought a huge tusked elephant to the platform so the couple could mount it. They sat on a small wood seat on top of the grey back while the mahout was seated behind the elephant's ears.

Once moving, the mahout actually used the ears to give direction to the ponderous rocking animal as well as tapping with the stick and calling out in a sing song voice. They rode, swaying with the rhythm of the huge beast, through the surrounding jungle. The elephant followed the mahout's direction but also made its own slight deviations to reach to grab tufts of grass with her long curling trunk and roll them into her mouth or once in the river, play with the water by splashing and shooting it. Lee watched this submissive gentle creature and while she was thrilled to have such a close experience with them, she also felt sad for its captivity and life in a kind of slavery. This was not how the animal would have lived in the wild, cowed for the amusement of tourists, but she also recognized that she was one of the reasons for its exploitation as well.

After the elephant ride, the group returned to the hotel where they had time to relax before their dinner. Lee chose to go for a walk to see more of the elaborate temples while Curt went to get a massage. He was actually looking for more than just a massage but Lee didn't have to know that. Meanwhile, Lee headed toward the old city and found the most ancient temple, Wat Chiang Man. She approached the gateway reverently; concerned that she might make some unintended cultural mistake that would be taken as disrespectful. She looked for a local person to emulate but she was alone on the path. She had read that each wat or temple was laid out with eight boundary stones around a center bot or ceremonial hall where the monks would study or perform their rituals.

This complex also had a pagoda with gold leaf and red lacquer painted carvings on the lattice screened facades along with a phallic shaped column in the center. She laughed when she saw the column, slightly embarrassed, then on impulse she moved to kneel on the steps of the temple in front of the Buddha, while the scent of exotic incense curled to her nostrils. This round bellied seated figure represented the philosopher Buddha, formerly Siddhartha, a man born in Nepal around 563BC into a wealthy family who spurned his inheritance to wander the world seeking to live a pure existence. Buddhism was a kindly belief system based on the individual never causing harm to any living creature and always seeking to improve oneself to achieve enlightenment. It did not harp upon being sinful, as Christian teachings, but instead seemed to have an uplifting optimistic message which resonated with Lee. She bent her head in the humble gesture of prayer and asked the Buddha to watch over her and her child. She continued with prayers to guard her family, for peace in the world and assistance to become a better person. Her life was no longer so easy and she felt helpless with so many things out of her control.

Chapter 19 - Dormer Framing

Once Lee and Curt had returned to Toronto, Lee was eleven weeks along and couldn't hold back her big news any longer. She called her mother then Curt's parents, who were thrilled, and eventually her friends who offer a variety of support from advice to strollers. The pregnancy went smoothly as Lee advanced through the second trimester then into the third with cravings for cherry slushies from Dairy Queen and heavily layered liverwurst sandwiches. The nausea had slowed down and she could continue swimming and playing golf or squash without any problems. In fact, she was pleased that her golf game had improved since she now had more weight and leverage behind her swing. The baby seemed healthy and kicked whenever she was relaxed just before falling asleep or when she took a bath. After she would lower herself into the tub and submerge into the warm water, the amniotic fluid drain would drain down towards her spine and small body parts began to emerge more prominently on top. She would see the images of small feet and elbows stretching the skin of her abdomen and she could watch the progress of the mobile twisting stranger within her body.

Into the third trimester, when she could only lay on her back at night to sleep, she could feel the baby get very active and once in a while she was sure that it had flipped over. She would excitedly tell Curt about what she as feeling and grab his hand to place on the part of her stomach where she felt kicking but he usually just complained that he couldn't feel anything and he just move her into a position for his pleasure. Lee was disappointed that she didn't have a husband who wanted to share this amazing experience but she was so elated about the new life she was carrying that nothing could dampen her enthusiasm. She loved this baby from the minute it was conceived, it was hers and she would protect this child from anything harmful she vowed.

While Lee continued to work hard at her job, Curt had decided that he had done enough selling of intangibles. He wanted to deal in marketable goods and build his own company. He told Lee of his decision in an announcement one evening and while it caught her off guard, she was not unreceptive to the idea. Lee had come to understand that playing the market really was gambling and no one really knew the answers so she was partially relived that Curt was leaving that field. However, she hadn't fully comprehended that she would now be supporting the family. Curt had not even asked her if she was on board for this scheme, he had just told her of his decision and of course she had supported him, as he had expected. He now had to figure out what product he wanted to sell.

Lee suggested that he go to see her family's business since it might give him an idea. She arranged a visit for Curt to travel to the Windsor packaging plants then the Brampton paint production plants. Upon returning, Curt claimed to have found his niche market. He was going to sell office supplies to industrial clients with Lee's family being his first customer, provided his prices were reasonable. Curt then cashed out his small retirement fund, rented an industrial space and registered a company name high in the alphabet. Then he went about getting suppliers and began the layout of a mail catalogue containing all of the products for distribution to potential customers. Lee helped with all of this, including doing ink sketches for the catalogue, flyers and pamphlets. She didn't see what choice she had since she needed him to draw a salary as soon as possible. Her belief in the economic stability of married life had been stripped away dramatically and she was on a roller coaster ride that she couldn't get off now.

Once her belly became noticeable, Lee approached the partners and verified to them that she was expecting in the summer. She also quickly reassured them that she had no intention of quitting her job, since she needed the money badly. She hoped that they wouldn't mind if she worked from home for a while and brought the baby into the office until she felt comfortable leaving the child with a nanny. Robert and Kamal were very supportive and reassured her that they could work around her schedule whatever she chose to do. In fact, they hovered like new grandfathers for the first couple weeks, concerned for her health, until everyone in the office realized that the pregnancy wouldn't change anything.

Lee continued to work on her projects at the same pace, never wishing to let anyone down or allow the pregnancy to affect her work but once she got to six months along she had to sneak off to rest at lunch hour. She would drive her car to the underground parking garage at the nearby YMCA, crawl into the back seat of her little vehicle and sleep for a half hour. She then returned to work refreshed and finish eating at her desk in the usual method, cramming the food in her mouth with one hand while sketching with the other. The partners did not want to tell the clients right away and Lee tried to conceal her pregnancy as long as possible. One client was completely unaware since the young man had approached Lee after a meeting and proposed to her they should run off to the South Pacific together. She had laughed, clutched her belly in the dark shirt dress and explained "I would love to go to the South Pacific with you if I wasn't married and five months pregnant". He chuckled, offered his congratulations and never made another personal suggestion again.

Into her last trimester, Lee was expected to attend bi-weekly ob/gyn appointments. It was during one of these exams a few weeks before her due date, that Dr. Treland told her that she was a couple centimeters dilated all ready. She explained that the baby was ahead of schedule and that Lee could expect to deliver anytime. Lee was pleasantly surprised at first. She had been so exhausted and heavy lately, with the baby dropped into the birth canal between her hips; it was like walking with a basketball between her legs.

It would be a relief to have the birth over with but then she began worrying about where the birth might occur. She imagined her water breaking in the middle of a meeting or contractions starting while she was in traffic jam on the infamous Don Valley Parkway, or Don Valley Parking Lot as it was nicknamed. When she voiced her concern, Dr. Treland offered that she could have the baby induced on a specific date, and then she could be better prepared for the arrival. This procedure would involve an appointment with the doctor to remove the plug in the cervix then booking Lee into the hospital for the next day where her water would be broken manually if it had not broken already.

Lee accepted this solution but declined any drugs since she wanted a natural birth with as little trauma to the baby as possible. She was nervous about the pain though. She had attended the prenatal classes and seen the videos of a birth. A woman would be lying exhausted and sweating while attempting to breathe in short deep puffs between puckered lips as a spouse held her hand and mopped her brow. Then the camera would move to an embarrassingly close shot between the woman's legs, showing stretched skin over a round protrusion that pushed out until it looked like it would split the woman. Lee winced each time she saw this but her questions to the teacher were always about what happened after the birth and the class leader would then usually praise her for seeing past the relatively short painful birth to the long term future care of a baby.

On July 20th, Curt drove Lee to St. Thomas, the older brick hospital in the center of downtown and Lee was taken up to a large private birthing room with flowered wallpaper, low lighting and pale colored vinyl floors. It was similar to the one she and Curt had seen on the hospital tour but this one was filled with nurses and young looking interns. Once she was prepped and lying on the hospital bed, Dr. Treland had broken her water with a quick flick of her hand. Lee had not felt anything until the liquid flowed down into a pan under her buttocks, then she just had to wait. The contractions started in a slow building rhythm until they were on the threshold of being difficult to bear. Lee hoisted herself off the bed and waddled into the adjacent washroom in the hopes of easing some of the pain. After another hour Lee considered that she could have avoided this if she had gone ahead with an epidural but it was too late now so she just focused on breathing between the vise-like grips of pain in her lower abdomen. Finally one of the interns checked between her legs and announced that the head was visible.

Lee was past caring, as she asked through clenched teeth that someone please put her out of this pain. The team of nurses and doctors then told her to push hard at the next contraction which she did with much of her remaining strength. Dr. Treland was in place at the end of the bed and gently held the baby's head as it emerged but suddenly creases formed between her eyebrows in a frown and concerned was etched on the nurse's faces who were watching. Lee looked from their faces down toward the doctor's hands and saw a bit of matted dark hair on a bluish colored puckered face.

Quickly the doctor asked Lee to stop pushing while she used her hand to gently spread the labia then carefully put one finger around the cord that was wrapped a couple times around the baby's neck. She uncoiled it and once released, she asked Lee to push hard which helped the shoulders and the rest of the body slip out. Lee felt the pull of suction as the baby left her body which provided immediate release from the pain. Then the infant was whisked over to a stainless steel table near the window where the team worked on the little body until a faint cry emerged from the angry newborn and its face turned a healthy pink. Lee finally exhaled in relief.

The child was a long limbed nine pound baby boy with a large round head, clear pink skin and dark puckered eyes that blinked in surprise at this new world of light all around. Curt was ecstatic. Lee had been so grateful when the child had cried out that she put out prayers of thanks to God and the universe. Overcome with exhaustion, she felt as though she could only now finally relax since she knew the baby was safe. Then once she had expelled the placenta, the nurses brought the baby over to lie on her stomach, congratulate her and suggest that she let him start feeding when he was ready. She gazed down at the perfect skin, tiny hands, sweet turned in feet and thought he was so absolutely perfect.

The new mother swelled with love for the tiny human being that she had nurtured and delivered. Curt came from the corner of the room over to kiss her and gaze at "His boy" then he started making phone calls to their relatives and friends. Later in the day, her mother, his parents and several other people started streaming into the hospital to see the baby and new parents. They brought baskets of flowers and gifts with blue balloons while Curt handed out cigars in return. He would then theatrically describe the entire event, though as Lee recalled, his vantage point for most of the birth was from the seat of a chair behind a newspaper. He expounded to each, that he had read that the pain of giving birth was equivalent to taking your lower lip and stretching it over your head. Also, that a woman's body released a chemical that made her forget the pain so she would reproduce again. Lee was too tired to dispute these myths but she did protest and ask him to stop when he began telling everyone that all new babies just looked like drowned rats. Other new mothers would not appreciate hearing that comment nor would they agree she knew, since she thought that her baby was beautiful.

Lee recovered quickly from the birth and she was able to walk to the nursery to get the baby so he could sleep in an open plastic hospital bassinet in her room. She had also convinced her doctor to check her out early so she could leave the hospital on the second day. There was no way that she could sleep and heal with nurses coming in constantly to check her for infection, take her temperature and nag her about breast feeding. It was wonderful to be back in her own home and she wondered if she should have considered a home birth, but dismissed this idea as she remembered seeing the blue face of the baby when he first emerged. She spent the first few days back home soaking in the tub, sleeping with the baby in the croak of her arm and resuming her life as normal as possible. She soon found out though, that no one had sufficiently warned her about what would happen when her milk came in. After the clear substance that the baby took for the first few days, the rich pale white milk came flooding in from ducts under her arms and Lee was in agony. Her chest was taught and extended like a pair of grapefruit despite her wrapping herself tightly, expressing in the shower and getting the baby to feed. She couldn't be touched since she was so sore and when the baby would first latch on, like suction on a new wound, Lee would grimace in pain until the feeding was over. But this did not stop Curt who after just a few days decided that his rights as a husband were just as important as this baby. So he would push into Lee's bruised body from behind and she would bite her lip again. It was all worth it though as she gazed at her gorgeous baby in awe. He was a total joy and a blessing beyond anything she could have imagined!

Lee's projects however, did not go on hold just because she was recovering. She had even been required to make a few phone calls from her hospital bed to ensure everything went smoothly on the construction sites. Once released, she tried staying home with the baby since her mother had stayed to help, but she was getting bored. So five days after the birth, she put the baby in the car seat along with a bag stuffed with lotions, diapers and wipes and drove to the office. The group was happy to see her back and they were equally fascinated with the tiny infant. She put the sleeping baby under her desk, still in the car seat, and went though her faxes, phone messages and did some sketching. She also couldn't help constantly gazing down in wonder at the beautiful child, contentedly sleeping with his small chest rising in tiny quick beats and the round soft spot on the head matching this rhythm. She stayed for a few hours and when she returned home, her mother announced that she was returning to Windsor since she obviously wasn't needed.

Anne's leaving was probably best since Curt seemed to dislike her mother's presence, which put pressure on Lee to choose again. So Lee started a routine that she would head to the office once the baby was ready, work for a while, breast feed the baby behind the locked door of her office, then drive back home when they had each had enough. She worked at home as well, mostly when the baby was asleep. He was a contented, good natured child who was now called Andy, though Lee had put Andreas on the birth certificate at the hospital. Both parents had agreed on this unique name originally, but right after the baby was born Curt had heard this name on the radio associated with an African American sports figure, so he had gone to the clerk's office the next day and changed it without telling Lee.

When he finally disclosed what he had done, Lee was not

pleased about it. She was disappointed to discover the prejudice he obviously held deeply since it was something that she hadn't known before. But she was even more surprised that he would change a legal document without consulting her. When she had confronted him about this he had gotten defensive and argumentative. She didn't like conflict and she was too tired to fight back, so she left it, yet again.

Chapter 20 – Rafters & Trusses

Early in her pregnancy, Lee had asked her friends about finding a nanny and she was directed to an agency that would help parents sponsor a foreign nanny to enter the country for a year contract. She was told that the candidates were usually Philippine women, with strong maternal instincts and deep Catholic roots. They tended to travel to work together, often migrating first to Arab countries or Greece before making their way to Canada. They usually spoke very good English, which they had taken in school, as well as the language of any other country they had worked in. They also often sent half of the income they earned back to their families in the Philippines, so they lived modestly and rarely caused problems. Lee was given a book of faces and resumes to select from and she picked a smiling young woman named Mary, who was presently in Athens working as a nanny but had a degree in business from a Philippine University. She would be able to arrive in Canada in a few months, should the working visa process go smoothly. Lee filled out all the paper work to sponsor the girl, paid the agency, then waited until they were to pick her up from the airport.

Baby Andy was several weeks old when Mary arrived and settled into the basement apartment. Curt had evicted the tenant who had been living in the suite below when they had bought the house which had been a conflict laden process. The tenant had been offended when shortly after the sale Curt had entered his apartment without prior notice as was required by law. He had threatened to report Curt if he ever did that again and Curt had laughed at this, causing the man to get even more upset. Lee felt badly for the tenant especially when Curt gave him notice claiming that a relative of theirs would be moving into the apartment, which was one of the few ways to break a lease and evict a tenant in Canada. Curt had consulted with a lawyer and found this loophole then lied in the eviction notice to get his way. Lee tried to distance herself from this situation since while they needed the apartment, she did not condone the method.

Mary seemed to be a competent, pleasant person, who had been trained by her previous employers to come upstairs early and start each day sweeping the house and washing the dishes. She was eager to take care of the baby and slowly, as Lee grew to trust Mary, she left the baby for longer periods. She missed him when she didn't take him to work, but he was getting more mobile, learning to roll and make sounds, so it was harder to get her job done and watch him. Sometimes when she had a meeting with a new client, she would leave the sleeping baby in the basket with a co- worker, but eventually she would be called out to sooth or feed the crying baby. In meetings with her regular clients, she would just bring the baby into the conference room and he became the center of attention.

Andy was such a good baby, sleeping through the night at six weeks so Lee was getting more rest herself. She had given him glucose water in a bottle for his night feedings as recommended at the hospital, which seemed to fill him quickly and set him up for a sound sleep, as well as giving her sore nipples a break. She had to be careful not to leak though her pads onto her shirts when she started leaving the baby with Mary to go to work since she wasn't successful in pumping her milk. She had bought a breast pump but it was too painful for her to use, so she abandoned the idea and had to rush back home for the afternoon feedings. After six months, Lee had weaned baby Andy off of breast milk and onto formula that could be heated in the new microwave oven. The medical books had recommended a minimum of six weeks of breast feeding to ensure the baby got the benefit of mother's milk for immunities, something that the previous generation had not valued when mothers all flocked to the easier modern bottle feeding, but Lee was determined to do what was best for the baby.

Adam's Architect had prospered and grown to a staff of twenty five including draftsmen, a book keeper, two architects, a secretary and even a full time receptionist. In order to accommodate all of these people though, the firm had been moved to new headquarters in a high rise building in Markham, north of Toronto. Robert and Kam then sold the little office building on Sheppard and pocketed a nice profit from the sale. They were optimistic about the future and perhaps influenced by the grand ideas of the developers to take a lease in this new building. There was a lot of money coming into Canada from Asia through the first born sons of the wealthy Hong Kong merchants. The Sino-British Joint Declaration had been signed in 1985 and the British were preparing to hand over the island of Hong Kong, Kowloon Peninsula and the New Territories back to the People's Republic of China. The ninety nine year lease for all of this territory expired in 1997.

It would be the end of British administration and rule after a hundred and fifty years in the highly prosperous colony. The thought of takeover by a rigid Communist government had caused the exodus of many Hong Kong residents and their wealth to Vancouver and Toronto. Lee was engaged to design large scale developments, calling upon her urban planning courses, to lay out acres of streets, buildings, parking and amenities. The process to actually re-zone a piece of land took about two years in the municipalities around Toronto and was an extremely arduous task. It required a huge amount of paper work, civil engineering drawings and applications to the many levels of government to seek approval of the plan through public hearings, administrative review and negotiations. Lee was told that Canada, with a population of only 26 million, had eleven levels of government, while the United States, with a population of around 242 million had only six levels but she didn't know if this was true, it just felt like it.

Lee had been shown the new lease for the office space since it was a ten year period that would overlap her partnership once Robert and Kam retired, but she had not been asked to give her opinion or be involved in the final decision. It had been five years since she had been brought into the firm and there was still no sign that the partners were going to be stepping down. Kam, however, was doing less work with the company now that it had expanded and shifted to higher end projects. He spent even more of his time on the golf course. Then the crash of the financial market had put a stop to development and slowed down the construction industry.

Lee's work began to dry up and the firm was experiencing a financial crisis. Robert confessed to Lee that both partners had been forced to put the profit from the Sheppard Street office back into the firm to pay salaries but they didn't know how long they could continue. Lee then asked why they weren't taking stronger measures to lessen the financial burden such as layoffs and cost saving measures, to which she received no reply. She drew up a list of thirteen items that would help ease the monthly expenditure including laying off several positions that were not needed and subletting part of the office, but this was ignored by the partners.

During this difficult time, Robert had been introduced to a potential project that might help keep the doors of the firm open. He had been invited to present a proposal to Jim Wallace, the representative of the company who owned the Canadian franchise of Kentucky Fried Chicken. They needed to renovate twenty five of their stores a year and Robert had convinced them that Adams Architect could do it. Lee was sent to meet with Jim at his office to discuss the design while Robert would deal with the fees involved. Upon entering the large imposing office with the dark wood paneling and the tough looking gentleman seated behind the massive desk, Lee was slightly intimidated. The man looked hard and calculating, like an armed services marine, which was unusual for Canada. He had short, brush cut styled graying hair, a square jaw and powerful arms but when he stood up to shake Lee's hand she was surprised to find herself looking down at him. He was actually quite a bit shorter than her especially since she was wearing heels with her black suit, so she felt a little more confident.

As he sat back down, he explained that most of their restaurants were older dating from the late '60's and had never been updated. The company needed to put forward a new image, along with the new trend for healthier food. He talked about starting with the renovation of the signature store on Yonge Street, the main street in the heart of the retail area of Toronto. As he talked he reached out for a form core board with materials and drawings on it next to his desk, raised it to show Lee then flung it across the room, which startled her.

"That is a design by another architectural firm, and it is crap! You have two weeks to come up with a great scheme. One week for a design that I like and another week to do a cost estimate to prove that it is within our budget" he stated.

Lee wasn't able to completely hide her surprise but she recovered quickly and asked a few more questions. Then she gathered her briefcase, smiled while she put out her hand to shake and assured Mr. Wallace that she would see him again within a week with a design that he would approve. He watched her determined form retreat from his office with a raised eyebrow and reluctant grin.

Lee did love a challenge, especially when it involved a difficult problem and finding a unique solution to impress a client. She had always been trying to prove herself capable, despite being a woman, whether it was to her father, classmates or other architects. This is what motivated her to be more than just a good designer, it made the adrenaline flow. So she immediately went to work on the drafting board, sketching and searching the sample room for materials then calling to check costs. She was inspired by the concept that the client had outlined; a two storey space which revolves around a KFC bucket. She didn't want it to be a literal bucket, just an impression of the form, so she envisioned sloping sheets of curved glass on the street facade following a cylindrical shape on the inside of twisting red painted sections of wall swirling around a center atrium with a curved stair wrapping the edges. She then consulted with Laura and found a faux wall finish that was durable, inexpensive and gave off an iridescence of subtle colors. She used drywall to frame out niches to highlight photos and create recesses for two topper seating alcoves. It was all big bang for a low buck and she was sure that this design would be within the budget. So she drew up some hand perspective sketches, put together a material sample board and set up a meeting with Jim for the presentation within the first week of the deadline.

Lee presented her design, passionately describing the aesthetics, simplicity and practicality of the solution. She had explained how the users would be drawn to enter the space then how they would experience the sense of light and color once inside. She went over the ease of movement, the attraction to go up to the second floor, areas for display and lastly, the building code issues. Jim had made a few comments during her presentation but they were in a team spirit tone, such as "we can solve this issue" or "we can work around that", so she believed that he liked the design. When she was done, she looked up and saw that he was smiling as he continued to review the drawings. Jim then congratulated her on the design, asked her to leave the boards with him and get the budget numbers to him as soon as possible. She was dismissed but she felt so good that she couldn't wait to get back to the office to report to Robert. She still had work to do but she was confident that she had already set the foundation for hitting that budget number with the material she had already selected.

This commission was not glamorous or potentially newsworthy, but it was more important than anything she had done before if it saved the firm. She thought about how her fellow graduate students at Yale might have scoffed at such a project. It was just a fast food restaurant concept that she might be repeating twenty five times a year for years to come but she was happy to be doing it. This was not the high profile museums, award winning schools, complex high rises or even high end custom houses that she imagined her classmates to be designing in New York or Chicago but it was a job that might help her family and firm survive this recession.

Chapter 21- Ridge Beam & Vent

Lee adored her baby boy and was soon absorbed by his laughter, attempts to imitate faces, grip fingers, roll over and eventually lift his head and crawl forward. His progress was astonishing and she was overwhelmed by the thought that she helped create this incredible human being. She wondered if you could have such instant love when you adopted, though she imagined you could, especially if the adoption followed years of yearning for a child. She also began to worry. She checked the baby's crib all the time while he was sleeping and set up a monitor. She looked for sharp objects that would hurt him, or things that he could swallow or choke on, then removed them from reach. He was so fragile is some ways, though resilient in others and she felt that she had to be constantly vigilant and protective, but not smothering. She set up a little plastic pool in the back yard and enjoyed watching him sit in the water with arms outstretched smacking the surface, laughing until he would accidently splash it into his own face. Then there was surprise in his wide eyes and sputtering with his small mouth before he went back to the game again.

Once Andy was mobile, Lee would work in the garden while he explored the small yard and she would laugh watching him lift his bottom and knees when he crawled since he didn't like the feel of the grass. Lee also enjoyed taking the baby in the stroller down the shaded one way streets to run errands to the health food store or drug store, and farther onto the boardwalk along the lake. They strolled past the muscle beach work out area near the public pool. Seeing the highly developed and toned bodies in the weight lifting section and the bikini clad girls around it, would inspire Lee to go to the club to run on a tread mill or hit squash balls while the baby slept in the carrier in front of the glass wall of the court. She was proud that her body had bounced back so quickly, though she would have to work hard to get rid of the final few pounds.

Curt had little interest in the young child, any young child Lee noticed, and he would boast when he was with friends.

"The kid will only be of some value when he is old enough to go drinking with me"

He did however, pick the baby up and carry him around once in a while or hold him while he watched TV. This allowed Lee to fix dinner and finish her other chores or house repairs. Curt also discretely watched the boy for signs of resemblance to himself. The round green eyes were not his but the large head, thick bottom lip and double jointed thumb made Curt smile. He was also extremely glad to have a boy. This was important to him and he felt that the world was as it should be, ordered and obedient to his wishes.

Now that he had a male heir, it was appropriate that he should begin to build a legacy, or empire as he would joke, that he could pass on to his son. His father had been a partner in his own business, a used car dealership, and it had left him comfortable in his old age. Lee had learned later that the early retirement was due to his partner buying him out after a nasty accident and liability law suit that may have been Mr. Richard's fault and a result of an alcoholic dependency. However, Curt admired his father who he called "The Old Man" and while he acted confident and cock sure in front of this father, he still wanted the man's approval.

So Curt worked hard on his fledgling company until it was moved to a new rental space with a conference room, two offices and a stock room. Lee was enlisted to help by painting the office, getting furniture and producing art work for the monthly marketing brochure. Soon Curt realized that he couldn't grow the industrial sales business alone and so he got the affable Ned to quit his job in order to join Boulevard Supply. Ned was now married to a woman who worked full time like Lee, so she could help support him with this startup. The two friends were compatible in work since Curt was the aggressive salesman and Ned the amicable people pleaser. Ned would manage the suppliers and future employees and Curt would round up business.

The company slowly started to make money, though Lee never knew how much. She just deposited her pay check into their joint account and hoped it was enough to cover everything. Curt paid the utility bills and mortgage while Lee was doing everything else around the house, including the book keeping for the nanny, the cooking, grocery shopping, doctor's visits and most importantly, the care of the baby after work. She was also still working part time for Curt's business and even though it was an uneven division of labor she wanted to support Curt while he was chasing his dream. She didn't think he appreciated her efforts much but maybe she would get a turn next to chase a dream of her own. Lee had also cut back on her spending by doing most of her shopping for Andy and herself at Walmart instead of boutique shops or even the Hudson Bay Department Store. She had planted a vegetable garden in the back yard and decided to cut her hair herself to save on salon expenses. Lee had always been fairly frugal but now things were extremely tight. Lee had even jumped at Curt's suggestion that they become vegetarian since she thought that it would save even more money, though he had assumed that she had been convinced by an article he had shown her about the health benefits. So to further play on Curt's new found health kick, Lee had suggested that he take a lunch to work each day and that they cut back on dining out. Curt had no desire to cut back on his own pleasures though and told her that he would pack a lunch occasionally to pacify her, but he never would.

Just as Lee would start to relax about their financial situation, Curt would suddenly demand that she empty the savings account that she had set up for Andy or ask her mother for a loan again. At one point they owed her mother thousands of dollars since Curt couldn't pay his taxes and his business had more expenses than he had anticipated. Lee had come from such a financially stable background, with her father managing everything quietly and efficiently, she had never experienced panics like this. Her family wasn't extravagant but they still lived pretty well. She knew that her father, the accountant, would be disgusted by such poor monetary management. Curt couldn't seem to be able save a penny and he was always owing money.

Then Curt asked that Lee sign a second mortgage on the house. The mortgage rates had finally gone down a little and they were able to get a lower rate for the first mortgage. He said that he would use the money to pay off the two cars and the rest would help the company since he couldn't get any business loans yet. Lee cringed that he even asked her to do such a thing. She was under enough pressure with the baby, managing the house, the nanny and her own demanding job. Why did he have to make it so much harder she wondered? He knew that her family was against having a mortgage at all, let alone a second one. Her grandfather didn't believe in loans and that was one reason that the business had survived for so long and prospered when others had failed. A second mortgage would take out all the equity that their parent's loans had given them. But Curt was adamant that they would be able to replace the money in the near future and so he persisted to badger Lee to give in, and eventually, over many months she finally did. Curt knew how to get his way every time.

It was in the midst of this next financial crisis, that Lee discovered that she was pregnant again. She had been standing at the kitchen sink one morning cleaning her breakfast plate, when she suddenly felt nauseous. An overtaking nausea, which forced her to clutch the edge of the counter, head lowered in anticipation of retching. As she stood again waiting for the nausea to pass, it tweaked a memory and she knew what this was about. She grabbed the baby in her arms, plunked him into the stroller and hurried down the street to the pharmacy. It wasn't open yet so she paced in front holding Andy on one hip, until the doors opened. Inside she grabbed the pregnancy kit, paid at the counter and raced home with the baby to perform the test, which of course came out positive. Then she sat on the bathroom floor and cried, she was exhausted, worried and in addition, emotionally and economically unprepared for another child. Andy was surprised by his mother's defeated posture and tears and so he tried to hug her but he could only wrap his little arms around one shoulder. This brought about a tiny smile in the crease of Lee's mouth. She grabbed the precious boy in a big hug and then called Curt to tell him between sobs, that she was expecting again.

Lee spent the next few hours reconciling to the situation so by the time Curt got home she was actually excited about the new baby. Curt didn't pay much attention to her mood, he just assumed that she was cried out for now. He suggested that they go out for dinner and since Lee felt like celebrating now, she was enthusiastic about it. The little family loaded themselves into the car and headed up Markham Road through Scarborough, the baby secure in the back car seat happily gurgling. Then Curt turned to Lee and said to her.

"You will need to get an abortion you know. We can't afford another baby right now, so you should get rid of this one. We can try again later"

Lee was shocked. She looked at this man next to her with amazement and incredulity, and it was like her eyes were suddenly opened after being blindfolded. She was studying a stranger, this man she had been with for years. But he was busy driving and too wrapped up in his own thoughts to notice, though he sensed something was wrong. A startling idea flew into her mind then and she realized that she would leave him before she would ever abort her baby. She knew that he would try to talk her into this devastating mistake and she hardened herself, she would never agree to abort. So she didn't respond. She just slowly turned to stare back out of the front windshield and felt inside her, all of the feelings that she had left for this man, shrivel up and die right then.

After this epiphany, Lee continued her household routines and duties in the marriage, even though it was only a shell to her now. She would not abort this baby and she did not want to divorce even though things had changed in her now. She was feeling stronger in her convictions and paying attention to her moral compass. She had been weak, deferring to her husband in the hopes that he would do what was best but she knew now that even though he appeared strong, he was a coward driven by selfishness and he did not make the right decisions. She also knew that she could do anything on her own, even raise her children alone if she had to, but with a new baby coming, she was not ready to make any changes yet. Curt had backed off of the topic of abortion. He had finally sensed in her quiet over the following few days that he should not press the point. So he instead he did an about face and decided to celebrate the existence of the new baby by suggesting that the family drive out to the country to tell his parents.

Mr. and Mrs. Richards lived an hour north of the city in a modern log and cedar shingle house that they had built on fifty acres of woodland. They had cut out a small area for the house, a front lawn and gardens but left the rest as thick forest. Mrs. Richards, a large boned, tall, kindly woman, with a wide square face, was a gifted gardener and the explosion of color and variety of plants in the beds around the house always delighted Lee. She was also an excellent cook and Lee looked forward to the fresh vegetables from the garden, rich pastas and moist cakes that were specially baked for their visits.

Mr. Richards, though jovial and teasing, had something about him that made Lee cautious. It may have been how gregarious he became as he drank more during the evening and then initiated arguments on controversial subjects. He would bring up government spending and suggest off the wall investments, which got Curt incensed. He would also talk about how affairs in a marriage shouldn't be such a big deal since they were just short flings, making Lee defensive. He claimed that quick physical gratification shouldn't harm the solidity of a marriage. Lee of course adamantly disagreed with him, saying that adultery breaks a sacred vow and trust. At the end of the evening he was often the only one still laughing but the couple adored their grandchild and Lee was happy that they wanted to be a part of Andy's life. They seemed thrilled about the new baby as well and so pleased with their son, though Lee doubted that they would have been quite so proud of Curt had they known what he had suggested to her in the car that day.

Once they were back in the city, Lee decided to work off the heavy food that she had eaten so she took the baby with her to Lakeshore. While she was on the stationary bike in the gym and Andy was sleeping in his car seat next to her, Cary, one of her work out friends approached to ride next to her and chat. Cary was an attractive slim blond woman from California who took aerobics classes until she looked as though she had no body fat at all. She wore very stylish business and casual clothes, and had regular massages and facials. She wasn't married so she did whatever she wanted and had money to spend on herself. She had her own business selling ultra thin speakers that could hide behind a painting or become the surface on a wall. It was the latest technology in surround sound, and Lee admired her for her independence. She also enjoyed their work outs together during which they would discuss business issues or projects but today, Lee confided that she was in a crisis. She was tired from excessive work and pressure, scared of the future and she wasn't sure what she should do.

Cary immediately told Lee that she should go see Mr. Harper, her psychic. When she saw the surprised look on Lee's face, she smiled and explained that it was not some fake who looked into a crystal ball. He had a talent and if Lee was skeptical, then she should just go and consider it an amusing experience. Cary said that Lee had to first call for an appointment, mentioning who referred her then she would be invited to their condo where Mrs. Harper would greet her and take her into the living room to relax for a few minutes. After this she would be brought into library to sit across from Mr. Harper while he held some personal objects, such as a comb or ring that she had worn recently. He would then proceed to describe the images he received, which could be present, past or future and he encouraged the clients to write down what he said for further reference. It sounded pretty harmless, so Lee took Mr. Harper's phone number from Cary and after a few more challenging days she called to set up an appointment.

As Lee was invited into the modest living room by the sweet elderly Mrs. Harper, she realized that while she was still skeptical, a part of her wanted this to be real. She also understood that this was the exact kind of desperate hope that would drive people to spend their money on the crystal ball frauds. She told herself that she was just looking for some good advice, and if there was a hint of direction for the future then it would be worth the visit, since the present was falling apart. After a few minutes of down time, Lee was escorted into the small den and introduced to a tall slightly stooped older gentleman in a navy suit jacket with thick brown hair, wire glasses framing warm brown eyes and below that, a trimmed mustache. He rose from behind his French provincial desk to shake her hand then graciously gestured for her to sit down. He then told her that he had been an advertising firm executive but he was retired and wanted to share his gift now that he had the time. Mr. Harper asked Lee to keep her arms unfolded and her legs together but uncrossed, in order to allow the energy to flow to him for the session. He told her that it worked in business meetings as well if she wanted to guard her thoughts, just cross her legs. He requested the personal objects that she had brought, so Lee passed him her wedding ring which he placed loosely on his finger and her hair brush which he held in his other hand. Then he closed his eyes and after a couple minutes said in his deep voice;

"You have been given a contract. I beg you to not sign it. Please have an accountant or lawyer look at it right away since it is not beneficial to you at all"

Lee's eyes widened at this statement. She had just been given a contract by Adams but she hadn't had time to review it yet. Robert had hinted that it was probably written too favorably toward Kam and himself, but he believed that the accountant was just trying to protect them. Lee was still digesting this while Mr. Harper was proceeding with more descriptions of images. He talked about her family, her work and then he paused, looked up at her and said in an excited voice.

"You are pregnant aren't you?!"

Again she reeled at the accuracy of the statement, and confirmed that she was indeed pregnant but she had only found out herself recently. He gave her a knowing look, smiled then continued.

"The pregnancy will go well and the baby will be a healthy little girl so don't worry anymore"

"Your children will go to private school for a period"

"You should give the children ginger ale for stomach aches"

"You and your children will be moving to the southern United States and it will be a good move for you"

"You will have your own business in the States and be successful"

"You will build a large house on the water without a basement and it will have a two storey section with wonderful views"

"You will be in a car accident on a rainy day in the place where you are living, but don't worry, no one would be injured"

"You will be married twice"

At this last statement, Lee stopped him, surprised once again, and asked him.

"If my husband and I had lived together, broken up and then got married, did that constitute a second marriage?"

"Your husband is an American with hair darker than yours, brown eyes and he will love you very much," Mr. Harper responded.

She laughed and explained that her current husband was a blond, blue eyed Canadian and he certainly didn't love her very much at all.

"I am just telling you what I see," Mr. Harper said with solemnity.

After Lee paid the fifty dollar fee and bade the couple goodbye, she went to her car and just sat in a daze for a while trying to digest all that had been thrown her way. It was a lot to take in but as she began to analyze the probability of each item, she realized that most of them could come to fruition if she wanted them badly enough. After all, it depended on what path she chose to take, but these powerful words had opened possibilities for the future. They made dreams and hopes become potential realities. Mr. Harper had known things that no one else could have known and he had stated her recent unspoken wish, which was to move back to the States. Perhaps he did have a special gift, like the Oracle of Delphi in Greece, who in ancient times foretold the future for kings and city states. Then there was the seer who had told Julius Caesar that he would come to harm before Ides of March which was when he was murdered by his lover's jealous son Brutus and his senatorial friends.

Lee had begun to realize that moving to a less expensive city with lower taxes might reduce their financial burden. The United States represented greater potential for success, as it did for every immigrant, and a bonus of better weather than Canada. Curt could go back to earning good money as a broker and their children could have a better life. Canada's socialism pulled the entrepreneur down with taxes and an expensive cost of living. In a way, this session with Mr. Harper had put some magic back into her life. Lee had thought that everything for her future would be just plodding, one foot in front of the other, just trying to survive. Recently with all the burdens she had encountered, she didn't see any lifting of this load, only more difficulties. She felt quite alone in the struggle, especially since her husband was part of the problem and she couldn't tell her parents or friends how badly things were going. Mr. Harper's words had given her confidence and pointed out an alternate destiny, like a neon sign glowing in the fog, she now knew where she could be heading and that the current challenges were only temporary.

As soon as she returned to the office, Lee faxed off the contract to her father to review. Shortly after this, the firm secretary put through a call from Joseph, which was a surprise since he rarely ever called Lee, so she knew that it had to be important. Her father opened with his usual business-like manner then got right to the point.

"Do not sign that contract. It is extremely disadvantageous toward you. You could make changes to it but it is so one-sided, I would just throw it away"

Lee thanked him for his quick assessment then assured him that she would not sign it at all. There was no rush and with the change in the economy, she didn't need to take on the role of ownership in an unstable architectural firm at this time. She was now armed with knowledge of a potential alternate future, as supplied by Mr. Harper, and she was calmed by it. She decided that she would go visit him every six months or when she needed an important question answered.

After some thought about how she would phrase it, Lee told Curt that she had been to a psychic. She paused to see his reaction and when he didn't respond, she continued. She described Mr. Harper's warning about the contract, their potential lifestyle in the United States and the declaration that the baby would be healthy. Curt asked her if he had told her the sex of the baby. When she quietly said that it would be a girl, Curt's tone dropped and he declared.

"The guy is wrong, it will be another boy" but he hesitated before he said it and Lee could tell that he wasn't sure.

Chapter 22 – Fireplaces & Chimney

The months passed and the imminent arrival of the new baby put Curt in motion. He had decided that the house needed divided rooms and the front porch enclosed to become a breakfast room, unknowingly recalling suggestions that Lee had made when they first bought the house. Curt needed to believe that he made all the decisions in their lives so he rarely asked Lee her opinion. His ego, which constantly required bolstering, wanted the ideas to be his own so his memory conveniently complied.

In response, Lee had learned to plant her ideas and then stand back to watch them germinate as her mother had done in her marriage. This may have been a regular practice in marriages of earlier eras especially when centuries before women had no land, money or power of their own. In those male dominated societies, the wife may have had to allow the man to feel as though he made all the decisions while she was subjugated. Subtle guidance or influence would have been required from minds that must have been just as brilliant and equal to their male counterpart as they are now, if lesser educated. So Lee tried to subtly act as a trainer directing an athlete and while she wasn't always successful, she did get some things that she wanted without a confrontation.

The change to the house was not an expensive alteration, but they had no money for even that. Curt was afraid that Lee would try to do the work herself despite her pregnancy, so he hired a local handyman. When the man came to build the new walls, Lee worked alongside him doing the framing and electrical wiring on the interior then she helped build two new side walls to the porch and relocate a window to complete the enclosure of the porch.

Curt also helped hang the drywall and in one weekend they had a new front breakfast room even though it was done without a permit. Lee had offered to do the drawings and submit them legally but Curt was in a hurry. He didn't want to bother to get a permit and he said that it wouldn't be a problem. Lee was too tired to argue even though she would have never advised a client to do this, especially in such a prominent location. She was concerned that neighbours would be watching their work and call the city to complain. Then she would be facing irate inspectors, a stop work order and they would have to get a permit anyway. But the neighbours were grateful for the improvements to the house that the young couple had done and more importantly, they were afraid of Curt. So no one filed a complaint and the Ponderosa was transformed again.

Another event triggered by the upcoming arrival of the baby, was the request by Mary for more money. She had gone directly to Curt, bypassing Lee who paid her wages, and told him that she deserved more money since she would have more work. She had then asked for a twenty five percent increase in salary and Curt had agreed. Lee was not pleased when Curt told her this news. She had to point out to him that they would now be paying more than the going rate for a nanny with multiple children and they couldn't afford that kind of increase. Curt told her to go back to Mary and renegotiate it, which she tried but then Mary announced that she would quit. Encouraged by friends to press for more money, she now couldn't back down.

Lee immediately turned to Laura to ask if she knew a good nanny who needed a job and she was able to connect Lee with a wonderful, kind woman named Joley. She was a thin tom boy styled girl, in baggy pants and a checkered work shirt, with a wide brilliant smile of slightly protruding but straight white teeth, and twinkling dark eyes. Joley explained that her last employers had moved to California and though they tried to get her a visa to work in the US, it had not been possible. Lee liked the girl immediately, so after the two agreed on wages, Lee checked her references then introduced her to Andy. This last step was a success with Joley falling in love with the sweet little blond boy and Andy reciprocated her affection.

Lee arranged for Joley to start a couple weeks later, during which time Mary appealed to Lee to keep her job. She had tried to find a new position and discovered that she couldn't get the wages she had imagined. Lee informed her that she had already hired someone and wished her luck in her search for new work. Mary was resentful during the last days of her employment, so Lee was grateful when the transition occurred and Joley was moved in downstairs. This change also pointed out how easy it was to have Joley in the house compared to Mary, who had needed a great deal of help adjusting to the new country. In a certain sense, she had been like another child, coming up the stairs weeping and inconsolable when she had a tooth ache or confused when she couldn't figure out how to send part of her wages back to the Philippines. Lee did not want to lose Joley, so she asked Curt to leave all items regarding the nanny to her. He agreed to this since his partner had asked him the same thing about their employee relations recently as well. After a few employee complaints about Curt's behaviour, Ned had asked his partner to leave all the personnel issues to him. Curt did not tell Lee this though since it hurt his pride to think that he might have messed up, something that he would never admit. Instead he reacted in a way that came natural to him, he blamed it on others.

"That employee was a jerk," he would say and soon he had convinced himself it was true.

As Lee lost her desire to exercise, due to being physically exhausted caring for the baby, she decided that she still deserved a little time for herself so she signed up for a class at the University of Toronto. She had previously taken Karate, Tae Kwon Do and joined Laura in a pottery class. All of her relatives received handmade glazed pots for Christmas that year. But while she was pregnant she decided to take another photography class. She was planning on learning to shoot good quality pictures of the children herself without the expense of a professional photographer. The class was in the basement of a university building downtown and there were twenty students who all brought their own cameras and tripods. The teacher was a talented photographer, who announced in the first class that they would have a live nude model to shoot. It was the first time that Lee had photographed a naked person and she was wondering who would volunteer for this. She remembered drawing classes that she had taken where they had various nude models, but they were usually gaunt art students or homeless people who needed the meager wages they were paid for the sessions.

The photography teacher introduced Greta, originally from Germany, and mentioned that she would be their model for a couple classes. She had walked in wearing an old maroon silk robe, strode up to the podium, adjusted herself onto a chair and then arched her back to drape herself into a pose. She was a young woman, with long brown hair in a tight bun and a heart shaped face with a clear complexion. Lee was surprised at how attractive she was and the men in the class had stopped adjusting their tripods and were now staring at the girl. Then Greta undid the belt at her waist, shifted her shoulders and let the robe drop to the floor. She was exquisitely built. Her flawless dark toned skin rolled over the perky upturned nipples of her small breasts then flowed down over a smooth stomach to an uncut patch of dark hair between her long legs. She was sure of herself, confident and even gave a small smile when she dramatically tossed her head to look up and returned the stares of the students. The men started out of their hypnotic trance, closed their mouths and embarrassingly turned back to adjusting the camera mount or settings. Lee felt a surge of envy, and then gave a short laugh as she sensed the lust emanating from the other students, all male, as they furtively watched the girl before aiming their cameras at her. Lee was five months pregnant, wearing a large baggy sweater of Curt's and she felt like the size of a house. "Good for this woman," she thought. She has a wonderful gift and displayed more confidence than Lee had ever felt.

The class went well and Lee got used to moving in close or zooming to get a silhouette of a shoulder line, breast or hip bone, then circling for a different angle. The men were clicking away and moving their cameras to adjust the angle. The model regularly shifted her position as well into beautiful artistic poses. She made sensual movements of her hands and head, tilting it slightly, toward the side, or down in a look of modesty or vulnerability while the teacher adjusted the umbrella on the side to give new lighting effects. Lee had taken many shots and when the girl paused for a break and donned her robe, Lee developed her film and got a student to do a proof sheet for her. She did not want to spend any time in the dark room due to the chemicals but she still was anxious to see the work. She didn't know if she was allowed to send these negatives to a lab for printing.

On the second day, just after Lee had set up her tripod several spots back from the stage area where Greta sat, the lights all went out in the building. It was a blackout and the teacher called out for the class to just remain calm. He further explained that this happened once in a while and he would go fix the situation. Except for a few small red lights from the battery operated cameras, the room was entirely black. Lee couldn't see anything. Her eyes could not find any illumination beyond the little red lights, so she remained in her position. Then she suddenly felt strong hands gripping each of her buttocks and a body move against her back. She started and began to turn to face the accosting person just as the lights came on and she found herself facing the naked Greta. She guessed that this was a pass, so she smiled at the woman and said softly.

"I am five months pregnant and married but I thank you"

How extraordinary that she had not perceived this coming and how flattering for someone to be attracted to her while she was in her stretch front jeans and baggy outfit. Greta just shrugged then she turned back to the podium as Lee dropped her head grinning while she pretended to adjust her camera. She missed the look of shock on the faces of her fellow students, though she guessed what was going on around her and she would remember this incident for years, smiling at the memory each time.

The second baby was much easier than the first. Lee had been booked to go into the hospital on Nov. 20th to be induced with the doctor breaking her water. But that morning just after she had stepped into the shower, she felt an expulsion from between her legs and looked down to see some pink fluid going down the drain. She finished shampooing and conditioning her hair then stepped out of the shower wrapped in a towel and informed Curt that her water must have broken. Lee completed dressing while Curt passed Andy over to Joley then got the car ready. It was a Saturday so they were lucky that they didn't encounter the usual work day traffic jams on their way to the hospital and Lee felt calm as she breathed deeply between contractions.

Once they arrived at the hospital, Curt went to park the car and Lee was taken to her room where she delivered the baby fifteen minutes later. Dr. Treland had just entered her room to begin setting up to induce when Lee explained about her water breaking earlier and the mild contractions that she had been having in the car. When Dr. Treland checked beneath the sheet for her progress, she found the baby crowning and just asked Lee to push. With little pain, a small wiry dark skinned baby quickly entered the world. Lee cried out "Thank God" when she was told that it was a healthy little girl. She had been hoping for a girl and it was a moment that she would never forget; the quiet birthing room, with just her doctor to assist with this simple, fairly painless but beautiful birth.

She was alone in the room with the baby on her breast when Curt came bursting into it ranting about the paper work he had to fill out before being allowed upstairs. He turned to the doctor who had just entered the room again and asked how long she might think it would be until the baby came since he was rather hungry. Dr. Treland raised an eyebrow and gestured toward Lee saying.

"You have a beautiful baby girl"

Curt turned in surprise toward Lee then spotted the tightly wrapped pink blanket held in her arm, at which sight he blurted.

"It would have been a boy if I had been here"

Lee sighed in exasperation, while her doctor looked at Curt incredulous, as the tender moment dissolved and reality was thrown over Lee like a thorny net.

Again, Lee was back at work five days after delivery with a sleeping baby Sarah in a car seat under her desk. She wasn't happy that first morning back since she had been stopped by the police and given a speeding ticket, mistakenly in her opinion, on her way to the office. She had pointed out to the police man that not only did her car have a limit to its acceleration but she had a newborn in the car which she would have never endangered by speeding. The car in the next lane had zoomed past her on the straight away, but since she was in the closest lane, the police man had pulled over her car instead of the real culprit. The policeman refused to back down, though he did tell Lee that she could fight the ticket in court. She would go to court months later and win the case, but that didn't help her mood the first day back.

During Lee's short absence, the firm hadn't picked up many new projects. The KFC jobs were the main bread and butter for the company and Lee noticed that the partners still hadn't applied any of her budget suggestions. She tried again to get some of her cost saving items implemented over the next few months but it was a slow and frustrating process. She did not have the authority required. This made her concerned about the firm and her job so she decided that she would have to start taking on some of the freelance projects she had been offered. Laura had been working with a new contractor who was looking for an architect to partner with for some design/build work. She assured Lee that he was a great guy, very professional and produced good work so Lee decided to stop in at Laura's office downtown office to meet him.

Laura was located in the glass and blue mullioned clad modern Ontario Design Center, which housed other designers, fabric and furniture showrooms and even a television and music studio. Lee remembered one time, when she had visited Laura's office, Rick Moranius, of "Honey I Shrunk the Kids" fame, had walked past the glass reception wall and waved to her when he noticed Lee watching him. So Lee had naturally thought that one of the music studio clients had lost his way when she had entered Laura's office and found a guy who looked like more rock star than general contractor standing in the reception area. Laura quickly made introductions and Lee was shaking hands with Jamie Bradley, a tall handsome man with a wide white smile and long shoulder length light brown hair.

Lee liked this man immediately and they discussed potential scenarios for working together. James mentioned that he had lots of opportunities to get residential work but he wanted a designer on his team so he could win bigger, more prestigious projects. Lee was intrigued, felt that she could trust him and agreed to try this new arrangement. Lee understood that this would mean even more work for her, but she felt it was prudent in this economy to take advantage of opportunities and possibly bring in more money for her family as well. It would not be in conflict with her current position but she would have to tell her partners that she was doing this residential freelance on her own time outside of the office.

Before she had a chance to do this, Robert and Cam asked Lee and the other two associates to all attend a meeting in that afternoon in the conference room. As they each gathered in the front conference room, Lee assumed this might not be good news and the look on each of the other participants reflected this concern as well. Robert lead the meeting while sitting at the head of the table, explaining the difficulties of the last year, the steps that they intended to take to reduce costs, which included many of Lee's suggestions, and the potential of new work for the future. Then he brought out a file folder and passed around a copy of a document for each person in the room. Robert said that they had fallen into a dire situation and their accountant, Greg Williams, who was seated next to Robert, would explain it for them.

Greg, a pudgy bespectacled man in a navy suit, turned to the group and began to throw out figures of expenses, rent, overhead and income. Then he said that he had come up with a potential solution which was noted in the document that each person held. The three associates looked down at the papers in front of them and scanned the numbers on the pages. Greg further explained that since the recession, Robert and Kam had been putting all of the profit that they had gotten out of the Sheppard Street Office sale, back into the firm to keep it afloat. However, this did not cover enough. They were now asking each person in the room to contribute fifty thousand dollars to cover the short fall. Lee's eye brows rose and a gasp escaped her mouth as she stared up at Greg, taking in the request.

"And how do you expect us to come up with this fifty thousand," Lee asked.

"Mortgage your house," the accountant replied, which brought another sound from Lee, a laugh this time that she could barely control.

"You are actually serious," she blurted after she had stopped laughing and saw the dour look on the man's face.

The meeting continued but Lee remained quiet for the remainder as she mentally calculated her next course of action. As soon as the meeting broke up, she was back in her office and had closed the door. She immediately called Laura and told her of this new development. She said that she would have to quit immediately and either find a new job, which would be very difficult in this market, or go out on her own. She felt that she had no choice. When she had stopped speaking, Laura nonchalantly told her.

"Well, you will have to move in with me then and start your own firm."

"Jamie will be thrilled, he has enough work for you and I would love your company"

This was such a perfect solution that Lee closed her eyes, offered a silent thanks to above, and then graciously accepted. Laura was already established in beautiful offices with all the amenities she would need and the office was closer to home so she could see the children more. The commute to her current job was over an hour in heavy traffic and that would be cut to about fifteen minutes now. She was concerned about initial income flow, but she hoped that work with Jamie Bradley would grow quickly, and it did.

The projects with Jamie were so enjoyable, partly due to his personality and partly due to the relaxation of her work schedule, though it didn't pay quite what she was used to with commercial work. She was however now able to go into work whenever she wanted, staying late at home in the morning to play with the children and avoid rush hour then working late in the evening at home when the children were asleep. Curt was rarely home so he didn't really notice any change in their lives. The clients for the residential work tended to want to meet after business hours but didn't mind children coming along so Lee usually didn't have to employ Joley for additional hours except when Curt wanted to go out.

Jamie also had a couple children and his wife, a beautiful well coifed blond woman named Sherri, worked full time at the Ontario Star newspaper so he often had his children with him as well. He did all the work organizing and caring for his children as well, such as registering them for school, buying their supplies, taking them to soccer practice and when they were sick he tended them. Lee was amazed at how caring and kind he was and how little his wife seemed to interact with the family. Sherri was the primary bread winner though since she had a regular pay check, while Jamie's income ebbed and flowed with the projects.

One of the first jobs that Lee did with Jamie was to renovate his own house, an unremarkable, faux stone and brick single storey house near Eglington a few blocks from the lake. Lee got the scope of work from Jamie then met with Sherri to go over her requirements. The woman didn't have long to talk, but swept Lee though the crowded house complaining about the lack of closet space, limited shoe storage and small bathroom. Lee was shown the stack of high heels crowded into the small master bedroom closet but didn't see any of Jamie's things in the room.

Lee decided not to say anything to Jamie but designed two large walk-in closets for the renovation and a spacious Master Ensuite. Mrs. Bradley would probably take over both of the closets but she tried to leave an area for Jamie since he deserved it. She reflected on how personal it was to design someone's home. You saw how a family lived and functioned, warts and all, and you had to be as non-judgmental as possible. Lee had to bite her tongue often when trying to offer a more efficient way to lay out a room, or set up a kitchen especially when the client wanted something that didn't make sense to her. The client is always right she learned, a mantra she repeated regularly to herself, and they wanted it at the least possible cost.

Once the Bradley house was complete, with its new grand front porch, creamy siding and bay window under the added second floor of spacious bedrooms, the neighbours started calling Jamie to work on their houses. Jamie had been a carpenter, learning his trade by apprenticeship, until he decided to branch out as a general contractor. He had surprising good taste, incredible honesty and common sense so he was amicable to work with, but he was new to this leadership position in the business, so he had challenges. He didn't have a steady team yet so subcontractors sometimes didn't show up when they needed to be working and at one point, Jamie's van with all his tools was stolen, when his assistant left the keys inside.

After much trial and error Jamie completed his own project and moved on to work on the various neighbour's houses with Lee. These renovations grew in size and number until the team was regularly adding large additions or second floors to the tightly spaced houses in the older neighbourhoods near downtown. Lee had to bring in a structural engineer to review each situation but the older houses were often able to bear the new floor joists on the existing block or stud exterior walls and just build upwards.

Soon, Jamie had attracted a good number of doctors and other affluent clients for renovation work and Lee was getting busy. These client houses were in areas where the price of real estate had jumped and it was too expensive to move to a larger house or the family just liked their neighbourhood and didn't want to leave it. Lee enjoyed collaboration with these people, though the work was more time consuming than profitable, but the projects were fun to do. Lee was told constantly that she was the only designer who listened or thought about storage and flow in a home. The clients, usually with the wife in a leadership role during the renovation, enjoyed working with a female who understood the functioning of a home with children, elderly parents and home offices. Lee came to understand that women tended to design from the inside function to the outside, while men designed from their exterior vision inward, forcing the spaces inside to conform. Lee thought that maybe her marriage was a little like this, forced to conformity so that it looked successful on the outside despite how it felt or functioned inside.

Lee didn't have time to dwell on the state of her marriage though since business was growing along with the children. Lee was careful to give each client fair warning in the beginning, that any renovation had the potential to go over budget, so they needed to put aside a fifteen percent contingency allowance for surprises and changes. This small amount of advice often made the difference in client expectations and allowed for a happy conclusion to the project. Lee got regular thank you notes from her clients, which meant more to her than the extra money she had earned while working at Adams. She had to give credit to Jamie as well though. He was accommodating and determined to make the clients happy with their projects, even if it meant a loss on his part.

In this attitude, she and Jamie were alike. She felt that people were either givers or takers as a basic ethical core, and generosity of spirit seemed to be a predetermined character trait, born within each person or lacking altogether. She guessed that some people could force themselves to do generous acts, but if they were not generous by nature, then there might be selfish reasons for the act to take place. She was a little late in understanding this elemental lesson in human nature when it came to Curt, especially if she compared him to Jamie. With Jamie, she felt his kindness, concern and gentle caring about everything he did. He would put other people first, especially his children, and she admired that. Curt still didn't pay much attention to their children and he was never affectionate or kind to her. Lee also found that with Jamie she could open up about her goals and dreams, joking at first, then more serious as she saw that he didn't ridicule her the way Curt would have. The rapport built up slowly, as they reviewed projects and building techniques, easily speaking each other's language of construction. Then they expanded into discussions of their personal lives and a friendship grew.

Chapter 23 – Sheathing

The baby Sarah was just over six months old when Lee's girlfriend Mandy, came over on Mother's Day with her young son. The two mothers sat in comfortable lawn chairs in the backyard chatting amicably while watching the antics of their well-loved off spring. The little boys climbed the steps of the deck, swung on the swing set or dug in the black soil of the garden. The baby was laying on a blanket absorbing the sunshine of a beautiful day, lifting her head to look around and trying to crawl to the edge of the blanket to grab the grass. Mandy was an interior designer who worked on large international projects and Lee was fascinated by her work and the exotic locations for these extravagant developments. They had met when Lee had worked on a prestigious project in Beaver Creek Colorado, where President Ford had a house.

Lee had been working on this project to help Christopher, who had been hired to design a dozen million dollar chalets, around a central hotel styled building that would be built into the side of the mountain, each with ski-in facilities. The main building would have rooms for guests or the employees to stay, as well as party rooms for use. Each chalet was a four thousand square foot home with a steeply pitched shake roof, double car garage with heated slab floor, hot tub on a stone patio. The interiors were organized around a great room with a soaring beam supported cathedral ceiling lit by an elaborate antler chandelier. The project would eventually earn The President's award for design though Lee's firm didn't usually submit their work for awards. Mandy had developed beautiful sketches for the interior concept of the main building which Lee admired and was asking about. The two were deep into a discussion when Curt came outside, stood in front of Lee, who glanced up smiling to see what he wanted. He looked down at her with a scowl and said:

"Are you two going to just sit out here all day doing nothing?" Then he added "You know Lee, your smile looks like a sneer the way your lips turn down at the corners. It makes you look rather ugly"

Mandy made a quick covering remark, saying that Lee had a lovely smile, while Lee could only look at this man in front of her in stunned silence. She had decided that she would not respond to his mean jibs, which were coming more frequently but this was the first time he had been quite so nasty in front of a friend. She turned back to Mandy, deliberately ignoring Curt, asked her about her next trip abroad for a project then leaned down to lift the baby back to the center of the blanket and caress the her head, which reminded her why she was still married to this man. Besides, it was Mother's Day and she didn't want anything to spoil it

After this incident, Lee noticed that Curt had gone back into what she referred to as his "extremist binge phase" again. These seemed to happen every six months and this time the topic was food again. Curt had picked up the new book "Fit for Life" and after skimming its pages he began to lecture Lee on the idea that different food types, like starches, carbohydrates and proteins, should never be mixed since it could cause digestion problems. Curt also expounded upon the book's theories of the evils of dairy products and white bread, quoting a passage from the book that humans had never be seen sucking off a cows udder, so it couldn't be natural to drink milk. Lee thought that this was ridiculous since humans were probably drinking vitamin rich cow's milk for thousands of years and now with technology we didn't have to drink from the squirt of an udder or a pail. It only proved to her that humans were resourceful.

The book's theories also countered many scientific nutritionist recommendations about calcium and vitamin requirements. When Curt persisted, Lee questioned the author's credentials but her logic didn't matter to him. He began throwing out any milk or white bread that he saw in the fridge. Lee would then just buy more, much to his chagrin. Then she decided to end this battle by inviting Molly Baker, the sister of her high school friend, over to visit. Molly was a certified nutritionist who was practicing at a local hospital. Lee knew that Curt would never listen to her so she thought that a professional might have more influence. She had to try for her children's sake. She could not let them go without valuable calcium just because Curt was on one of his binges.

Molly came for lunch on a beautiful spring day and the three of them sat out on the back deck while the children played in the yard. Lee had only met Molly at curling matches with her sister so she hadn't been sure what to expect. She was pleasantly surprised by her professional countenance and well-spoken manner. When Lee brought the conversation around to the book and its theories, Molly was able to praise its promotion of eating fresh vegetables and fruit but gently discount its lack of proper research and the danger of applying the book's premise to children.

"Children absolutely need the calcium offered through milk products, especially when they are young. Pill supplements cannot fulfill their dietary needs and unless breast feeding continues for several years, milk is a good substitute for young children," she pointed out.

"There is no problem with white bread beyond the lack of vitamins in it. Though homemade or vitamin enriched wheat bread would be better," she continued in a serious tone.

Lee tried not to look at Curt during this discussion, she just prayed that he would relax his grip on the fridge contents and let her feed the children what they needed. She had conspired with Joley to keep the milk and bread in the downstairs apartment fridge for now but it was very inconvenient and she didn't like sneaking around for something so illogical. Finally, Curt conceded that the children could have milk but he wanted the bread to be wheat. Lee said that she had the right to eat what she wanted but she would continue to buy wheat bread for him and the children. He relented finally and Lee was so grateful to Molly for her help. It was like she had just won a court case - little did she know it was just the beginning of such battles, and ironically the author of that Fit for Life book died surprisingly young.

Lee had settled into Laura's office well. She enjoyed the short commute, excitement of the downtown area and often brought the baby in with her since there was only two other women in the office usually, Laura and her draftsperson, Sandy. Lee would breast feed in the section where her desk was located, behind a short wall that separated her from the rest of the office and the entry area. If a courier or client entered the office and the other girls weren't available, she would lean her head out and ask them if she could help. Then slowly, she would disengage the baby's mouth from her breast, wrap her up and go out to assist. She had a drafting board to work on for design and a bulky computer for drafting and administrative work, and that was all she needed. Laura had a plotter to send drawings to by cable connection for printing. Then these large drawings were then couriered to a printing company to make the sets for permitting and construction bidding. Her collaboration with Jamie was going well and they had several doctor's homes to design, each in more expensive neighbourhoods as their reputation grew.

As Jamie built his business and became successful, his marriage deteriorated even more. Jamie was still doing the majority of the child care while also organizing each project with the clients and subcontractors, chasing down new leads and running jobs as a superintendent himself. He was exhausted but always had a wide grin on his face and a goofy sense of humor but he was also very endearing. He had an incredibly happy disposition along with his optimistic nature and when facing difficulties, approached them head on with humility and the goal to resolve them at all costs. So when his wife finally confessed to having an affair with her boss and announced that she was leaving the family to move in with him, Jamie took it hard, hit to his core. But he rallied, agreed to a generous separation agreement with joint child custody and even helped her move. He then continued, one foot in front of the other, wading through the mire of marital failure and keeping his heart break to himself. Lee couldn't understand how his wife would give up such a kind and thoughtful husband, something she would have cherished.

Lee was at her desk when her mother called to tell her that her grandmother had passed away. It was a shock to Lee since she did not even know that her grandmother had any serious problems regarding her health. Grace did have angina, chest pains due to narrowing of the arteries to the heart, but she had been having these attacks for years. She had never complained about any of her maladies or health issues so the family had become complacent about them, Lee included. This time however, she had been taken to the Kitchner-Waterlou cardiac care hospital St. Mary's for further tests and while there, she had gotten severely worse.

Anne had not bothered to tell Lee about this development, only informing her sister Mary, so she could join her at the hospital. When Lee had asked about visiting her grandmother, Anne had told her that it wasn't necessary and her grandmother wouldn't want visitors anyway. How sad that Lee had not had a chance to say goodbye or see her grandmother one last time. She put her head on her desk and sobbed. She felt a piece of her childhood slip away; the grief of loss along with the thought that her children would not get to know this wonderful woman. She also felt recognition of the pain that her grandfather must be feeling right now after losing his lifelong companion.

The funeral was held a few days later at St. Matthew's church in Olde Walkerville where Lee's great grandparents, Archibald and Lucy, rested in a small graveyard behind the old stone church. Lee and the children had driven down to attend and she had also been asked to give the eulogy. She had prepared a heart-warming, admirable account of her grandmother, mentioning her artistic abilities, her bridge lessons and her stoicism in facing hardship. But as Lee stood before the filled church and saw her grandfather's long sad face, she almost couldn't go on. Lee paused to gather herself, blinked the tears away, lifted her chin to look up over the heads of the audience and instead she began to tell stories about her grandmother. "Life is only a series of stories after all" she thought. How little is left once a special soul is gone.

Lee wanted the audience to appreciate her grandmother in a more personal way so she put aside her notes and regaled them with tales of their trip to New York when she charmed the waiters, her grandmother's deep and revered spiritualism, her classic "There, there, there" whenever she tried to comfort a baby. She told of her grandmother's regal bearing despite her difficult childhood and of the time she ran around the dining room table with a broom to chase a disobedient child, never intending to catch her. She told of the complexity of the woman but most importantly, she reminded them of her lovely laugh and kindness. Then she offered a prayer to the God who her grandmother loved dearly.

Shortly after the funeral, Lee began to research the possibility of moving to the States, her grandmother's home country, and the chances of getting visas or green cards. The free trade agreement had opened up work visas for certain professions and Lee had found that architects were on the list. She also located an immigration lawyer and set up an appointment. Her next move was to get Curt to start thinking about potential relocation. The border was opening up and she wanted to take advantage of it. This was a sore point for many Canadians, as Lee found out once she started to tell friends what she was doing. They couldn't understand why she wanted to move somewhere that had drive-by shootings and where handguns were prevalent. They quoted the latest violence in the news, the statistics of murders and the information about gangs who roamed the urban blight of so many US cities.

While living in Toronto, Lee had often noticed that groups of people socializing often dropped comments about the US wanting to make Canada the 51st state. Fears that the big bully country to the south would try to absorb the lightly populated, but resource rich northern neighbour were prevalent. Lee would roll her eyes when she heard this and say that she never heard that kind of talk anywhere she had lived in the US. Americans do not think about Canada much at all let alone talk about annexing it. She began to consider this concept like an analogy of a dog and a flea. The flea, which is living on the dog, is aware of everything the dog does, every move, every attempt to scratch itself and even every times it sleeps. While the dog is vaguely aware of the flea, it is just an unsolicited companion, and an irritation once in a while, that has to be tolerated.

Discussions on moving to America increased as Curt started getting bored with his business. It was stuck in a spot where he couldn't expand it without a boost of new capital and he couldn't find anyone to loan him more money. He did however, in his conversations with clients, find a one company who offered to buy him out. This prompted Curt to consider the move more seriously. So he joined Lee at the appointment with the immigration lawyer in his plush office overlooking the harbour. After asking questions about their background and reviewing their preliminary information, the lawyer discussed options for their potential migration and long term residence in the States. He explained the background of the Nafta free trade agreement on the border crossings and situation of Canadians going to work in America. He said that it was possible that they would each be eligible, as professionals on the free trade list, to get the one year H2B work visa that could be renewed three times.

After these visas ran out, they would have to be sponsored by their companies for extended work visas then hopefully green cards or they could also be sponsored by Lee's mother as a child of an American since she was eligible for citizenship automatically through her mother. Once they had gotten green cards, it would be five years of living continuously in the United States after the cards were issued before they could apply for American citizenship. As an architect, Lee was clearly listed on the Free Trade list of professionals, but Curt would have to be classified as a manager to qualify even though he would most likely be getting a job as a broker, a glorified salesman, which was not on the list. Despite this one risky part, they left the office buoyed at the possibilities.

Lee decided to tell her parents that they were thinking about moving to the States. The family was quite used to the quick step across the border since they had now had set up a plant in Dearborn, a suburb of Detroit. It was a minority owned business partnered with a Native American man. The work had poured in as companies satisfied their minority employment quotes through this new firm and the cousins had then gotten work permits to cross the border to work in the new plant. The company had purchased an old warehouse building which was a million square feet on two floors in the heart of a disintegrating neighbourhood.

The old brick offices of the building butted up to the cracked sidewalk on Warren Avenue in a section of Dearborn that had seen better days. The parking lot on the side, now filled with pot holes and loose gravel, had once managed hundreds of tractor trailers for the former furniture business. The buildings was lined with loading dock doors and the back faced a railroad siding which had been critical for shipping product.

When Steward's purchased the building, the single pane glass windows of the offices were replaced with double glazed with bars on the outside, the flooring replaced with new plush carpet and the entire facility was renovated to prepare for the new packaging business that would occupy it. It was an island of progress in an area where adjacent structures were dilapidated cafes, vacant retail spaces and garbage filled empty lots. After the extension of highways, the introduction of busing and riots of 1968, the population of downtown Detroit steadily dropped from almost two million to nine hundred thousand by the end if the twentieth century, and it never fully recovered. The "white flight" sent the Caucasian population fleeing for the suburbs. Places like Oakland and Macomb Counties filled with the middle class while Gross Point, the wealthiest section of the city, restricted its access to a single road which protected it. Any areas outside of this were reclaimed by the chaos of the downtown and left to wither.

Detroit had begun as a primarily French settlement, as demonstrated by the names for many of its landmarks and streets, but after World War 1 there was a large influx of British, German, Polish, Irish, Jewish immigrants as well as transplants from the southern states. The city depended upon these immigrants and the border crossing with Canada, where eventually up to 150,000 people commuted and over 13 billion in revenue crossed between countries. This border defined the nature of the city with the core centered on the river's edge and roads radiated out like spokes of a wheel from there. The center of the hub featured the Renaissance Center, a glass clad multi-towered development designed by John Portman and completed in 1977. It housed the tallest building in Michigan and at one time its 73 storey hotel was the tallest hotel only tower in the world. Portman, who created similar structures in other cities including Atlanta, San Francisco and Los Angeles, was popular for his massive circular glass and concrete constructions with interior oval cantilevered pods and walkways protruding into soaring atriums linking each tower.

The RenCen, as it was nicknamed, was surrounded by some classic old limestone and granite clad skyscrapers including the Penobscot and Fisher Buildings and the lower brick warehouses making up the popular Greek town, where restaurants and entertainment spots shone in an oasis amongst the decay of urban blight. This was also the base of rich cultural and technological invention as the home of Thomas Edison, Henry Ford, Motown and the Detroit Tigers. More recently there had been an increase in the Arab population in Detroit suburbs, mostly Lebanese, and these people had settled in Dearborn around the new plant so they made up the majority of the new plant employees. The Steward family hired an interpreter and learned the unique needs of this segment of their work force, who turned out to be hard workers and very good employees.

Lee's parents were supportive of their plans to move to the States, understanding that they couldn't stop the couple if they wanted to anyway. Some of Anne's cousins had been born in the States then grown up in Windsor, like her sister, but during Vietnam, they had been forced to choose countries since dual citizenship had been revoked. The boys had chosen to remain Canadian to avoid the draft, while most of the girls remained American. Later, when dual citizenship was allowed again, their children would apply for American citizenship in order to work in the States.

Lee and Curt had both gone to school on student visas and with assurances from the immigration lawyer about their prospects of getting working visas, they decided to visit a potential area in the southern States to look for jobs and a house. They wanted a warm climate, a fairly large city and reasonable cost of living. Washington was still too cold a climate and Florida too much tourist and retirement oriented. As they were deciding on what area to look into, Lee called her former professor, Kevin Malloy, who had left Miami to become an accreditation officer with the AIA, the American Institute of Architecture and central review board for architects. He now spent his time traveling across the United States, visiting each architectural college and reviewing their courses, teaching methods and compliance. She asked him where, in the entire Unites States, he would recommend they should move.

"If you have children then the best place in the United States to raise them is Charlotte, North Carolina. If you want an academic atmosphere, then the triangle region near Chapel Hill is the best, which is also in North Carolina" he replied in his charming southern drawl.

Once Lee had mentioned this advice to Curt, he was able to be persuaded to consider a trip to North Carolina. Neither of the pair had spent much time in the state, beyond their wind surfing trip, so they decided to head straight down to Highway 95 to check out Raleigh first, then over to Charlotte. They left the children with the nanny and on a dreary late March day drove out of the slush covered city of Toronto and headed toward the border crossing in Niagara. It was a fourteen hour drive, through a brown rolling hills covered in skeletal trees barren of leaves. It got slightly warmer as they went south but the air was still cool and landscaping muted.

After Richmond, Virginia, the sun emerged from behind the dark clouds and the sky began to clear. They crossed the border for North Carolina and looking about, saw an ocean of stately green pine trees, blooming white and pink dogwoods, delicate redbud trees drooping with rich scarlet color and brilliant azaleas bushes peeking between trunks at the base. It was an incredible sight. Curt directed the car into the first visitor station turn off, and as they opened the car doors, they were hit with a succulent blast of warm lightly perfumed balmy air.

"This is where I want to be, somewhere in this State!" Lee exclaimed as she spun around to take in all of the natural wonders.

Curt shook his head in agreement as they removed their heavy pants and changed into their shorts with Curt stripping at the side of the car and Lee using the washroom. This initial euphoria was subdued though as they toured the capital city of North Carolina. The white capital building was graceful rising out of its central park surround, but the rest of the city was small town in nature, a bit shoddy and uninteresting in its design and structure. It was the seat of power for the state but not business it seemed. The couple decided to immediately continue west toward Charlotte, a place that Lee didn't know much about, beyond the demographics that she had researched.

The Queen City, as it was known, had a population of about seven hundred thousand inhabitants and 1.5 million in the metropolitan area. It had a subtropical climate and was situated along the Catawba River system and at the base of the Appalachian Mountains. It was the second largest banking center in the United States, behind New York, and most of all, it was a city on the rise. Companies were relocating to Charlotte because of the weather, low cost of living and attractive life style. So the couple pushed west along Highway 85, through low undulating hills with expansive fields of tobacco, corn, soybeans and wheat. They went through the outlet and design center in Burlington and the small towns that once dotted the wagon routes for pioneers or soldiers going west.

As they approached Charlotte, they saw a small collection of modern high-rise buildings, set inside a ring road highway. Outside of that core spread well designed low rise developments, both office and residential with fluid street layouts ending in cul de sacs. The exclusive residential neighbourhoods even farther out tended to have entrances with brick guard houses, sweeping curved stone enclosure walls, immaculately trimmed bushes and colorful planting beds. Overall the city was attractive with an air of wealth, expansion and progress. They also noticed the number of churches, one on almost every corner. They were in the Bible Belt which was the land of the Southern Baptists, evangelist Billy Graham and The PTL Club under Tammy Faye and Jim Baker. This part of the culture would be very foreign to them.

While Curt went on job interviews, Lee began researching real estate with an agent and she couldn't believe the incredibly low house prices. In this city they could afford a five bedroom home on a horse ranch, a large lakefront property or a substantial historic house in the city, for the price of their little place in Toronto. Curt however insisted that they only consider houses in South Charlotte since he would most likely be working in brokerage firm near that area. He didn't want them looking at any lake front or country properties. Lee was disappointed but held her tongue. She was excited at the prospect of an escape from their current tight little house, congested city and the financial nightmare. They had toured a neighbourhood called Oak Park which had rolling hills, something the Charlotteans didn't like; they wanted land "flat as a pancake".

In Toronto the ravine lots were treasured so Lee She asked Curt to drive through the Oak Park neighbourhood again. Once they passed the curved brick entry walls, Lee popped out of the sunroof with the video camera and began taping the view of the beautiful houses. She exclaimed to the camera that they could have any of these mansions for much less than the price of their little house in the Beaches. She just looked around her in wonder and realized that she couldn't wait to move here, into the warmth and security of this well planned and welcoming city. This was where she wanted to live!

Chapter 24 - Doors & Windows

When the couple returned to Toronto, they were in an excited mood especially when several firms made offers to Curt including the ability to sponsor him for a work visa. In order to satisfy the requirements of the H2B visa, the firm would be required to post the job position open for the entire company to prove that the professional was filling a unique position that another American could not. The couple began telling their friends of their plans to immigrate and how everything was falling into place. Their friends only shook their heads and questioned the wisdom of this decision. Weren't they afraid for their children, to grow up in such a violent place and worried about their own safety.

The incredible amount of crime, gun violence and gang warfare that the US news put on the TV every day was daunting. Then there was the terrible health care system where people lost their homes if they couldn't pay their medical bills. Why would anyone want to go there and live amongst those aggressive, arrogant people! Curt and Lee ignored their concerns, since each had already lived in the States and didn't find it so scary. Curt soon accepted an offer from Piedmont Brokerage, hammered out terms of employment and then concentrated on the negotiations of the sale of his company more rigorously.

Lee broke the news to Joley, who was not pleased that this same situation was happening again to her. Lee promised to ask the immigration lawyer if there was any way she could come with them but she wasn't too confident that it would sort out, especially considering how tricky it was going to be for Lee and Curt to get their own visas. Lee then gave Laura an update on their progress, estimating when they might be ready to do this move. She would miss Laura, especially since it had been such a comfortable, reassuring experience working in her office.

Laura was so well organized, generous with her space, staff and equipment as well as encouraging about Lee's work. Lee had had looked forward to going to the office each day. She and Laura had an easy rapport, whether discussing children, husbands or clients and their friendship had deepened with the extra time they spent together. They were both extremely driven and hard working women and to have found a similar type of friend had helped Lee's confidence. Laura was one of the few people who were genuinely pleased for Lee about the move. Possibly since she knew more about her personal concerns than anyone else and also because her husband had a green card and they were also considering moving to the States one day. It was their dream too.

There was only one incident that occurred to mar Lee's enthusiasm for the move. One Saturday morning a couple days after their return from Charlotte, Lee was getting breakfast ready for the family when she saw little Sarah hovering around the breakfast area. She had grown into a beautiful, highly intelligent but sneaky little girl. She went through all the cupboards of the house, Curt's wallet and irritated her brother by running off with his toys until he burst into indignant tears which Lee had to sooth. Lee watched her little brown haired girl now with a smile on her face, so full of love for this small creature, as Sarah checked her father's position on the couch reading the newspaper, then her mother at the stove.

Lee could tell that she was up to something so she kept an eye on her with her peripheral vision. This time, Sarah's goal was the house keys. Lee hid hers but Curt left his on the side table until he was ready to leave the house. The little girl quietly snuck up to the table and lifted the set into her palm then sprung to go up the stairs. Lee stopped her escape with a stern voice asking that she return the keys right away. The little girl, with defiance held the keys behind her back and replied.

"I don't have any keys"

Lying was the one trait that Lee could not condone so she asked again for the keys to be returned. Sarah refused so Lee said.

"I saw you take them sweetie, please do not fib to me. It is very important"

Meanwhile Curt had picked up on this incident and got up off the couch to see what was being done for a reprimand. He asked Sarah himself if she had his keys, and while her eyes grew large at this unexpected turn of events, she once again said no. Lee was obviously not being forceful enough in his mind, so Curt grabbed Sarah's arm from behind her back and found his keys in her hand. Then he said that she had to be punished and this time it would be something Sarah would remember.

He was tired of her disobeying him; she had to respect her father. Lee was shaken with this sudden burst of anger and she was further routed to her spot near the stairs when Curt grabbed the child with one hand and dragged her into the kitchen to get a metal spatula out of the kitchen drawer. He then carried Sarah over to the couch, her panic spreading so that she was crying in fear. He growled through gritted teeth, as he yanked her pants down.

"You are going to behave now"

He began beating the instrument on the child's bare bottom, the smack of the metal on the bare skin and the screams from the girl broke Lee's hesitancy and she yelled for Curt to stop. He did not stop and Lee could see welts beginning to spring up from the pale smooth skin of her small daughter's buttocks. Then there was blood as well. Sarah's eyes were wide with terror and Lee saw small droplets of blood spraying into the air then dropping onto the carpet. The tool must have broken the child's skin.

When she realized that Curt was in such a state that he would not stop by her voice alone, she sprang into action. She moved in with her back to Curt and scooped the girl away from him, taking one blow to her shoulder. Then she backed herself against the stair wall and turned to face the raging man who was surprised by this interference. Tucking her daughter protectively within her arms Lee looked up at her husband with fury in her eyes as she prepared to defend both herself and her child.

"You are never to do that again," she hissed.

He squinted at the defiant woman with barely suppressed anger as he caught his breath but didn't approach any closer. However he did still hold the spatula up in the air with the intent of swinging it again, but he paused and regained his senses as he contemplated his next move. He didn't dare hit his wife since she would report it, but he would make sure both of them paid for this someday soon. So he lowered the spatula and turned to head out the back door.

Lee was extremely shaken after the incident with the beating and more frightened of Curt than ever. At first she had been worried that a worker at the French school might see the damage and report them to Social Services. She could lose her children if this happened, which tore at her heart, so she decided to hold Sarah back from attending class for a week. She was also worried what Jolie might think but the welts had reduced by the time Joley was back to watching the children and Lee explained that it was an accident that should not happen again. Joley just looked at her solemnly and nodded. Lee did not dwell deeper into what kind of man could lose control like that or what he would do next. Instead she concentrated on getting the house ready for sale and packing up their belongings.

The house was in very good shape so there was little to do except follow the instructions by the realtor. They had picked a top agent since they wanted it to sell quickly. Unfortunately the agent had suggested an asking price that matched what they had bought it for six years earlier, so they would lose all their sweat equity, renovation expenses and some of their parent's loan once they paid the broker fees. Curt insisted that it was the best they could do and the agent had said they would get more action and possibly a bidding war.

So they took her advice and listed the house. Lee had baked a Pillsbury dough bread roll just before the Open House to add the heavenly scent throughout the house, as the Realtor suggested. Then she took the children in a stroller through the park and along the beaches all afternoon while excited buyers viewed the house. A few offers came in the first night and soon they had accepted the best one but it had a closing date much sooner than they had wanted. Lee had to ask her aunt if they could live at her house in Brampton for a couple months. Aunt Mary agreed right away and was sincerely pleased about having her niece and family for a little while before they left the country. She would miss them since she hadn't had any family in the area before Lee moved there, and she loved the children. Andy and Sarah adored Aunt Mary as well for she was kind and gave them candy.

Once the deal was closed on the Beaches house and they had the money from the sale of the business Curt and Lee went ahead and put in an offer on a house in the Oak Park development. They first tried to purchase a four bedroom house that had been the showcase house for the neighbourhood and was cleverly decorated with built-in shelving, a full library and amazing landscaped private back yard. The disadvantage was that it was backing onto a very busy thoroughfare, and it had synthetic stucco exterior. The realtor phoned them to say that the house already had an accepted offer on it. Curt told her to find out the name and contact number of the buyers. He then called the buyers to offer more than their bid if they passed the house over to Lee and Curt. This scheme did not work, it only made them more determined to keep the house.

Lee, though disappointed, suggested they consider the less expensive house in the center of the development. She was asserting herself more, especially when she recognized Curt's lack of good judgment. It was an attractive stately house, with a red brick facade and the typical white columns on the front porch, set into an open yard that blended into the neighbours and appeared larger as a result. However the interior was not very attractive with an odd color scheme, damaged pre-finished wood floors from the last owner's dog and a cheap looking kitchen. Lee did a design and estimate and determined that she could renovate the interior to suit her family with very little money. So they put in a low bid, after learning that the last owner, a doctor, had been transferred to Seattle and he was anxious to sell. A deal was agreed to and the sale closed quickly once the mortgage was approved. Non-US citizens had to put down twenty percent for a mortgage and since they had paid back Curt's parents loan, they decided to use the remaining part of the loan from Lee's parents for this down payment.

Lee began to work on a new design for the house, keeping the renovations to a minimum. She found a contractor, through the realtor, to do the work before the family arrived. The floors would be refinished, walls removed and the entire house repainted. Lee would renovate the kitchen herself once they arrived. She had picked out hand painted Mexican tiles for the counters and selected a pale cream antiquing paint for the cabinets. She was excited about the move once again.

Curt wanted to be sure that everything was ready for their move, so he suggested that they cross the border and get the visas early in case there might be problems. The family all loaded themselves into the Jeep Cherokee and headed south to Niagara Falls. Once they crossed the long arched bridge to the immigration and customs booths on the US side, they told the officer that they needed to get H2B visas. He then put a yellow card under their windshield wiper and directed them toward the building to the right. Once in the INS parking lot the car was surrounded by very serious looking officers. The family all emerged, Lee pulling the diaper bag out from under the seat, just in case it was going to be a long process.

In the building, Curt and Lee with babies in tow, approached a desk with several officers and put forward their request for a H2B visa for Curt and visas for Lee as spouse and the children. A stern looking officer came to collect the papers that Curt held out, asked a few questions then retreated to his station. It took over an hour, with the children fidgeting but fairly good, and finally the officer returned, asked a few more questions about Curt's potential job and his education, since a degree was required for the H2B, then he went back to his desk. Lee felt like a criminal being readied for prison. She wasn't sure what she had done wrong but every glance from the other officers made her wish that she could melt into the walls or turn around and go back to Canada.

Finally another officer, a thin, dark haired man with a smile, approached the family. He seemed more amicable and so the couple chatted with him a bit about their relocation. He mentioned that they could renew the visa for three years but then Curt said that they were planning on staying longer. Lee winched since she knew that the requirement of the H2B visa was that the applicant did not intend to stay indefinitely. The officer's face grew hard and he briskly admonished Curt.

"I will pretend that you did not say that to me"

He then held out a paper, welcomed them to the United States and directed them on the route to Highway 75. Curt then said that they were actually headed back to Toronto, and again Lee winced, because the officer then grabbed the visa from Curt's hand and scolded him stating.

"You can only apply for this visa on your final trip into the US. Any trips back to Canada or any other country, once you have the H2B, require special permission".

Curt just stood there sputtering that he had a job and they had bought a house in Charlotte and they had sold their old house in Toronto. The officer then looked at the foolish fellow hard and said that they would just have to come back again and apply when they were ready to cross the border for the year. He muttered to himself.

"They are lucky they had gotten me instead of the one of my fellow officers or they would never be crossing the border again"

Red faced Curt lead the small group back the car and across the bridge.

When the family had moved into Aunt Mary's house, Lee had to commute into the city with the children an hour and a half each direction in order to drop them off at the French school or Joley's new apartment then head into work at Laura's office. One morning in November while driving into the city on the Queens highway that ran along the lake, they were stuck in bumper to bumper traffic when Andy got sick, throwing up all over the back seat. That smell then prompted Sarah to toss her breakfast and soon the car was a quagmire of heavy nauseous smells and liquids. Lee got out of the car to retrieve a box of wipes from the trunk and spent the rest of the time in the traffic jam, cleaning off the children, their car seats and the rest of the car, with the windows open to the cold fresh air. She would be happy to leave this.

Curt meanwhile, went into Boulevard every day where he continued as President, as per the sales agreement, until they left the country. Ned would then be made President and continue in that capacity for a minimum of a year. The new US parent company was motivated to keep Ned with them, since they did not have any other representatives in Canada, so they increased his salary as well. Ned had been pleased with the monetary windfall of the company sale and the promotion, so he didn't seem to mind losing his portion of ownership. Lee again was grateful that such an easy going fellow had been Curt's partner.

At Lee's own family business, Steward Packaging, there were problems in the Windsor plant. The Big Three car company, the main customer for this plant, had decided to cut down the number of packaging companies they used and this was after they had already told all suppliers that they had to take a forty percent cut in pricing for all future business. Steward packaging had scrambled and changed their services from inclusive to a la carte. The company survived the cut mostly because Steward had no debt to carry, unlike many other companies. Lee's grandfather William had a policy of only buying what he could afford, not borrowing from the bank and this had carried over to the next generation and it is what had saved the company many times.

After nervous anticipation, the Steward plant was chosen to continue as a supplier, while the unselected companies, some quite old and established, loyal to the customer for generations, folded shortly after the announcement. The Steward plant got even busier and had to expand into the entire three hundred thousand square feet of the old Brandon Machinery building on Lauzon Road that the family had purchased. The challenge with this new influx of work was that they had to hire many new full time people. The company always had temporary workers since it was unpredictable how much work would come in on the tractor trailers each week. They even provided an office in the plant for the supervisor for this section of the labor force. The family was known as a fair employer and they were hard workers themselves, since the younger generation often labored shoulder to shoulder with the rest of the staff. The new group of full time workers at Stewards however, did not have time to understand the bonus structure, flexible work schedule and complimentary coffee and snacks, before the union got their tentacles into them. It turned out that many of the new employees were union sympathizers, possibly sent to infiltrate this family business that had been immune to union organizing for over sixty five years.

Once in place, these instigators began to spread unrest and union propaganda. When an interest in union organization was expressed by the workers, according to Lee's mother, the management of a business in Canada was not allowed to address the employees about it until after a union vote occurred. Unions in Windsor were also known to be less reasonable than the ones in the United States, so with their hands tied, the family could only watch as misinformation was fed to the employees, incompetent leaders were chosen to represent them and unreasonable expectations were promoted by the union. Soon the leaders organized a vote, on scrapes of paper so no one had to show their inclination, and the union was voted in. Their first task was to go on strike. Unrealistic demands were leveled at the company, for increased wages, removal of all temporary workers and the establishment of swing shifts instead of fixed shifts. The company knuckled down to negotiate, offering the items that they thought they might be able to afford, but there was no movement on the union side. Instead they shut the plant and set up pickets.

Steward Packaging tried to function, but there were threats to office staff, blockage of driveways and turning away of trucks. Office staff could not join the union, so they had to go to work each day, but it was stressful not knowing if the union would allow them to enter the building. The family finally had to hire police to ensure the safety of the office staff and family. The Big Three client grew frustrated and gave Steward's a date that the plant had to be back up and running. The family offered to open the company books for the union to inspect, to demonstrate that there was not enough profit to give the full amount of raises demanded without bankrupting the company. None of the union representatives had enough education or understanding of accounting to decipher the books, so they refused this offer and stood firm. They had to prove to the workers that they could bully the company and get what they had promised.

The workers got the raise they asked for, which mostly helped cover the new union dues they were all required to pay, but they also got the swing shift. This type of work schedule was meant to rotate people through each of the three shifts of the day every two weeks, so no one only had the less desirable night shift, but instead it caused great difficulties for the workers. They could not establish a regular home life and single mothers were especially hard hit as they tried to organize babysitting or daycare around a changing schedule. Others, who had previously signed up for the night shift so that they could alternate in the care of a child or parent with their spouse, were also scrambling to readjust their lives.

After the first year of the union, which had forced Steward's books into the red, the family had to discuss whether they would have to close the plant. In January the union took that decision out of their hands. The workers were instructed to go on strike again, even though many were disheartened by then from the last strike. They couldn't afford the lost wages of another strike, but worse, the client had decided that they had enough as well. The Big Three client decided to move all packaging out of Canada and back to the States and Steward's lost all of their contract work.

Most of the five hundred employees of Steward Packaging had to be laid off. Some of those original workers, who had been with the company for decades, would have a very hard time finding another job in Windsor, especially with the recession. Steward Packaging became a shell of a company, doing small amounts of piece work as it came available and subletting the rest of the plant. The long heritage of the business steadily supporting the family and its employees came to an end.

Chapter 25 – Brick Veneer & Ties

When the moving date arrived in early December 1993, Lee and Curt packed up the car and headed, with some trepidation, across the border to get the visa again. Everything went smoothly this time though, and the family left their homeland and headed south to Charlotte to introduce their young children to life in the States. Lee still did not have a job when they settled into the new house but she was busy researching day cares and schools, getting familiar with new types of grocery stores and shops as well as sending out more resumes.

A couple of the biggest bonuses of this move turned out to be the return to the imperial system of measurement, Canada had gone metric, and the extended hours that stores stayed open. In Canada, there were few stores open on Sundays or late on the other week days, so the 24/7 grocery store was a huge benefit when Lee ran out of diapers or milk. The people of the area were also surprising friendly as well. Neighbours stopped in with welcome baskets of fruit and baked goods. They brought lists with the days that garbage was picked up, the streets were cleaned and the neighbourhood Christmas Party occurred. When Lee and Curt sat out in the Adirondack chairs in front of the house in the wonderful sixty degree weather, the neighbours drove by and honked in amusement at the silly Canadians.

"Its winter you crazy people," they called out.

Then one day, as Lee driving back from shopping, she approached her driveway and saw that it was blocked by a massive brown Cadillac. She proceeded to maneuver her car around the well cared for antique and continued down her sloped driveway. After getting out of the car and extracting the children, she turned to look up toward the street where the driver of the Cadillac had gotten out and stood silhouetted with arms outstretched. The woman was in a long fur coat with white running shoes peeking out of the bottom, and her hair was lit bright red from behind by the setting sun.

"Welcome to Charrrrrrrlotte," she drawled in a heavy southern accent.

This was Eve Milton, Lee's new neighbour who lived directly across the street in the large imposing grey stucco house. She was a seventy year old widow of Jewish descent, who had been a diamond merchant with her husband for many years. They were originally from

Poland but had lived in Czechoslovakia for years before escaping to the United States just before WWII and changing their name to blend in the melting pot. Her house was up a hill with a long set of steps to get to the front door, but she welcomed everyone and kept cookies for the children who visited. She spoke multiple languages and had traveled all over the world. She told extraordinary tales, with the enthusiasm of a life well lived, which enthralled Lee. Her house was filled with valuable antiques including oriental screens, oil paintings by European masters, Dutch blue delft pottery and delicate paper thin English china. She told Lee the story of traveling to Beijing to bargain with the clever Chinese merchants, who could also speak many languages but would hide this knowledge so they could listen in on their adversary's conversations.

One time when Eve and her husband were in negotiations with a Chinese man, they tried switching languages to communicate with just each other but each time it was clear that the gentleman was following their discussion. So finally they switched to Yiddish, at which the man started gesturing and insisting that they stop speaking something that he didn't understand. She told stories of how her house had been hit with lightning twice and how she was sure there had been a bobcat in her back yard one evening. Curt scoffed at these stories and called Eve an "Old bat" even though she as the first to sign up with Curt as a customer. But Lee found the stories endearing and she enjoyed the woman's company. She gave Lee wonderful advice and wise sayings, such as "Friends are like elevators, they can take you up or they can take you down". She was also one of the first people to gently warn Lee about her husband's poor choices when selecting stocks for his customers and his tenancy to move the stocks around in order to make more commission.

After Eve's warning, Lee began to pay more attention to what her husband was trying to sell to their new friends and neighbours. She was concerned that they might lose money as Eve had and she didn't want to compromise their friendships. Before she took any action though, she had decided to look over their previous year tax return a little closer. The preparation of their return was something that she had just handed over to Curt to do and signed where he told her. As she checked the columns of figures closer, she silently wished her father had given her more thorough instruction in his field of expertise. Then she noticed a page for declaration of losses and saw that it was filled out in a section for a large five figure sum in stock losses. Lee was shocked since she had no idea he had even invested any of their money in the market let alone lost such an amount.

While she decided not to bring this loss up with Curt, it would just start an argument, she did want to protect their new friends. That evening, she suggested to Curt that he avoid doing business with their neighbours but he laughed at this idea. He had cultivated the trust and friendship of a doctor who lived across the street, Greg Sandor, and Curt was using him to meet other doctors to recruit as clients. Greg was an attractive and kind natured fellow so he didn't seem aware of Curt's motive for the friendship or chose to ignore it. He had an athletic home maker wife nicknamed Slim, the daughter of a local minister and Lee enjoyed their friendship.

The couple had taken Lee and Curt to their first fish camp, a popular local restaurant with fried food. In fact, most of the families on their street came along caravan style and drove the forty five minutes across the city to this white concrete block structure with the long line of people outside waiting to be seated. Lee had first assumed that the food had to be excellent but once they were inside she saw the piles of greasy fried fish and oysters at the other tables and dismissed that assumption. This was a southern tradition that they had just been introduced to by their new friends and Lee was worried that these same people might now be betrayed by her husband.

While Curt was out trying to make new contacts and sign up clients, Lee could barely get herself dressed in the morning before being overrun with maternal and household duties. She was exhausted each evening but her mind was not being stimulated and she was bored during the day. She needed some adult interaction or a job. In Canada all the women she knew worked outside of the house but in their Charlotte neighbourhood, many of the wives seemed to be stay-at-home-moms who spent their free time volunteering at the schools, the Junior League or just playing tennis at a club. Lee also decided to volunteer and join a club, but the club she joined was the Women in Construction where she eventually became the chairman and helped run a city wide drafting competition. The volunteer work she did was at the Thomas Home for abused children.

At the Home, Lee was matched with two children to tutor each week. One child was a thin sweet African American girl with cigarette burns up her arms, apparently from her mother. She also suffered from a mild form of mental retardation, which Lee guessed may have also been from beatings and abuse by the mother as well. The other child was a sullen, distrustful boy, who wouldn't sit near her as she read to him or looked over his work. She brought treats for each of the children and while the little girl became affectionate and trusting, the little boy stayed far away.

These children all had to have extensive therapy, but they were so damaged Lee wondered if it they would ever be able to function in society. Lee would sit in the classroom of eight children, next to her student, while the young teacher and her assistant attempted to do their best to educate them. They were a disconnected bunch with little sense of decorum, too caught up in their own inner torments. Their pain and hurt painted the walls, the desks and crept into the air of the room. Lee was affected by it as well as it entered her lungs and she was pulled down into a sad helplessness.

During one visit to the Home, while Lee was in the classroom bent over her young ward's notebook, a tall girl in the back row suddenly stood up and in a fit of uncontrolled anger, attempted to pick up her desk to throw it across the room. She screamed as she pulled at the heavy desk, her face contorted in fierce hard edges and strained muscles. Guards had to be called in to wrap the girl in a straightjacket, and then drag her down the hall to the padded "quiet room". Lee couldn't understand what had triggered the fit and was surprised that this kind of room really had to be used. She was mesmerized by this bizarre situation. It was the kind of scene that you saw in a movie, not real life. She asked the teacher what would happen to the girl and Lee was told that she would be held in the room until she calmed down. Then the therapist, who arrived the next day, would spend some time with her to again try and sort out her many problems. This was said in an almost bored tone, as though a disruption like this happened all the time.

It was frustrating to Lee to stand back and watch rather than help in a more significant way but she had no training and she had not been allowed to see the children's files. She had undergone the required background check by the Royal Canadian Police and the intimidating police fingerprinting by the US police, in order to be able to have access to the children's files but she was ignored. The home had lost its director and the temporary director in place was not very qualified or organized. In this transition, the volunteers were being overlooked in order to deal with more critical issues.

Then one day Lee did get a call from the temporary director but it was not what she had been expecting. He introduced himself, even though they had meet a few months before, and he explained, trying to stifle a laugh, that Lee's sponsor child had been found to have lice. He suggested that she disinfect her home then quickly hung up on her. Lee was hurt by the callous way he had given her this news but she immediately began vacuuming, washing sheets and towels and headed to the drug store to purchase medicinal shampoo for everyone. Curt laughed at her as well when he found out, until he realized that he was susceptible to getting the nasty bugs himself. Then he pushed for her to quit the volunteer position. He pointed out that Lee had never been allowed to do much despite her efforts and she should pay more attention to her own children instead of kids who were too messed up to fix.

Lee was not happy with his implication that she wasn't already doing the best for her children. This criticism from a man who rarely paid attention to them himself and never attended their school functions or birthday parties, but she didn't say anything. She believed that she was doing a good job with her children, certainly compared to what she saw at the Home but that was not a fair marker. At the Home she saw the needy, sad red haired boy desperate for attention, who sat on the ground close to her legs at recess, or the one who whimpered uncontrollably or the scared wide eyed girl who was brought in by the police hugging a teddy bear, and her heart went out to all of them. Lee had never been aware of this kind of situation in Canada. It must exist in that country too but she didn't know where they put the young victims or if it was just worse here in the United States.

An afternoon shortly after this, Lee dusted off a business suit, checked for spit up on the shoulders and headed off to attend an Women in Architecture luncheon. This monthly event took place in an elegant private dining room of a downtown restaurant and it attracted both male and female architects, landscape architects, interior designers and business women. Lee entered the space, paused and breathed in the smells of business with pleasure. It was new paint, wood polish and the rich scents of roasted meat and garlic. She took in the attractive dark wood paneling, low lighting and the thick patterned carpet as she wove between tables and groups of suited patrons toward the back room. She found her name tag in a table and then joined a group already clustered in the center of the room. As the women adjusted to her presence, they began asking her questions such as where was she working. Lee told them that she hadn't found a job yet. One woman quickly exclaimed.

"Cheryl's company is hiring and they need senior architects"

Then she tipped her head toward a tall blond woman in a navy suit next to her. Cheryl stepped over to shake Lee's hand while offering a broad smile. She mentioned that her boss had probably buried her resume in a huge pile that he had on his desk, without even looking at it. She promised to retrieve it from the stack and point it out to Stavros Theopolis who has the head of retail division of Scope Architects. The event then moved into the presentation about the proposed new South End light rail commuter line that private groups were promoting for Charlotte. The line was to run from the south suburbs into the uptown along part of the abandoned Norfolk Southern rail line once the company came to an agreement with the city. Lee left the group afterwards with envy that they all had jobs to rush off to, and headed back to pick up her children at preschool.

The next morning, Lee got a call from Stavaos in which he requested that she come in for an interview the following day. Lee was excited to finally have an interview, even though she knew that the job would probably be a lower position than she had held for a long time. The following day Lee dressed in her suit again, dropped off the children after giving them long hugs and kisses then headed downtown. She parked in the employee parking lot for the firm and went up to the reception area in the two storey red brick building. Stavros, a stocky dark haired man with a determined stride and a scowl came into the waiting area after a few minutes. A large forced smile broke on his swarthy face as he spotted Lee and approached her with an outstretched hand.

Stavros then graciously directed Lee to a small glass walled office, where he got right to the point. He told her that Cheryl had recommended her for a job. He had then reviewed her resume and determined that she was well qualified. He asked a few of the standard interview questions then mentioned that they were hiring project managers if she was interested. As he said this, he looked up to check her features to determine how she had taken this. He detected a slight eagerness, which helped him choose his position on a salary. The wage he offered was less than he had given to the men applying but Lee didn't know this. It was also half of what she had been earning in Canada but she was no longer a partner and she was in a new country with lots to learn. She then explained that she needed the company to sponsor her with a letter of employment so she could get a work visa, and when he agreed, they shook hands on the deal. She was to start the job as soon as she could get the visa.

Lee's parents paid for her and the children to fly to Detroit where they picked them up and drove to Windsor for a quick visit and before re-crossing the border for her visa application. Her mother was thrilled to see the children who had grown so much since their previous visit. Andy was tall for six years old, with blond curly hair, dimples in his fair skinned face and bright green eyes. Sarah was a darker wiry little girl with beautiful wide set round eyes, a button nose and mischievous smile. They were both highly intelligent and well behaved, for which Lee was grateful but took little credit out of modesty. Lee always took advantage of their trips to see family as a time for her and the children to do adventures together. They went to carnivals, amusement parks, rode ponies, went boating and to the movies. She loved her time with them, though physically tiring, but everything they did fascinated her. She felt incredibly lucky to have such beautiful children and fearful that something might happen to them.

So she tended to be very protective, always holding their hands through parking lots or crossing streets and making sure that they had life jackets on before they stepped onto the dock to go boating. She had been having severe anxiety dreams about one of them falling into the black water and disappearing before she could reach them or a house collapsing on them and she couldn't get them both out. Sometimes she would wake up at the most fearful point in the dream, shaking and in a cold sweat, sure that it had really happened. In her parent's house though, the dreams and nightmares, had stopped and she was able to sleep deeply.

Curt had called once but she had not thought of him much during the visit. It was a relief not to be under his scrutiny and constant criticism. She felt safe here under her parent's roof as she hadn't for a long time. Finally it was time to go back and Anne drove her to the tunnel, where they were motioned to pull over into the parking near the immigration office on the US side. Officers stood guard over the car while Lee went in to get her work visa. She breathed a huge sigh of relief when it went smoothly and then joined Anne and the children in the car to continue to the airport.

Lee arrived at Scope on her first morning and was given a brief tour of the office then taken to a large interior room lined with work stations by an apologetic colleague, who explained that this had been the materials library but they were growing so fast they had to put cubicles in it. She was assured that it was temporary. The colleague then showed her the basics of starting the computer, the password and elementary commands then left. Lee waited for a little bit, assuming that someone would come over to introduce her to the company standards or give her a project to work on but no one came by. She then began to play with the computer, accessing its software programs and trying to understand how to use the Auto CADD. She had been hand drawing her designs to pass to the draftsmen in her last firm and had not worked on the computer much herself.

As Lee was punching the keys, in an attempt to figure it out by logic, she thought that she heard a stifled sob behind her. She stopped and listened again then leaned around the adjacent cubicle and saw a young girl with her head in her hands and her back shaking. Lee touched her shoulder and the girl started then looked up. Her pretty face was streaked with tears and her makeup smeared under large dark eyes. Lee gave her a reassuring smile and asked her what was wrong. The girl told Lee that she didn't know how to work this computer and she was afraid to ask anyone. She and the other two girls had been brought in after graduating from the community college and they had been told to start drawing but none of them had ever used a computer before.

They had asked for help and been told that the printing company salesman would give them preliminary tutoring, but he had left. Lee introduced herself then citing little knowledge herself, pledged that she would help as much as she could. When the other two girls heard this, they left their computers and leaned in to hear what Lee might have to offer. Lee recalled all the CADD drafting techniques that she had been exposed to at Adams as well as what she had figured out earlier, and gave a rudimentary lesson in computer drafting. When each one had tried the technique with success, they thanked Lee then immediately got down to work, faces toward the bright screens, right hands clicking away on the mouse and left on the key boards. They each needed this job badly.

As Lee returned to her desk, a large man in a disheveled white shirt, loose tie and dark wrinkled pants stood in the center of the room and called her name. When she answered, he strode over and handed her a sketch showing a site plan in Madison, Wisconsin. He asked if she could have the drawing in CADD done and faxed to the client's number before a scheduled call at two pm. As he spoke, his breath wafted over to Lee and she picked out the heavy sent of liquor. While she turned to glance at the clock to see that it was already eleven o'clock, the man disappeared. Lee shook her head then went back to work on trying to figure out drawing on the computer. At one forty five she printed her work and found a secretary to help fax the plan. Then she went to find the sloppy man to give him a copy as well. The sloppy man had to be one of the senior employees so she checked the cubicles along the windows and found him in a middle one, leaning on his desk while talking into the phone. Lee slipped the site plan onto the desk in front of him then turned to leave. The man then grabbed her arm and yanked her back into his cubicle. As he held her arm he spoke into the phone.

"I have the person who drew the plan right here. I am sure that she can tell you about the time it takes for re-zoning and permitting in Madison"

Lee was surprised as he handed her the phone since she had no idea the site needed to be rezoned or permitting periods for Wisconsin. She stammered into the phone that she would verify everything right away and call him back. The sloppy man had been unprepared and let her take the fall. It was incredibly unprofessional and she was tempted to just walk out. She was being treated as a draftsman but labeled project manager. She later found out that many architects in this office were expected to do all their own drafting as well as design work. She also discovered that architects in the United Sates had given away many of the responsibilities and subsequent fees to civil engineers or independent project manager consultants who usually had no architecture degree and sometimes very little construction experience either. She had quite a bit to learn about this system.

A couple days after the site plan incident, the sloppily dressed man was fired. He had come in drunk again and this had been the last time to be tolerated. Stavros had told Lee this as he stood in front of her cubicle and announced that she was now in charge of the Harry & Tom grocery store expansion working drawings. They were going to be doing extensive renovations to the existing stores and building many more new stores each year. Lee was going to be given a team of draftsmen and they have a section of their own. She asked if the sloppy man was to be helped into a Rehab program but Stavros laughed.

"Don't you worry about him. Just start moving your things into the empty executive office around the corner."

It had formerly been occupied by a Vice President of the firm and it was between the CFO and the President's office. This was a step up she wryly thought to herself as she entered the twelve by twenty foot room with a large sheet of glass facing the park next door.

Shortly after Lee's move to the office, Stavros brought in a sweet, young blond man to join her production team. Nate Randall was originally from Ohio, a trained draftsman with a certificate from a community college. They were given two new stores to draw up as their assignment with very tight deadlines. Lee quickly outlined responsibilities with Nate and they set to work in an agreeable manner. They were both surprised the first Friday morning of their employment when the entire staff was called into the atrium for a prayer session. "You have got to be kidding" Lee thought as she watched everyone bow their heads as the President, mounted on the stair landing above, gave a sermon. She had already heard the rumor that this guy was having an affair with a girl in the graphics department so the hypocrisy of the situation made it hard for Lee to keep a straight face. "The Bible Belt" she thought wryly.

After a few weeks a third person was added to their team, making the once spacious room seem much smaller. Devin McCoy, a recent architecture graduate and world traveler, came complete with a dry sarcastic wit and unconventional attitude. He was so urbane and charming that Lee could hardly connect him with the Hatfield McCoy legend that he claimed a family connection. It was a tight fit in the room but the three eventually got along so well that their laughter would eco down the hall until the receptionist came in to reprimand them.

"This is a serious office where everyone is expected to work hard and not fool around," she scolded after she had thrown open their door.

This sent the group into more hysterics until the woman turned in a huff and went back to her desk. They certainly understood about the working hard. The draftsmen and architects who were running the projects tended to put in over 70-80 hours a week but they did not necessarily declare all the hours on their time sheets. It was a matter of pride that their jobs not go over budget with too many billable hours. Besides, the firm wouldn't pay overtime anyway. They were offered comp time instead, but the employees could never afford to take the time off due to deadlines. So the hours for architects were extremely long, vacation limited and the pay was low. What a profession Lee mused!

Chapter 26 - Poly Barrier

At home, Curt was becoming even more erratic. He had started drinking heavily after he got in late from work and barking orders to everyone in the house. Sometimes he didn't get home until everyone else was asleep and Lee wondered what he was up to when his clothes smelled of smoke, beer and the slight whiff of perfume. Any kind of liquor that was in the cabinet was poured into the largest glass Curt could find, mixed and tossed back while he sat alone watching TV. The children were afraid to go near him so they stayed in their rooms or near their mother. Then Curt began to bring home expensive organic steaks and announced that he was on a protein only diet now. Lee and the children were still vegetarian so Curt barbequed his own meat on the grill which he ate in front of them. His criticisms became more biting and hurtful while his voice grew louder. At one point he was talking down to Lee so much that she pointed out to him that her IQ was actually over 140 and not 20. A couple days later she found a book in the living room, face down on the side table entitled "How to Increase your IQ" which made her laugh in spite of her inclination to find it pitiful.

One day while Lee was at the top of the driveway watching the children ride bikes, Greg and Slim joined her to chat. When Curt, who was trimming bushes, saw them he came over to the group began to talk about a Commitment Keepers meeting that he was attending with Greg. Slim then turned to Lee.

"You know what those meetings are all about, don't you?"

When Lee shook her head, curious now, Slim continued.

"They talk about men being superior to women and gays being an abomination".

"You must be kidding," replied Lee surprised.

"Listen to the tapes yourself," Slim said.

"They have tapes?" she sputtered.

Lee turned to Curt and asked him if he actually listened to tapes. When he acknowledged having tapes, she asked to borrow these to listen to as well. He embarrassedly told her that the tapes were in his car and she was welcome to listen to them. She immediately went to the garage and found a sleeve of ten tapes in his car and one in the tape player. She pulled out the one in the player and transferred it to her car.

The next day after she had made the children's lunches, dropped Andy off to school and Sarah to the day care, she listened to the tape as she drove to work. At first she wasn't sure what she had actually heard and rewound the tape to play over. Slim was correct; the tape had started with the concept that women were put on this earth to be men's helpers.

"Women are not inferior beings, since they were after all, made of one of Adam's own ribs, but they were also not meant to be equal. Women were destined to be helpmates. Men should be responsible for them so they don't have to work outside the home and in return, their wives will be a great support for their success," the commentator enthused.

It went on to warn men to stay away from displaying any "female traits"– these had to be suppressed. It was against the laws of nature to have men behaving like women, being soft, emotional and worst of all, fornicating with each other. She was late for work as she sat in the parking lot listening, but she couldn't believe what she was hearing. When she finally entered the building and sat down at her desk, the boys asked what was wrong and she told them about the tapes. Devin made a remark warning her about cult-like religious zealots and cave men types while Nate just said that it didn't sound like the real Commitment Keepers agenda. They were just supposed to encourage men to honor their promises to their wives and children.

Lee thought long and hard on the way home that night and by the time she had picked up the children and pulled into the garage she was prepared. She gave the children their nightly bubble bath then wrapped their clean pink bodies in thick towels before transferring them into their warm pajamas. She brought them downstairs to say goodnight to their father then read them a story in their beds, as she did every night until they fell asleep. She kissed their soft cheeks and brushed aside their fringe of bangs before she left their rooms. When she got back downstairs, Curt had been through several glasses of liquor but appeared to be focused as she spoke to him.

"I listened to those tapes and I have to tell you that I think they are harmful and wrong. I will not give you an ultimatum but I will say that if you continue to be involved with a group like this version of Commitment Keepers, or whatever they call themselves, we will have a serious problem in our relationship"

When she had finished Curt just said that perhaps she should come to meet the leader of their group to debate their beliefs. This group included a lot of doctors who were good for potential business clients and contacts so he didn't want to quit. She just quietly replied.

"My rights and equality are not debatable" and she left the room.

It was shortly after this that she got a call from Jamie Bradley. She was surprised but very pleased to hear from him. He was such a good person and he was from a period when she had been a valuable coworker, admired designer and this reminder made it hard for her to keep her voice steady without breaking as they talked. He asked how it was going in the States; if the construction business strong and could he find work if he wanted to immigrate as well. She told him that everything was going fine, work was busy and the Charlotte area was booming in the construction field. She gave him some names of contacts for work and promised to keep in touch.

Lee knew that she would not be able to keep in touch - Curt would forbid it and start accusing her of devious intentions if he even knew about the call. Afterwards she sat for a long time, trying to sort out how so much could have gone so wrong. All her dreams about moving across the border had come true but she was still not happy. She loved being in the United States, with the aggressive entrepreneurial business mentality, the friendly people and the beautiful warm weather in the South but the pieces were not fitting together yet. The round puzzle piece was trying to fit in the square hole again.

Then Lee got a call from Bob West, the president of Whitmore Architects. He had the resume that she had sent out a few months ago and wanted to talk to her about a job offer. They were looking for someone of high qualifications to head up a new Commercial division for the firm. She said that she could meet right away and the next afternoon she was in the modern lobby of the sleek metal and glass building shaking hands with Bob. He was a distinguished man, with white hair combed carefully to the side, in a crisp white shirt tucked into pressed suit pants. He had a precise way of speaking that drew Lee's attention and her respect.

She was given a tour of the building, which Bob owned, and introduced to various partners as well as the director that she would be working with for marketing this new division. The salary they offered her was higher than what she was making at Scope and they added a percentage of the profit. Lee was excited about this chance to get back to a position similar to where she had been in Canada so she accepted immediately.

Nate and Devin were disappointed when they heard that she was leaving them but they weren't surprised. Devin had been asked by Stavros to attend a meeting with the Harry & Tom client to go over the working drawings. This didn't make sense when Lee was the project manager until he discovered that the client didn't want any women involved in the project. When he told Lee this, she just said that it confirmed her decision to leave and she wished him luck in taking over.

Devin then proposed that they meet once a week for lunch to keep in touch. Devin's wife owned a popular restaurant on High Blvd so they chose it as their lunch gathering spot. Lee was touched by this and the trio began a tradition of regular lunch meetings once Lee joined Whitmore. Eventually after a year Nate had moved away but Lee and Devin would continue to meet for many years to compare experiences in architecture, travel and personal challenges, during which they cemented a lifelong friendship.

As the kids were getting older, Lee noticed that they needed a play room to take their friends for TV and games, away from the adults. Lee decided that she could build a playroom in the crawlspace if she dug out a couple feet of dirt and poured a slab. She had done this in Toronto for clients and she didn't see why it wouldn't work here in Charlotte. She checked the foundations to ensure that they all went down deep enough and consulted a structural engineer about removing certain brick columns. She then decided that the stairs down could be cut into the floor of the closet beneath the stairs to the second floor. She presented her plan to Curt who was skeptical but agreed to it especially when Lee said that he didn't have to pay for any of it if he didn't want to. He just insisted that a professional electrician check Lee's work if she was going to do the electrical herself as she had proposed. She agreed and soon she and the children were spending their time together under the house with shovels and the wheel barrow moving dirt up a ramp from the crawlspace to a depression under the deck. The children were enjoying helping their mother. Sometimes they helped her shovel dirt into the wheelbarrow and other times they just rode their bikes around while Lee did the digging. Curt remained upstairs and just continued to watch the television every evening by himself.

Lee was actually pleased with this arrangement since she didn't completely trust Curt around Sarah any more. The girl had been wary toward her father ever since the beating and wouldn't give him the kiss

-202-

on his cheek that he insisted on some days. At school when the teacher asked the children to draw a picture of their family, Lee noticed that the little bus Sarah drew had her mother, brother and all their pets in the windows but did not include her father. Curt had also been bullying Andy whenever he got a chance. The boy would be playing basketball with his friends and if Curt saw Andy wearing pants or a shirt that he didn't like, he would insist that the boy stop playing and go change immediately. Curt would further humiliate him by taunting him that he wasn't manly enough. Andy would wind up in silent tears as he was wrenched away from his friends for a variety of trivial reasons.

Curt wasn't any better around Lee either. When they went to a neighbourhood dinner party together he would make teasing and rude remarks about her basement efforts or her architectural work. He told her book club friends that she didn't really read any of the books. Sometimes he would simply disappear during a party without telling her where he was and then laugh when she finally found him outside with other guests or sometimes even at another house. He liked to see her discomposed, it amused him. These incidents only convinced her that she had to do what was best for her and the children, like building the basement play room, since Curt wasn't interested in their happiness. Lee also rationalized that if the children stayed with her in the basement after school then she could make sure they were safe from him.

It took months to complete all the digging but once they were down deep enough to allow for headroom clearance, Lee called a concrete supplier to bring a hose to pump concrete for the four inch slab. When the slab had set properly, she began to build the wood frame of walls on the ground and then swing them up into place against the block foundation wall. She expanded the existing door opening to allow for a new French door, making it a walk-out basement. She then rented a masonry saw to cut an opening for a new window facing the back yard. Lee started this cutting herself one Saturday and soon the air was filled with pink brick dust that spread over the entire neighbourhood.

When Curt saw the dust he became concerned that Lee was destroying the house so he went out to check her work. As he watched her cut the forth side of the window opening he noticed her arm was tiring of holding the heavy saw so he volunteered to finish the last cut. Lee was grateful as she handed over the saw but regretted it just as quickly when Curt turned to her.

"I will be glad to help you in this little project but you owe me. I expect some extra favors in the bedroom if you know what I mean, maybe with a special outfit or handcuffs" as he leered at her, his eye brow rose in an arch. Lee backed away, thoroughly repelled and feeling dirtier than the pink dust that coated her skin.

The next job was the wiring and Lee had gone over the books from her electrical classes in order to wire the three way switches for the lights properly and the outlets. She called in an electrical sub contractor to check her work, as Curt had insisted, and when the head of the company had reviewed the wiring, he offered her a job with his company. She laughed and thanked him for the compliment but she said that she already had a job. Besides it was not easy work twisting fingers into such tight places all day. When she told Curt of the fellow's offer for employment he didn't respond. He had thought that her wiring would have been a mess and need to be redone. He could not imagine that she would have done it correctly and he reminded himself to call the electrician and confirm her claim.

Now that the wiring was complete Lee and the children stapled the thick plastic vapor barrier on the studs then installed the heavy sheets of drywall. Andy was the one to help set the screws while Lee balanced the four by eight sheets. He enjoyed using the drill and set many of the drywall screws. Lee also taught Sarah to do it, holding her small hand steady on the drill as they both pushed. Once the screw was set deep into the board, the little girl's smile would light up her round face and she would look to her mother proud of her accomplishment. Lee then did the taping and millwork and they all painted the walls. It was not perfect, some of the mud joints were visible or the paint uneven but Lee and the children were very pleased with their work.

Once the pool table that Anne had given them was installed, along with an old couch and TV, the room became the most popular in the house. The neighbourhood children began coming to the basement door to ask to play with Andy and Sarah. Lee then moved the trampoline directly outside of that door so she could watch all the children while they played. Soon even Curt came down there and spent most of his time watching TV in the basement as well, in the cozy spot which the family had built without his help.

The basement was complete and Lee decided to relax a little. Work was not very busy since she was being introduced around Charlotte to all the heads of the big development companies but they didn't have any projects yet. The firm had also signed her up for a leadership course to further familiarize her with the area and people in positions of power. She had attended talks by the head of the airport, chairman of the Chamber of Commerce, visited the coliseum and listened to plans by the school board for improving the system. But the really interesting part of the class was the visit to the prison. She was to join a group going to the Spector Drive prison which was a minimum security facility. Lee had never even seen a jail or prison and she wasn't sure where these were located in Canada, but of course even that country had to have some criminals.

Crime was so low in Canada though, most likely due to the lack of guns, drug wars and poverty, that most Canadians were terrified of the violence in the US. The newspapers and television news programs blasted gory details of murders, muggings, robberies and rapes in America, competing with each other for the most devastating and dramatic of these events to boost ratings. Lee just refused to watch the TV, read newspapers or listen too much of the news on the radio and this allowed her to feel relatively safe. She was still cautious but her neighbourhood was a sanctuary of the middle class where home owners didn't always locked their doors. She was curious though how the people with fewer advantages in marginal neighbourhoods survived and what happened to those who were caught breaking the law.

On the day of her visit, Lee wore a baggy shirt and pants, pulled her hair into a pony tail and parked her car with the license plate facing away from the prison windows. She admitted to herself that she was a bit nervous as she walked to the door, imagining inmates watching her. In the entry, the leadership group was gathered for an introduction of the facility. An older uniformed guard, with sparse hair and a sagging belly, described the holding cells, the number of pods and the lifestyle. The current inmates were actually Federal prisoners with serious records even though this was a minimum security facility. The city was in the process of building a new federal prison near the court house downtown so these prisoners were being temporarily housed at Spector he explained. Lee's heart jumped and she scanned the room to check the number of guards around them. It didn't seem like enough but soon the group was being escorted through the facility.

Each pod they passed was configured with a security control desk in the center and the rooms radiating out around it. The doors to enter the pods were set so that one pair had to be closed and locked before the next set would open. Lee found that the painted block walls, bright florescent lighting, heavy wire glass doors and colorful but sparse furniture reminded her of a community college or high school environment as the group began moving through the building. "Interesting what that says about our society" she thought as she walked past large wire glass windows with views into classrooms of orange clad students. The prisoners got access to a variety of classes, a library, cable TV with limited stations, various workshops, one hour per day in an chain link enclosed outdoor court, and three meals a day. The guard explained that many of the prisoners also used their library time to research the law and became well versed enough to file law suits on their own. Lee had read that these law suits often clogged up the legal system with such frivolous issues such as a prisoner's complaint that his food was not hot enough. It seemed like an incredible waste of tax payer money and court time. Maybe the US should follow Canada on their restriction to frivolous law suits. There would be no more fake whip lash law suits any more, let alone prisoners suing about their conditions.

The guard lead the tour deeper into the facility past more classrooms which held many African American men with shaved heads in orange suits and some rather scary looking white men who stared straight at her with a fierce intensity that made her turn away. When they stopped in a corridor in front of one of these classrooms, Lee tried to squeeze into the back of the group and hide her name tag. She was amazed at the women who had dressed in tight clothing and flaunted their name tags on the chests while the prisoners filed past them.

Lee also watched the female prisoners go by, including one attractive young girl holding her extended belly as she walked, obviously far along in a pregnancy. Lee wondered if the girl had gotten pregnant before she had been admitted or after. They visited the health room where an older nurse explained that the staff did not have experience dealing with this harder type of criminals.

"They are unpredictable and dangerous in many ways. Over ninety percent of them are H1V positive or have full blown AIDS"

"My son is a guard here" she continued "and I worry about him since the prisoners throw feces and other mucus at the guards in an attempt to infect them"

Lee wasn't sure that the nurse was supposed to be saying these kinds of things to the visitors. It definitely made her even more nervous and they hadn't even gotten to the scariest image of the visit. At the end of the tour they came to a pod that was empty except for one large powerful but manic fellow, obviously deranged as he raced around a pod that would normally have held eight prisoners. He was like a rat in a cage as he ran up the metal stairs then across the top mezzanine balcony and down the other side before grabbing the phone off the wall and slamming it. He kept repeating this sequence the whole time the group watched and the young guard explained that this was the man who had been recently sentenced to death for strangling thirteen women. He wouldn't be with them long the guard hoped. "I have now seen pure evil" is what passed through Lee's mind as she watched his frantic race.

Chapter 27 – Air Space

One Thursday in February, Curt asked Lee to meet him in the den. Dread filled her as she entered the room and sat down. "This could only be bad news" she thought. Curt cleared his throat then explained that he was going to cut up their charge card and split finances from now on. She would have to get her own bank account, charge card and then contribute half of their expenses to a common joint account that he had already set up.

Lee was hit by surprise and needed a minute to comprehend what Curt was saying. Then she asked Curt to give her a little time to organize and get herself a new charge card. He confessed that it was too late and he had already cancelled their mutual card. Once again he had not consulted her but she held her temper as she faced him and told him that the arrangement was fine. He was slightly startled that she had not protested and his smug smile faltered momentarily as he leaned back in his leather chair. She turned to leave the room when an idea struck her. She realized that with this arrangement she would wind up paying for more of the household and children's expenses since she did all the shopping. She turned back to him.

"This will not be fair since I pay for all of the expenses for the children and the house"

Curt thought this over and replied.

"Just organize all the receipts and submit them to me and I will reimburse you for half"

Lee laughed at this and commented that it would just add more work for her in a day that didn't have enough hours in it already. Instead she just accepted that she would have to pay more than her share if necessary. Then she realized that he could now spend without restriction or her knowledge. He had gotten out of the chair and was going past her to the door when she stopped him with her words.

"I will need a post-nuptial agreement"

He turned back to look at her, squinting his eyes even more than usual to scrutinize her and cautiously said that would be fine. It was followed with a laughing snort as though he had just placated a child who had asked for something they would never get. Lee wasn't sure what had motivated this sudden split of finances until she saw the new computer and printer the next day in Curt's office. She had told him that they couldn't afford a computer when he mentioned wanting to buy a new one the week before. Now she knew the reasons behind Curt's latest surprise. This marriage was becoming a line of battle and Lee had to take action.

Lee recalled a magazine article she had read while waiting at her printers about a fellow who was considered the toughest lawyer in Charlotte. He had won more cases than any other lawyer despite his less than professional appearance. He was often seen in the office in jeans and a baseball hat over long grey hair. His favorite tactic was to starve out the wives of men who wanted a divorce by limiting their support and causing a lot of delays to the court decisions. This way the women became more pliable, especially the ones who didn't work, and often settled for less. Lee did not want to be on the other side of that firm, so she made an appointment with them the next day.

She was assigned to an associate by the name of Carol Rogers, an attractive dark haired woman in a black suit who stood when Lee was escorted into her office. When Carol sat down behind her desk, she began to question Lee, who was surprised by the woman's soft low pitched voice. But as the interview proceeded, Lee began to glimpse the intelligent and tough core in the woman. She soon felt confident about trusting Carol to handle this part of her life and they discussed writing the post nuptial agreement. Lee and Curt had already made a listing of all their furniture and possessions to cross the border so Lee just divided those up and added the list to the agreement to be drawn up. She been as fair as possible and she hoped that was good enough for Curt.

After her meeting with the lawyer, Lee next dealt with getting a charge card, which was not easy since it turned out that she had only signing privileges on Curt's card. As a result, she had no credit rating of her own in the United States. She was finally given a basic card to set up her accounts. Eventually she discovered that this new financial arrangement left her with more money than she had been using previously. It turned out that Curt had been spending more than his share so now Lee had the ability to invest in a retirement fund of her own and college funds for the children. She also treated herself to a new miter saw and she knew just where she could use it, to finish up the basement trim.

When Lee got the first version of the post nuptial agreement she gave a copy to Curt. He had told her that they would just use her lawyer since he trusted her and it would save money. He reviewed the document and said that it looked fine but he seemed hesitant to sign it. Instead he began to write apology letters to her which he would then leave on the bed. These notes usually said that everything was his fault because he had treated both her and the children so badly. He would agree to whatever she thought was best. Curt confessed that he should have believed in her abilities more and offered to pay for half of the basement work. He should have also recognized that she was contributing more than her share to everything in their lives.

Then one evening he caught her in the basement alone and asked her if she was mad at him for all that he had done. She was buoyed with hope at this approach and thought that maybe they could finally talk honestly and start to work out some of the ugly issues. So she sat down near him and told him that she wasn't mad but she was disappointed.

"I haven't had any strong feelings for you one way or another for some time. You have been very hard on all of us. We have problems to sort out in our marriage and it will take a long time but I am willing to do the work. The children need both of their parents so I am not going anywhere"

"Well, I love you and I will do whatever it takes to work things out," he said quietly and gently took her hand.

She smiled at him, with warmth and new hope in her feelings towards him. Then a child came running down the stairs and launched herself into Lee's lap. Lee hugged Sarah tight and she knew that the conversation was finished for now.

After this, Curt did an about face again, surprising her by saying that he had gotten his own lawyer and he wanted changes to the post nuptial. The lawyer he had picked was constantly rewriting and sending drafts back and forth so the process was delayed and Carol's billable hours went up. However, she liked Lee and felt sorry for her, so she tried to charge as little as possible. Meanwhile Curt became even more belligerent and hard on all of them again. The children cringed away from him and stayed close to their mother as much as possible.

Lee was still going into the office and found herself leaving later each evening in dread of being with Curt at the house until one day a teacher contacted her and asked her if there were any problems at home. Andy was suddenly not doing very well in class and she wondered if Lee had been traveling. The teacher knew how attached Andy was to his mother. She had never seen the father at the school and the boy never mentioned him so she didn't think that he could be of help. After this news Lee returned to picking up the children early since she did not want them to suffer in any way. She spent even more time with them, working at home, in hopes of deflecting the tension within the house. She didn't know what to do beyond protecting them as much as possible. So she signed the next draft of the post-nuptial just to get it out of the way.

While her personal life was in a shambles, Lee finally got a break in establishing the commercial division business at work. She was asked by one of the developers she had met to do a small retail building in the university area to the north of Charlotte. The challenge for this project was that Lee would have to get approval from the University Design Committee which had the Dean of the Architecture School and a professor of architecture as members. Fellow architects were the worst critics since they all believed that they knew the best design.

In order to prepare for the presentation, Lee had decided to do a rendering of the building design that would be even more realistic than an air brush or water color rendering. She looked for a way to use a photo of the site and render a building in place as with air brush, but on the computer instead. She consulted with the IT expert at the firm and he suggested that she try the software program Photoshop. She got him to order her a copy and it arrived right when she discovered that both her children had started to develop small red spots on their faces and bellies. Lee rushed them to the doctor who confirmed that they had chicken pox and they had to stay out of school for a week.

Instead of panicking, Lee decided to take advantage of the situation. She sat out on the deck while the children played on the swings or in the tree house and skimmed through the Photoshop user manual. Then she began experimenting on her laptop with the drawing techniques and soon she had produced a rendering with the desired effect. She returned to the office once the children were given the doctor's approval to go back to school, printed out the images in large format mounted them on foam core boards and she was ready for the committee.

The meeting was held in a university classroom with tied seating where various developers and other architects were waiting their turns to present. Their project boards were lined up along the wall but Lee kept her boards at her seat, covered from inspection. She watched the other architects presenting and realized that her boards were far more high tech which calmed her nerves a bit. She witnessed each project get torn apart and disapproved for various missing details or non-conformance. Finally she was called up to present and she lined up her foam core boards on the ledge facing the audience. Immediately several viewers leaned forward with interest and the architectural professor's mouth opened in surprise. She then began talking about the axis and viewing angles of the site, the practical issues regarding the parking then the building design, materials and details. The Dean challenged her on various trivial design items, which she successfully defended, before he reluctantly told her that the project was approved. She sincerely thanked the members of the committee and headed out of the room through the double doors with the boards tucked under her arm without looking back. She had made it into the corridor when she heard someone running behind and turned in surprise to see the professor of architecture catching up with her.

"Where did you come from?" he asked with incredulity as he approached.

"Canada," she replied with some amusement since she knew that was not what he was expecting.

"That was the best presentation we have ever seen!" he exclaimed. At which she thanked him, smiled, then she turned to continue down the hall. The professor watched her retreating form in admiration before heading back into the occupied room.

Lee did not know it at the time but the ramifications of this one presentation actually set the stage for the future success of her architectural practice in her new home city. Shortly after the University approval, Lee was wandering through the International Shopping Center Conference at the Charlotte Convention Center, when a tall man in a well cut suit spotted her and approached. He was pointing a finger at her as he came forward and she recognized him as a member of the audience during the University presentation. .

"You are good," he said staring intently at the trim young woman while she stumbled to say "Thank you".

"I will be calling you to do some work for me," he stated then turned on his heels and disappeared in the crowd.

Lee was pulling out a card from her wallet to give to the man but when she looked up, he was already gone. How odd she thought, but it was also exciting if he really was going to send some work to her. She told Curt about the encounter that night but he was only interested to know if the man had gotten her phone number then warned her that he probably had other things on his mind. She dismissed his comment and headed up to play with the children before tucking them into bed and reading them a story. When she returned downstairs, Curt announced that he had something to say to her. Her heart sank since this kind of pronouncement usually meant bad news for her.

"I have decided that I will move into the bonus room. I plan on having to work late at the office a lot"

Lee felt a wave of incredulity spread over her, though out of caution she didn't show any of this on her face. "What had happened to his great pledge to work on the marriage?" she thought. Instead she only said.

"I will abide by your decision if that is your choice, but if you want to attend marriage counseling to try to resolve our problems I would be glad to do it."

He rejected this with a sneer then left her to her thoughts. Secretly she was flooded with relief that she wouldn't have to tolerate his unwashed body smells, noxious flatulence and noisy snoring any more. She didn't know if the sexual demands of his body would also move with him but she would go along with whatever was required of her - she wanted to be a good wife. She had observed that many marriages were more like two people living as roommates, rather than loving and affectionate couples. She had also read that fifty percent of marriages had little or no sex within the relationship. Perhaps this occurred after many years with the same person from boredom or a loss of love. There were so many factors that were roadblocks to a successful and long term love. She had accepted years earlier that her marriage was just a shell of her original hopes but she could live her own life without separating or divorcing since she didn't want to do that to her children.

During the first week of sleeping alone, Lee was pleased to discover that her anxiety dreams had stopped. She was able to relax a little more and could fall into a deep contented sleep. She felt truly rested for the first time in years. While she appreciated this new privacy, the solitary also allowed for insecurities to sneak in. She began to think about how her body had faired during the pregnancies and if she was physically attractive any more. Laying in the big king size bed one night she made an assessment of it. Her hands followed her contours from her neck down to her hips and across the top of her breasts. She had softened and thickened but she was still in good shape.

Lee thought about how women were supposed to do self-examinations of their breasts so she methodically moved her hands to knead the tissue around the left one then the right. As her fingers explored the heavy part of the right one near her right arm pit, she suddenly felt a hard nodule. She paused, her mind slowly registering the unexpected discovery. She moved her fingers more intently to push and prod this intrusion, hoping that it would dissolve but she knew it was not going away so easily. It might just be a cyst filled with water she tried to convince herself but she began to worry and sleep eluded her until early morning, when exhausted she finally drifted off for a few hours.

The next day Lee went over to the neighbour's house to ask about doctors specializing in breast cancer. Slim had been diagnosed with breast cancer and after a year of treatment she had been declared cancer free. The woman, whose hair was still growing back from the chemotherapy, recommended the female doctor at the Breast Medical Office as a most compassionate and skilled specialist. Lee had never heard of it but she called their office and after describing her concern, was able to get an appointment quickly. The receptionist warned her that they did not take insurance and the appointment would cost several hundred dollars but at that point Lee didn't care what it cost, she just felt lucky that it wasn't too exorbitant.

On the day of her appointment, Lee located the sparsely decorated clinic off the atrium of a multi-storey office building. At first she felt awkward seeing the name of the office "Breast Medical Office" emblazoned on the glass and she found herself embarrassed to be entering the doors. "Anyone who sees me will know what problem I have now" she thought. But the center was quiet and she decided that this was the least of her problems depending on what the doctor said today.

She didn't have to wait long before she was lead into an examination room and introduced to a surprisingly thin young Indian woman with a mop of dark hair who was the clinic's staff doctor. The doctor asked Lee to change into an office gown and lay on the table while she prepared some instruments. She was very professional and soon Lee was relatively relaxed while the doctor probed her tissue and asked questions. She stopped over the lump, moving back and forth and asking about how long she had known about it and whether there was any pain associated with it. Lee mentioned the throbbing ache from her breast into the tissue under her arm. A sensation that felt similar too when her milk flowed into the ducts when breast feeding but in reverse and the doctor said that any pain was good since it was rare in cancerous legions. The manual examination confirmed Lee's fears that it was a serious lump but the doctor said that it could be a cyst or fibroid rather than a malignant growth especially considering Lee's young age Then the doctor squeezed clear gel on her chest and moved an ultra sound scanner, which was a little wider than a curling iron, down and across her breast as the images it produced were projected onto a computer screen in front of them. She pointed out the different dark and light masses to Lee, explaining what each one potentially represented. The doctor then frowned for a minute while squinting at the lump shown on the screen then told Lee that she would probably rule out a cyst since there was no fluid sac evident. She wasn't sure how dangerous this lump was though since it didn't look like standard fibroids either and she recommended a mammogram.

Lee was asked to move to an adjacent room with a massive piece of complicated stainless steel equipment in the middle of it. As she hesitated at the door, a nurse briskly pushed Lee forward and asked her to put her chest against the protruding shelf. She unceremoniously lifted Lee's gown, grabbed her breast with her plastic gloved hand and moved it until it was lying on the cold steel plate. She then brought down another plate on top of it and squeezed the plate down until the breast tissue was flattened like a pancake. Lee winced at this pressure but the nurse just told her to remain very still.

"As though I could move now anyway" she thought wryly as she was pinned to the machine. The nurse then left the room and triggered the x-ray. It was an unpleasant procedure which left Lee sore and embarrassed. She wondered how so many women could be subjected to this on an annual basis without complaining. Then she was ushered back to the first office to sit while the doctor reviewed the film from the mammogram. Finally the doctor looked up directly into Lee's eyes with concern in her own.

"I suggest surgery to biopsy the lump so we know exactly what we are dealing with in this situation The mass does not look right, but as I mentioned, the fact that you have pain is a good sign"

Lee swallowed and took a deep breath before consenting to the surgery. She didn't see how she had a choice.

The surgery appointment was rushed to take place at the end of the following week and Lee was pleased by the importance that the staff placed on her situation. It had hit her when she had gone into the washroom to change back into her clothes after the examination. She had started to shake uncontrollably, as fear began to overwhelm her.

Lee braced herself by placing her hands on each side of the sink as she fought the urge to vomit. The rigid pose eventually helped stop her body's shaking and slowly she looked up into the mirror at her drained white face, with the frightened eyes. She felt pity for herself right then, at all the unfairness of life especially if the surgery verified a malignant growth. Everything she had experienced; her successes, failures, challenges and hard work had culminated to this moment in time and they fell away as insignificant. None of it would help her now. She would have to gather her strength and move forward.

Lee's mind kept repeating "nothing is known yet", "do not panic" and "you can handle this too" so eventually she was able to walk out of the washroom with a certain amount of fragile control. She approached the checkout desk and collected the documents for the surgery while the nurse gave her instructions for preparation. Then she said a quiet goodbye to the nurses and headed to her car, where she lost that tenuous control and began to sob. She cried with her hands and forehead on the wheel; out of fear for her children, the pain to come and for her potential loss of a future.

When she returned home later that day Lee hid herself in the bedroom to think over everything that she had learned at the doctor's and begin to sort out her options. She had to hang onto the hope that since the lump was painful it would not be cancer. Then the children came streaming into the room. Curt had picked them up from school as she had requested and she was so glad to see them. She hugged them each as though she would never see them again, and they melted into her then eventually squirmed within the overly tight embrace. These two little ones were the most beautiful part of her life. They were pieces of her heart and precious to her beyond words. She would sacrifice anything for them but what would she have to do to save her own life.

Later that night after dinner, she told Curt about the lump and surgery. He didn't seem too concerned so she dropped the subject and sat quietly. Her parents would probably have the same reaction so she didn't bother calling them about the surgery either. If the results came back positive then she would tell them and she was sure that they would be supportive and help her if she needed it. Lee also couldn't tell her boss right now either since that might lead to the loss of her job, so she was once more alone facing one of the most difficult situations in her life.

On the day of the surgery, Lee packed her bag and then took

the children to school early before heading to the hospital. Curt had not even mentioned the surgery or offered to attend so she didn't press it. She would probably be better off without his cynical comments. Lee had been a bit nervous since she knew that there were risks with any procedure but the day had begun so hectically that she didn't have time to dwell on it.

After being prepped in a pre-op room, she had the catheter dug into her arm and was started on a drip with general anesthesia then wheeled into the operating room. An hour later she came aware that she was talking but didn't know what she had said, just like last time she had come out of surgery. She stopped, looked around confused and saw two nurses sitting beside her bed looking at her with amused grins. Then she smiled as well and laid back – she had gotten through the surgery fine. She thought of that carpe diem saying "Each time you wake up from sleep is a great day because you are alive."

After she was released the next day Lee took a cab home, slid into her bed and began the vigil of waiting for the results of the tissue tests. She had to consider what would happen if the tests came back positive. A malignant tumor would be a big challenge and she would have to fight hard to survive. What kind of partner would Curt be if she couldn't work or take care of the kids while she was going through chemo or radiation treatment? He had showed no interest when she had mentioned the doctor's report nor had he offered to help in any way and this was the easy part. She knew that she did not want to die while living with someone who did not care for her; this was a clear thought that keep going through her mind.

Lee had a hard time focusing over the following days and so she almost missed noticing that Curt had started staying out even later than usual some nights. She couldn't deal with that right now since her main concern was her health and the future well-being of her children. It was taking so long to get the results of the test that she could hardly sleep or concentrate on work. Her only relief was her time with the children when she could forget about all her problems and wrap herself in their unconditional love.

Then her doctor finally called two weeks after the surgery and said that the test had come back negative, it was not a cancerous lump but just fibroids. She suggested that Lee have surgery to remove the fibroids or she could leave them since they often reduced in size once a woman went through menopause and didn't have as much estrogen in her system. Lee was so grateful and acutely happy that she didn't hear the rest of the doctor's report. She thanked the doctor, told her that she would think about another surgery then put her head in her hands to cry with relief.

Now she had to address the next problem, Curt's obvious straying. She decided to catch him upon his return to the house one morning. So she slept lightly, waiting to hear the overhead garage door open and when it did at five o'clock one morning, she went downstairs to confront him. She stood with her arms crossed in the breakfast room as the door from the garage slowly opened. He stumbled in with his clothes partially on, hair disheveled and shoes and jacket in hand. He was startled to look up and see her waiting for him. This caused him to fumble with the items in his hands nearly dropping them.

"Where have you been?" She asked in a calm but firm tone.

"I stayed over at Rob's house since we had a few drinks. I didn't think that it was wise to drive back home after I had been drinking," he said after a pause.

Then Curt looked directly into her face to see how she would take this comment. As he did this she noticed that his eyes appeared larger and the blue iris was more noticeable than usual. He had widened his normally squinting eyes to scrutinize Lee's reaction which told her that he was lying. Disgusted with this knowledge, she just turned and left the room. A few weeks later the same thing occurred and Curt just scurried past her this time. "So much for his desire to work on the marriage and how he loved her still" she thought.

Shortly after this Lee got a letter from him left on the bed. This time he had written that he had met someone, a woman of similar age who owned a very attractive house. He wrote that Lee would have eventually heard about their lunches and outings together. He wanted to be with this woman long term but he wasn't going to leave home yet because he needed to get his Green Card through Lee first.

She laughed when she read this. Could he not see how unbelievably bizarre this letter was – had he considered the children. No, he had not even thought about the children. This declaration made it impossible for her to continue as a wife to someone who had slept with at least one other woman and probably more. Some couples continued after adultery, working out the problems that caused the infidelity but Lee could never respect or trust Curt after this deceit. It was the final culmination of all her fears and humiliation.

Lee realized that her marriage was probably over but she didn't know the next step so she wrote the words "This is considered adultery" on the note and left it in the bonus room. The next time he tried to sneak back into the house in the early morning, she was waiting for him in the kitchen again where she blocked his escape and declared.

"You need to choose between your girlfriend and your family"

Thinking of the bed and woman he had just left, Curt laughed and said that he would choose the girlfriend. Lee was somewhat relieved since it was not her decision to destroy the family but it was the death blow to the marriage.

"It only takes one person to end a marriage," Lee recalled the minister's words.

In order to expedite the separation, Lee had to agree to joint custody since Curt said that he wouldn't move out without it. He had his pride and he needed to tell his parents and friends that he had an equal share of the children, as though they were property. Lee however insisted on being named the primary care parent and to have final decisions on all education and medical for the children. She had learned over the years that Curt had never made a decision that benefitted anyone but himself, so she had to protect the children.

During the negotiations, Lee also had requested only a quarter of the child support that she was entitled to under North Carolina law which she hoped would limit the amount of tension with Curt since he seemed to mostly care about money. This was a mistake on her part and it would cost her dearly by the time the children turned eighteen, but she believed that she could give her children all that they needed. She did however insist that the agreement mention that she and the children could live in the house for a year before it would go on the market. Curt had originally wanted them to move into a rental so the house could be sold right away, but Lee had stood firm against this. She wanted the children to stay in a familiar and comfortable situation as long as possible to ease the transition. This made her think though about where they would live once the house was sold.

If she had her choice, she would move to a lake front location, just like she had growing up. In fact, her mother had encouraged her to look for lake front lots while they were visiting last time, as an investment and vacation spot. This had planted the idea and now Lee began to research all lake front properties in the northern Lake Norman area and southern Lake Wylie.

She had called her mother to tell her about the adultery and separation, ashamed at having to confess this failure. But as the conversation lengthened, Lee pulled herself together and asked if Anne had been serious about offering to help her to get a lake property. Anne had just bought a waterfront cottage a couple doors down from her own house for Lee's sister, so maybe it was her turn. Anne agreed that since Lee's grandfather had left a good inheritance, if Lee found a nice property, she would help her pay for it. She told Lee the amount that her sister's house had cost and said that if Lee found something within that budget, they would set up a family trust and put the house in it.

Lee began her real estate research immediately. This was the best news she had gotten in the months since the doctors report. She toured every house for sale and walked every lot on both lakes near Charlotte until she had a better feel for the neighbourhoods, schools, socioeconomic groups and taxes for each. She decided that Lake Norman would not work for her due to price, traffic, lake levels and density, but Lake Wylie was still relatively natural and undeveloped by comparison. Then she visited a small community called Terra Harbor on a peninsula protruding in to the southern region of Lake Wylie just above the dam. It was a community developed in the 70's with houses that had been designed in very modern styles with clerestory windows, steep roofs and colors that blended with the surrounding environment. Trees could not be cut down so it was thickly forested with many parks and a marina for outdoor activities. The older sections of the city were not always well maintained, giving it a beach town quality, but there were a few newer sections of development near the entry that had attractive custom homes being built.

Seven developers had gone bankrupt trying to manage and develop the city but the new owner was a developer with deep pockets so there was hope that revitalization was potentially on its way. Lee liked the new neighbourhoods and she especially liked the school system for the residents. Terra Harbor was part of the Fort Mill school system, an area that was originally formed as a mill town for South Creek Industries, a textile manufacturer. Generations had worked at the plants producing textiles before the business was relocated to South America.

However due to local tax incentives and its proximity to Charlotte, many other industries had moved into the Fort Mill district and the area was thriving. Lee had heard that in the past the South Creek Company had trouble getting executives to relocate to the area due to the school system. So the company had decided to subsidize the Fort Mill schools in order to allow them hire better teachers and build new schools. The result was an exceptional school system which had the quality teachers, facilities and the opportunities of a private school while still in the South Carolina public school system. Families concerned about their children's education flocked to the area.

Lee was one of those concerned parents. She had originally enrolled Andy in the Charlotte-Mecklenburg school system despite its poor reputation, under the impression that since they lived in a good neighbourhood, the local school would reflect this - she was wrong. Busing had brought almost forty percent of the children from the urban core into her neighbourhood and these children were often uninterested in their classes and disrespectful if not threatening to their teachers.

As a result some of the most talented and dedicated teachers didn't want to work in the CM public school system and instead applied for jobs in the growing private schools or in the outlying communities like Fort Mill or Waxhaw. Lee had enrolled Andy into the Harris Woods Elementary school near their house and made sure to visit him for lunch at least once a week to monitor his transition. She found that she was the only parent who did this and one of only a handful of parents who attended any class functions.

Andy's new teacher was a harsh woman in her fifties, with dyed black hair and scarlet lipstick, who had never taught school before but Lee wanted to be open minded about her potential. Unfortunately just when Andy first entered school he had a severe hearing loss in one ear due to an infection. Lee conveyed this information to the teacher and her assistant the first day. The weeks passed and his hearing had not improved.

One day when Lee arrived to have lunch with Andy, she couldn't find him in the lunch room and asked the teacher where he was. The teacher told Lee that Andy had been belligerent and he was in detention. Lee was surprised and asked the woman what he had done. The teacher explained that when she had called him to stop working on an assignment, he didn't listen to her. Lee asked what position Andy was in when she had spoken to him and pointed out that the teacher had addressed him from the direction of his bad ear. Lee left the teacher sputtering and immediately raced up to the empty classroom where her son had been banished. She found the small boy sitting in a chair trying to eat his lunch with tears running down his face. Lee swept him up into a strong protective embrace and carried him out of the room and down to join the rest of his class once he had recovered sufficiently.

The next day Andy declared that he did not want to go to school. "Who could blame him" Lee thought, but she quietly explained that it had been a misunderstanding and it wouldn't happen again. However, a few weeks later when Lee went to have lunch with her son, he was again missing. Lee asked the teacher where he was and she said that he had been caught cheating. She could not believe this and asked the teacher to elaborate. The teacher took Lee to the classroom where she showed her one of Andy's test papers. It was a small sheet with smudges above the lines where her son had erased then written answers on top in his looping careful left handed printing. Lee could have wept as she pictured her diligent son with his head down concentrating on both analyzing the math questions and controlling his left hand movements to form the numbers. She then realized that she didn't understand how this constituted cheating. The teacher pointed out that since he had erased his answers then rewritten them, he must have copied the correct answers off another student.

"I believe that all children lie and cheat. They can't help it," she stated looking directly at Lee.

Lee was stunned by this statement and she found that she was having trouble controlling her anger with this poor excuse of a teacher. Memories of her own harsh elementary school experiences flooded her mind and she went into a protective mother mode.

"This does not prove that he cheated at all - it only proves that he figured out that he hadn't been using the right formula on these problems and he went back to correct his first answers. You have made a pretty big leap to assume that he was cheating unless you actually witnessed his leaning over to spy on another student's paper," she exclaimed as she stared scornfully at the teacher.

The teacher stepped back from Lee in surprise before she regained her composure and then declared that Andy would not be released from detention. Lee left the room before she said anything more, went directly to make an appointment with the principal and then remove her son from school for the day. Andy could not remain in this atmosphere.

When Lee met with the principal the next day she relayed all of the recent events and asked that her son be moved to another class. The principal said that while he sympathized with her ordeal, especially about the hearing loss, he had to support his teachers and her son could not be moved.

Lee then stood, calmly declared.

"Then my son will be moved to another school within the week," and she left the office.

It took just under a week for Lee to find a Montessori School that they could afford which seemed perfect for her gentle and intelligent child. It was a small school with just three classrooms, similar to the school she had attended, but here the teachers engaged the children to develop their talents and let them work at their own pace. It also was environmentally oriented with a large park behind it where the children were encouraged to explore nature with their teachers. This was so much better for Andy. Curt, who had not paid any attention to what was occurring, had just left it to Lee to make all the arrangements.

Chapter 28 - Wiring & Lights

After the separation, Curt disappeared and the family didn't see or hear from him much for almost a year. He was consumed by his new relationship. Lee got a call from him only when he wanted to discuss financial issues - usually about how he could get more money. Curt had initially moved into the bonus room of a house in the neighbourhood owned by another man who had also just separated. Lee heard all this from the neighbours, who were distressed that this man had abandoned his family for another woman. They were all good Christians and adultery was not a Christian thing to do, though by this time most of the neighbours were not very fond of Curt anyway. They had seen his attempt to kick their cats, his unkindness to their children and heard his sarcastic unflattering remarks to each of them, which he thought was funny but they did not. Lee winced when she heard their complaints since she felt guilty about bringing this person into their neighbourhood. They would be glad to see the last of him.

Then her next door neighbour called Lee to tell her that they had seen Curt sneaking around the property and spying in her windows a couple times. This information alarmed Lee and she had to get her lawyer to reinforce the contract agreement that he couldn't access the property without her permission. Another neighbour and his wife had actually seen Curt at the airport within a couple weeks of their separation with a woman, rather tall with short blond hair. He had been fondling her in public, running his hand all over her backside. The couple had been reluctant to mention this to Lee but she had taken it well, hiding her embarrassment and even smiling back as they relayed their disgust at the scene.

Once shortly after Curt left the house, his girlfriend had called the house by mistake and left a message. It said "Hey honey, you must be in the shower. Call me back. Love you sugar!" in a thick Southern accent. Lee had called the number back and quietly told the woman that she had called the family house and not Curt's cell number. The woman laughed and thanked Lee as though it was a perfectly normal thing to do, then she hung up in order to phone her lover on the correct number. Lee shook her head and congratulated herself on being so calm and rational about it all.

One time Curt's adulterous behavior actually worked to Lee's advantage. She was trying to get Sarah into the Montessori School that Andy attended but they didn't want to accept a child her age since she was between learning periods. Lee had been able to book an interview for enrollment with the teachers, though she had been warned that it was unlikely that Sarah would be accepted.

Just as the group was in the middle of the interview, sitting on cushions on the floor with shoes removed as required by the school policy, they heard a heavy stomping sound in the hall. Two people emerged through the doorway of the room wearing matching black leather jackets, sunglasses and wood clog shoes. It was Curt and his new girlfriend to the shock of the teachers in the room.

Curt wore a huge grin on his face while he steered the pair between the low tables until he was in front of the small group on the floor. Then he pushed the woman next to him forward to introduce Joan to the teachers and then to Lee. She was a big woman, tall and shapely, with short blond hair and dark eyes that looked straight at Lee appraising her. Lee said hello, shook hands then dropped her head to concentrate on her daughter and hide the tears of humiliation. After a few comments, then awkward silence, the pair turned around and clomped out of the building.

One of the teachers turned to Lee and exclaimed.

"Oh I am so sorry. I can't believe what just happened. That was the first time you met the woman isn't it!" The next day Sarah was accepted to the school. "Probably out of pity" Lee thought.

Following the school incident, Curt had come to take the children out for dinner but Sarah refused to go. She had actually seemed happy about the separation when Lee had first explained that Daddy wouldn't be living with them anymore. It made Lee wonder if any more abuse had occurred. So she asked Sarah and the little girl said that Daddy had hurt her when she was upstairs. Lee was alarmed but had to find to out more. She pressed her daughter to tell exactly what happened and how often. It seemed that Curt would try to catch Sarah alone in her bedroom room then yank off his belt or grab a nearby object to hit her.

"I wanted my Mommy but you were downstairs and couldn't hear me when I cried. But Daddy said that it would be bad if I told you and he would have to punish me again," her daughter sobbed.

Lee's heart broke as she heard this from her sweet daughter. She felt like a failure as a parent - how could she have not seen this. Were there bruising or welts on her daughter's skin that she hadn't noticed or had Curt been clever about it, ensuring that he didn't break the skin this time. She should have paid more attention to Sarah's withdrawal from her father. Now she had to determine her course of action carefully. Lee decided that the one protective recourse she could take to help stop further beatings was to draft a letter to Curt and copy her lawyer. This would create a physical record of the action as well as clarify what she needed to say. She wrote that she knew about his secret beatings of Sarah and if he was to ever do it again, she would bring in Social Services and let them determine if he was a fit parent to continue to have visitation with the children and how often.

Curt called Lee soon after he received the note, first excusing himself to shut the door then clearing his throats a few times, which gave Lee the odd sensation that he was going to tape their conversation.

"I did not do anything wrong. Sarah must have been exaggerating as kids tend to do," he said in a formal rehearsed fashion.

"I only did the same as my father who belted me when I was a kid and I turned out all right"

"That is a matter of opinion" Lee said wryly. "Either way, this cannot ever happen again," she emphatically stated.

She also realized that, as with all of their conversations since separation, the first statements out of his mouth were usually untrue and she could just never trust him, as she had thought years ago.

They talked a little more about schedules then Curt cleared his throat again, the sign of something more difficult to say, and asked her to sign the papers to sell the house. Lee refused.

"The children need more time to adjust to the separation by staying in the old house a little longer and I need the time to decide where we will live. It has only been a few months and our agreement says that I have a year," she replied.

Then the talk turned ugly. Curt began shouting that he wanted to sell the house since he needed the money. Then he hit her hard with is next statement.

"Maybe I need to protect the children from you. I think that I will file to get full custody and take them away from you," he yelled.

This froze her. The thought of losing her children acted as a poisonous drug penetrating and flowing through her body until it convulsed with fear. She didn't remember saying goodbye or collapsing onto the floor, but minutes later that is where she found herself. He was going to try to take the children. She could tackle almost any challenges or hardships but this one was a nightmare that she didn't think she could recover from. It took a few days of worry and tears before she decided to stiffen her spine and do all she could to fight for her children. She started to write down all events, medical care and conversations that she had with Curt or the children's teachers, as she had always done with her business calls. She consulted with her lawyer to prepare for a law suit against her and ask for any advice on how to proceed. Her lawyer assured her that there was no way that Curt could get full custody especially with his abusive and adulterous history, but the case would probably go to court in an expensive and messy fight if he did file.

While Lee was making a decent salary she was worried about the legal fees of a custody battle and extra costs that might come up as a single mother. Her job setting up the new Commercial department at Whitmore was going well with steady projects but Lee had been living paycheck to paycheck. She eventually had enough work to hire new staff for her division and she was given a raise which relived some of her financial concerns. Her parents also said that they would set up a reserve for her and college funds for the children, as William had done for them, if she ever needed it.

In hiring the new staff, she was instrumental in bringing on board several female architects, despite typical concerns that they might get pregnant and quit. The women each had excellent qualifications and would bring some diversity to the firm. Lee eventually became especially close to a petite blond architect named Trudy who had attended a prestigious university in Virginia for her undergraduate degree. She had then worked in that area for a few years before moving to Charlotte. The two women had many lunches together during which they slowly began to reveal the personal details of their lives as their trust in each other grew. Once the walls of restraint were breached though, the flood gates opened and the two confided some of their most intimate secrets to each other.

Trudy had been married previously to a fellow who had abused and beaten her. It had started with small slaps in anger, which he apologized for afterwards and professed how much he loved her. She believed him and since he seemed to have such remorse, she actually felt compassion for him to some degree at the beginning. He seemed so tortured by his mistake that her indignation would fade and she would forgive him. This did not last and soon he would get more violent and threatening, triggered by any small infraction of the strict rules he set in the house.

Despite her injuries Trudy loved him and stayed in the marriage but lived in fear of his anger. At times in his heated rages, he had screamed that he would kill her if she ever left him. Trudy never told her family since she had hoped that things would improve so she wouldn't have to admit the humiliation of being a battered wife. Eventually she researched shelters, hid money away at work and planned her escape. By the time she had left him, Trudy bore the scars of several visits to the hospital and was isolated from her family. This was the reason she had fled to a city large enough that she could hide in and where she hoped her ex-husband would not find her.

Neither woman had expected to have such experiences in their lives. They had been so hopeful and convinced that marriage was what they needed to do to be happy. Disney movies told girls that they could find a prince and live happily ever after and they believed it. Cultural expectations and parental pressure encouraged these girls to get married but now Lee and Trudy were grateful to be out of their former marriages. They were also glad that they had an education and a good job so that they could survive on their own and take time to heal.

Previous generations of women did not have this choice and Lee wondered if the divorce rate had increased so dramatically in her generation because women could now be independent and leave a bad marriage. They didn't have to put up with the adultery and abuse. Western culture was more accepting of single mothers and professional women now than it ever had been in thousands of years. If Lee and Trudy had been born in India or a Muslim country, they would have been tied to their husbands forever or thrown aside to die as a divorced outcast. She was grateful she lived in a country that was far more advanced and didn't have those barbaric ancient customs. Besides if women worked at equal paying jobs then they could support themselves and their families as well as contribute to society in a meaningful way. At least that is what Lee wanted to do.

Soon Lee and Trudy were going out after work to have a drink or go to the movies when Lee's children were with their father for dinner. The girls' nights out were great fun and Lee was able to slowly see her single life as having more potential for happiness. Though she did miss her children when they were with their father, she was gaining confidence and making new friends again. Trudy's boyfriend also began to join them on gallery crawls or out to dinner. Ryan was an extremely handsome man who attracted a lot of attention with his six foot two muscular frame, thick dark hair and intelligent brown eyes. He had an olive completion that was due to Latino heritage on his mother's side and while he spoke of her often, he rarely mentioned his father.

Ryan was working at a manufacturing plant doing basic administration work to earn money enough to finish his Masters in Computer Sciences. It made no sense to Lee why he had such a job when he was obviously brilliant, but that was his choice. When he was with the two women, Lee felt very protected and supported by his presence. Ryan had heard a little about Lee's difficult former husband and she had confessed that she dreaded running into him. Ryan responded by saying that a bully usually needed to face someone their own size then they weren't so tough. He assured Lee that Curt would not bother her while he was around. When she heard this Lee laughed.

"I just need to borrow you from Trudy and take you to all my functions," she joked.

Then she blushed as she realized how forward this sounded but luckily Trudy was preoccupied hunting for her lipstick and didn't hear the comment.

Chapter 29 – Bridging

Lee determined that it was time to find her own place, far away from the bad memories. She had discovered a beautiful lot on the water in a newer development of Terra Harbour. The lot was on a cliff with a forty foot drop to the water so it had been considered unbuildable and it was the last waterfront lot available in this section of development. Lee had looked at the waterfront houses on the market but none of them interested her, so she got the idea that she could design and build her own house. This lot was on a cul-de-sac and it was pie shaped with over two hundred feet of waterfront on a private cove. There was a small sand beach and it was covered in a beautiful variety of mature trees. It was everything that she was looking for and she knew that she could design to a house to work structurally and overcome the topographical challenge. Also if she did a lot of the construction work herself then she might be able to build within her budget. The only conditions on the purchase of the property, besides the design criteria, was that an 1800sf minimum sized house had to be built within two years of the purchase and the owner had to use one of three approved contractors for the construction.

When Lee and her realtor sat down with the selling agent to discuss the deal, the agent said that two of the contactors listed would not be able to build any house under one hundred dollars a square foot. This was too high for Lee so she asked again if there was any way that she could act as her own general contractor. This was not possible but he did suggest that the third contractor, a fire recovery specialist, might be able to do a cost plus agreement with her. Lee set up a meeting with the owner of Better Than Before Contracting, a grizzled older man with a large pot belly and balding head. She started the discussion with a description her new lot, her architectural and construction background and then her request to do a cost plus contract. In a thick southern drawl, the contractor told her:

"It'z poussible but I'ah need plans to take a look at befor I'ah can give ya an estimate" Then he shook her outstretched hand and left the meeting bemused.

So Lee went straight to her drafting board, putting all the ideas of what she wanted in her dream house on paper. At first she sketched her thoughts on velum by drawing the cliff with layers of living space ordered by public spaces on the main level and private ones above. She thought of the home she grew up in which had a master bedroom on the ground floor, a sun room and hidden attic areas that she loved to play in as a child. She also thought of the wonderful openness of a cathedral ceiling with light spilling from high windows. French doors opening onto cascading decks to create indoor/outdoor living areas and a kitchen with a view of the lake. She also refused to have one square foot of wasted space just for show, she couldn't spare that. All of these wishes had to be incorporated into a house that she could afford to build. As she worked with her head bent over the board, the hours streamed by until the light of morning shone into the basement. By then her ideas were hard lined onto Mylar and the design had culminated into a compact but open concept multilevel residence with simple but elegant elevations.

When she was satisfied with the details she gave copies of the plans to the GC for a cost estimate. She outlined the items that she would do herself, like the finishing of the basement, all of the painting, wood trim and tile then crossed her fingers to wait for a number. After a couple days, the GC came back with a reasonable estimate, still a little high but encouraging enough to allow Lee to write up a contract for purchase of the lot. Her offer was accepted and Lee became the owner of an acre lot on Lake Wylie in the Fort Mill school district. She was so excited when the paperwork came back signed. She had done this on her own and she was thrilled to be in charge of her own destiny again. Lee was also extremely grateful to her parents for the opportunity and she offered a prayer to her grandfather who had paved the way to this exact moment in her life. She was once again on an exhilarating path in life and despite the failure of her marriage, she was free now to make her own decisions, manage her own money and hopefully celebrate many more of these successes in the future as well.

Once the deal for the land closed, Lee used a small inheritance from her grandmother Grace to get a dock built. She had drawn a sketch of the design on the survey in order to get a permit from Duke Power, who owned the water rights to the lake. Then she had given it out for bids to local marine contractors. Lake Wylie was first formed in 1904 when the Catawba River was dammed to allow a hydro-electric power plant to be built at the southern end. Since then the lake had been increased in size and a second dam was built in on the northern end at Mountain Lake. It was part of a chain of eleven lakes on the Catawba River, which was named for the Native American tribe the

Catawba or "people of the river", and despite its unappealing function, it was a beautiful, relatively clean waterway with dense tree growth and rolling hills on each side. It was rich with fish and wildlife populations so ducks, muskrat and blue herons were seen most every day. The houses were tucked away behind massive oak, dogwood and pine trees which gave the shoreline a natural park-like appearance.

Once her dock was completed, Lee and the children went on weekends to swim and kayak in the cove. They were all excited about the new house and Lee was making sure that they started to get familiar with the neighbourhood. The earth moving equipment was usually on the lot when they visited since the contractor had started to clear the house site and dig the footings. It was a surprise each time they drove the twenty minutes to the property how much work had been done. Lee had asked that as many trees as possible be left so the house would be nestled in them and she would have less erosion problems. The foundations would act as retaining walls to hold back the hillside and they were made of recycled material with concrete poured inside which was better than concrete block in this situation. When the foundation walls were complete the framing crew began to erect the lower floor and its walls. Lee visited the site most every day before driving to work and noticed that there were only three carpenters for the framing crew and one didn't look very healthy. She introduced herself then asked if this was all the crew that they had. The thin sickly looking man, Jim, answered.

"I am the head framer and we had one more carpenter but he got arrested for a drunk and disorderly charge and taken off the job"

"Great," Lee muttered.

She had a deadline to complete the house and not enough crew. So she told the men that she had worked as a carpenter and wondered if they minded her joining them in the morning to help. They were skeptical at first, looking at her as though she had lost her marbles, but agreed to her request since it was her house and she was paying the bills. The next day Lee arrived at seven in the morning with her skill saw and tool belt on her hip and started assessing where she could jump in to work. The guys had paused to watch her with amusement, expecting it to be a farce. But once she had started using the nail gun, blasting the studs in the end wall in the rhythmic fashion of a pro, they had hurried back to their own work to keep up.

At break time Lee chatted with fellows and found out that Jim had just gotten out of the hospital for by-pass surgery after a heart attack, which was why he was so fragile and gaunt. He drank a bottle of Mountain Dew in the morning just to wash down the fist-full of pills he had to take. The other two framers consisted of a tall thin boy just out of high school and an amicable dark haired man with such a large beer belly that his belt strained to keep his pants on. Lee was worried about Jim's health but the other carpenters told her that he was fine and this was the crew's third house this season. Besides, Jim needed the money badly since he had so many medical bills to cover.

So Lee would drop the children off early at the Montessori school each morning and joined the crew until just before noon then leave for her real job. She was lucky that Bob West had agreed to this temporary change of schedule. He had allowed Lee to finish her work at home after hours to make up for the time she was spending on the site. This went on for several weeks until the house began to rise out of the concrete encased hole in the ground like a giant Jenga set. Lee worked on the main and upper floor structure as well as the walls, gable roof & dormers along with the framers who soon treated her just like one of the crew.

As it turned colder the only warmth the crew had was a barrel with the burning scrapes of wood which the group huddled around in the morning and on breaks. Lee didn't mind the cold or harsh conditions since she loved the work even though she was sure that the walls she had framed were probably the most crooked. It gave her great satisfaction though, both to be an accepted member of the crew and to contribute to the building of her own home. They all joked around with each other while bracing walls and passed tools but they functioned like a well-oiled team. Soon the framing was complete and Lee had to thank the guys and regretfully say goodbye. They were off to their next job. The roofers, electricians and plumbers were scheduled to start work the next week.

Once the framers white pickup truck pulled away Lee went back into the house to walk around and admire their work. It had always fascinated Lee to stand in a space and look over the skeletal forms of a structure before it was draped in the skin. She would piece together the puzzle of the room functions by tracing plumbing pipe and electrical lines. She would imagine the flow of the structural forces as they descended down through wood and onto steel beams then posts into the concrete walls below. It was the building in the raw condition, exposed for all to see, and it usually left Lee in awe when she stepped onto a site in the middle of construction and just looked up at the rafters.

Lee was enjoying the challenges of her position at Whitmore and she had managed to transfer her qualifications from Canada as a registered architect to North Carolina, something that had not been done before. The AIA, the American Institute of Architects, had recently opened up reciprocity between Canada and the United States for architects registered in one country to apply for registration to practice in the other. Lee was registered in Ontario, where she had written her exams and done her internship, but Ontario did not recognize the reciprocity yet. Lee would have to rewrite the qualifying architectural exams all over again before she could call herself an architect in the US.

Frustrated, she researched some more and found out that British Columbia was the first and only province to recognize the agreement so she applied for registration in BC through Canadian inter-provincial reciprocity. Once that application was approved, she was then able to apply for registration across countries. She was advised that her university qualifications would have to be screened closely but she wasn't worried about that since she had attended one of the best schools in the US. If Yale was rejected then the system here was in big trouble. Soon she received notice that she was one of the first Canadian architects to become registered in the United States and the first in North Carolina through reciprocity.

When she had been at the firm for almost three years, Bob West and the other partners had decided to bring in a marketing company to do an analysis of the firm so it could go national with their Health Care division. Everyone in the firm was interviewed candidly and their work assessed. Once that process was complete, then an extensive report was submitted to the partners. In the action column of the summary page was a big surprise – in a red highlighted note at the bottom it stated that the firm was a potential target for sexual harassment law suits. This sent waves through the firm's management and they immediate set out to contain the situation. Bob West had been skeptical when he read that part of the report so he called Lee into his office to find out what she knew. Lee confirmed that she had personally experienced instances of harassment and heard of some events that had happened to women as well. Bob was genuinely concerned and asked Lee to be more specific.

"Well, the head of engineering won't address me at meetings and charges hours to my projects when he isn't even working on them."

"Then my draftsman threatened me with physical harm after I had given him an assignment. He got in my face and looked like he was going to hit me but apparently contained himself from actually striking. I am not the only one he has threatened"

Bob could only shake his head and ask her why she didn't report this to him.

"These are not really tangible complaints that could be verified - so it's just my word against theirs. The engineer could just say that there was an accounting error, and that is what he told me when I confronted him. The draftsman could claim that he didn't know what I was talking about"

Right after this, the firm's leadership asked the five main culprits who had been identified, to take an in-house re-education course taught by experts on respect and equal treatment of co-workers. These listed men when confronted became either very sheepish or angry, depending on whether they felt guilty about their behavior or defensive. Over the next several months the courses were discreetly conducted during lunch time in a private office and even though their names had not been revealed, everyone knew who they were.

Once this problem was resolved, management went on to the next item on the action summary. It was a suggestion that the firm should close down the other smaller divisions and concentrate on Health Care primarily. So Bob called Lee into his office again and made an offer to her in his smooth southern drawl.

"We have been advised to eliminate your Commercial division, and I apologize for this after we had just set you up and your efforts have begun to bear fruit"

"You are closing the division," Lee blurted, her eyes opening wide in surprise.

"Yes but we would like to offer three options for you. The first one is that you stay with us in charge of an MOB division focused on medical office buildings. Second, we would partner with you to open a new firm that does commercial work. Option three, you are welcome to take all the clients and work you have generated and leave this firm to start your own firm"

Lee needed a minute to consider what had been said to her as well as push down a strong urge to cry out "Don't do this to me now when I have had so many other challenges". Her eyes had also begun to water so she tilted her head up slightly, so tears didn't spill on to her cheeks, and tried hard to focus on the positive advantages to this proposal. She then gathered herself and told Mr. West that she was very grateful for the options that he had presented. It showed that the firm still valued her and trusted her leadership. She recognized that the offer was extremely generous; she thanked him and then asked for a day to consider. The timing for this offer was potentially fortuitous. She had just gotten permission to apply for her green card with her mother as sponsor, so she was now eligible to be self-employed instead of requiring an employer to sponsor her for a work visa. Her own firm was now possible.

At one point during her years of waiting for her green card, she had been told by her immigration lawyer that the law had been changed and her mother could no longer sponsor her. She had panicked and worried about what would happen to her, her children and their home. She could only guess that this was how an illegal immigrant lived every day, in fear of being deported and losing all that they had worked for. She was especially concerned that she might be forced to leave her home and children. Curt would never allow her to take Andy and Sarah back to Canada. He would definitely sue for full custody then and she might face jail time if she tried a border crossing. She didn't want to keep her children from their father but she had to be near them to make sure he didn't do any other damage to them until they were old enough to stand up for themselves.

So she began to ask her family and friends if they knew of any solutions to her dilemma. After hearing about her problem, her brother-in-law, a kindly lawyer who had married her sister a few years earlier, suggested that she have a consultation with one of his colleagues who was known to be an outstanding immigration lawyer. Lee arranged for an appointment with Terry Walter on her next visit to Windsor and nervously awaited the date. She couldn't think of any other way to stay in the States unless she married an American or started a business which hired a minimum of six employees with an investment of at least one million dollars. Marrying anyone at that point was a remote occurrence since her divorce wasn't even complete yet, and she didn't have a million dollars.

So Lee said a quick prayer before pulling open the etched glass door to Mr. Walter's office in the historic Fisher Building in downtown Detroit. The room she entered was very shadowy due to the classic dark wood paneled walls and small exterior windows, but the gloom disappeared when Mr. Walter's booming jovial voice welcomed her in to sit down. There was no secretary to greet her, just a smiling dark haired man wearing wire rimmed glasses and a crisp navy suit jacket sitting behind a large polished wood desk that dominated the room. He reminded her of Perry Mason from the old black & white TV show and she relaxed. She sat opposite him and began to describe her situation and desire to secure a green card.

Mr. Walter asked Lee a few questions then confirmed her fear that the law had changed. However, he went on to say that the interpretation of this new law may not affect her application and he asked if she would excuse him while he made a phone call to confirm. He picked up the phone and after a few quick comments into it and a delay for listening, he thanked the person on the other end and hung up. He then turned to Lee and told her that her application should be fine and she should be able to keep her place in line for a green card but he would reconfirm this once he had her additional paperwork.

Lee couldn't believe that it was so simple after months of worry; she could have hugged him she was so relived. Mr. Walters went on to describe the process that she and the children would go through next. There would be more photos and applications, a personal interview and a swearing in ceremony which would be done in either Charleston or the small town of Greer, South Carolina. He assured her that they would be fine but offered to guide her through the process and attend her interview if she paid his expenses, which she quickly agreed to do to avoid any more problems.

Lee was grateful for any help she could get with the immigration process since it was so intimidating and confusing. She couldn't imagine how an uneducated migrant worker could ever navigate the labyrinth of bureaucracy and she felt great compassion for the illegal aliens and their dilemmas. In the early stages she was told that the waiting list for the "Married Child of an American Citizen" to get a Green Card would be approximately fifteen years. Luckily when she separated from Curt, she was changed to the list of "Single Child of an American Citizen" and that was only a ten year wait. Once her application was in, she would get highly official looking documents in the mail scheduling her appointments for various required meetings and document deliveries. These letters also mentioned that if she missed an appointment then her application could be set aside; so she worried about her mail going astray.

The first appointments were in Charlotte and she had to bring both children to the office building off Woodlawn where hundreds of other immigrants were also waiting until their numbers, pulled from a ticker tape upon entry, were announced. All of the children of these applicants would get tired and hungry, moaning or sleeping in their parents arms while they waited in the mass of humanity. The officials who checked identification at the door offered little information to the questioning mothers. So they would go back to their children, sitting in groups on the floor or those lucky enough to have sequestered a chair or two, and wait until their turn to approach the counter. It was the Ellis Island of the South.

The next series of appointments were in Charleston so Lee and the children would drive the three hours then stay overnight at an inexpensive North Charleston hotel with an indoor pool for a short holiday. The INS offices were in a brick building on Meeting Street across from the historic market renovated by the Daughters of the Confederacy. The inspectors there were courteous and many of the applicants were sailors from the nearby naval base who were there to get green cards for their new foreign brides or grooms. After waiting several hours Lee and the children were photographed, finger printed or interviewed then they were free to go to the beach for the rest of the day. But the worst appointments were in Greer. This office was a couple hours west of Charlotte situated in an older industrial complex of a small town off the highway. It was difficult to find, unpleasant to endure and the staff were especially rude.

Upon entering the building, applicants were interrogated with harsh questions by a highly intolerant good ol' boy police officer, subjected to a metal detector and frisked then told to take a seat in the over-lit waiting room and where they were ignored for hours. The sign-in officer often went out of his way to intimidate them, which offended Lee and scared the children but they were helpless to object. Lee was also often harassed by the INS officers at the airports when she returned from any international flights. She would be pulled over to the INS desk upon arrival and the officer there would aggressively question her then review her paperwork looking for inconsistencies. One officer screamed into her face.

"If I find one thing wrong in your paperwork, I will bounce you right out of this country. You will be deported immediately"

Lee had reported this event to her lawyer who reassured her that she couldn't be deported so quickly no matter what the man said. She would have rights to remain and prove her case which would take time. However Lee figured out that if she brought an American citizen with her to the INS desk when she was signaled over the threats would not occur. So she started doing this each time she traveled with an American and she hoped that once she got her green card, the nerve wracking scrutiny would be a thing of the past.

Chapter 30 - Roofing

After all of these challenges, Lee still felt sure that she was making the right decisions now, her instincts told her this felt right. She had made some poor choices but now the future offered so many possibilities. She believed that she could start her own firm and succeed. So she researched available shared office space, costs for printers, computers and other expenses as well as what she needed as income to support her family. With her parent's assistance, she would just be able to make it through the tough first years of a new practice. So she accepted Mr. West's offer to take her clients and open her own firm. She had found a high quality key man professional office located near the airport. It had a lobby with rich dark wood paneling, plush stylish carpet and elegant millwork for the reception desk and conference room paneling. It also had a perfect corner office with a view to the fountains of the development, which Lee immediately leased. It came with staff to manage the office and these girls became good friends to Lee. They helped her find office supplies, organize meetings and they dropped off fresh baked cookies to make her feel welcome. So she set up her registered company and got her own professional stamps. It was official now; Harding Architect LLC was open for business.

It took very little time for Lee to get used to her new business. Her clients had transferred without any concerns and she was now set up in one of the most attractive environments she had ever worked. She designed her own logo and business cards then printed them herself on stock paper. They might not be as slick as some but they worked for her budget. She purchased a good laptop computer so she could take it back and forth to the house, set up an Internet account and brought the children over to see the place where their mother would be working. When the staff discovered that her children were visiting, they plied them with cookies and sodas which weren't very healthy but Lee didn't object. She wanted the children to enjoy coming to their mother's office since she would have to bring them when they couldn't attend school due to holidays or illness; unless it was serious and then they would all stay home.

The staff adored the two well manner children who said "Thank you" with big smiles and played hide and seek in the conference room. Lee tried to always corral them into her office where Andy & Sarah would take turns twirling in Lee's chair, looking through her drawers or drawing pictures with her pencils. Eventually they would get bored and ask to go home. Lee soon learned to stock the room with children's books, toys and videos. "Anything so they can be happy and I can make a living," Lee thought wryly.

After getting settled in to her new office, Lee started designing and drafting. She had several franchise projects where the clients built the same restaurant concept in multiple states. There was a Mexican fast casual concept, a pizza joint and a self-service deli. She also had a great custom upscale restaurant in Columbia, a pet care retail store and a child development day care to work on. Lee had also been given the exciting job of designing the headquarters for a Japanese manufacturing company by Andrea's husband Jeff. He was the president of the American division and he had insisted that Lee do the project. She had been flattered and especially grateful to him since she needed this kind of kick off project for her firm. Jeff had found it difficult convincing the Japanese to use a female architect, but he stood his ground as her advocate. After sending her resume and sample project material over to the Japanese CEO, she was finally approved and Lee began preparing sketches and plans. She did computer renderings of the proposed building which made approval from overseas easier.

Her team of engineers got to work on their drawings and once complete Lee put the drawings out to bid to three contractors. They waited for the numbers to come in on the bid submission day and when the low one was tight to the budget, they signed a contract with the GC. Then they conducted a ground breaking ceremony, which Lee was invited to attend along with all the company employees and contractor representatives. It was a gloriously bright sunny day and on the red clay site stood a white tent shading a table of h'ordeuvres and champagne in plastic cups. Jeff in his double breasted navy suite and dark wavy hair looked like a politician as he shook hands with everyone.

Jeff eventually called the group over to a spot near the future driveway. There Jeff stood with his head up, an erect stance and obvious pride while he announced the official opening of the new headquarters building. He grasped the handle of a silver plated shovel that was handed to him and dug it into a small pile of dirt that had been set in place for this occasion, then looked up for the photographer to snap the historic moment.

After getting settled Lee invited Trudy to come for lunch and tour her new offices. The staff supplied some sandwiches and drinks then the two women sat down, with Trudy facing the expanse of glass, to catch up on office politics and friends. This was when Trudy dropped the bomb shell. She was moving to Phoenix. Lee was stunned. She thought that everything was going so well for her and she had such a wonderful boyfriend.

"What is going to happen to your relationship with Ryan - is he moving out there with you?" she asked.

Here Trudy became evasive, just hinting that their relationship wasn't working out and Ryan would not be coming with her. They had been dating for over a year and he had never moved to any further commitment or deeper feelings as she had hoped. So she had started looking into the Phoenix area for jobs since she had terrible hay fever and she had heard that the air of the dessert was a great remedy. When an office in Scarsdale had expressed interest in her job application, she had flown out to interview and fallen in love with the vast beauty of the jagged mountains and reddish plains of rock and sand. The firm later sent her an offer of employment and she had accepted before even telling Ryan. She just felt that she needed to take advantage of this opportunity and start new.

Lee missed Trudy when she left and Ryan must have as well since he began calling Lee often, perhaps to keep two of the trio together after the split. In one call he asked if there was anything that she needed for her computer. He was a genius programmer and rebuilt computers for fun after hours so Lee jumped at the opportunity to have help with her machine, and to see him again. Ryan began a regular routine of coming to Lee's office to help out or they would just have lunch together. He had a serious but creative nature so their discussions were often about art, philosophy or just future dreams. Lee also talked about the house construction which was progressing steadily until one day Ryan asked if he could get a tour of the site. Lee thought that it was very kind of him to humor her this way and she said that she would be glad to show it to him any weekend. Ryan offered to come to her house the coming Saturday and they could all go together. He had met the children several times before when he had come over with Trudy so they were excited to see him when he pulled up in his white truck. Both Andy and Sarah thought Ryan was cool and when he offered to swing them around in the yard and play video games with them afterwards, the adoration was complete.

Lee looked wistfully at the three figures as they chased each other in a spontaneous game of tag in the back yard. The tall muscular young man with an irresistible smile; running just fast enough to keep the game entertaining, and the two laughing blond cherubs racing behind. It was so comfortable with Ryan at the house and Lee sometimes wondered if there was any interest besides friendship. She was certainly attracted to him, but she didn't want to cross any line. After Ryan finally allowed himself to be tagged, he announced.

"Who wants to go swimming?"

The children both screamed that they did so the group got into his truck and they all headed to the new house. When they pulled up to the site Ryan whistled his approval. "Lee this is great; you kept all the old growth trees. It's like a fabulous tree house". This caused her the blush but she appreciated that he noticed. The whole group then walked up the temporary ramp to the first floor, holding tight to the children's hands as they moved toward the edge of the future deck to look out over the panoramic view. It was a spectacular sight with the light sparkling off the rippling emerald green water and the hillsides of thick dark forests. Ryan asked what amount of the shoreline was hers and she pointed out red flags near certain rocks and trees that marked the widely spaced property lines. He congratulated her on such a great find.

Then the little group went carefully down the back stairs and out the garage door opening onto the worn path to the lake. The children raced once they were on the familiar the path until they reached the dock. When Lee and Ryan had caught up, she gave permission for them to go onto the dock and into the water, which they did with great joy. Lee was a bit embarrassed to be in a bathing suit in front of Ryan, so she removed her shirt then quickly dove in. She turned back in time to watch the well sculpted form of Ryan in his surfer shorts jump in a cannon ball next to the children to splash them. The children squealed with screams and laughter when he came up spouting water at them. They all played in the lake for the next hour with Lee taking peaks at Ryan's back and chest while watching the kids dive off his shoulders. After the swim, the group headed back to Charlotte and Lee invited Ryan to stay for dinner. She was surprised when he agreed and then joined her in the kitchen to help make the stir fry.

"I love to cook. Maybe one day I can show you more of my

abilities" Ryan said quietly as he leaned a little closer to her.

Lee wasn't sure exactly what he meant by this but chose to relate it to food for now. She was tempted to brush past him or accidentally touch him while they worked but dared not. In fact she kept a good distance when possible. Then after dinner Ryan helped clean up before saying goodbye to the kids and heading to the door to leave. He thanked her, hesitated, dropped his eyes and then turned to leave without looking back. Lee wondered if he had thought about kissing her as she slowly shut the door and leaned against it in a dreamy state.

Trudy and Lee had kept in touch and whenever Trudy called she always had exciting news about her new home. She described how much she really enjoyed Arizona with its dry air, rolling hills, gullies and bright sunshine. The climate had helped her hay fever and she had taken up horseback riding which she had loved as a child. She rented a beautiful chestnut mare with white booted legs and rode all over the desert mesa. She was saving up to buy her own so she couldn't fly back to Charlotte to visit for a long time. The work at her new firm was keeping her challenged and she enjoyed the multifamily condo projects she had on the boards. She was being promoted to a project manager she stated with pride and Lee congratulated her. Their calls were often about work and not very personal until several months after moving she had called to ask how everything was going in Charlotte and Lee could not hold back any more. She told Trudy that Ryan was helping her out with her computers. Lee had felt guilty about hanging out with Trudy's old boyfriend so she asked if it was all right.

"We broke up before I left Charlotte. It just wasn't working out. He is a great guy and it's cool that you guys are hanging out," Trudy then explained. Lee was relieved, since Ryan hadn't mentioned the break up.

"I'm sorry about the break up but I had wondered how you and Ryan were going to sort out things for the long run when you moved out there. I hope that you meet someone amazing in Phoenix. You deserve it!" Lee exclaimed.

She missed her friend but she wanted her to be happy. Then Trudy said something that surprised Lee. "Why don't you and Ryan go out for dinner some time" Lee sputtered that they could maybe do that but only if Ryan wanted to. He was so much younger than her; why would he want to be seen out with someone her age. He reminded her of her old roommate Warren, a fellow who could have anybody he wanted with his looks, intelligence and personality. Lee laughed to cover up her racing thoughts, finished up the call and said goodbye to her friend. After hanging up, Lee just sat thinking, a little gleeful and a little nervous. She couldn't get that suggestion of dinner out of her mind. It had been six months since Curt had left and she hadn't been interested in going on any dates until now.

As Lee sat reflecting over the content of the call, she realized that she was actually the happiest she had ever been in her whole adult life; despite the legal threats by Curt. It was so liberating to be free of the weight of another person who was pulling you down. It had been like frantically treading water while someone kept putting overloaded scuba belts on your waist to drag you under. All she really wanted to do discard all the weights and float, looking around with amazement at the world surrounding her and enjoy it. She was tired of dealing with bullying and money worries.

Lee had drawn herself deep into a shell for years to battle emotional attacks and pain. It was a defensive measure and she didn't want to be ashamed of her behavior but now it seemed so sad. She was recently finding her own strengths and defining her identity but she didn't know if this would have happened if she had still been married to Curt. She had been afraid of him in a way. His bizarre, unexpected behavior and his verbal abuse had slowly eaten away at the vulnerable areas of her self-esteem. He seemed to use it as a way to crush and then manipulate her. When she had actually begun to gain the confidence to push back at him, that had been the point when he had thought the marriage had failed it seemed. For Lee it had taken time for her to open up after he had left, like tentative first steps, but she could now express herself freely. She could run through sprinklers with the children, wear the clothes she liked, climb a tree, eat white bread, drink milk, laugh and not be criticized or feel threatened by anyone in her own home. Life was so good!

Chapter 31 – Stairs & Landings

The next time that Ryan called Lee, she described her talk with Trudy to him. He confirmed that they had broken up before she left but he had thought that Lee had known that already. He was also still in touch with Trudy but just infrequently to stay friends. He then shyly suggested that they do as Trudy mentioned and go to dinner together. Lee smiled to herself, tried not to sound too anxious and accepted his offer. They arranged to meet at a cozy Italian spot on the following Thursday when the children would be with Curt.

After she hung up the phone Lee twirled with her arms outstretched then pitched herself onto the bed with a flop. She was giddy with excitement like a teenager. She had never felt this way about someone before and it was intoxicating but a bit scary as well. He was such a kind person, so good to her children, handsome and with such a brilliant mind. But he was a young single guy – what would he want with an older mother of two just going through a messy divorce. She began to analyze what might be going on, second guess the situation, and look for hidden motives but that felt all wrong. So instead she looked up to the ceiling, said a thank you and tried to imagine which dress she would wear for their date.

The week went by very slowly but on the big night, Lee was ready. She had splurged and bought a form fitting black dress and high heels for the occasion. The looks she got from men as she entered the restaurant's bar section made her feel pretty good but she ignored them as she searched for Ryan. She saw a bartender glance her way.

"I think your date is here," he said to the customer in front of him on the stool in a navy blazer with white cuffs.

The man stood up, tall and imposing, then turned around and Lee's breath caught. It was Ryan and he looked so handsome in his preppy jacket, khaki pants and crisp white shirt with a couple buttons open at the collar to expose his tanned chest. His hair was combed back with a bit of gel and his strong chin framed the white gleam of his smile as he admired Lee. She had never seen him dressed up before and this seemed like another person, an older more mature man. He moved forward, gently took her hand, kissed it and said she looked beautiful with such sincerity as he looked directly into her eyes that the rest of the room disappeared. All Lee saw was this strong and attractive man waiting for her. She couldn't believe that she was so lucky.

The food they ate was an indistinguishable blur but Lee noticed the details of the man across from her that she had not paid attention to before. She saw the cow lick of his hair line, the smooth contour of his cheek stretched over the bone and the slight turn of one of his front teeth. He was beautiful and so fascinating to look at that she couldn't turn away. She also felt every beat of her heart in its nervous pounding. She had been a little self-conscious at first, worried that she may have misinterpreted this date but that worry had disappeared once he had taken her hand and complimented her. The two had also delved into more personal subjects than they had approached before.

Lee learned that Ryan's wish was to buy a sailboat and sail around the Caribbean one day. She loved that idea and told him that she had always wanted to travel more and explore other countries. She then revealed that she also hoped to begin painting again and enter some local art contests. Maybe she could even begin to sell her work again. He enjoyed art galleries and offered to take her to NoDo in Charlotte, an art oriented community that had a gallery crawl every first Friday of the month. She was thrilled as they made plans and compared their dreams. But the night ended too quickly as the restaurant closed up and the pair, awkward again but holding hands headed out to the parking lot. When they got to her car, Lee thanked Ryan for the wonderful evening then invited him to her place for dinner the next Thursday. He smiled and readily accepted. The two then leaned in towards each other until their lips touched gently at first, then with intensity for a long passionate kiss. Ryan's hands slowly caressed Lee's waist, while she wrapped her hands around his neck as though she wouldn't let go.

The following Thursday Ryan came to the door of Lee's house with a bouquet of red roses and a chilled bottle of wine. He looked intensely at her as he passed these gifts over the threshold into her open arms while Lee's response was a quick thank you and a drop of her head to hide her flushing cheeks. He had brought the items of a lover she thought, which thrilled her. They both had expectations for this evening that they had not spoken out loud and it made the first few moments awkward. Then Lee welcomed him into the living room and asked him about work. It was a safe conversation which eased them into their usual comfortable rapport again. Lee had prepared salmon with mashed potatoes and grilled vegetables which they ate on the couch in front of the fireplace. The good food and crackling fire helped Lee relax and as Ryan cleared their plates, she leaned back on the couch and closed her eyes.

Suddenly she felt his fingers running over her shoulders and neck in a massaging motion. She smiled and leaned into them - they felt so good. She hadn't been touched by another adult in a long time. Then the fingers slowly dropped to caress the hollow of her throat and down her chest to the edge of her bra. She inhaled sharply and felt her body's arousal. But he worked slowly building her anticipation. He leaned down to trail his lips over the same skin that his fingers had just touched. Then he reached under her shirt to follow the form of her breast, tracing the lines until he had pulled her bra to the side and ran his tongue over her nipple. She responded even more with small moans of pleasure. Then he raised his head to look into her eyes, as though asking permission, and she pulled his head toward her so she could press her lips onto his.

The kiss was long and hard, expressing all the pent up longing and lust of months. Their fingers explored each other's bodies while pieces of clothing were unbuttoned and unzipped. Consumed with passion and wrapped in each other's arms, they lowered themselves on the couch then onto the floor in front of the fire with various discarded clothing scattered around them. Ryan then intentionally slowed himself and began to explore Lee's body. He traced a line of moisture on her skin from her neck down between her breasts, drawing a faint line and giving her exquisite pleasure. Then he moved down her belly to hips and thighs, her muscles clenching in anticipation. When his fingers dropped down between her legs, she was transported. All of her energy was focused on this one area of sensation and she felt a rushing noise in her ears. She exhaled as spasms raced through her body and she greedily moved her hips to maximize the effect while his other hand cupped her breast.

Then when he felt she was ready, Ryan lifted himself over her, his lean muscular frame balanced on his strong arms while he lowered his face to kiss her swollen mouth and neck again. She felt his body become a part of hers and gasped. They were locked in movement as the light of the fire cast shadows across their bodies, unaware of anything around them, focused only on their points of contact. Ryan moved them subtly into various positions heightening the sensations each time, while Lee only marveled that she could feel so much physically. She then let herself go emotionally as well, releasing all her fears and gave her explicit trust to this man. Her heart had opened, cracked like a stubborn nut and she exposed all of herself to the experience. She then felt an even stronger spasm course up her entire body as Ryan tensed and she blurted out a groan of pleasure. He collapsed with a gasp and she held him tight so he wouldn't move off of her body, as tears began to stream down her cheeks. "This is making love" she thought "This is how it is supposed to feel"

Afterwards they lay relaxed in each other's embrace, tangles of arms and legs looped over each other. The fire had dropped to a pleasant yellow and red crackling glow. Ryan began to speak, slowly at first, just a whisper.

"I have wanted to do that for a while. I think that you are a very sexy and amazing woman"

Lee smiled, grateful for the compliment but then demurred saying that she was too old for him, probably by ten years, while someone like Trudy was a better match. He chuckled sadly and then explained that Trudy was a wonderful person but she had serious damage from her former marriage and he was not able to help her with the issues. They had not been intimate very often since it brought back too many bad memories for her and she couldn't enjoy it. The rest was private but he wanted Lee to know that he had never been attracted to anyone as much as he was to her. Their age difference shouldn't matter if they cared for each other. Lee accepted this for now, pushing away images of her mother's disapproval, and looked at the beautiful man beside her. His warm brown skin was shiny with sweat, enhancing the curves of his muscled back and arms. His short dark hair was thick and she couldn't help running her fingers through it as his head rested on her chest. Nothing else mattered but this moment.

Lee and Ryan were together every Thursday night at her house learning about each other and enjoying their private time. Then during the weekends, they spent the days with the children taking them to their base ball games, playgrounds, swimming or out to movies. The children would say good night to Ryan then scramble up stairs with their mother where she would cuddle with them in her bed for reading time. They had gone through all the Maurice Sendak, Silverstein and Robert Munsch books, the beautifully illustrated Whales Song and Opus books and they would eventually get to books geared for older children like Enders Game or Harry Potter. Then she would tuck them each in their own beds for sleep with a big kiss. She also always told them how much she loved them. She thought that this was so important, something that she had never gotten as a child. One day these beauties would be too big for this cozy time together with their mother and it would probably break Lee's heart when that happened. After the children were asleep, Lee and Ryan would sit intertwined while she read and he worked on his papers. They would talk about all kinds of subjects, intimate histories of family, disappointments, surprises and achievements, secure that this person they were confiding to would not break their confidence.

During one of these evenings, Ryan revealed that his father, Eric Walker, had been a US military soldier deployed for a tour in Vietnam then eventually stationed in Panama to assist training recruits in jungle warfare. It was here that he had met Ryan's mother, Maria Diaz. The young girl had been working as an interpreter for supply purchases, having learned English from a local missionary. She was from an old Creole family that had fallen on hard times, so her relatives had been encouraging when she brought the handsome American soldier home to meet them. They expected the match to improve their fortunes.

She was proud and very beautiful, Ryan said as he described her, and he believed that his father must have loved her very much at one time. There was sadness in Ryan's voice as he spoke, so Lee gently took his hand in hers as encouragement, patiently waiting for him to proceed. The pair had gotten permission to marry just before Ryan's father was redeployed back to the States. Eventually Maria was able to get US citizenship through her husband and when his service ended, two moved to Buffalo where Eric had been raised. They were happy for a while even though the weather was a torture for Maria, who was used to the humid tropical air of Central America. In Buffalo, part of the infamous Snowbelt region, she would pile layers of clothing on her small frame before venturing out to the market or take Ryan and his younger brother Brad to school. Still she shook from the cold all through the hard winters.

As the years wore on, Eric became more dissolute, troubled and violent. He had taken a job at a hardware store after his discharge but he quickly became disappointed with the mediocre chores that he had to perform; each day a reminder of how little he had achieved in his life. He was angry that his wife couldn't fit in with the neighbours more, though he didn't understand that it was their prejudice and not her lack of effort. When the couple had bought their new house, Maria had gone to visit some of the neighbours, offering savory arepas and roasted banana dishes, but she was shunned because of her darker skin, accent and strange food. Eventually she just stopped trying and accepted her solitary life. Eric also began suffering from nightmares and flash backs from the war. He took out his frustrations on the boys, often screaming at them, hitting them and locking them in the basement for long periods while Maria wept upstairs begging that they be released. He had instituted military rule in the house which the boys and Maria had to live by. Everyone had to be up at the crack of dawn, make their beds to tight standards and attend to assigned chores. At the table, they had to eat each meal in strict military fashion - fork to the front, then up, then forward to the mouth, then down. All performed with eyes forward, just as Eric had been trained. Ryan realized now that his father must have been suffering from Posttraumatic Stress Disorder but at the time, it wasn't widely known then that these veterans needed serious help. By the time Ryan was old enough to understand, it was far too late.

It was an overcast day in September when Ryan was getting ready to start his first day of sophomore year in high school. He had gotten up early, prepared his back pack and then gone to wake his brother by throwing a shoe at him through the crack of the door. Brad came immediately flying out of the room in his boxer shorts to chase after his brother with the first thing he could grab, the shoe, calling out to him that he was dead now. Ryan had just hurried around a corner when Brad threw the shoe after his fleeing brother with such force that it bounced off the walls and knocked over the vase and picture frame on a side table. The vase unleashed its contents of glass marbles everywhere, with a pelting noise as they hit the wood floor. This caused Brad to stop in surprise as the disaster unfolded before him, watching the beads bounce as though in slow motion. He had forgotten about his father for a minute in his early morning stupor but looked up from the mess on the floor just as the heavy set man burst out of his room as though in response to gun fire. The tall thin bare chest boy just stood in the hall while fear crept over him. His father was in just his dress shirt, boxers and socks, which would have been funny under other circumstances.

Upon seeing his son staring at him wide eyed and guilty, stammering "Sorry Dad….. I'll clean it up", Eric's face began to grow a deep red as the flush of anger moved from his chest, up his neck to his forehead. He was furious and began to lose control of his temper. He grabbed the boy by the arm almost dislocating it from the shoulder socket and dragged him toward the stairs. At that moment Maria came out of the bedroom in a rush with wild eyes, concern for her children painted all over her face. She grabbed at Eric's arm that gripped Brad and pulled to try to separate them murmuring.

"Everything is fine, it was just an accident"

As the interlocked group moved toward the stairs Ryan came back down the hall from the opposite direction just in time to see his father swing out his other arm to knock away Maria's grip. This hit her across the chest and sent her sprawling down the stairs; her neck was broken when her head hit the fifth step. She collapse like a rag doll and slid the rest of the way down.

After the tragedy, Ryan had left home to live in a small room above the garage of friend's house in order to finish up his last years in high school while Brad was sent to their uncle's house. He hadn't seen Brad much since then, just on holidays when his uncle and aunt invited him over. He refused to visit his father at all, either in the jail or once he was released after being acquitted of the accidental death. Ryan only had school to sustain him and help him survive on his own. He won scholarships and grants to the public college but he still had to take out student loans to cover the rest. He refused financial help from his father and worked multiple jobs in the back of restaurants to afford books.

Ryan was a brilliant student, with an exceptional work ethic and he held a straight 4.0 GPA throughout his undergraduate years. The loss of his supportive and kind mother had paralyzed him and he could barely cope those first months but now there was only an ache and sadness that would creep up on him once in a while. It forced him to retreat to be alone where he would think of her, tears sometimes welling up in his eyes as he contemplated how he would have done things differently. He had so many questions that he wanted to ask her and things he wanted to tell her, but that could never happen now. After a few hours, he would force all of these emotions down, burying them deep and head out into the world again. Lee held him tight as he relayed this story, her heart breaking for his loss and they just stayed in that position for almost an hour before Lee quietly encouraged him to come with her up to bed.

Chapter 32 – Gypsum Board & Paint

Finally Lee's lake house was on track to being complete and she told Curt that she was ready to put the marital property up for sale. Curt then had bargained with Lee to allow her to select the realtor if she took all responsibility for anything that came up in the inspection report on the house and especially the basement. She consented and called in her neighbour Andrea to list the house. Andrea wasn't necessarily the top selling agent at that time but she was very good and most of all she knew what Lee was dealing with. She would help Lee through this process. Meanwhile Curt had his new lawyer draw up another legal agreement for Lee to sign regarding the inspection report for the house. Lee knew that in North Carolina that once a real estate deal was final it came under the Caveat Emptor clause in law or often called "Buyer beware". There was no going back to ask for anything or sue for surprises once a sale was complete, the buyer took the property "as is", but Lee made sure that there were no issues.

When the inspection was finally done Andrea said that it was one of the cleanest inspection reports that she had seen and Lee was proud that she gotten the house to such a great condition. She had seen that single mothers often couldn't maintain a house properly due to budgets, abilities and time so she didn't want that stigma on the house. Andrea then talked to both Lee and Curt about comparables and a suggested sales price for the house. They both agreed to the number then Andrea got the papers prepared for signing. In order to sign the papers though, Curt had insisted that Andrea drive to his new "love nest" rather than meet her at his nearby office. He had moved in with his girlfriend to the house that her third husband had given to her in the divorce settlement.

It was in an attractive gated community on a hill near Gastonia, a blue collar suburb of Charlotte, and Curt had wanted to show it off. Andrea had gone to the house, been given a tour and witnessed Curt's lustful pawing at the woman before they sat at the dining room table to review the papers. She was uncomfortable with this arrangement and told Lee this. So Lee had to call Curt to request that future transactions occur at his office. He didn't care about the next meetings since his point had already been made. He wanted Lee to know what he had now - a sexy woman with a big house.

The marital property was shown often and Lee scrambled to clean it and take the children out each time a potential buyer came to see it. After a month, when they didn't have any offers, Curt insisted that they drop the price ten thousand dollars every week. Andrea was appalled at the suggestion, since this would affect her own house value, but Lee told her that they had no choice. After a couple weeks of price dropping, the house read like a distress sale and three bids came in on the same day. Andrea faxed over the offers to both Curt and Lee to review.

One was from a pair of lawyers and it was low so Lee was glad that it had gotten eliminated. The next two were for the same amount but different closing dates. Curt immediately picked the one with the shortest closing date of just two months. Then he marked up the counter offer with an even shorter closing date of just one month and offered to drop the price even more if this was acceptable. Lee was not happy with this since she needed the extra month, as well as the money, but she didn't argue. She just wanted this last piece of the common property divided and closed out. Luckily the buyer couldn't make the closing any shorter and the original deal was accepted. Lee breathed a sigh of relieve and told the children that they were moving to the lake in a couple months.

All the contractual papers were signed and everything seemed to be going well until Curt threw a wrench in to the proceedings a day before the closing by deciding to refuse to sign the final papers. He had called Lee and told her that he didn't care if the buyers sued both of them since he was not giving back his share of the down payment loan from her parents. He told her that she could pay them back herself. He needed all of his half of the money for himself. Lee had to notify Andrea who said that if Lee was willing to sign tomorrow, then she would not be sued. Andrea also then had to tell the buyer's agent to prepare for a serious problem at closing. The next day when the two real estate company representatives came to the table with their clients, each was prepared to recommend legal action against Curt if he didn't sign over the house.

Lee was the first to arrive and Curt came sauntering in shortly after her. He nodded hello to Lee then looked for a chair as far away from her as he could find. He lowered himself into his selection, crossed one leg on top of the other and set his elbow on the chair arm so he could use his fingers to support the side of his head, a pose that spread his arrogance like a coating on the walls of the law firm. She watched with incredulity and wonder at how different they were. She had come to understand the hard way that he didn't have the same morals as she had, but now she was seeing that contractual agreements meant nothing to him as well. She was worried about the buyers in this transaction since it would be so disappointing and hard on that family if the sale didn't close. Lee had heard that they had two little girls so she would do what she could to help but it was out of her hands.

As soon as the buyers arrived, an attractive blond woman in a form fitting dress and a dark haired man in a tailored dark suit, everyone was ushered into the conference room. Papers were passed around and introductions were made. When Lee found out that their names were actually Ken and Barbie she had to stifle a laugh since they fit that image perfectly. They were a very attractive young couple, she was a curvy blond and he was tall and dark haired. It wasn't so funny when shortly after this Curt repeated that he would not sign the papers if it meant that he had to pay Lee's parents back their note on the property. The closing attorney then formally stated that Curt would be committing a breach of contract and he would be liable for law suits from real estate companies from both sides. Curt just pointed to Lee and said that she would be liable as well, but the attorney clarified that this was not true since she had already signed the contract and completed her obligations. The attorney then suggested that Curt join him in his office for a discussion where they could hopefully come to some arrangement.

Lee and the buyers had to wait over an hour before Curt and the attorney finally came back. It had taken four attorneys, including a personal friend of Curt's, to finally talk him into signing. He had only agreed in the end when a compromise was made to hold the disputed money in trust until Curt could sue Lee for it later. As they were all leaving, the closing attorney leaned down to Lee's realtor and whispered.

"The real problem was that the seller was out to be as mean as possible to his former wife, who seems to be a nice person"

Andrea whispered back in a tone that emphasized her words.

"She is a very nice person"

Once the house was settled, Curt insisted that the children begin a schedule where they stayed over with him every other weekend from Thursday through Sunday. Lee agreed but tried to see the Andy and Sarah most every day by having lunch with them at school on Fridays. She also did all the driving between the two houses since Curt otherwise insisted on keeping the children on Sunday night so he didn't have to back into town to drop them off. If she wanted the children back Sunday she had to go pick them up. Lee had to swallow her pride to do this as well because Curt would not let her use the front door when she came to get Andy and Sarah. He insisted that she go through the open garage to the mud room door where he made her wait while he played the role of doting father. She had to watch as Curt had the children gather up their back packs and shoes then forced them to kiss his girlfriend goodbye.

It was painful to feel like an outsider viewing this domestic scene with her own children on the other side but when those two raced out to hug her and said that they missed her, she melted with relief and love for them. Lee soon discovered though that the children were often difficult after a few days with their father. Once in the car, they seemed more belligerent toward her and fought with each other, something they didn't do at her house. She would have to immediately remind them to behave better and that her rules included being respectful to each other. When they arrived at home, which would be after seven thirty, she had to hustle them to finish homework, check for papers to sign since Curt would have forgotten that, read them a book and tuck them into bed. Then she would sometimes just sit in the hall, listening to their breathing and sending out a prayer for their safekeeping.

One day when Lee went to the school to have lunch with the children, the teacher approached her to mention that the children were falling asleep in class on some Fridays and they never had their homework or school slips signed. Lee discovered that it was after the Thursday nights with Curt and she went back home with a mission; to ask Curt to get the children to bed earlier and help them with homework. But he just couldn't handle it and the problems persisted. He tried to get his new girlfriend to do it but she was more interested in her tennis game and sometimes her own child, a spoiled overweight boy the same age as Andy, who she shipped off to "fat camps" in the summers. Curt was also going out of town on weekends when he was scheduled to have the children, so he left them with his girlfriend. The children were upset with this and when Lee asked to keep the children herself on those weekends Curt would not agree. Lee had spoken with Joan, the girlfriend, but that conversation had been difficult. The woman had called Lee one day, her deep southern accent making it hard to understand.

"How arre y'all" she drawled in false concern. "I jest wanted to talk to you about how we'll be rais'in the children. I realize that you'll be wanting us to take them a whole lot more. I know that I can't git my son out of ma hair to go to his father's enuff, if you know what ih mean"

Then she gave a giggle at the end of this speech. Lee was too stunned to talk at first and then she had to hold back the choke in her throat to cry out.

"I love my children, I want them with me as much as possible and you are not raising them!"

She realized instantly that she would never be able to understand this woman and their views on child-raising were miles apart. She was obviously rather insensitive and perhaps not very bright but maybe she was just functioning on lies that Curt had told her. If this was the case then perhaps it wasn't her fault and Lee would keep this in mind.

When the Easter celebration at the school approached, Curt had sent her a fax that read:

"Our family has decided to attend the school Easter event together so you are not required to attend"

Lee found it hard to believe what she was reading. She was hurt once again by his callous action. She had not asked Ryan to attend the event with her since she didn't think it would be appropriate at this time in the separation. Obviously Curt did not have the same consideration toward her and the children. Then she discovered that he had been changing the children's legal and medical paper work without telling her. A nurse had called Lee when she became a little suspicious about Curt's requests to alter the forms. She showed Lee the forms which listed Curt's girlfriend Joan as the emergency medical contact and another stranger to Lee as being allowed to pick the children up.

"That just didn't seem right so I had to call you," she confided to Lee.

Lee thanked her and revised the form but she found out that she had to go into the school and doctor's office on a regular basis to recheck the records to make sure that the information had not been tampered with again in any way. She had requested a block on all records and left a copy of the court order at each office but Curt was still able to bypass that once in a while, depending on who he spoke to at the offices. Lee didn't care if he wanted to get revenge on her for some imagined slight but she begged him not to harm or endanger the children in any way by changing the medical forms but he ignored her.

Curt then wrote a letter to one of the children's teachers saying that he was now living with a woman named Joan and if the teacher had any problems with the children, they were to contact Joan right away. The teacher called Lee in to her class to show her the letter and explain that she was appalled by receiving it. She was a Christian and did not want to know that this man was living with someone.

"I certainly will not be calling this woman!" She declared hotly.

Lee apologized and thanked the teacher for letting her know. When she told Ryan her frustrations, he had teasingly offered to go straighten this out with a few physical threats. She said that wouldn't be wise but she thanked him for his support and clung tightly to him, feeling fortunate to have someone like him during this difficult period.

The house was almost finished now and they were excited about moving in. Lee was doing all of the painting herself so she rented a compressor after the one she had bought broke under the strain of painting so many cathedral ceilings. For a week Lee wept white paint from the corner eyes as the fine spray of primer and finish coat penetrated her goggles. Next she inhaled the dust of the tile cutter as she finished the countertops and the shower floors for the washrooms. Her hands became calloused and red from the mortar trowel for the concrete block post work and the nail gun for the trim but she enjoyed all of it. She had taken over the contracting when the GC had neglected to pay some of the subs and once she had sorted out the lien issues, she found some good deals on the materials and labor to complete the house as well as using her own sweat equity.

When Lee's parents came to help with the finishing touches, the electricity had not been fully turned on due to the contractor issue. So they had to sweep, install trim shelving for the closets in over one hundred degree temperatures. They were all dripping with sweat in the confined spaces but they worked hard. Lee's father went for swims in the lake on breaks after which he declared.

"The water was so warm it didn't even cool me off"

After the closets were done Lee set up her wet saw on the back deck and cut granite tiles for the kitchen counter while her parents cleaned up until they all eventually gave in to exhaustion and left to pick up the children at school.

The next day the group all helped the movers shift Lee's possessions to the new house and when it was done they went back to the old house where they slept on air mattresses until the electricity was finally turned on at the lake property. After everything was complete and power booted up, Anne and Joseph drove Lee and the children one final time to the attractive new white house perched on the edge of the cliff overlooking the lake. They stood with Lee on the deck, viewing the forested back yard with the trampoline and hammock that Ryan had set up, the dock extending into the green blue water and told her that she had done a great job. Then they kissed their grandchild goodbye, gave Lee big hugs and drove back home to Windsor. Lee missed them when they had gone.

Chapter 33 – Cabinets & Trim

The children and Lee had been living in the new house for several months when Halloween arrived. They had met a few of the neighbours but Lee was looking forward to knocking on front doors for trick or treat and introducing herself and the children. One of their next door neighbours, a straight backed strong fellow with wavy tousled hair, had paddled over in a canoe the first time he had seen her on the dock to introduce himself as Reginald.

"We are German and we drink beer on Saturday and Sunday. You are welcome to come over any time to join us," he told her with a slight Germanic accent.

She thanked him and mentioned that she would love to come over. He explained to her after they had been friends for many years, that the reaction to his introduction was his way of determining if she was a bible thumping Baptist or not because they wouldn't drink on a Sunday. She had then asked the age of his two boys since she had seen them paddle off in their canoe and thought that they might be close to Andy's age. She wanted the boys to meet and once they did, they became very close friends. These two neighbor boys spent each afternoon at her house once they had finished their homework and Lee cared for them as her own children.

In fact, there was a large group of boys the same age and a couple girls that were Sarah's age who lived down the street and soon they all began coming to Lee's house to hang out after school. Lee had moved her children to the local school, a new brick building on a large campus complex within a ten minute drive to the house. Andy and Sarah enjoyed all their new friends and Lee's heart warmed when she saw her children laughing and playing with the others. She had set up a recreation room in the lowest level in the house complete with a pool table, ping pong table, dart board, video games and a fridge for drinks.

When the children got tired of inside games, they headed to the trampoline or asked Lee if she would watch them swim. She bought kayaks so they could paddle around and tubes for swimming. Eventually with Ryan's help they all built a tree house on the hillside overlooking the water, with tire swing made out of an old tire they had found on the property. Ryan also cleared an area and set up a vegetable garden for the children to help plant. It was all she could have hoped for and she was content.

On that first Halloween, Andy had decided to go trick or treating with the neighbour boys, so Lee and Sarah went on their own. Sarah was dressed as the Little Mermaid and Lee was dressed as Esmeralda, "Enriching Disney even more" Lee thought but her daughter was very excited about her costume as she ran up the sidewalk to a tastefully designed stucco house perched on high the corner. Once the door opened, Sarah held open her bag and Lee explained to the owners that they had just moved in cross the street. The couple, Nina and George Murphy, said that they had watched the construction and then invited Lee and Sarah in for a quick visit. It was a well furnished home with traditional Queen Anne replica furniture and overstuffed couches in rooms with views out of French doors to the green of the fifteenth hole of the golf course.

The couple offered Lee and Sarah a seat on the couch and then asked where they had moved from. Lee told them that they were originally from Canada but they loved living in the South now. They discussed the advantages of the area, the reduced taxes and the great school system. Eventually they asked Lee if she was married and she explained that she was divorced but she had a boyfriend who was a computer programmer. At this comment the couple sat forward on their couch. Lee thought that maybe they were prudish about her having a boyfriend but it turned out that they were interested in his computer skills. They explained that they owned a company which sent programmers all over the country to set up new software and they could not find enough talented people to hire. Nina was the one who hunted for the new employees and after hearing how many computer languages that Ryan knew, she suggested that Lee ask him to call her for an interview.

Lee immediately called Ryan to pass on the potential job information and by the next morning he had made an appointment for an interview. Lee was actually invited to attend the interview as well and after some pleasantries, Nina began to ask a series of technical questions to Ryan who answered them with confidence. Then the conversation moved onto issues regarding travel and availability. Nina apologized to Lee as she described the amount of travel required during the week for the position they had in mind for Ryan. She wanted to make sure that they both understood the demands of the job so it would not hurt their private life. As the interview wound down, Nina explained that she and her husband would discuss Ryan's potential employment and call him in the next few days.

Ryan was a little anxious to find out if they were going to offer him a job and at what salary. Since dating Lee he had begun to understand that he needed to make a better living so they could do some of the things that they had talked about in the future. This job opportunity might change his life. A few days later Nina called and Ryan was offered a position with a salary that was three times higher than his current job. He accepted immediately then called Lee to give her the good news and to thank her. Ryan was so happy about his new position that he insisted on taking Lee out for a celebration dinner. Lee's divorce had just been finalized recently as well so she was definitely in the mood to celebrate.

The two went to a charming French restaurant in the historic district of the South End and they were given a table outside on the patio. It was a beautiful balmy evening with stars out, the sound of crickets and the smell of honeysuckle. Ryan was animated as he described his new responsibilities to Lee who grinned as she watched his handsome face light up. She felt her heart swell with love for him and understood that she was incredibly fortunate. He explained that he would be traveling during the week but home to Charlotte each weekend. He promised that he would still be able to see her often though they would lose their Thursday sleepovers. He also reassured her that he would continue to watch the children's baseball games and join them swimming. Then he smiled and took her hand.

"I have so much to thank you for and I am not talking about the job. I am falling in love with you - but I hope that doesn't scare you away"

Lee blushed then and felt even younger than him at this moment. She smiled back at Ryan and quietly said.

"I am falling for you too"

It was corny but it was true and he leaned over and kissed her.

Meanwhile, Curt's anger was growing. He imagined that Lee was getting all kinds of money from her parents while he had to start all over with very little. He had hidden his retirement fund that the company had vested for him and a bank account from Lee, but that wasn't enough. He had also seen the younger good looking guy that Lee was dating and that had affected him more than he had thought. He had gone to one of Andy's baseball games and even though Lee and the fellow tried to be inconspicuous, Curt had seen them. He had always been very observant. The guy had waved bye to Andy, given

Lee a kiss then jumped on a Ducati motorcycle and driven off. He rode the bike with incredible confidence, one hand on a knee while the other revved the throttle. At the last moment though, Curt thought that the guy had actually turned and looked right at him in an almost challenging way just before the bike and driver were lost from view behind the trees.

The incident had unsettled Curt and made him a bit more cautious about confronting Lee in person. Attending these baseball games was something Curt didn't do too often since it just burned him to be anywhere near Lee or her new neighbourhood. The kids should be doing sports in his area not hers. He was a two parent household and she was not, which had to be more important. He began refusing to allow the children to attend their sports or school functions if these occurred on his days. Lee had called and sent notes to Curt asking him to please allow Andy to go to his baseball and Sarah to go on her class trip or gymnastics. She had even offered to do all the driving but he refused.

Instead he signed the children up for tennis lessons in his community and told Lee that he would make sure that the guard at the gatehouse refused her entrance if she ever tried to see them play. He took the children on trips to the beach in his new RV and forgot to tell Lee. He ignored the pickup times when Lee was supposed to come get the children at his house or he refused to answer the phone if he saw Lee's number on the caller ID so she couldn't talk to the children. All these things were in violation of the separation agreement but he didn't care. Lee wouldn't do anything about it except whine, like she always did, he figured.

Lee didn't like the inconsideration and acts of spite that Curt was initiating but the worst for her was sharing the children for holidays. It was a new situation in that she wouldn't see her children for Christmas or Easter on alternate years or weeks at a time in the summer. Curt would never consider splitting Christmas Day or Easter like many divorced parents. Instead he would be taking the children to Canada to visit his parents or keeping them at his house through Easter holidays without giving her any access.

In order to distract herself from this sad jetsam of divorce, Lee decided to plan wonderful holidays for herself on those dates. The trips she researched and booked included drives in the mountains, kayaking in Annapolis and beach holidays to Hilton Head or Savannah. She also flew to Canada or Florida to visit her family especially during holidays.

Ryan went with her on many of these trips but his new job was extremely demanding so he couldn't join her on the longer ones. He was however making so much more money now that he had decided to look into fulfilling one of his dreams, which was to own a live on-board sailboat.

Ryan researched the type of boat he wanted and eventually found an older thirty eight foot Morgan Out Island that was within his budget. Morgan's were thick hulled, wide body, mono hull blue water sailing boats. They were meant to sail across oceans. He took Lee with him to Edisto Beach to go see the boat in person and look it over for defects. A full inspection would be done by a professional during the sale but Ryan knew what he was looking for. He was a very mechanically inclined person and he could repair anything just by reading a book on it, but he also had a lot of experience. He had a gift for figuring out how to fix engines, repair fiberglass or just get rid of stains on fabric using an everyday product. When he saw the Morgan, he knew that he could fix this boat.

The couple had found the marina on the east side of the island then began hunting for the boat in the slip the owner had indicated. It was at the end of the last set of docks, tied up where their approach was to the boat's side so they could see the lines of the deck rail with its blue stripe below and the matching bimini and dodger covers. It was a good looking sail boat though the teak on the deck was dried out, the paint mottled and the canvas faded. They introduced themselves to the agent waiting on deck then asked permission to go on board. He introduced the boat as having thirty seven foot length, eleven foot width and four foot draft. She was wide which made for much more comfortable cabin living space below. There was a Perkins diesel engine, roller furling jib, spinnaker sail, air conditioning, depth finder, radar, microwave and propane stove.

"All the comforts of home are in this boat," the salesman enthusiastically spouted.

Ryan walked along the rail checking all the lines, sails, self tailing winches and fittings. They went below to the spacious cabin next where there was a kitchen and a chart table near the hatch opening, a washroom with marine head and small shower stall, V bunk at the front and a second bunk to the side. There were skylights and port holes but it was still dark due to all the stained wood throughout. Lee sat at the small dining table that could fold down to make a living room space while Ryan opened all the floor hatches to check the through hull fittings and pipes for leaks, rust or damage. When he was satisfied he came and sat with Lee then asked her if she would consider sailing with him on his boat some day. She laughed and said that it would a great adventure but she couldn't go very far until her children were all grown up.

"That's a deal!" he exclaimed.

"We can also take the kids with us - just on safe trips down the Intercoastal or sailing in the bays," he said, a grin on his face as he moved his arm over her shoulders to give her a grateful hug and kiss.

Once the purchase was made, Ryan asked Lee and a friend to help him deliver the boat down the Intercoastal to the slip he had rented at the old Navy Marina in Charleston, now open for private use. They left Edisto early and motored the boat out of the harbor then sailed out along the coast. Ryan had taught Lee some of the basic sailing techniques using the winches, captain's wheel, compass and various ropes for adjusting the sails. He also showed her the wind arrow on the mast that indicated the best point of sail for efficiency and speed. After sailing north to the jetty entrance, they cranked up the motor and cruised on horsepower the rest of the way to Charleston. It took the team six hours, after grounding the boat once on a sand bar, to get it to its new slip. It had been a beautiful day, with the sun, wind and spray off of the water, so Lee became hooked on sailing.

It was a sport of contrasts – one moment calm and peaceful, the next requiring urgent activity to tack or reef the sails. Lee enjoyed the challenging work but she also just wanted to relax and watch the water all day. She actually felt meditative when the horizon looked endless and it was quiet except for the lapping of waves on the hull. She would then offer up wishes for her loved ones to always to always be safe and happy. She thought about other people in this world who were not as fortunate. Lee had grown up hearing the pleas on TV from spokespeople like Sally Struthers to assist impoverished children in Africa and she always thought that she would help as well someday. She had signed up as a parent volunteer in the children's new school and she had been invited to join the city's Board of Variance but Lee wanted to work with people who really needed help and didn't have the opportunities of those in the US. This was a dream of hers yet to be realized.

The boat was settled into a well next to similar sized sailboats, with neatly ordered equipment, trim sails and shiny varnished wood. In order to get his boat in comparable shape, Ryan decided that he would need to spend his weekends working on his new boat. He asked Lee if she would mind driving to Charleston on Friday nights with him to live on the boat over the weekends that the children were with their father. Lee loved Charleston and the water so she immediately agreed. She also thought that it would be great to spend even more time with Ryan and see how they get along on the boat, whether sailing or repairing it. As the months sped by, they found that they were quite compatible. Ryan was patient with Lee, teaching her aspects of boat repair as well as rigging and sail making. This made him seem older, more mature to her and their age difference was forgotten. Ryan had worked in a sail making shop during summer breaks and he owned a commercial sewing machine so he could sew as well as she could. On the weekends, there were usually lots of boaters around and soon they got to know other couples who were live-on-boards as well. These sailors invited them for dinner on their boats or to group barbeques on shore.

Many of these sailors had done some serious blue water sailing and Lee was enchanted with their stories of far off sailing adventures. They sailed to hidden coves and islands that could only be accessed by water. They walked beaches looking for shells, snorkeled remote locations and hiked jungles hunting for waterfalls. They met amazing people like the man who sailed the world in an open dug out rigged with a center mast. This fellow had even found a new wife in the Philippines to join him in his small craft and they cruised between ports trading goods when possible or living off the sea's bounty. There was also a couple who sailed in a twenty five foot fiberglass sailboat and wrote about their adventures for magazines to earn money to continue to sail. They eventually had two children who sailed with them around the world for years. There were also horror stories which involved boats nearly being hit by a freighter or colliding with lost cargo containers in the middle of the ocean at night. Tales of storms and hurricanes that drove boats off their moorings or aground and these always made Lee a bit more respectful of the power of nature but it did not deter her desire to sail.

When they were alone for dinner, Ryan would take Lee to catch shrimp and he would make a gumbo or low country spicy shrimp dish with corn, potatoes and Old Bay seasoning. He was an excellent cook and Lee had never had anyone cook for her besides her mother. It made her feel a little spoiled. Afterwards they would lie together on deck under the stars contently before making love in the bunk below. During the day they would work on sanding the teak or repairing the lines and stanchions then jump in the water to swim. Dolphins often circled the marina and came to investigate the noises they made on the boat. One time during an amorous mid day coupling below deck, they heard fierce knocking on the hull, which startled them until they realized it was their friends from a few boats down playing a prank. They had seen their boat rocking and knew what it meant.

Lee also learned to follow the rhythm of the tidal current which was very strong during the ebbing or surge tides and potentially dangerous. They lived by its rise and fall and Lee took advantage of the slack tide, when the current was least active, to swim or clean mollusks off the hull. They were busy all the time but their time together still had the feel of a holiday. Ryan was an easy companion and he was confident enough in himself that he was not threatened by Lee's abilities. Instead he was respectful of her ideas, interested in her opinions and they fit together so well, in both mind and body. Lee still missed the children but it was a wonderfully free period when the couple could pretend that they would travel far away one day together.

Chapter 34 - Toilets & Fixtures

Everything was going so well for Lee in her new life and then the law suits started. Curt's anger had boiled over. First he sued her to get back the money that was held in escrow – her parent's loan for the house down payment. Curt had a new lawyer since his last two had quit. Lee had accidently met one of his previous lawyers at a fund raiser for a judge. When the woman that she had been chatting with found out whom Lee's ex-husband was she had laughed and then explained.

"Your ex-husband had a nickname at the firm, and it was a four letter word. Everyone who had to deal with him used it behind his back. We were all glad to when he switched firms"

This was probably a breach of lawyer privilege but Lee was grateful to know that someone else, who understood the situation, shared her view of Curt's behavior. It was actually pretty amusing when she thought about it.

Curt's new lawyer had filed the suit to be heard in South Carolina, thinking that Lee's firm couldn't represent her there but the big firm had lawyers who could practice in that state too. In fact, Lee's lawyer for this case knew the magistrate of the little town where the trial would be held very well. He told Lee that that the man was very fair and she had a good chance. Before the trial, Curt offered to settle with Lee if they split the money but Lee left the decision to her parents who rejected the offer. On the day of the trial, which had been a last minute booking, Lee's parents had fortuitously been driving through the area from Florida to visit her on their way back to Canada so they were able to attend. This support, along with Ryan's, was a great help to Lee. She was grateful to her parents and she began to feel solidarity with them for the first time in her adult life. They had helped her with the house and now they were by her side for the next challenge.

The group had driven to the small town about a half an hour away and met with Lee's lawyer in an associate's office to prep before the hearing. Lee had never been in a courtroom before and she had been nervous. As the time approached, they walked across the street to the older brick municipal offices and entered a dingy room with a desk and a low wood stained wall separating the front section. It was smaller than she imagined a courtroom would be, even for a magistrate, and rather outdated in appearance with yellowing paint and bench style seating. Eventually the magistrate entered through a back door, a kindly but weathered heavy set man. He took his seat and shuffled through papers on his desk before looking over the group facing him. Lee's mother was in running shoes, due to bursitis, and a casual golf outfit while her father, with his thinning grey hair and glasses, was still wearing his navy golf wind breaker. They were a modest looking couple. Curt had arrived in a dark power suit and proceeded to try to control the room; shaking Joseph's hand while pounding him on the back like a presidential candidate, grinning at the magistrate then proceeding to plunk his well shod feet up on the wall of the witness stand until it was motioned for him to drop them. His lawyer was a thin serious fellow who seemed embarrassed by his aggressive client but tried his best to act professional.

When Lee took the stand, she calmed herself so that her answers would be clear. She talked honestly and directly to the magistrate, turning to him on key points. She was embarrassed to talk about her scare with cancer so when he asked her about that time period, she just said that "there were difficulties" and cast her eyes down. The magistrate could tell more by watching this former couple than the documents he received earlier could ever disclose. He had been considering in Lee's favor even before she had taken the stand but when he saw the arrogant plaintiff try to explain why he didn't need to pay his former in-laws back with unsupportable justification, he was convinced. During his years on the bench the magistrate had seen these kinds of characters who preyed on people they viewed as weaker and he was in a position to rectify this. He was a southern good ol' boy, who was looking forward to retiring to fish every day that the good Lord provided fair weather. But right now he would try to ensure some justice was done in this case as he dismissed the group, wrote a note to himself on the main points for his ruling in the woman's favor and began to imagine the pot roast dinner waiting for him at home.

After the hearing, Lee and Ryan said goodbye to her parents who drove off north on Highway 77 toward Canada. Then the two headed down south on that same highway, through Columbia and onto Highway 26 towards Charleston. They took the exit ramp that lead them straight to the naval yard and passed through the military check point, where Ryan had registered when he first leased the slip. Once inside the barriers, they drove past abandoned multi storey barracks, office buildings and ship repair facilities. The small marina was at the end of the service road next to a high concrete commercial dock where massive tankers and container ships were unloaded. They had brought groceries for the boat and used the public cart to wheel them down the long gangways out to the boat. Once everything was put away, Ryan popped open a bottle of sparkling wine, poured them each a glass to toast the end of the court case. Then they lay back on cushions to watch the sunset from the cockpit. The water in the marina, protected by the surrounding break wall, was like glass. Its reflections described scenes of glistening lights, white hulls and dark edges. Once the sun set, with its vibrant orange and red luminance reflected off the clouds and water, they lay wrapped in each other's arms to wait for the stars. It was a perfect evening as they listened to the musical tones of the halyards clanging with the movement of the slight breeze and rocking of the boat as they made love.

The next day Lee and Ryan decided to drive into the city to wander the market area looking through the woven baskets, painted shells and t-shirts. They ducked into galleries to view the realistic styled paintings of marshes and historic buildings then they walked along the high stone break wall past Rainbow Row, the stately colorful mansions that lined the Battery area facing the bay. Off of a cobble stone street with gas lanterns they found a little restaurant where the hostess seated them in a private corner booth. A candle on the table flickered in a silver holder casting shadows across Lee's face while they looked over the menu. Lee was still disturbed about the hearing but this dinner was a reward for the event being over. She ordered mussels for an appetizer and salmon in a puff pastry with crème sauce for her entre and they also shared a bottle of Chateau Neuf de Pape. After the delicious food and the smooth oaky wine they relaxed and sat a little farther against the back of their seats, smiles on their faces. It was then that Ryan threw out the remark that changed everything.

"So when are we getting married"

He had blurted it, a grin of mischief playing on his mouth. Lee took the remark as casually as it had been delivered and responded without thinking.

"I have just been through enough grief with one marriage. I don't want to even think about that again for years"

She knew that she had made a mistake the minute the words left her mouth. She looked up at Ryan to see his reaction. His features were frozen for a minute then his mouth shifted into a straight line before he turned away to look for the waiter. When he turned back, he had recomposed himself and asked Lee if she wanted anything else.

The conversation had turned practical and impersonal. Lee now felt uncomfortable and guilty about saying something that had obviously disappointed him. He paid the check and they left the restaurant to go straight to the car for a quiet return to the boat. The rest of the weekend was spent staining woodwork, preparing a few meals, closing up the boat and then driving back to Charlotte, all with a slight tension between them. Lee had tried to ease things a bit by explaining to Ryan that she had just meant that she needed a bit of time. She didn't want him to think that she wouldn't marry him. They could get engaged if he wanted but she just couldn't go straight to marriage right now, she had just gotten divorced. Also, she hadn't been sure that he had been serious either; it had been a surprise to her. He did relax a bit once he heard this but he was still slightly cool toward her when they parted.

Now Lee was worried. She may have just jeopardized the best relationship she had ever had by misunderstanding Ryan's expectations. He had never been married so perhaps he was in more of a hurry than she was at this time and she had not seen it coming. Maybe it was due to her involvement in the house, children and law suit that she had missed his intentions. Ryan must have been making signals to her over the last months. She had lain on the bed once he left with a deep melancholy settling over her, as she tried to reassess what went wrong and what she really wanted for her life. She was confused, fearful of the handcuffs of marriage again and wasn't even sure she deserved someone like Ryan. Soon tears were flowing uncontrollably down her cheeks until exhausted with distress, she couldn't cry anymore.

Eventually she had to go pick up the children at Curt's house. He had made his girlfriend sell her house and they had purchased a larger house which had a view of the golf course. Lee thought that was a big mistake on Joan's part and she felt a sudden stab of pity for the woman. She was being taken down the same path that Lee had been on with Curt; overextending for the sake of the image and the ego of a man who only cared for himself. This made her realize how much better a person Ryan was for her; his kindness, care for the children and love for her seemed to surpass anything that Curt had ever shown toward them. The long drive gave Lee time to think about Ryan and how she wanted it to work between them. She just couldn't consider marriage yet so she didn't know if she could save their relationship. She would have to wait to see if they could get back to where they were last Friday. It would be hard and words once spoken could not be taken back.

Ryan continued to call Lee from the road though their conversations were not quite the same as they had been. There was a wariness and coolness to his voice, at least in Lee's perception. Their relationship wasn't as easy going and intimate as it had been when they got together on weekends anymore and Lee didn't know how to fix it. Her business was doing well and she immersed herself in the design of new projects during the week. She could almost forget all the other issues if she just worked hard enough. She had a new restaurant chain and a daycare franchise that had hired her for multiple projects throughout North Carolina.

Lee's engineers, who had also become good friends, were doing a great job on performance and delivery of these projects. She had a mechanical and plumbing engineer, a tall lean man with a mustache and thick hair who could charm any client and had an excellent reputation with the city inspectors. His partner was an electrical engineer, a shorter solidly built man with a thick southern accent, who did quick and precise work. The structural engineer she had found was a cantankerous fellow with a wicked dry sense of humor. He entertained her whenever they spoke on the phone and used his sharp mind to produce excellent work for reasonable fees. So she had a team that she could trust. This one aspect of her life was steady and reliable, but she knew that it wasn't enough for her. She needed to take Uncle Jack's advice and find a way to help others.

One day when Lee was skimming through the local Lake Wylie paper before throwing it into the recycling bin, her attention was captured by a photo of a dozen people on a mountainside with the caption "Team Hikes Kilimanjaro for Kenya Orphanage". Lee was immediately enticed to read the article. It was about a charity founded by a woman in the Lake Wylie area that was looking for sponsors for children in an orphanage in Nairobi, Kenya. Lee read about how a group had hiked up Mount Kilimanjaro in order to raise money for the orphanage. It was a fascinating endeavor for an admirable cause and Lee was drawn in. The article affected her so much that she immediately emailed the contact at the bottom. She got a call back later that day from a woman with a slight French accent who introduced herself as Sophia Duluce. She gave Lee the background on the orphanage foundation by explaining that she had been about to run the Chicago Marathon for her fiftieth birthday when she decided that she didn't want to run just for herself, she needed a cause to motivate her to raise money.

A friend had introduced Sophia to a Kenyan couple who were trying to set up an orphanage on land that they had secured just outside of Nairobi and the concept of collaboration was formed. This couple, Reverend Jim Wanjuiri and his wife Carol, wanted to help the children of AIDS victims who were left as orphans in the Kibera slum. There were over six million orphans in Africa from the devastation left by the AIDS epidemic and many of these children, if their grandmothers couldn't raise them, were left to fend for themselves.

Kibera, one of the world's largest slums, was located about five kilometers outside of Nairobi's city center. It was formed originally when Nubian soldiers returning from their service in WW1 were given allotments in the forest near Nairobi. Eventually more tribal groups located in the area but when Kenya was given independence this kind of settlement was banned and left without services. So the cost to live in Kiberia remained low and as a result many poor people were drawn to reside there until its population spread to over three hundred thousand. Many of these inhabitants, who had no clean water, sewers or schools systems, were street children, left orphaned and Sophie was determined to save as many of them as she could – so the Nairobi Orphanage Foundation or NOF was formed.

Sophia was an energetic individual whose passion for her cause was infectious. She enthusiastically explained to Lee that she would have the option to sponsor a child for as little as two hundred and fifty dollars a year. This would provide all the food, clothing and education for an orphan child in Nairobi. It was amazing that so little could do so much, Lee thought. Her children weren't so inexpensively sustained for a year. Lee then invited Sophia to come her house for their introductory meeting during which the necessary forms would be filled out and a book of children available to sponsor would be reviewed for selection. When the thin woman with short grey hair and a broad smile arrived, Lee invited her in and they all sat at the breakfast table to talk. The children looked curiously at the foreign woman but kept their ears tuned into her story about the orphans of faraway Kenya. They had been told about the poverty in Africa in school by their teachers and they couldn't believe that people might not have a car or television, let alone food or clean water.

The two little blond heads leaned closer as Sophia placed the album on the glass table then turned the first page. The book revealed a small child with large deep brown eyes set in an oval coffee colored face with a shaved head looking appealingly up to the camera. She wore a tattered green sweater and in the background was a crude concrete block building set in a mud. Sophia flipped the next page to reveal another thin child with round anxious eyes set in a sweet face staring out of the page. There were dozens of emancipated children, with hopeful looks on their lovely dark faces and Lee felt slightly nauseous at the sight of poverty and starvation so blatant. She asked that Andy and Sarah pick out two children whom they would like to adopt, a boy and a girl. Then she left the room with the excuse of using the bathroom in order to collect herself. Any problems in her life were so minor compared to this stark brutal reality she reflected, while taking a few deep breaths. It was so different than the TV appeals to have a person in your house with evidence of real need witnessed firsthand. She had to help. She returned to the breakfast area where Sarah looked up with a big grin on her face and exclaimed.

"We have picked out our new sister and brother. Come see them mommy"

Shortly after this, Curt struck again and Lee got a certified letter informing her that she was once more a defendant in a law suit. This time it was in family court regarding the children. Curt claimed that "circumstances had changed" which was the only way that the courts would open up a separation agreement for reassessment. It seemed outrageous to Lee that this was allowed to happen since Curt was with the same woman, in the same neighbourhood and on the same schedule with the children for that last few years but the lawyers had to be called in and the money would start going out. The only real change was that Curt had married Joan. They had snuck off for a weekend in Virginia after requesting that Lee keep the children and she was sure that the timing had been due to his visa running out. He could now get a Green Card through his American wife and it would only take a couple years. This kind of application was called the IR Green Card and there were no restrictions on the number of applicant cards awarded each year.

Lee's Green Card application would take a lot longer since she had applied under the F3 category for married children of US citizens over twenty one. Once divorced though, Lee had actually moved into the F1 category which had a shorter waiting list, her lawyer explained, with 20,000 annual spots. She had been looking at a twenty year process to become an American but now it might only be fifteen years in this new category. Refugee categories had over 70,000 spots and Political Asylum was wide open but she certainly didn't qualify for those. She had also submitted her name into the Green Card lottery, or DV for Diversified Immigration, which had been established for countries that may have not been equally represented in immigration to the United States. Ireland, Finland, Australia were amongst the lucky countries whose residents were welcome to participate in the lottery the last few years, along with Canada. Lee's sister had entered the same lottery and when she actually won a spot, she didn't even bother to finish the process because it required her to go live in the States right away. She hadn't counted on that part of the deal. Lee would have given her eye teeth to get that winning spot and her sister had just thrown it away. It was exasperating to Lee, whose future was tenuous until she got the security of a Green Card. More frightening was that Curt would have his Green Card soon and if she didn't get hers, she might have to return to Canada then lose her children and everything else she had worked for so hard.

The court date was set and Lee started to prepare for a battle. Her lawyer had asked her to draw up some lists of parental responsibilities and the division of care for the children. Lee got to work and soon had produced multiple charts and lists of all that she had done for the children for school, sports and activities. She also had all the medical records on visits to the doctor, dentist and urgent care for ear aches and sprains. It became blatantly obvious how little Curt had been involved with the children or spent time with them. In a period when fathers were taking a more active role in their children's lives, this father hadn't done much. Even when the children were injured at Curt's house, he didn't bother taking them to the hospital or doctor, he just let Lee pick them up. So she couldn't really understand why he was suing her. Lee told Ryan of her frustrations and worries when they were together but she held back some of it since she didn't want their relationship, already strained, to bear the burden of her former marriage.

Ryan listened and was supportive but Lee didn't think he really understood how fearful she was and how important all of the legal actions and visa issues were to her right now. She was also concerned about how a younger boyfriend might look to the courts if it came up. These concerns weighed on her mind daily. She spent many hours working out strategies for presenting her case, hunting material for court documents and most of all, making sure that the children were happy. She didn't have the time or attention to dedicate to Ryan and she knew that at some point any decent guy would pull the plug on this kind of relationship and move on. They were also in different phases of life. He wanted to start a family, after his dream of sailing, and then settle into a house that he had a hand in creating. She had already done all that and she wasn't sure that she wanted to start the process all over again. She loved and respected him greatly but the age difference between them crept into her insecurities and she wondered how she would look to him as her body began its decline while he was still youthfully virile. Her age would also be a factor putting pressure on the time line for more children and increasing the risk of birth defects. Maybe she should just let this relationship slide into the death of neglect. Then Ryan could find someone who could dedicate themselves to him alone and their future. He deserved it. He was such a kind, affectionate and loving person and what she had to offer included the burden of another man's children and a nightmare of an ex-husband.

"Proceed with one foot in front of the other" was the motto that came to mind again as Lee dealt with all of the pressure and complexities that were assailing her now. Lee had to inform the children's teachers about the law suit as well. She asked them to keep her aware of anything that happened with Curt and if they would testify for her. Both of the women sympathized with Lee but they would not be allowed by the school board to go to court for her. They could tell that she was a good mother who cared deeply for her children so they supplied her with other help. The teachers informed her when Curt neglected his duties, didn't check the children's homework or sign forms. They told her all the times he avoided parent teacher conferences, or assemblies or special class events and even when they knew he had lied to them.

Lee also had to fill in for Curt during the Father/Child Day in the classroom and she sat next to Andy helping him make a toothpick bridge while the other fathers sat with their children eying her suspiciously. Andy was brave though and hid his disappointment but Lee could tell he was hurt. She had anticipated this and brought homemade cookies to ease the situation. Soon the other children were excitedly gathered around Andy as he passed out the cookies to everyone, no longer embarrassed that he had his mother there and not his father. All of it reinforced Lee's resolve to protect and fight for her children but it was a sad situation when they were all so intertwined with a person who was so damaging as a husband and father, like barbed wire stretched tight around a tree choking it as it tried to grow.

Chapter 35 – Gutters & Downspouts

By the time the day of court arrived, Lee had recruited her neighbour and her mother to attend to testify for her. She was especially grateful to both women since she was very nervous about the whole event. She felt as though her abilities as a mother were under scrutiny and the risk that she might be ordered to give up her children terrified her. It was an intimidating ordeal as well. They had to go to the large limestone courthouse facility in downtown Charlotte, a place Lee had never visited before, check their briefcases or purses through security and walk past the gruff policemen who eyed them suspiciously. Then they waited outside of a set of large wood stained double doors until a bailiff opened them so they could enter the court room. "This has to be a similar procedure to what criminals go through" Lee thought, as they entered the large oak paneled courtroom.

At the front on a raised dais was a long wood trimmed desk behind which sat a black robed figure leaning on elbows with hands clasped in front. "Just like in the movies" Lee mused. The judge was a dignified African American woman with short wavy coiffed hair, manicured nails and a carefully made up face with a stern look on it. This judge would expect concise, accurate information Lee realized. Lee's lawyer Carol joined the small group on the left side of the bench, while Curt, Joan and their lawyer, a short stocky aggressive looking fellow, sat on the other side of the room. The line was drawn in the sand.

Since Curt was the plaintiff, he was put on the stand first to testify. He wore his usual arrogant smile but he was a little more subdued than at the magistrate hearing. He was sworn in and his lawyer began the questioning with basic facts of his name, address and inquiries about his current job. He asked about events in the marital home about a year before separation. Curt described the situation as "The marriage was obviously failing" and then, surprising Lee and her lawyer, he launched into a detailed description of how he had met and dated Joan while he was still married. He said that he had found someone new and they had set up a wonderful life together. He then talked about how Lee had begun an intentional campaign against Joan to exclude her from the children's life. His lawyer started framing his questions with the phrase "Your psychotic wife then did…"

Lee was surprised that someone could make this kind of statement without proof or challenge. Lee looked to Carol who sat attentively assessing the opposition but offered no protest to the libelous dialogue. So she sat back and just listened as her character was not too subtly attacked before she was even called to the stand. Carol had seen this lawyer in action before and had warned Lee that he would try to intimidate her. She had prepared Lee not to show any reaction to any insulting remarks or crowding while she was on the stand since this was his method of intimidation. Lee wasn't worried about him. It had just occurred to her that the whole situation was like a game. The opposition had nothing against her as a mother it was just that Curt, in his prideful macho way, was trying to push her aside to pretend that Joan was the mother of his children. Lee was the troublesome game piece that had to be knocked out so Curt could win. This was theory was even more apparent as the questioning continued and Carol finally turned to Lee perplexed and whispered.

"Do you have any problem with this woman?"

Joan had never come up in their court preparations and Lee whispered "Not at all" then turned back to watch as the lawyer then asked Curt what income he expected to make this year. Lee's jaw almost dropped when he braggingly answered.

"I should clear over three hundred thousand this year"

Was he a fool, Lee wondered - who would voluntarily expose their income in family court when he was paying so much below legally required child support? Carol immediately leaned over to Lee and whispered 'We can appeal the child support on Tuesday." But Lee shook her head as Carol was called to cross examine. She asked Curt some preliminary questions then moved in for more specific hard hitting ones. She asked if he had altered records at the schools and medical offices, waited until he acknowledged it. Carol then entered several more pages into evidence and asked why he would put down a girlfriend as an emergency contact when Lee had never put her boyfriend on the forms.

"We were living together as a family and Lee was just a single parent not a family," Curt said.

"But you were just living together, not married"

"There are all kinds of families," Curt burst out in reply.

Carol laughed at this hypocritical remark then said there certainly were all kinds of families but in North Carolina living together was not common law marriage and Joan was still a girlfriend only.

Then she pulled out the long list of violations to the separation agreement, went over each one to verify their accuracy. After this she asked if Curt allowed the children to have friends over to his house.

"Of course" he exclaimed.

"In fact the kid's best friends who live next door to Lee come to stay overnight all the time"

At that blatant lie, Lee saw movement on the other side of the benches as Joan opened her mouth in protest and shook her head. The judge saw it too. Then Carol asked about his hitting the children.

"I just hit them with a spatula or belt like I had been spanked as a kid. Besides, it was a mutual decision between Lee and me"

The judge looking incredulous at this statement couldn't help interrupting and she asked Curt.

"Are you telling us that the children's mother agreed to your beating them"

Curt replied with an adamant "Yes" and everyone turned to Lee who shook her head visibly denying any such an agreement. She felt a sense of shame creep over her as well as she realized that she had not protected her children enough. Carol's eyebrow had shot up at Curt's response and she dug in to pursue this questioning further, like a bull dog tearing at a bone, exposing the lies. She tried to find out how often these beatings occurred, how many objects were used and where these incidents took place. Curt began stumbling with his answers, knowing that this was tricky ground and his lawyer broke in to rescue him by regularly calling "Objection" to this question or that. The judge overruled most of these but the interruption served its purpose giving Curt more time to consider his answers. He began answering that he couldn't remember. Lee looked over at Joan at this point and noticed that she had a very concerned almost angry look on her face with her brows furrowed as she stared at Curt. She obviously hadn't heard any of this before. She might be worried for her own child now.

As the questioning of the plaintiff wound down, Carol asked Curt one more time what he wanted and why they were all in court. Curt's lawyer then stepped forward to submit a document that he stated was the list of demands that the father had in this case. Carol immediately requested a copy and upon receiving it, called out.

"A recess to review this document please your honor"

When the judge agreed she also stated that they should have already seen this request long ago. Carol slid next to Lee on the bench to look over the items together. The demands were not nearly as severe as they had both imagined. He was asking for control of medical decisions, dental care, the ability to list Joan as an emergency contact, extension of the children's visit to include every other Sunday and four full weeks in the summer. Lee shook her head; all of this fear, tension, money and anxiety over such minor things. She wasn't going to lose her children and she could have wept with relief. Then she saw that she had been played like a mouse caught by a cat. This was about power and control; it was not about the children. In fact Andy and Sarah had not been mentioned in the questioning by Curt's side at all and they should have been the focus of everything. Lee slumped in her seat as some of the adrenaline drained out of her system. She sat for a minute in this posture until her mother slipped her arm around Lee's shoulders and tugged her to get up. The lunch break had been called.

After a quick lunch of cold sandwiches in a cafeteria, the court session began again and Lee's neighbour and then her mother were called to the stand to testify. They stated that Lee was a devoted mother and a person of excellent character. Anne was asked if she had witnessed any times when Curt did not look out for the best interest of children. She verified various incidents of neglect and abuse. Then Carol was asked if she was aware that Curt had threatened Lee. Anne said that she knew of various threats and that Curt had said that he was going to take the children away from Lee. When the questioning was turned over to Curt's lawyers turn, he just asked a couple trivial but safe questions. He wanted this woman off the stand so he quickly wound it up and said.

"No more questions your honor"

Anne seemed disappointed to have been dismissed so quickly but she returned to her seat, smiled triumphantly at Lee and placed her hand on her daughter's arm for support. Lee was then called to the stand. She gathered her inner strength and mounted the dais to be sworn in. She felt comfortable, and while she was aware that she was perspiring under her arms, she didn't believe that it was staining through the suit dress. Carol opened the questioning with the simple

"Do you have any problems with the woman named Joan who is now the plaintiff's wife?"

"I do not have any problems with her. In fact I am grateful that she has been kind to the children"

Lee looked straight at Joan while she answered to add conviction to her statement. It was like a bubble bursting for the opposition though since they had based their entire attack on the "psychotic jealous ex-wife" They would be at a loss when cross examination took place since their fire power was significantly reduced. Carol then questioned her about the separation, the care of the children while Curt was busy with his new relationship and the children's successful transition to their new home and school. She guided Lee's testimony skillfully, maneuvering through descriptions that allowed her to enter pages of evidence into the record. When answering questions about how the children were doing in school and all their activities, Lee turned to the judge, looking directly at her and stated.

"They are doing very well. Their grades actually improved when Curt left the house and they really like their school and neighbourhood, but it is a balancing act to keep everything going well. It takes a lot of work and any changes might upset that balance."

The judge would understand this she was sure. Then Carol asked if Lee had actually given permission for Curt to beat the children. She adamantly denied this then glanced down as she spoke.

"I found out later from Sarah that she had been beaten other times by her father but I hadn't known"

Curt's lawyer immediately jumped up crying "Objection, hearsay!!" Lee stopped speaking and looked to Carol as the judge replied.

"Granted - the witness cannot quote second hand sources"
Confused, Lee looked to Carol who said "You have to word it differently"
Then Lee understood and tried again.

"I found out that Curt had beaten Sarah in secret which I didn't know until after he moved out. It didn't stop then either. At one point I was at Sarah's school talking to her teacher about her work when something we were discussing triggered her to drop to the floor and cry out "Don't hit me, don't hit me!!" We were stunned and asked "Who hits you" and as I picked her up off the floor and held her, she said "Daddy".

There were murmurs in the courtroom which the judge's strong voice silenced as she summoned the attorney's to come to the front of her desk. She leaned down towards them and told them that they needed to meet in her chamber immediately. Then with the gavel she banged out notice of a fifteen minute recess. Lee was escorted from the box and she slid in the seat next to her mother while the others left the courtroom. Just before the fifteen minutes were up, the group of lawyers and the judge filed back into the courtroom. Carol slid next to Lee and explained quickly that the judge wanted to know why this case had come before her with such a history. Curt's lawyer had explained that it was rare that a father wanted more time with his children but the judge had silenced him with a look. Then Lee was back on the stand where she was turned over to Curt's lawyer who began to strut in front of the witness box staring at Lee in an attempt to intimidate her. She stared back at him unflinching. Skillfully, he dove in with a question that Lee did not expect.

"How much money did you make last year?"

This was so odd since it implied that Lee hid something and it seemed to be off topic again. Lee replied.

"I made around sixty thousand last year"

He looked scornful and pushed again.

"I mean the total of all your income including what your parents have given you. And why don't you know the exact amount!!!" he screamed.

"I earned about sixty thousand including anything that my parents have given me. I have my tax return over there if you would like the exact amount. I can get it for you"

"No, that won't be necessary," he blustered.

This had collapsed his argument and he paused then turned to walk back towards his seat to gain time as he considered a redirection. His client had insisted that this woman was getting hundreds of thousands of dollars from her parents, information that he was going to use to his advantage. Instead, the quietly composed girl on the bench was just a sap who his client had pushed around and fabricated stories about to everyone. He had not seen this coming – his client had pulled the wool over his eyes as well.

It was just as the lawyer was pacing back to the bench that Lee and others in the court noticed the movements in the Plaintiffs' bench. Joan, who sat with her mouth dropped open, had begun to use her elbow to jab back and forth into Curt's side. The real figure of Lee's income must have been a surprise to her. She turned in anger toward him with her brows furrowed and everyone in the courtroom could tell that he had lied to her about something, especially the judge. It took Curt's lawyer some time before he could reassert his dominance over the court room. He tried a few more questions then he asked Lee why she had so much documentation for this trial. Lee replied that in her job she documented all her phone calls and any information on projects for liability reasons. The lawyer did not accept that and moved closer while hammering at her about why she had been so obsessed. He asked the question again and again, moving even closer to the bench. Lee's lawyer called out an objection to his crowding the witness and this gave Lee time to think. She realized that he was trying to make her break in some way and expose a psychotic personality. But she was calm and she knew what she had to say. She turned to Curt, staring hard at his now humbled figure and told the truth, which silenced the courtroom and ended the trial.

"He threatened to take my children away from me"

In the closing statements Curt's lawyer tried ranting again about Lee being an obsessive psychotic but his argument had lost its power and the closing statement was just a hollow collection of words. Then Carol stood for her final statement and dramatically pointed at Curt. It startled the few witnesses in the courtroom as she loudly declared her summation.

"This father is a control freak who through his extreme behavior has withheld the children from their activities, altered legal documents, broken the separation agreement and endanger the children's lives as a result. We also cannot forget the beatings he gave to his daughter in secret. The court should not grant any additional time or consideration to this father"

She continued to reiterate other points from the trial and when Lee looked over at Curt, she saw that he had turned a deep red. He looked like he would burst out in rage at any moment but Lee was distracted by a thought that came to her suddenly. A puzzle piece had been slid into place. She had heard the words "control freak" and it had solidified so many scattered ideas in her mind about her marriage. Lee had heard that expression about people who try to smother and control other people. They tend to be crave being the center of attention and in order to secure that attention they often push their spouse's family and friends away. It is the selfish behavior of an insecure person. Lee remembered this part especially and now understood its application. When Carol concluded her summation, she sat down and turned to Lee to whisper.

"Did you see how he lost it when I mentioned the words "control freak"? I should have used that when he was on the stand!"

A week after the trial had concluded Carol called Lee to announce that the Judge's opinion had been filed. She congratulated her client and told her that the decision was completely in Lee's favor. Curt wasn't given any more time with the children or control but he was expected to pay for medical and dental, a bonus that Lee hadn't expected. Lee breathed a sigh of relief. The document also required that Curt allow the children to go to their events and sports even if they occur on his visitation days. So it was worthwhile to some degree if the children benefited from the whole legal mess but Lee was glad that it was over. It was such an expensive and emotional process during which there was no real punishment for this father who beat children. The courts almost ignored this aspect and Lee began to see the legal system as an area of grey rather the than black and white of right and wrong that she had grown up believing. This system for justice felt like it was a coin toss - who had the better lawyer and who was better prepared won the day.

Chapter 36 – Telephone & Cable

Lee had tried to reconnect with Ryan after the trial, but he was travelling and it was hard to explain what she was feeling over the phone. She wanted him with her, to hold her and let her vent her frustrations. She wanted to feel protected and loved. Eventually when he recognized Lee needed him in person he had called her and suggested coming to visit that weekend, but by then she had pulled back into her shell and didn't respond with encouragement. She wasn't sure what she wanted and with the memory of Curt's bullying and deceit so fresh, she was hesitating to commit. He moved onto other subjects but the conversation dwindled until he just quietly said goodbye and hung up. Lee thought that this might be best right now for her and certainly best for Ryan. She was getting stronger now and could continue to build a new life for herself without needing the support of a man. She also knew that if he had come that weekend she might not have been able to end the relationship. She loved him but she just couldn't see the future together as clearly as he could. She was damaged and trying to recover but he could do better for himself she thought. Silent tears slid down her cheeks for the loss of such a fine man.

Several days later, Lee received an email from Sophie that NOF was organizing another service trip to Kenya in a few months and everyone was encouraged to sign up. Sophie had known that Lee would be interested. Lee did a careful review of dates to make sure that the children were with their father, checked all of the costs, her bank balance and anticipated receivables then decided to jump in. The ground costs were very low since they would be staying at a Missionary Hotel but the flight was expensive even with the group discount. They were planning a construction project of building bunk beds and desks for the children. Most of the little ones were sleeping two to a small bed and currently there were not enough desks in the class rooms for all the students so they were sitting on the bare floor to study.

Lee attended NOF's preliminary meeting at the assembly hall of a church across the Buster Boyd Bridge in South Carolina. There were people of all ages in attendance; young girls, middle age couples and retired men. Everyone seemed very well organized and excited about the trip. The volunteers were told that they would be allowed to carry two suitcases up to fifty pounds free and that there would be materials each participant had to bring with them. The leaders then asked everyone to line up in front of large containers to each receive their packages of desk tops, screws, and nails, saw blades, candy, shoes and party favors to bring in their suitcases. There were drawings of the bed and desk designs done by a volunteer so they could calculate materials. Most of the materials were donated and they hoped to build eight bunk beds, a dozen desks, distribute shoes for each orphan and throw a birthday party for all of the children Lee was so impressed with the organization of the entire program and she was very glad that she had signed up. Now that the messy court fight was behind her, she was looking forward to this new adventure wherever it would take her.

During the weeks before the trip, Lee was excited and very busy making sure that all her clients had the drawings that they needed and she had all the materials for the work at the orphanage. She had gotten so many shots for the trip - yellow fever, typhoid, tetanus and she was given pills for malaria that she had to take ahead of the trip as well as weeks afterwards.

She had thought about Ryan a lot and wished that he was joining her. He had skills that would have been so beneficial to the group and his compassion for the children would have been inspiring. They had talked so much about traveling the world together. Most of all she just wanted him with her. A piece of her heart was missing and she ached to fill it again. It would just take a phone call but she couldn't do it yet. They had exchanged emails on a weekly basis but these were more friendly correspondence than passionate connections though neither could not let go completely and Lee missed him. She had called him to tell him all about the trip and he wished her safe travels along with hopes that it went well. He especially asked her to be careful in a tender tone which melted her heart and she gripped the phone hard not wanting to let go. He then quietly told her that he loved her just before she reluctantly said goodbye. She had whispered "I love you" too but it was after he had hung up.

Lee had also told the children all about her trip, prepared them for their vacation with their father and packed the pictures that they had made for their adoptive siblings. When Lee dropped them at their father's house on the day of her flight, each of the children had run to her to give her bear hugs before she got back in the car. She almost couldn't leave when she saw their bright smiling faces waving good bye but then they turned and ran in to the house through the garage door.

Lee heard her ex-husbands gruff booming voice welcoming them, the squeals of laughter and she pulled away quickly before the hurt of exclusion crept in. She then drove straight to the airport and joined the NOF group in the departures area. They had organized a volunteer to stay with all the bags while the cars were unloaded and parked. Each bag was counted and then the group checked in. While in line Lee began chatting with the person next to her, a small dark haired woman with glasses and a thick southern accent named Pat. Another young athletic blond girl and older dark haired woman joined them to introduce themselves and they all began the process of bonding over a common goal. Then Pat confessed that she was here due to her brother's insistence and this would be her first flight ever. The other women were incredulous and looked more closely at the woman to see that the statement was true.

Then Lee laughed as she said "Well, you certainly don't do things halfway. This is a big trip for anyone"

Pat turned out to be a dynamo of good humor with a feisty nature to her character. She had a few questions about the upcoming flight which the women answered and Lee offered warnings about things that might startle her unless she was aware of them; such as the when the wheels are taken up or dropped in the housings for landing and when there was air turbulence. Pat was grateful for the pointers and confessed that she was nervous, though it was said with a big grin on her face.

This first flight was to Chicago where they would catch the next leg to London then hop on a short plane ride to Nairobi. The flight from Charlotte however had been delayed and then with the storms on their route, the plane was very late in landing. Pat, who had fared well during the flight decided to follow Lee when they landed so the rest did as well as she hurried to cross from the domestic terminal to the international. It was going to be close and they had made it to security in good time before they were stopped and asked to get new boarding passes. They hurried back to the ticket line but by the time they got to the front of that line, their plane had already left. The attendant then tried to rebook them and casually said that she might get some of them on a plane in a couple days and the rest might have to wait even longer.

"It is the busiest traveling season to Europe after all," she gushed. Lee interrupted her by stating in a quiet but firm voice.

"All of these people are going on a charitable mission to work in an orphanage in Kenya. A delay of a couple days is not acceptable and could produce negative press. Please look into this immediately"

The woman's smile drooped as she finally noticed the matching shirts with the Nairobi Orphanage Foundation logo on the twelve people in front of her. Luckily for the NOF group, the next domestic flights were also delayed, and the attendant quickly booked the group to take the places of others passengers who would miss their flight to London. The group thanked Lee then finally relaxed until boarding this next flight a few hours later and had uneventful flight over the pond to land at Heathrow. Their layover in London was enough time that Lee was able to jump on the train into the city to explore for a few hours. She toured the British Museum, watched a protest movements key note speaker then wandered the streets and bridges over the Thames before returning to the airport. She had invited the others to join her but they were too worried about missing another flight. The quick stop over invigorated Lee and reminded her how much she loved travel.

When the last flight dropped to land in Kenya, Lee strained in her seat to peer out the window at the thick green rolling land below. Tin roofed shacks dotted the hillsides and soon the regular grid of streets and commercial buildings created their patterns on the land as well. The plane landed smoothly and taxied to the front of the terminal building. The warm humid air seeped into the plane as the doors were opened and the passengers were directed down the steps onto the tarmac and into the high ceiling airport where they waited for their luggage. The room was filled with people from all over the world and Lee couldn't stop watching them with fascination as they moved past her. There were stately Indian women in brightly colored saris, solemn Muslim men in white robes and turbans, tall dark skinned proud Africans in tribal fabrics.

The dusty baggage area with chipped vinyl tile floors and warped ceiling had long sheets of glass windows into the baggage handling section where the workers loaded the bags onto the conveyor belt. Sophia saw Lee's look at the window and explained that it may have been installed to discourage stealing from luggage. Nairobi had the nickname of "Nairobery". Finally the group's bags arrived though some were still missing including one of Lee's. Once they had filed missing bag forms and been given assurances that the bags would be delivered to them, though looking back at the glass again, Lee wondered. Then the group headed out of the sliding doors of the terminal toward the two small white vans that were waiting for their arrival. As they emerged into the dark night Lee marveled at the exotic feel to the air, the tropical landscaping and the chaos of people jockeying to carry their bags for a small fee. There was the unique smell of wood smoke, loamy soils and tangy floral plants. This continent was the birthplace of humanity and Lee felt its inexplicable ancient pull.

When they approached the first van, the driver Joseph, a tall well built older man with an easy smile, took their bags and loaded them in the back. The vans drove into the modern downtown with the driver pointing out the main sights in his accented English including the Parliament buildings, International Conference Center and markets. There were massive glass and metal high rise buildings with small older brick buildings between or green landscaped parks and planters with varieties of palm trees and flowering hibiscus. The van continued on four lane roads crowded with vehicles and motor scooters until they came to a roundabout which slowed the traffic to a crawl. Here vendors wove between the cars and trucks to sell newspapers and dried fruit.

As they sat, Lee suddenly noticed movement in the odd umbrella shaped trees surrounding the traffic circle and the silhouette of massive hunched shapes with long beaks. They looked to be the largest vultures that Lee had ever seen but Joseph explained.

"Those are Marabou Storks. They are a kind of scavenger but also they have one of the largest wing spans of any bird. We do not like them but you can't get rid of them"

The van eventually cleared the roundabout then took turns that brought them into a residential area. Then they pulled into the driveway of the Methodist Hotel, a low squat brick building surrounded by fanning trees and a high metal fence. A stern thin dark skinned guard donning a military styled hat came out of a small telephone booth size building and lifted the gate for entry after a brief exchange with Joseph. Once stopped at the curb, the group gratefully spilled out of the van and into the dark shabby reception area to check in. A tired clerk welcomed them with "Jambo" then passed out room keys.

Sophia and her husband Bill, a burly red faced man, lead the group to a small meeting room to review the itinerary and rules. They were to leave at six each morning for an hour ride south east to the school bringing with them all the materials for the construction work. Once the work day was finished they would leave around five o'clock to return to the hotel then go to dinner either across the street or at a hotel nearby. No one was to walk alone at night since while it was a fairly safe city during the day, it was dangerous at night and foreigners were targets due to their perceived wealth. They hauled their heavy suitcases up to the second floor and many of the volunteers passed out on their beds fully dressed until being rounded up for dinner downstairs.

The next morning the vans pulled into the courtyard just as the sun was rising for loading and soon the group was driving east onto narrow roads with swerving cars and overloaded trucks. As they traveled, the buildings became more dilapidated and pieced together while the roads gained pot holes and dust. They passed hundreds of people walking across fields and along the road toward the city or gathered at stops for the matatu, small colorful buses. They all tended to be lean tall dark people in clean but worn clothing Some were chatting and laughing together but most were alone or in pairs, silent as they took long determined strides toward their destinations Lee was immediately drawn to watch them as she realized that they were up this early to walk so they could cover many miles to get to their jobs before the work day started. She was in awe of their incredible fortitude.

The vans continued past small commercial strips that looked like they were part of a war zone except for the watermelon sellers in front with their wares spread across old blankets. Then the development became more sporadic and they saw the tin shack villages of squatters on the hillsides. A few tattered pieces of laundry hung on ropes strung between tree limbs that acted as roof posts for uneven sections of corrugated metal. Lee's heart went out to these people as she solemnly stared out of the vans window. These people had to endure so much with so little that she became embarrassed by her comparable wealth and excess. "How spoiled and selfish we are in North America" she thought when we have so much.

Eventually the van turned onto a dirt track pitted with pot holes and drove past goats being herded by young boys carrying long sticks. The only buildings now appeared to be corner stores consisting of a small shacks pieced out of remnant wood planks covered with the remains of once vivid paint and metal bars covered any openings. Then they turned into a driveway where a scrawny bent man pushed open a large blue metal gate which the van pulled through to the school grounds. They continued to drive past uneven corn fields and sections of unfinished concrete block structures before they stopped on front of a series of matching gable roofed block buildings with red painted metal doors that Lee recognized as the children's dormitories from the pictures.

Dozens of smiling children with shaven heads in well worn uniforms of tattered green sweaters and long plaid shirts stood as a welcoming committee in front of the buildings when the volunteers emerged from the vans they broke rank to run up to Sophia and Bill for hugs and recognition. Several approached Lee tentatively so she sank to her knees to be at their level and smiled. When she stretched out her hand several moved forward to clasp it. Then Lee pulled out her camera and began snapping shots which drew more children to her. She took their pictures and turned the camera around to show the children their own image. The little ones broke out in laughter as they saw their own faces, maybe for the first time on a screen. Then Lee showed them how to use the camera and gave it to the closest child indicating that she should now take the pictures. Lee posed with various children and watched as they shot close ups of their friends in various poses. Then having remembered what buttons Lee had pushed to display the shot, they laughed heartily as they reviewed their own pictures.

The matron of the school, a heavy straight backed woman whose height was emphasized by the hair piled on top of her head and wrapped in a scarf, assembled the children for a welcome ceremony. They lined up by age which was also by height and a young boy stepped forward. On a cue from the matron he began to sing al Capella, a soulful tune that echoed between buildings His voice was deep and full as he skillfully wove the tune through stanzas. The rest of the children eventually joined in a harmonic background chorus that built in crescendo until all the children were all clapping along as well as the guests. Other solo singers came forward next to lead both Christian and tribal songs as the rest of the children sang along.

Lee was enraptured with the quality of the singing and the rhythmic movement it inspired. All of the children were moving in time and most of the adults as well. The last song called "Jambo Jambo" was a song of welcome very popular in Kenya Sophia explained to the group before the familiar melody started. After the show the children went into their classrooms and the volunteers were directed to enter a courtyard surrounded by a low wall of concrete block whose back wall had a lean-to shed with a corrugated metal roof. Underneath the roof were stacks of fresh cut white wood, mostly full 2"x4" members. Lee noticed that many were twisted and had a variety of lengths but this was the material they had been supplied and was probably standard for the country.

Some of the group then went to collect the generator that they had previously bought for the school and gathered the tools out of an unoccupied office to set up in the shed. The plans of the bunk beds were pulled out and Lee volunteered to cut the pieces along with Pat's brother Phil who had also worked as a carpenter. The teams for fitting and assembly organized themselves ready to collect the cut wood and transform it. They armed themselves with power screw drivers all connected into the noisy generator and they were ready for action. Soon Lee and Phil were feeding the volunteers wood pieces but the first desk and bunk bed to be assembled were slow going. The group had to sort out the exact hardware to be used and what team members were to perform which task. Then the group made templates for screw locations and started the assembly line.

Lee worked hard without a break for the first three hours until lunch was called. The volunteers then went to the kitchen, if one could call a tin shack with two large vats over a wood burning fire a kitchen, to line up for food. The children were given their plates of ugali, a slab of corn mash, and greens then handed a small cup of milky tea. They were excited but well behaved as they snuck curious glances at Lee and the other volunteers. Lee smiled at each child who looked her way then asked Sophia when she could meet her two sponsor children. Right after lunch she was told but she still couldn't help scanning the faces to see if she would recognize them while she took spoonfuls of the ugali which tasted similar to the grits and collard greens of the south.

When she had eaten Lee decided to explore the grounds. She could hear children laughing and shouting in the distance so she followed the sounds until she immerged behind the building into a field where barefooted nimble boys were chasing a rag wrapped object substituting as a soccer ball. Lee had come prepared for this and she pulled a new soccer ball out of her backpack and began blowing it up with the small portable pump she had brought along. The children watched her with curiosity. When the ball was blown up Lee approached the edge of the field and offered it to the players. They whooped with delight when they saw the ball, called out "Assante" which was thank you in Swahili then motioned for her to throw it.

Once the shiny white ball was in play, the children raced after it and some of the delighted children motioned for Lee to join them. Lee used her hands to verify that they wanted her to play and when they shook their heads in consent, she picked the side that had a smaller number of players and ran across the rough field into a middle position. She just wanted to help out the defense, not change the way they played. Soon the ball was shooting across the wild grasses toward one of the bent metal goal posts on one side or the other. Lee felt awkward in her heavy running shoes as she ran alongside a quick bare footed team mate to help bring the ball down the field. She saw the lithe young boys jump over each other and skillfully redirect the ball with incepts of their feet. They were like gazelles with their quick lithe movements and it was beautiful to watch.

Lee hadn't played soccer like this since she was in at Colburne Elementary School and she had not kicked a ball since coaching in Terra Harbour. It felt great to run with the children but when she got into close contact with the other players, she worried about injuring a child with her kicks or body so she tried to direct the ball away before kicking. Sometimes she had to leap over children when they dove or fell attempting to take possession of the ball from her. The boys laughed hard when they tumbled and saw Lee jump over them. Lee was laughing as well and when she paused to gather her breath, she noticed various girls gathered around the field watching the play, so she signaled them to join in. A couple of the bolder ones ran onto the field to join the teams while the more timid stayed on the sidelines or grabbed the skipping ropes that Lee had brought along and jumped rope nearby, with eyes still on the curious smiling stranger.

Finally the children were called back to classes by a gong and several gathered around Lee like an escort, grabbed her hands and looked up at her with large bright white smiles. A volunteer dentist had come the week before to do a clinic for the school and all the children had their previously brown stained teeth cleaned and repaired. Lee felt a warm sensation of camaraderie with these lovely affectionate children. Such cruel beginnings to their lives and yet they were happy with this meager living. Their parents had been taken from them, they received small rations of food, shared beds and their total belongings fit into a shoe box but they retained a joy for living. Lee grasped this lesson and sent an offer of appreciation to the heavens for this miraculous experience she had been able to witness and its lessons.

When Lee returned to the work area Sophia was standing in the courtyard with her hand on the shoulders of a young girl whose shaved head was bent. When she heard Lee approach the girl looked up at her and Lee recognized Julia. She was smaller than Lee imagined, just coming up to Sophia's shoulder and she seemed even more vulnerable. Once introductions were made, Lee came forward and warmly embraced the thin frame. She slowly back up, still holding Julia's hands, she said.

"It is so wonderful to meet you finally Julia. We loved all your letters"

She smiled reassured into the beautiful intelligent eyes that looked shyly up at her. The girl had lovely smooth chocolate skin and high cheek bones in a delicate oval face. Her shoulders were held square and her long elegant fingers draped over Lee's as she patiently stood in the hot sun. Lee asked a few questions then let her go back to class with the promise that she would seek her out later. Sophia gave Lee the times when she could visit with Julia then Lee inquired about David. Sophia hesitated before she explained.

"David was claimed by his relatives last week. They had left him at the orphanage after his parent's death because they thought that he had the same wasting sickness. But we test all the children and can only keep the HIV negative ones. Once they discovered that he was free of disease they picked him up and took him back to their home"

Lee was disappointed that she could not meet David but she was happy for the boy. She returned to cutting wood while the assembly teams carefully put together a sample bed and a desk by the end of the work day. It was a slow start but Bill assured them that the production would go faster after this. It did improve each day and soon they had produced not only the number of beds and desks they had planned on, but a few extra as well.

Pat was in the assembly group and she welded the electric screw driver with such force that Lee smiled as she watched once she was finished the cutting. Then Lee jumped in to help move beds when she saw three of the farmers enter the small compound to help lift the bunk beds. Lee took hold of the forth leg of a bed as the skinny Kenyian men each wrapped their arms around a leg and heaved. Lee was able to lift her end but she had to almost run to keep up the pace of the men. She was considered very strong but these wiry men were like steel with no extra flesh on their muscular sinews. They walked the beds around the tight corners of the dorms, past the open sewer of the outhouse with its offending smells then settled the beds between the existing bunks with their thin foam mattresses and worn light blankets. Lee thanked the men, paused to look around at the scant belongs on each bunk, peer at the colorful cards from kindly strangers tacked to the walls, and then headed back to the shed to pack up the tools. At the end of each day the team packed up all the tools and locked them in the spare office. Stealing was a big problem everywhere in this country but as Lee was beginning to understand it was an act of survival not malice since the many of the Kenyan people seemed to be hard working and good natured. They just had limited food and opportunity to improve their lives. Unemployment was at around fifty percent and only half of the people complete an education through elementary school. There was also a lot of corruption and that just bred more corruption. She thought about how decadent the grocery stores in the States would seem to these people let alone the houses and cars of even the middle class. "We are so spoiled" she thought as she sat in the van on the way back to the hotel looking out on the squalor they passed, and this was not even one of the massive slums that ringed Nairobi.

One early evening on the way back to the hotel from the orphanage, Sophie instructed Julian to detour toward Kiberia, the great slum where the children had been found. She then turned to face the group and told everyone in the van to refrain from showing any cameras or cell phones.

"There is no reason to tempt any desperate characters. This is a dangerous place we will be seeing"

Shortly after this Julian pulled the van over to the curb and out of the left windows, spread before them stretched thousands of rusted low pitched roofed shacks smashed together in chaos. Some of the shacks wove in a slightly bending pattern and Lee realized that those were the ones facing streets, if a mud covered narrow path with an open sewer on one side could be called such. This was Kiberia, a breeding ground of poverty, sickness, hopelessness and crime. It was a city unto itself with its own methods of ownership and governing. People lived here in ten by tens, the name for the small rental shacks, because it was inexpensive and they were desperate. It had been ignored for years by the Kenyan government but every once in a while, an international NGO or church group would reach out to help, sometimes to get their hands slapped and at other times to establish a medical clinic, food distribution or education center. The most successful ones utilized the local talent to administer and man the clinics. There were still people who cared about each other even in this seething mass of incredible pain, undiagnosed illness and hunger.

Then Lee started to hear the children's own stories about Kiberia as they slowly opened up to her. First she learned of their different tribal affiliations. Some were Luo or Luya which were tribes from the west of Kenya, while others were Kikuku, the largest and most politically powerful tribe. There were about forty tribes in Kenya and many spoke different languages or dialects as did the children. She also heard the heart wrenching stories of what had happened to them in Kiberia before they came to the orphanage. Little Carol had been left in the gutter to fend for herself at four years old – lucky to find garbage to eat and corners to sleep in. Stella had been forced by her uncle to work as a prostitute at the age of eight. Jeffrey had been beaten and abused then left for dead before a kind soul cleaned him up and left him at a clinic door. Julia had a brother somewhere in the slum that she hadn't seen for years.

All of the children had arrived at the orphanage as just skin stretched over bones partially covered in rags. Lee had felt tears come to her eyes as she learned the state of these children who each now seemed happy and well adjusted. It amazed her that none of them ever complained or wallowed in their misfortunes as American children did for much less horrendous situations. It was a matter of perspective and Lee's eyes were being opened. She could see how easy her life had always been despite what she and her children had suffered under Curt's abuse. They still had opportunities to get help and support whereas these Kenyan people had very few alternatives. Life continued, Lee thought, sliding right past us whether we chose to swim beyond our problems or drown in our sorrows.

On the last day the matron announced a birthday party for all of the children. Since most of the children did not know their actual birth date this party was a celebration for everyone. They would receive new shoes and a bag of candy but the meal would be special as well. They would each get a full glass of milk with a spaghetti dinner followed by ice cream Most of the children had never tasted noodles or ice cream and they were brimming with anticipation This tantalizing meal would be something that they would talk about for months. The day their bellies were full and their tongues tasted the flavors of cold vanilla and chocolate. They would dream of this treat and hope that Miss Sophia would come again next year.

The group's final goodbye with the children was very hard on Lee. She didn't know what to reply as the children begged her to come back the next year. She had found a calling that would combine her love of construction with her compassion to help other people but whether she could afford to do this on a regular basis would be a challenge as a single mother. She knew that Ryan would have loved this experience as well and she drifted off into a day dream about the two of them one day coming back to the orphanage together. She was snapped back to the present when a small hand tugged at hers and a high voice asked to use her camera for a picture.

The rest of the group was also having trouble saying goodbye as they swept children into embraces and clicked last minute pictures. Finally they all boarded the vans for the return trip along the dirt roads back to Nairobi. After leaving the orphanage the group sat in their vinyl bench seats gazing out of the windows in a contemplative mood or reviewing picture on their cameras. They thought warmly of the new connections they had made here in Africa but slowly some of them began to think of home. Once the van pulled up in front of the hotel, the volunteers went directly to their rooms to pack their bags. Some would be checking out in the morning to return to the States while a small group, had booked to continue on a two day safari in the Maasai Mari National Reserve in the Great Rift Valley. The activity of organizing for this adventure revived some of them out of their lethargy but memories of the children hung thick in the air and the group were quiet on their last night. The next day though the excitement of the safari had loosened their tongues and they were teasing each other before they hurriedly joined the rest of the group downstairs. Julian awaited them with their carriage.

Chapter 37 – Exotic Landscaping

The drive to the Rift Valley took the group toward the famous Ngang Hills, a ridge of peaks named for the Maasai word meaning "knuckles". The road left the city and wound past pockets of slums where wood and tin shacks blended in an undulating mass that stretched through valleys filled with the litter of humanity or along polluted river beds. Without this debris, the countryside reminded Lee of North Carolina. There were winding roads through thick forests of the foothills or over ancient rounded ridges. They also passed small farmsteads called shambas, often carved out of old British plantations that were taken over after independence. As they drove farther, the farms got bigger, they appeared to be more prosperous with well tended crops and sturdy built fences and structures. Then the road left the low rolling terrain and entered the heart of the mountains.

The van hugged the steep sides of the cliffs on sections sliced like raw cuts out of the earth as they wound down the road. Suddenly Julian pulled the van over onto the side of the road near some tourist shops and encouraged everyone to go across onto a viewing deck to take a look. They did as he suggested, some distracted by the carved ivory statues and wood figures in front of the shops and the rest migrating to the flimsy wood platform with a rail guard, not sure what to expect. As Lee approached the edge she caught her breath. It was her first glimpse of the majestic Great Rift Valley. Spread before her was shimmering golden plains that unfolded below the shadow of the mountain range that wrapped it in arms of dark green. The valley stretched to a haze of infinity under a clear turquoise sky. She was entranced by the beauty laid out before her and it was with reluctance that she pulled away from the sight as Julian called them to leave.

Once they had descended to the valley floor they passed many low scrub bushes at the mountain base but this slowly was replaced with neatly gridded fields of crops carefully tended with modern sprinklers and irrigation systems in the valley floor. Here were the bright heads of sunflowers, squat tea or higher coffee bushes, rows of beans and maize; the staples of the Kenyan diet. This was the bread basket of Nairobi, feeding the four million people of the area. These crops slowly gave way to dry sand colored scrub and the group saw their first giraffe, an elegant lopping creature with a dark brown hide covered in a geometric white spotted pattern. This was a reticulated giraffe, Julian explained since the pattern went all the way down its leg. They would see several other types including the rarer Rothschild giraffe that had five horns if they were lucky. Next they came across a few zebra, muscular sturdy looking beasts with short thin legs that were grazing near the road. Julian said that when the Europeans came they tried to domesticate the beast but its legs could not carry heavy loads and its irascible nature defeated the attempt. Lee was amazed that these creatures were so close to civilization-she had never considered that there would be modern farm houses with wild beasts in their back yard.

They soon slowed as the vehicle approached a set of high portals with gates and guards. This was the entrance to the famous Maasai Mara Park of the Rift Valley which flowed into the Serengeti. They were in the "cradle of humanity" as it was commonly referred to. As they stopped at the gate, the only vehicle for miles, Maasai women wrapped in bright red plaid blankets with layers of elaborately beaded neck pieces and large holes in their sagging ear lobes left the shade of nearby acacia trees and swarmed the van. They had ropes of beaded jewelry and wood carvings in their withered dark arms to sell to the passengers through the windows.

Julian warned the group that the women would expect payment if anyone took their picture, so they each dropped their cameras into their laps. The women got more aggressive as the van started to move forward. They made intentional eye contact with those nearest the windows and called out in English words to describe their wares "Bracelets, necklaces, hand carved". Lee had seen pictures of these women in National Geographic and here they were before her, in traditional dress that their tribe had worn for hundreds of years. They were an ancient people known as fierce warriors and cattle rustlers and she couldn't help staring in fascination until the van left them behind

After a few miles through swaying grasslands with great umbrella arching Acadia trees like islands on the horizon, the van turned onto a narrow dirt path. They had been bouncing for hours on unfinished dirt roads with many unexpected pot holes that lifted them right out of their seats. Lee was wondering if the van or her bottom could take much more when Julian announced that they were at the lodge. The group perked up as they wove through a narrow gate in a ten foot high chain link fence enclosure. When Lee looked back, a fellow in safari clothes was hurriedly shutting the tall gate tight which made her joke about what was out there to get them. They pulled up to an impressive open air Porte cohere with natural tree post supports rubbed to a gleaming finish supporting a thatched roof. The group spilled out and another safari clad bell boy guided to the lobby which was also open with a cathedral beamed ceiling. Standing in one corner of the lobby, straight backed, spear in his right hand and staring straight ahead like a guard at Buckingham Palace, was a Maasai warrior.

Lee was fascinated and she left her bags to go look closer at the fellow. As she approached his eyes suddenly dropped down to stare at her. They were dark as coal with bright white around the pupil, distant and calculating which made Lee a little nervous. As she greeted the warrior reverently

"Jambo!" then said timidly "Do you speak English"

A huge grin broke out on his face and he laughed. In her relief Lee laughed as well and relaxed. He introduced himself as Dan and asked in fairly good English if she would like to see how the Maasai live by visiting a village or going on a tour of medical plants. Lee said that she would be thrilled to do that and arranged to meet at the desk between safari outings the next day. The group was then escorted through the lodge grounds toward their tent rooms and given descriptions of the local plants and animals along the way. Lee scanned across the beautiful manicured lawns with flowering bushes and then saw the natural pool encased in rock formations in the center. She silently rejoiced at the discovery. Then she spotted a small creature standing stock still next to a tree near the pool. It looked like Bambi but even smaller and more delicate with huge dark eyes. Then she remembered its name just as the guide explained.

"It is a DikDik, the very smallest of antelope. They sometimes are able to get into the compound"

Lee wondered what else could get into the compound just as the guide advised the guests.

"We do have various animals who may wander through the lodge at night. We advise that you stay in your tents with the zippers down all the way and do not leave any food nearby to attract them"

No problem Lee thought as she assessed the items in her bag to throw out immediately, the guide continued.

"If you must go out then take one of the flashlights provided and stay on the path. We have guards out at night to assist you as well. Do not worry. If you follow these simple instructions then you will enjoy your stay with us"

As the group absorbed this interesting warning, some with

smirks and others with concern on their faces, they rounded a pathway and saw a series of tent structures ahead, each under a shed roof supported by wood poles on a concrete platform. "This looks interesting" Lee thought. She was rooming with Pat and when the guide unzipped their tent and ushered them inside, they were both amazed. The tent material, while crude on the outside housed a small gem on the inside. On a gleaming polished wood floor stood two beds with carved wood headboards, a fur throw on each of the colorful tribal fabric bedspreads. A pair of curved folding safari chairs and an ivory side table topped with a wine bottle and fluted champagne glasses stood in the corner like a still life painting. Running along the back of the beds was a wood slab table and in the corner was a built-in desk with an exotic wood top and indirect lighting. The modern bathroom, which had sleek European fixtures, was in a three sided block structure attached to the tent. The shower door was just a sheet of glass on hinges open above.

"This here's a pretty fancy safari tent. A'h wants one of these at home" Pat exclaimed and they laughed while they unpacked their bags.

The next morning at six they had breakfast in a huge cone shaped space with an elaborate buffet spread overflowing on tables in the center. There were every kind of luscious fresh fruit, French pastries, egg dishes, cereals, juices and savory meats. After stuffing themselves, the group gathered out front where Julian waited for them with the van adjusted so that its top was popped up allowing the passengers to stand to see out through a two foot open section. Early morning was when the animals were most active so they drove off to find them, followed by several other vans, all trailing dust clouds.

The sightings started slowly with Julius pointing out unique colorful birds, long faced grizzled back wart hogs then fat Gravy's zebra and antelope including the elegant long neck gerenuk and impala. Then they spotted a beautiful stately Beisa oryx and several massive black skinned water buffalo with horns off each side of their head as Julian eased the van near the river. He told them about how dangerous the crocodiles were and pointed out some of their inconspicuous long dark forms in the river to the visitors.

Julian described the migration patterns of the animals, and elephant herds which came to quench their thirst and bath in this same spot. Some of the group then asked about the Big Five game animals and how many were in this park. They had already seen a buffalo so that left the lion, rhino, leopard and elephant. Julian explained that they would probably see all of them but the leopard. Leopards were well hidden in trees during the day and usually only came out to hunt at night when it was too dangerous to do a safari.

The radio crackled and Julian responded by backing up and turning the van onto the dirt road driving at a quicker pace. He told them that a large lion pride had been spotted and they were feeding on their water buffalo kill from the night before. Drivers were required to call in sightings of animals so all the vans could join the viewings. When their van arrived, there were already a few others in a semi-circle around a pack of ten lionesses and one massive lion with an impressive mane, all sprawled languidly on a small hillock overlooking the plains. Three of the lionesses were at the kill tearing at the body of a massive black skinned water buffalo lying on its side in the dirt. Two of the lionesses took jerking bites out of the back end of the beast and one had actually tunneled a cavity in the side which it entered then pulled out entrails that she brought over to a couple cubs Lee hadn't noticed before. They were light brown in color, playful and extremely cute, tumbling over the lionesses and pawing at each other.

The lion ignored them all, poised in a lounging position a few yards farther away as he stared into the direction of the wind assessing the scents on the warm breeze. He was stately and remote in nature, a spoiled king. Cameras were all clicking almost non-stop as the excited tourists with their lens balanced on the roofs of the vehicles as they zoomed in on the pack. In between the shutter noises Lee could hear the crunch of bones and the tearing of the flesh and she winced. It was just like the nature movies but even more brutally real. Then Julian pointed out the small jackal with long pointed ears that hovered in a perimeter area away from the pack, pacing impatiently while watching the tantalizing raw meal. He said that there would be hyenas too but they couldn't come as close or the lionesses would chase them. Lee noticed that many other animals were also feeding nearby. There were antelope, gazelle and wildebeest with a football field distance, though they watched the pride warily while they chewed on the wild grasses. Lee was surprised that all of these animals, both predator and prey lived so closely together and then she smiled as she realized that the same was true for the human species.

When they returned to the lodge, exhilarated and hungry, Lee grabbed a few items off the lunch buffet, ate them quickly then found Dan at the lobby desk for her tour of Maasai medical plants. He was in full tribal regalia again, with long braided hair tucked into a headband with chains, woven thread and coin shaped decorations, arm bands and a red blanket wrapped and belted. He guided her along the perimeter of the fence and pulled at various leaves and pointed at trees giving the Maasai name for them. The soft light green leaves were used for bedding, stuffing their ears holes when they were enlarge and bottom wiping. The root of the aloe vera plant was used for making beer and the leaves can be stripped to make string. Olive leaves were used during the circumcision ceremony for a bed and the blessing tree leaf, shiny and dark green like a holly, used to heal foot & mouth disease of the cattle. They also buried their dead with it. The thorns of the umbrella acacia were put around village to keep lions and cheetahs away and its bark also makes a beer. The orange leaves of the Groton plant were used for insect and snake repellant which Lee thought was clever.

Dan continued to describe without embarrassment, some far more unpleasant ailments and point to the appropriate plant remedy. It was when he mentioned a plant for nausea that caught Lee's attention since she felt that she could use it right then. She had been feeling queasy and was wondering if she had eaten something bad. As they rounded a corner Lee saw a small fenced compound with several mud coated huts in it and Dan explained that this was here the Maasai stayed when they were working at the resort. He explained that he was only at the resort for three days a week and he got a ride back to his village in between. After this they came upon a row of small crudely built tents of heavy duty green canvas drooping from the support of ropes tied to limbs and sticks in the ground to prop a cover over the entrances.

"That is where the van guides stay when we are at the resort" Dan said and Lee's eye brows shot up at this revelation. They were such poor accommodations that she felt she would have to give Julian a bigger tip just to ease her guilt about his discomfort. Then Lee's eye was drawn to sudden movements on the other side of the fence and she saw a bunch of baboons, at least a dozen all scrambling across the top of a hill. Some were aggressively pacing and baring their teeth while others were swatting picking through another baboon's fur.

"That is the garbage dump for the lodge. The baboons eat out of it and then at night they still sneak into the compound to cause trouble"

"I will definitely keep the tent zipper down at night now!" she exclaimed as they turned to head back to the lobby.

The next morning the van headed out again and Julian spotted additional carnivores hiding in the savannah. He pointed out tuffs of ears above the grasses that turned out to be a hyena or civet cat. Later they had heard on the radio that there were three cheetahs on the move in the vicinity. When they arrived in the area that the cheetas had been spotted there were several vans were crowded in one spot. Julian ignored this section and took the van into the middle of another field. Lee was chagrined and pointed out that all the other vans were over in the other area. Julian just grinned and said "Wait". After a few minutes, the other vans had started their engines and were racing towards them.

Then Lee saw a head pop up above the grasses. It was close cropped with small ears and a sloping forehead over eyes that scanned the horizon. As the body emerged, she saw the beautiful golden pelt with silver dollar sized black spots over sleek rippling muscles. Then she saw two more heads emerge in the distance, all turned directly toward the van. Lee stood poised with her camera in the roof opening as the first cheetah passed right behind the back of the van and she got excellent close up shots of the handsome cat.

Julian explained that this was their hunting path and they were three brothers who had always been together. He knew these cats and where they were going. Then the lead cheetah stopped on a distant hill dropped its behind to the ground, arched its neck and made a loud chirping sound. The call was so unusual that it startled Lee. It was the kind of sound a large bird would make, not a regal cheetah. Out on the grasslands the other cats responded and hurried to catch up with their brother. Once together they all looped off over the crest and were lost in the high grass. Lee was amazed; she had never known that they made that kind of communication with each other. She realized too that this was a moment that she would never forget.

After they returned to the resort for lunch, Pat and Lee were brought by Julian to Maasai village just outside the gates of the Park. They were told that they had to pay a fee of twenty dollars US for this privilege, which would become a contribution to the support of the tribe. The Maasai were a wise and determined people since they still they owned much of their own land in the area. Their ancestors had stood strong against enslavement and resisted the forces of European marauding. It was only through treaties with the British at the turn of the 20th century that they had lost about sixty percent of their land in order to section off farm ranches and game parks.

As the van approached the village, they saw a group of sinewy dark men in colorful red wraps, lounging under the elegant spread of an acacia tree. Behind them was a rough collection of branches, piled to a height of about eight feet with a small opening in the front. As the van pulled up several women ducted through the opening and stood forty feet away under the shade of another tree. Lee and Pam were introduced to the chief, tribal elders by their guide for the tour, Sam. He was a twenty five year old Massai in the full dress of long tight braids woven with beads and knotted with coins at the ends, layers of necklaces and a plaid robe tossed over one shoulder and belted with a beaded rope slung at his hips. He had a proud bearing and fierce look until he smiled and then his face softened and it disarmed the women.

They were an extremely poor people and Lee noticed torn and dirty clothing under their bright robes for impressing tourists. Tourism now brought in valuable revenue for the tribe to survive. In the past they had been a nomadic people with cattle as their most valuable commodity but since being located outside of the park and far from the river they did not have as much to sustain them in the dusty plains. Their mud and dung huts were roofed with sticks covered in dung with grass growing on the top that Lee could see over the thorn enclosure and had not been moved in a long time.

Sam gave them a short history of the village in surprisingly good clear English then told them that he had gone to college to learn it. He wasn't married yet since he couldn't afford a wife. It took ten cows to buy a wife he explained and he had used his money to pay for school. The single men must sleep outside the village compound on the ground until they are married. Most of the tribal men of the younger generation, men who tend to take the public jobs, only want one wife but many of their fathers had three to six wives. Then the men all gathered in front of the women. Sam explained that once the men had their bride price, they would jump to show their prowess to attract a woman to be his wife. Then the men lined up, each holding a long staff and one of them started to beat a drum. With backs held straight and chins thrust out, starting with the far left, they each took turns coming forward and jumping from a standing position. Some threw their heads back as they jumped, others bent their legs and bounced, their tall lean frames stiff as their beaded necklaces bounced on their chests.

Lee didn't think any of them actually jumped very high, especially since she had read in National Geographic that they could jump their own heights. Then the women lined up closer to the village, in their layers of patterned shawls draped and knotted, and one came over to beckon Lee and Pat to join them. She was a young girl with a smooth oval face and she gave a small smile as she draped beaded necklaces over their heads and led them by the hand to the circle, where each of the woman sang as they began a bouncing dance in a more subdued but rhythmic version of the men's athletic gyrations. They pulled the Lee and Pat into the group and indicated that they were to bounce as well. They passed Julian their cameras to take their pictures as they danced among the brightly decorated woman, beaded necklaces bouncing on their chests and wide grins on their faces.

Once the dance ended, Sam led them through the opening in the thorn bushes into a large courtyard with circular huts along the perimeter. The ground was uneven due to the hoof marks of many cattle and Lee knew that they were walking on a bed of manure though she couldn't smell it. Sam explained that cattle were brought into the village at night to protect them. Cattle were a sign of the wealth of a village since besides being used as barter for a bride or other goods, their milk mixed in a bowl with blood drained from small lacerations in the neck of the beast, was their main food source. They also used the cattle dung to build their houses and as fuel for fires. Surprising to Lee, they did not kill the wild animals they living amongst, since they valued all life, unless they were a threat to the tribe or cattle. She also noticed as she looked around that the women tended to do the majority of the work. She saw women carrying children, sewing, weaving and hauling water while the men relaxed under trees or in the shade of a hut.

Sam led Lee and Pat into one of the huts to see how they were arranged inside and the tools that the villagers used. The small rounded shape seemed larger inside as they saw that it was divided into several rooms. The front room held a valued bicycles or a calf that needed tending. Then there was a central area with a corner used as a fire pit, blackened with use for cooking or heating the hut. On each side of the pit there were wood shelves built to hold a few carved utensils or plastic bowl. In the back were openings to small bedroom niches with pallets of the soft leaves. While they were in the hut Lee asked Sam if the tribe still practiced circumcision on the women which he confirmed with a sad shake of his head.

It was a disfiguring practice often performed on very young girls with clam shells or rusty knives used to scrape off their vulva. Then the remaining tissue was sewn shut often so tight that they were unable to urinate or give birth without extreme pain, sometimes causing infection or even death. It was estimated that the shocking practice was performed on about 100,000 women annually in the world. Sam said that in his college classes he had been taught about the dangers of female circumcision and he had tried to persuade the elders to stop the practice but it was hard to convince them. Lee and Pat just told him to keep trying. They left the hut, thanked him for the tour with a good tip, and returned, a little more somber, to the van where Julian sat waiting for them.

In late afternoon the group gathered again at the van for the next safari outing. The animals would now be active again as they headed out to hunt. Julian took them back to see the lions at the water buffalo kill again and this time the lionesses were all lounging on the hillock or next to a jeep in the shade but there was an air of expectancy; a tenseness in their poses. All of their necks were stretched tall and their faces were turned toward the direction of the evening breeze. Then suddenly, one of the lionesses stood and paced off in a determined but casual stride in the direction they had been watching. She paused and fell into a crouch next to the van to lick at the puddle of water in a tire track. Lee was fascinated by how much the gesture looked like that of a domesticated cat. Then she saw the lioness's large face in the reflection of the water looking up at her with the intense penetrating golden eyes and she shivered. This was no tame cat. The lioness then rose in a fluid motion, the thick muscles in her shoulders extending, and padded off down the track. Slowly each of the other lionesses stood and followed her until only the male and cubs were left.

The group saw several more lion prides in the savannah as well as a group of massive elephants casually ambling across the road with their ears flapping and tails swinging, and a few stately giraffe but finally they had to turn back to the camp. As they drove the dusty rutted road, the sun was setting, with a glorious spread of rich color across the darkening silhouettes of the trees and the undulating land. Both Pat and Lee's faces were covered in powder except where their glasses had protected their skin, as they gripped the lip of the van roof while they stood scanning the ground speeding by for sightings of more animals. Just as they had given up and sat back down in their seats, Julian drew their attention to an eerie spectacle. Just outside the gates to the lodge, deep in the high grasses, were pairs of laser white points of bright light. It was another pride, their tawny bodies blending with the golden tinted grasses. Lee hadn't noticed them until Julian pointed out their eyes reflected in the lights of the van. They were on the right side, a group of six lionesses and the male, their tawny hides blending with the high golden grasses. Their eyes looked like laser points of bright white casually tracking the van and it made Lee shiver. She didn't think that zipper would do much good if these fellows got in the gate.

Lee had looked forward to each safari outing since it reminded her of Christmas; there were big surprises each time you opened a present or in this case, turned a corner. It was so exciting to go around a bend and unexpectedly see a couple ostriches racing across a valley, a herd of majestic elephants sauntering across the road or stop for a panoramic vista and stumble upon some hippos playing in the river, snorting as they emerged from below the muddy water. It was sad that the adventure was coming to a close as they each packed their bags then gathered in the lobby to check out and leave. It had been a perfect experience except that she couldn't shake the nausea that kept reoccurring. Each meal she would chew on some crackers and bread to keep from getting sick and she was suffering headaches. She was worried that it might be malaria since she had forgotten the pills that she was supposed to take but she would wait until she was back home to check with a doctor unless the symptoms got a lot worse.

Chapter 38 – Home

The group had returned to Nairobi over dust filled roads where they were dropped off at the airport by Julian with hugs goodbye and promises to return some day. Then they dragged their bags and newspaper wrapped gifts through the unconditioned customs area to the gate where they waited for the plane with all the exotically dressed Africans and a few tired businessmen. After the passengers were finally called to board the plane to London and Lee was navigating the narrow passages, it finally occurred to her what was going on - she was pregnant! She tripped in the aisle of the plane just as this thought filled her mind and was barely aware that Pat had caught her then gently directed her to their seats toward the very back end of the plane.

"Are you all right? Is it the food poisoning again?!" she exclaimed concerned.

"Oh, I'm fine - thanks for the help. I'm just tired and not paying attention" Lee mumbled as she organized her bag under the seat in front.

She then took the flat airline pillow and tucked it under her head. She pretended to sleep as the plane took off so she could consider what she was going to do. It was such a turn of events, wiping all thoughts of her African experience from her mind, as harsh realty flooded her thoughts. She would have to tell Ryan and then he would insist on getting married – he would feel trapped. She didn't want that to happen. Then she thought about his smile, his touch and how very happy he would be about this news. It was what he had wanted.

Lee couldn't remember exactly when she had her last period but she determined that she must be a couple months along, since that was when she was last with Ryan. The baby would be fully formed now. That was an exciting idea and she was curious whether it was a boy or girl, but most of all she was worried if it would be healthy with all the shots she had taken for the trip and conditions she had been exposed to in Africa. She had not been eating well or taking any vitamins either. Then she remembered that trip to Thailand when she had been pregnant with Andy, and relaxed. She would have to get tests done when she returned and hopefully everything would be fine. Then after the health of the baby was confirmed, then she would call Ryan. That would be an interesting conversation- just like out of a soap opera.

"I know that we haven't seen each other for a while and maybe you are even dating someone else, but guess what, I'm pregnant"

Lee guessed that she could sell tickets to that show.

The plane landed in London and instead of going off to the city for the layover Lee just remained in the International terminal and tried to read a book and shop for gifts for the children. She thought about Andy and Sarah's reaction to a new sibling as she fingered a baby outfit that said "Big Ben". They might be thrilled, like acquiring a new doll to love or maybe they would be jealous of the attention that a new baby would get from everyone. Then the boarding call was announced and the remaining NOF group got on another plane for the leg to New York. The flight was fairly uneventful until they approached the coast of North America. Then the turbulence began. It was not much to begin with, just small shudders and bouncing while the lights were out.

Then the captain put on the sign to fasten your seat belts with a ping and the red light glowed over each seat. A little later Lee saw movement in the cabin as one attendant rushed up toward the front and another dropped the jump seats and strapped herself in. The cabin lights came on then and the Captain announced that everyone was to remain in their seats with their seat belts on. There were storm conditions along the Eastern seaboard and they were waiting for instructions about their approach. Just then the plane had a sudden loss of altitude and was plunged down violently Dishes rattled and flew in the air. The passengers were jerked tight against the seatbelts and anyone who hadn't heeded the captain's instructions to belt them rose off their seats a few inches or higher depending on their position and weight. Screams irrupted throughout the plane and Lee, though she wanted to join them, maintained a calm appearance she so she could help Pat who had gone pale and rigid as a statue as she white knuckled the arm rests between them. Lee reassured Pat that everything was fine and the planes were built to withstand this kind of force. Pat looked at her skeptically but when she saw Lee's calm face, she relaxed a little.

"We would like to apologize for the recent turbulence that we have experienced," the captain announced in his soothing professional voice.

"The storm has extended across New York State and planes are circling waiting a chance to land or being diverted. We are one of those being diverted and we have been instructed to land in Toronto The airline staff will sort out your connecting flights and hotel rooms for those who will have to wait out the storms. We appreciate your patience"

There were groans throughout the cabin but Lee was secretly please since she could go visit her Aunt Mary if she was delayed overnight. So once the plane landed and they went to the counter to get their new flights, she asked the group if anyone would like to come along to her aunt's house. They thanked her for the offer but they all decided to wait at the airport in case any flights got out that night. Lee called her aunt then rented a car and drove to Brampton. Aunt Mary had baked her special cookies while Lee was on her way and the house smelled of rich melted chocolate cookie dough when she entered. Lee was engulfed in a big hug, handed a drink then enticed to sit in a comfortable chair and talk. Aunt Mary was very happy to see Lee and hear all about her trip. She was such a kind and considerate person. There were really good people in the world; which was enough to give a person hope Lee thought.

The next morning Lee hugged her aunt then set off on the ten lane highway for the airport to catch her flight to New York then Charlotte. Toronto hadn't really changed that much, it still had the worst traffic of any city she had lived in. The freeway was four lanes each direction with additional express lanes and they were all full bumper to bumper. After eventually getting off at the airport exit, Lee steered to the rental car parking, left the car then checked in at the busy ticket area. After getting her new flight boarding pass she went through security before heading to her gate. She did not see any of the NOF group but they had probably gotten a flight later that evening.

At the entrance to the gate there were several serious looking uniformed US Customs and Border Protection officers reviewing passports and baggage: Lee involuntarily cringed. There were several countries in the world where preclearance for immigration and customs was done before the passengers got anywhere near the soil of the United States and they included Ireland, Bahamas, Bermuda, Aruba and most major airports of Canada. Lee lined up and could feel the sweat of nerves start to form on her scalp. When she got to the front, a burly man took her papers and began to scrutinize them. Just as she thought she was clear, he looked up and briskly told her to step aside and follow the other officer to his right.

She stammered "Why?!!"

"The seems to be an irregularity with your papers"

"But I have a green card application in place. It was cleared in

Charleston so these papers should all be correct"

"Ma'm, just follow the officer please".

"My children and home are in the States. I have to get back!!" She blurted out as real panic engulfed her. She started to shake as she looked at him wide eyed and desperate. Some of the other passenger's attention was drawn to the commotion in curiosity. The officer just turned to take the next passenger's passport, dismissing her while the one next to him took Lee's elbow, trying to avoid a scene and led her to a small office nearby. He told her to sit down and wait while he took her papers to review. He was making phone calls and flipping through her Canadian passport. Lee was feeling sick again with the outbreak of nerves but she didn't want to show that in case it hurt her situation. She wanted to project a calm professional attitude worthy of a potential American citizen but it was so difficult, she was scared.

Eventually the officer came back and said that she was not supposed to be in Canada since she did not have permission. She would have had to get advanced parole to do this and now her application for citizenship was in jeopardy. Lee explained, between gasps of air, that she wasn't supposed to stop here but her plane had been diverted. She had stayed overnight at her aunt's house so she had entered Canada last night.

"It doesn't matter ma'm. You weren't supposed to enter Canada unless you had gotten prior authorization. You will now have to wait for your Green Card in Canada"

"Nooooo" burst from her lips as Lee's voice escalated "My children, my home, my business are all back there – I have to get to Charlotte. You have to let me back in!"

She leaped up to argue her point and make him see sense but he was on the phone again calling for back up, with his arm out to keep her away. She tried again to explain, her hands gesturing and her eyes wet with tears, but it was going nowhere. He told her once again to calm down and motioned for her to sit. She did as he requested then she asked what her options were and he told her to check with the INS office. She should have filed an I-131 form for advanced parole to leave the US, but she had not. What she didn't know was that any immigration violation made at this border point could not be punished with the usual fines or even prison, since it was on Canadian soil and not allowed under the governmental agreement for that check point. They could however restrict her entry to the US. Lee didn't know any of this but she thought of her lawyer just then and decided to call him as soon as he would be in the office. He would sort this out and she could return to the US really soon if not today.

As she looked up she saw another officer enter the room, a tall dark fellow with a military haircut. He began consulting with the one who had given her the bad news. Then the first one said.

"We will need to escort you to get your baggage then out of the building"

The two officers each grabbed one of her elbows and Lee reluctantly allowed them to guide her to the lower level. They explained that she could not enter the US now until she was given approval of her Green Card application. She would have to notify the INS of her new address right away and if she tried to re-enter the US again without permission she would lose her work status and possibly be banned from ever entering the States again. Lee pleaded the entire way out of the terminal but it fell on deaf ears. The officers took her to the baggage area, sometimes holding her up if she staggered, and waited with her until her luggage appeared on a carrousel. After the two deposited her on the sidewalk outside of the building, Lee slumped in abject misery against a light post. "This could not have happened to me. What am I going to do!" she thought. The options were too horrific to consider. The pregnancy was difficult enough but now she had an even bigger problem. She then realized that she could not do it alone any more.

Lee called her surprised aunt to ask for a ride. She explained the immigration problem while they rode on the 401 and Aunt Mary turned to look at her, a worried on her face, and asked "What are you going to do dear?"

"I don't know yet but I think that I will need to go to Windsor to sort this out. If you could give me a ride to the train station, I will catch the first train"

She once more thanked her aunt as she dropped her off at the Via Train station. A few hours later, she was riding a modern, clean and sparsely populated high speed train southeast through flat well-tended farmland dense in crops of corn, wheat and tomatoes to Windsor. She was worried about the children and her business but hopefully something could be worked out quickly. She then began to draw up scenarios in which she was stuck for months or even worse, years, but she did not want to even contemplate that one. She would have to get her mail diverted, cancel appointments and most of all, she had to prepare the children for her delay. That would be heartbreaking but so would the closing of her business. She couldn't work remote for long since eventually someone would need a meeting or a site visit. She thought of Ryan as will, with such longing and sadness. She would lose everything she thought, and she dropped her head to hide tears as she quietly wept. Eventually the self-pity waned and she fell into a fitful sleep, her head against the hard cold vibrating glass of the window.

One jarring motion of the train woke her and she sighed as she slowly gained alertness and memory of her position. She pulled herself upright and decided to distract herself with a book during the remaining hours. It was hard to concentrate but she tried to read the bouncing lines in front of her. Then her nausea flared with the motion of the train. She ran to the washroom, yanked open the thin narrow door and retched over the low toilet until dry heaves were all that was left. This new life within her had reasserted itself and she realized that she had someone else to think of first of all. She settled in her seat again, got out some crackers from her bag and just watched the rows of high corn stalks roll past the window.

The train sped past gleaming silver silos and red painted farm buildings stately asserting ownership over sections of pasture land. The view reminded her of Africa in the Rift, with its rich farm land and tidy rows of crops. "How far away yet how similar each place could be" she thought. The people as well were similar in many ways; each valuing family, caring for their children, laughing with each other, loving, struggling and working hard to have the right to do all of those things each day, though the results were so extremely different. She fell into a collage of memories from her past, flashing images of events and people. Eventually she even smiled as she thought of her last train ride, the one from Detroit to Chicago when she was in college. Sometimes disasters turned out all right. She would just have to see if this cloud had a silver lining, as the old fashioned saying foretold.

Her mother was waiting for her when the train pulled into the station behind the whiskey factory started by the bootlegger who had once owned Peach Island. Anne had a forced smile on her face which was offset by lines of concern etched on her forehead. Lee just hugged her and got in the car. Anne began talking immediately, trivial topics of food recipes, parties and the antics of her gal friends who played bridge or curled, speaking as though her daughter had just come back from a weekend holiday, not a life away. It all slid past Lee, she didn't care about any of it.

Finally when she couldn't block it out any more, she blurted

"I'm pregnant!"

Lee's mother stopped the stream of talk then. She paused for breath and while looking straight ahead, she asked what Lee intended to do. Lee had not wished to tell her mother about the baby so soon. She had wanted to talk about staying at the house and borrowing a car until her lawyer could sort out the immigration issue. But she was actually excited about the baby, which was why she had spoken out so quickly, until she understood the tone of her mother's question. It had actually meant, "You are not married, how can you keep it". She reacted by pulling into herself, doing what she had done so many times, mentally closing the doors to others who tried to hold her back. In a gesture of defiance, she tilted her chin up and straightened her back then simply said "I am keeping this baby".

Once back at her parent's house, she dragged her bags, filled with the remains of her African service trip wardrobe and the gifts she had purchased, up to her room. The bags had been lightened quite a bit since she had given away most of her work clothes and used all of the supplies. When she was saying good bye to Julia, the young girl had handed her a scrap of paper. It contained a list of the items that she wished for – a request that Lee had asked of her earlier. It was a sad little list including socks, hair elastic, pencils and a mirror. Lee had immediately pulled off her shoes and socks then handed the pair to Julia, apologizing for the fact that they were not clean. Then she pulled the hair band off of her pony tail, took a pen from her pocket and gave these items to Julia as well. Lee was worried that she might have offended the girl. She may have wanted new items as any American would, so Lee waited to see her reaction. As Julia's beautiful dark face with the large solemn eyes looked up at her Lee saw that she beamed in delight. Then in a quiet voice she said.

"Thank you and May God bless you!" with such genuine feeling it moved Lee's heart – both from guilt at the smallness of the gift and pleasure in the gratitude.

Lee reflected on this as she looked around the large house on the water with new eyes. It had so many conveniences and luxuries such as washer, dryer, cars, televisions not to mention clean running water, indoor toilets and showers with hot water by comparison to Julia's world. It didn't make any sense that fate would distribute comforts and opportunity to groups of people so unevenly. What fortune had allowed Lee to be born in a wealthy country, go to college and make a good living - how did she deserve this much while the

African orphans got so little. These thoughts naturally lead her to consider just how much she could change this discrepancy. The small contribution she had made over the past two weeks in Nairobi was less than a drop in ocean, and now she had caused herself a whole lot of problems as a result. She sighed and prepared herself to call her children to tell them that she would be away for a little longer, if Curt would pick up the phone.

Lee had contacted her lawyer who reassured her that he would try to straighten all of this out as soon as possible. He couldn't give her any idea of time but he did not think that she would have to spend the next few years in Canada waiting for her Green Card. Meanwhile she scrambled to sort out and complete her clients work long distance. She had arranged with her engineers for them to file permits and take pictures of sites if she needed them but eventually she would start losing business. She just hoped to keep it all going until she could return. She had called Laura who immediately came to Windsor to see her. Laura was such a good friend and Lee sank into her embrace as she welcomed the stylish woman into the house.

Laura had also visited Lee in Charlotte when she had first separated from Curt, arriving to make sure that Lee was doing all right. Lee was so grateful for this wonderful gesture of support and caring. On that visit they had taken their drinks down to the dock and sat watching the sun set over the glistening water as they poured out their secrets to each other.

This time Lee told Laura all about the constant threats and law suits that Curt had filed, his abuse of the children and the adultery.

Laura patiently listened, a small gasp of sympathy escaping her lips occasionally as Lee spoke. Laura then told her.

"I have never seen anyone work so hard at maintaining a marriage, so always remember that you had done your best"

Which made Lee feel better, just knowing someone else could see that she had tried very hard to keep the family together. Then Laura told of her own frustrations with her business, her marriage challenges and dealing with her mother who had been diagnosed with Alzheimer's. They purged their feelings about these private problems knowing that neither one would break this confidence. It was a sacred but unspoken pledge of friendship. There were so few people who could understand how they not only "wanted it all" but they would fight for the opportunity to be mothers, business owners, wives and volunteers if that is what they wished. They would work hard to be successful even if other people threw wrenches into the finely tuned mechanism of their lives. Under their best efforts they believed that they could overcome the challenges.

As they sat in chairs on the lawn of Lee's parent's house overlooking Lake St. Clair, Laura just listened. Lee told her of the pregnancy and the refusal of entry to the States. She talked about how much she would lose if she couldn't get back and she especially spoke of her children, who she missed fiercely. She feared they would suffer while they lived full time with Curt. Lee also told Laura of her recent call with Andy. She had finally gotten one of the children to pick up the phone and when she talked to Andy, he had innocently blurted out:

"That lady Joan left daddy's house. He probably wouldn't want me to tell you this but they were screaming at each other outside the house and a neighbour called the police. We haven't seen her since some guys came to move her stuff. I helped too. But dad has hired a lady to take care of us and she is nice."

Lee was surprised by all of this and not happy that Curt hadn't told her the new arrangements with the children when she had called him about her delay. She talked to Sarah next and the little girl sounded good but when she had asked her mother when she would be back, Lee almost couldn't answer. So she cleared her throat, blinked away tears and tried to sooth Sarah's worries with reassurances that she would be coming to get them as soon as possible. It was a very hard phone call but Lee was so glad to finally speak with her children. Laura put her hand on Lee's shoulder and kept it there until she could continue.

Lee then told Laura about her parents friends who had told her horror stories of someone they knew trapped outside of the US, separated from spouses and children for years as they waited for paperwork and permission to cross the border. Her parents had even joked about dropping her off on a dock in Detroit and while it sparked a hope in Lee, she had no intention of crossing as an illegal. She would not risk being banned from the US or getting her architect license revoked, and besides Curt would turn her in if he ever found out. Then she spoke of Ryan, and her voice softened. She had not called him yet but she thought about him all the time. Her eyes moistened and she sighed. Laura then reached across and touched Lee's arm gently.

"You need to talk to him. He loves you and he can help"

"I know. I just was putting it off because of how he might react," Lee said.

"What, he might love and cherish you and the baby. He might

want to marry you and then you would get citizenship through that union. You are right, it is a horrible idea!" Laura declared sarcastically.

Lee looked over at her friend and grinned. Then a blushed rose up on her cheeks as she thought of Ryan loving her. She knew that Laura was probably right. She had been caught up in a stubborn pride that made her refuse to accept his assistance since she thought that she could take care of herself. Her Uncle Jack had said that no one was given anything that they couldn't handle and she believed him. She could deal with all of this but she was still a little scared for her children and her future. Maybe this was a situation that would be easier with someone to help to carry some of the load. Lee would like to talk to Ryan and hear his deep strong voice conveying wise and non-judgmental advice. Lee then took a deep breath, gave Laura's hand a squeeze of gratitude and promised that she would call Ryan soon. Laura replied a little sternly with "Tomorrow" and Lee shook her head sheepishly in agreement.

So Lee was standing at the edge of break wall the next day contemplating all that faced her. She had hugged Laura tightly that morning as they stood in front of her car saying goodbye and Laura had whispered into her ear "If you need me, just call", then she was gone. The wind was blowing out of the north. Squalls would follow from the dark clouds that started to roll in from the Detroit side. She thought of the baby and dropped her hand protectively to her stomach. She was not showing much at all and could still fit into her old jeans.

Just then another hand slipped around to rest on top of hers, covering it completely. It startled her but when she looked down she saw that it had a darker skin tone with long fingers that were strong yet gentle as they cupped her hand and Lee knew right away who it was. She exhaled and a small smile spread across on her face lighting her eyes as she turned to face Ryan. He kept his hand on her waist and pulled her close as he searched her face for any sign of displeasure at seeing him. Lee looked up at his handsome features, his dark eyes, strong chin and her heart literally skipped a beat.

"I have missed you" he softly stated as he wrapped his arms around her, buried his head in her neck and breathed in her essence. Lee leaned into his comforting strength.

"I suppose my mother called you," she said closing her eyes.

"Well, actually I called her when you didn't answer any of my messages at the house. She told me about the baby and I have to tell you that it took me by surprise. But I am so excited about it. Lee, we have a baby!" he exclaimed in reverence and hope.

"I wasn't sure that my mother liked you enough to confide the family secret," Lee said with a wry smile to diffuse the seriousness of the situation.

"Well I guess she wanted to give me the option to volunteer to step up to the plate before your dad had to come after me with a shot gun"

Lee flinched and tried to pull away from him after hearing what she had feared, but he wouldn't let her go and pulled her back chuckling as he explained that he was just kidding. She relaxed a little and just muttered into his shoulder "What are we going to do" but it felt good to think that there were two of them working together on these problems. She had missed him so much she realized. Then he outlined a plan he had devised and she just clung to him as he talked. It consisted of his coming to stay in Windsor and commute to his job while she was stuck here so they could plan for the future no matter that direction that future might take. He would rent an apartment nearby if her parents didn't want them cohabitating under their roof. He grinned and looked down at her as he said this. Next they would have to engage the immigration lawyer to file for a different kind of visa, one that might get her back into the US immediately. She looked up expectantly at him with new hope.

"What kind of visa?"

"I thought that you would never ask!" he laughed.

Then he leaned in to gently kiss her and she tasted the peppermint on his lips, smelled his light enticing cologne and kissed him back hard. The wind was swirling around them now and the dark clouds overhead were pregnant with rain but they didn't notice. Ryan then dropped to his knee in the damp grass while still holding her hand and declared.

"Lee, will you please consider marrying me sometime in the future. We can file a fiancé visa to get you into the US and back to the children quickly. Then we can slowly, at whatever pace you are comfortable with, try a life together as a family"

When she didn't respond, he spoke again "I love you and I don't care about the age difference or timing or whatever you are worried about. We can work that out. I just want to be with you – what do you say?"

He was looking concerned now as he watched her face for a reaction. She ran his lovely words through her mind, caressing the delight they brought, and thought about how Curt had tried to control and crush her, to make her feel small and unworthy in order to feed his ego. Then she thought of all the others who had tried to stop her every time she wanted to do something different or unconventional and while she had overcome most of these barriers, it was hard. She was tired. Now here was a wonderful, kind man who wanted to help, on bent knee, waiting for her, and he had declared that he would wait as long as she needed. She realized now that he had been waiting for her all along and had loved her enough to give her the space and time needed until she understood this. She believed all that he had said. Then she ran her hand over the new life in her belly, then across the smooth cheek of this loving man in front of her and said "Yes".

THE END